EYEWITNESS

When the Russian Army liberated the Ukraine from the Germans in 1943, Godfrey Blunden was brought to the city of Kharkov as a correspondent; it was there that he witnessed the scene with which The Time of the Assassins *ends. Later investigations, his long experience reporting Russian affairs, and his observations at the Battle of Stalingrad, established the facts on which this novel of terrifying immediacy and authenticity is based.*

"His commitment is to fact and to essential truth, which he serves no less by his imagination than by his experience and research. There is no page of his work that does not compel our admiring interest."—From the Introduction by Lionel Trilling.

Petite veille d'ivresse, sainte! quand ce ne serait que pour le masque dont tu nous as gratifié. Nous t'affirmons, méthode! Nous n'oublions pas que tu as glorifié hier chacun de nos âges. Nous avons foi au poison. Nous savons donner notre vie tout entière tous les jours.

Voici le temps des ASSASSINS. *Rimbaud*

THE TIME OF THE ASSASSINS

GODFREY BLUNDEN

Author of
A Room on the Route

With an Introduction
by Lionel Trilling

BANTAM BOOKS
TORONTO · NEW YORK · LONDON

This low-priced Bantam Book has been completely reset in a type face designed for easy reading, and was printed from new plates. It contains the complete text of the original hard-cover edition. NOT ONE WORD HAS BEEN OMITTED.

THE TIME OF THE ASSASSINS
A Bantam Book / published by arrangement with J. B. Lippincott Company

PRINTING HISTORY
Lippincott edition published April 1952
Bantam Modern Classic edition published January 1968

Published simultaneously in the United States and Canada

Bantam Books are published by Bantam Books, Inc., a subsidiary of Grosset & Dunlap, Inc. Its trade-mark, consisting of the words "Bantam Books" and the portrayal of a bantam, is registered in the United States Patent Office and in other countries. Marca Registrada. Bantam Books, Inc., 271 Madison Avenue, New York, N.Y. 10016.

PRINTED IN THE UNITED STATES OF AMERICA

TO LYNN CARRICK

AUTHOR'S NOTE: In the English rendering of Ukrainian place names the Ukrainian style has been followed, e.g. Kharkiv (Kharkov), etc.

Fiction and History
by Lionel Trilling

I have no knowledge of what literary model Godfrey Blunden had in mind for his remarkable novel, *The Time of the Assassins.* But if I had to guess by whom he had regulated his tone and attitude, I should think it was not a novelist at all. My own reference as I read Mr. Blunden's book was to certain historians, to Thucydides and to Tacitus, and, in a lesser degree, to Josephus. Like them, Mr. Blunden tells a story to which the only possible response might seem to be despair. Like them he maintains the power and fortitude of his mind, and of ours, before the terrors of actuality.

This is, I believe, a very considerable achievement, possibly a great one. It is first to be thought of as a literary achievement. Nothing could be more difficult than to present human extremity without, on the one hand, falsifying or mitigating the facts, or, on the other hand, assailing and subduing our minds with the details of horror. It is also a moral achievement, of the intelligence put at the service of the emotions.

The historical occurrence with which Mr. Blunden deals is the German occupation of the Ukraine up to the time when the Russians first retake the stricken city of Kharkov.

Perhaps nothing that the old historians describe was quite so dreadful as this, although it is not unique among the events of the last war. The Athenian genocide at Melos is one of the great crimes of the ancient world, yet this awful act was understood by its perpetrators to be exactly what it was, or so Thucydides leads us to believe. But the modern slaughter of the Jews, in the Ukraine as elsewhere, was undertaken, like everything else that the Germans undertook, not as a contravention of morality for the sake of expediency, but as a cogent example of a cultural faith, the hideous fruit of a carefully nurtured theory of ghastly morality. And the rationale of the Russian courses of action is a negation of human decency no less complete than the German.

And then those who suffered in the ancient world were likely to have had but a single enemy, dreadful as he may have been. But the victims of the situation that Mr. Blunden sets before us had two enemies, equally implacable, equally evil. If the Russian cruelty is more formal, less personal and fanciful—one almost says less fancy—than that of the Germans, it is no less ready and no less terrible; as one of the characters of the novel says, the MKVD, equally with the SS, provides its members "with the opportunity, within the rule of society, to experience the pleasures of absolute freedom," of which the most intensely enjoyable is the killing of the defenseless. Between these two opposing powers, it is not only men who are destroyed but even the idea of man.

Yet if what Mr. Blunden tells us is more terrible than what we read of in the old historians, still Thucydides' account of the Melian massacre, or of the plague at Athens, or of the death of the Athenian army in the Sicilian quarry, or, again, Tacitus' record of the tyranny, torture, and treachery of the Roman civil wars, or Josephus' narrative of the war against the Jews, are the ancient analogue of what the modern world has experienced in more extravagant form. And in the attitude of the historians, in their determination to maintain the power and integrity of the mind before the decay of the very fabric of society and the human soul, we have the tradition in which Mr. Blunden has put himself.

Yet there are novelists to whose work, in one aspect

or another, one does compare *The Time of the Assassins.* Flaubert, out of his great disgust with humanity, imaged in *Salammbo* scenes and atmospheres which make his Carthaginian novel in some ways comparable with Mr. Blunden's book. But Flaubert was corrupted by his subject. Its horrors "interested" him. They suggested to him the extremes of aesthetic response. The militant objectivity of his prose and pose is, as it were, the license for a kind of luxury of emotion. By this luxury Mr. Blunden is never tempted. He is not concerned to make us shudder even in a good cause. His moral resistance to evil does not fail for an instant. It is at all times supported by his intellectual, by his moral and political, commitment. His prose, with its stern restraint and precision and its grim pitying irony, is the sign and instrument of a mind that will not abrogate its function of asserting the order and worth of things even though the skies are falling.

And then it is inevitable that *The Time of the Assassins* should be compared with two other novels of contemporary history, Malraux's *Man's Fate* and John Hersey's *The Wall.* Mr. Blunden brings to his story gifts which are comparable with, even superior to, those of Malraux. It may be said, however, that as a novelist he is less fortunate than Malraux in the subject that history has given him. The historical circumstance of *Man's Fate* permits Malraux's characters to have the sense of the future, the awareness of history itself, the belief in the possibility of victory, the expectation that, even in defeat, their lives and deaths will have *counted,* even if only symbolically. And in *The Wall,* although the characters are without the hope of personal survival, still the past exists for them; the ideal future exists; the social group exists and is believed by its members to have an ideal permanence which makes the quality of its action important, however futile this action may be in a practical way, and the recording of its behavior an act of piety.

Mr. Blunden is not permitted to avail himself of the inestimable novelistic advantages which are implied by these circumstances of relative moral freedom. For example, the Ukranian Communists he represents are not free agents, thinking men and women, like those of Malraux—people who bring their minds, their hearts, and their pasts to the service of a cause, and who enter into a living relation with that cause, which implies that they may quarrel with it, or leave it. Almost three decades have passed since people could be in this kind of relation to Communism. Now, in *The Time of the Assassins,* the old Bolshevik, Lydia Artemova, may at moments feel dim stirrings of the free humanism of her student days, but she scarcely understands them. She has wholly identified herself with the Soviet regime and has made herself its entire tool. To her fellow party members in Kharkov, before the Germans took the city, she had been an awesome being because she had survived so many purges—for one naturally asked, "How many lives did you deliver that you are here?" And the young Communist *partizan,* Fomin, the type of ideal Soviet citizen, he has been bred up as the creature of the Party, capable of great courage and efficiency and wholly without the power to think or feel what has not been prescribed.

As for the two men of Mr. Blunden's novel who do have some vestige of the power to choose, they have virtually no real choices to make. Dr. Karandash, formerly a Ukranian nationalist, formerly an anarchist, formerly a Communist, now an agent of the SS in charge of certain politico-cultural manipulations, is the most fully developed character in the novel in the sense of being the most fully articulate, the one person who believes that he might possibly have charge of his own fate. His situation is somewhat similar to that of one of the ancient historians I have mentioned, Josephus. For Josephus, although in spirit a Jewish nationalist, was an official of Rome, attached to the army of Titus, and it was from this sad vantage-point that he observed the ordeal of his people. Dr. Karandash had been absorbed into the German apparatus through no original will of his own but with his grudging consent. A man of essential innocence, he accepts, while trying vainly to meliorate, the German methods, because, in the "long view," which his early Communist training made it the easier for him to take, any means of destroying the corrupt Soviet power are acceptable. Yet he cannot inure himself to the horror with which he has made common cause. With a naivety which is at odds with his knowingness, he commits himself to the Communist underground in Kharkov, only to be betrayed by it to his German masters. A fate of a similar kind befalls another ex-Communist, the German Muller, who, having suffered at the hands of the Russians, had accepted enlistment in the SS in order to gratify his hatred of Russians. Muller too is destroyed by the vestiges of the old humane values. Unable to endure his guilt as a member of the SS, he permits himself to be betrayed to the Communists.

In the grim ambiguities of their situation, Muller and Karandash are trying to reach, not faith—that, in the circumstances, would be too much to ask—but simply some ground for believing that they are, in the old sense of the word as they had once understood it, human. Only two of Mr. Blunden's characters are secure in their humanity and have no occasion to question it. Professor Shevchenko —he bears the name of a great Ukranian poet—had once been an eminent philologian, a lover of cultures and languages, in especial his native Ukranian. Under Soviet rule he had for a time been in favor with the authorities until a turn of the line had thrown him, not into the outer darkness from which there is no return, but into a limbo from which, should a counter-turn ever seem desirable, he might be drawn to be useful again. For many years before the German occupation he had scarcely lived at all, yet he knew himself to be the repository of the past, of the unique life of his people, and so his humanity had survived.

Shevchenko is, as it were, preserved in humanity by means of an idea, even though it is not, as Mr. Blunden presents it, an idea that has extensive power. The most luminous character in the book has no ideas at all, and perhaps she is the more enduringly human because of this. The young schoolteacher Maryusa had never been, as a Soviet citizen, political. Although entirely loyal, she had never joined the Party. When the Germans come she knows nothing else to do except keep open her little schoolhouse to receive and care for the children whose Communist parents had been summarily shot by the SS. But Maryusa is not long permitted to indulge her simple humanity and to run the school simply as the agency of natural mercy. The orders come that she must maintain "party vigilance" even though this is certain to mean the destruction of the school and its little inmates. When, in common humanity and common sense, she refuses, her doom is sealed.

The narrowness of the circumstances in which Mr. Blunden's characters must exist, the limitation of their power of choice, is, as I have suggested, a disadvantage to the novelistic imagination. It is a measure of Mr. Blunden's quality, of his literary power, his intelligence, and his moral commitment, that he overcomes this disadvantage. He overcomes it by realizing the power of the historical imagination. Like Thucydides, he derives his information in part from personal observation—he was for many years a correspondent in Russia and in that capacity was with the Red Army at Stalingrad and when it made its first reinvestment of Kharkov—and in part from careful inquiry. His commitment is to fact and to essential truth, which he serves no less by his imagination than by his experience and research. There is no page of his work that does not compel our admiring interest.

PART 1

In the late fall of 1941 the German Army, sweeping through the Soviet Ukraine, entered the city of Kharkiv. The people of Kharkiv came out into the streets to meet the Germans. Many people hailed the Germans as liberators. But on the morning of the third day the city was silent.

About eight o'clock that morning the door of the Krasnaya Hotel swung open and a man in a Homburg hat and a black overcoat stepped into the street.

The only other people to be seen were two young officers in long-skirted cavalry greatcoats who were standing before a neighbouring building. The officers were discussing the suitability of the building as a headquarters for General von Paulus. There had been a frost during the night and their voices rang loudly in the cold quiet air.

As the man in the Homburg hat walked by the officers he stopped.

"If I may be permitted," he said and he indicated a sign by the doorway of the building, "you are now looking at what was, until a few days ago, the home of the All-Ukraine Central Committee."

The officers stared at him.

"A handsome building," the man in the Homburg hat went on. "Allow me to point out to you the eighteenth century windows. In my time it was said to be the finest in Kharkiv." He wagged his head. "Ah, but in my time it was known as the Club of the Nobility."

The man in the Homburg hat resumed his walk, wondering why he had gone out of his way to practise this deceit. He had never been inside the Club of the Nobility; indeed he remembered that in his youth he had despised the whole street, which he had known as the

Nikolaevskaya, because it had been composed of such buildings: institutions, banks, houses of the great trade organisations. Looking at them now he was sure their character had not changed; though without a doubt renamed commissariats, they were as he remembered them: aloof, remote, impenetrable.

Turning off the old Nikolaevskaya the man in the Homburg hat made his way to a group of buildings he had known as the University of Kharkiv. Put up some time in the eighteenth century as a palace for the Russian governors of the Ukraine the University was not unpleasant to look at. Next door there was the Uspensky Cathedral with its high belfry tower. From the tower, he remembered, there had been a fine view over the city. The doors of the Cathedral were closed and there was the body of a man lying on the Cathedral steps, so that he was dissuaded from entering and attempting to climb the belfry tower.

The man in the Homburg hat remained looking at the old buildings. This little hill on which the buildings stood, the University Mount it had been called, was in fact the campus of his Alma Mater. Incongruous thought! Yet, here he had taken a degree of sorts. More important, here, in these precincts, thirty years ago, he had made the acquaintance with, and then passionately embraced, the libertarian ideas of his time. How sincere, inspired, brave and gifted his friends had seemed then!

This he said to himself, but he was not deeply moved. The street was narrower and the buildings smaller than he had thought. All were in need of repair. They were shabby in other ways too. Although he had approved of the old religious institutions being turned into museums, he was now a little ashamed for them, a little embarrassed for their pretensions as museums. They were not very old by European standards, nor were they very good examples of their style and age. The architecture was imitative of whatever had been fashionable in Europe at the time of their planning. But they were not exact imitations, always somewhere an exaggeration, or a too-strict formalism; always in cupola or cornice, a Byzantine or Baltic dramaturgy had crept in through the chisels and trowels of the workmen, so that the effect, intended to be worldly, cosmopolite, was in truth somewhat muddled.

The man in the Homburg hat entered a wide plaza. Around the plaza were a number of splendid modern buildings, among them one of fourteen stories. Standing in the plaza he became aware of the silence of the city. It was an oppressive, tense silence. Since passing the young officers he had not seen a living person.

He walked across the plaza, his footsteps echoing hollowly against the tall buildings. He thought he detected, in the distance, some slight sound, and now he walked towards the source. He turned into a long thoroughfare which he remembered as the Sumskaya.

Down the entire length of the Sumskaya there were the bodies of men and women hanging suspended by the neck from first- and second-story balconies.

There were so many bodies, and the reality was so improbable, that it appeared at first sight as though a great deal of merchandise had been hung out for sale, and this momentary confusion was prolonged by the mind's failing to identify the shapes, here and there, of those who had been hanged by the feet, head down, and whose garments had fallen over their heads and whose arms were stiffly semaphored. But then, in a flash they were seen for what they were.

And now, from the far end of the street, there was the muffled sound of a machine-pistol, coarse jests in German, and another body was flung over a balcony, dropping to the rope's end, there swinging pendulum-wise. An SS officer and two SS men came out of the building and entered the building next door.

The man in the Homburg hat waited. Then, with a nervous hand, he adjusted his dark glasses. He had noticed a furtive movement in the still, quiet street, a quick running from doorway to doorway under the heels of the dead. He saw that it was a boy making his way out of the street.

A few paces from the man in the Homburg hat the boy halted in his tracks.

The boy was about seventeen. He had big bony hands and a gaunt face with big cheekbones. Above the cheekbones, as though supported by the cheekbones, was a pair of direct-staring agate-coloured eyes.

"Come here, boy," said the man in the Homburg hat.

It is probable that Sumsk Street, or the Sumskaya, has never been called anything else by the mass of people in Kharkiv, but at the time of these events, and for some time before, it had been officially known as Karl Liebknecht Street, after the late German Communist leader of that name.

In a small apartment at the rear of a large building in Karl Liebknecht Street resided a family of Communists named Andrenko. They were young people of peasant origin, industrious, credulous, impregnable. Five years earlier their position had been one of slight importance, but a large number of vacancies occurring in the Party ranks about 1937 had made for them a rapid advancement. They had become functionaries of the Commissariat of Trade. Before them had opened the prospect of many years of enviable service and entrenched privilege. Jealous of their attainment, and being anxious to maintain and further their position, they had cultivated in all relationships, even between themselves, the forms of loyalty, obedience and enthusiasm.

The Andrenkos had one child, a son. Almost as soon as he could talk Fomin Nikolaevich had been entered in the Pioneers. He had worn the red kerchief, repeated faithfully the slogans, repeated after his teacher's "Be ready to fight in the workers' cause," the resounding, "Always ready!" In the Pioneers Fomin had learned to confess his own mistakes and, on occasion, those of his parents, though avoiding, and this was appreciated, the more obvious fantasies. Thus had candour been made serviceable, invention inhibited, and the ability to dissemble disciplined; the infant self-indictment, faintly foreshadowing the great Party cleansings (but so entertaining to the other Pioneers, among whom, so soon as the cue was given, there would be vociferous condemnation and the fun of shunning), had another function: the emotion of loyalty had been transferred from human and temporary objects to the abstract and permanent. Fomin had been a good Pioneer and had risen to be a Link leader, thus avoiding the fate of most boys his age, namely being drafted into one of the many labour schools or collective farm organisations. Earlier in the year Fomin had entered the Communist Youth League. Receiving at once high marks in Leninism he had readily understood the nature of the anti-Party leadership saboteurs and was learning to recognise and be armed against the foreign bourgeoisie.

The news that the Germans had entered the city had been brought home to his parents by Fomin.

After a brief and desperate stand at the bend of the Dnieper, Budonny's forces had retired to the Donetz. Kharkiv, lying between the two great rivers, was of small military consequence. Soldiers had passed through, and bombers had been seen over the city. But there had been no organised evacuation of Kharkiv, no proclamation, no Party directive, no warning of any kind, just the intelligence, passed from mouth to mouth that the *Nemtsy* were here. There had been no order to close the commissariats, but they were mostly closed, because the people who worked in them, like Fomin's parents, had remained at home, or had gone out into the streets. Nevertheless the Andrenkos had been confident that they would be told what to do. When Fomin had told his parents that thousands of people had come out to welcome the Germans and that the first thing these people had done was to direct the Germans to the *Narodny Kommissariat Vnutrennikh Djel* the Andrenkos had looked grave. But they still had not ventured out and they had bidden Fomin stay with them.

Early this morning, the third day after the arrival of the Germans, the door of the Andrenkos' apartment had been kicked open and an officer in a black uniform and a black helmet had stamped into the room. In his hand he had held a paper. Reading from the paper he had called the names of Fomin's parents.

"Nikolai Andrenko! Anna Andrenko!"

Having received no instructions to the contrary the Andrenkos had answered to their names. Whereupon an SS soldier had stepped from behind the officer and with a skilfully-short burst from his machine-pistol had shot them both dead. Erasing their names from his list the SS officer had debated whether the bodies should be added to the material of the demonstration, had decided against it, and gone away.

He had paid no attention to Fomin.

For a long time (measured by the retreating, spaced bursts of the machine-pistol) Fomin had stayed in the room. His parents had died without sound and so swiftly there had been little blood. Fomin had looked down on the fallen man and woman, on the still-soft hair of his mother, on the rough cheek of his father, and he had known that this was the end of life and that all he himself had was just such a life, held tight, dry-palmed, dry-mouthed, tremblingly within his breast, but at some time to be as easily expended. He did not touch the shapes which had contained the lives that had been his parents, nor did he attempt in any way to sustain the illusion that those lives were extant, but, when the machine-pistol no longer sounded close to him, he had taken his own life out of that room, holding it cunningly, feeling it nestling dry and hard in his breast, moving with soft catlike fluidity into the outside.

Staring at the stranger in the Homburg hat Fomin felt his world revive.

There were a few people in Kharkiv, as in other Soviet cities, who wore ordinary felt hats after the modern fashion. Time was when the wearing of felt hats had been encouraged. But none had ever appeared in Kharkiv wearing headgear such as this. It was a sooty black hat with an upcurling brim. It was a hat which boldly exposed the face. It was a complacent hat. It was not the hat of a responsible worker. It was a *foreign* hat!

"Tell me, boy, where is the *Narody Kommissariat Vnutrennikh Djel?*"

Not only did the foreigner wear this challenging hat, but he was otherwise provocatively garbed. He wore dark sunglasses. His overcoat of fine black cloth had a broad sable collar. His dark striped trousers were neatly creased. His shoes were black and glossy.

The fear that had almost dried up Fomin's heart now gave place to a profound needlelike suspicion. Suspicion was a familiar sensation. Fomin embraced the familiar, needing it.

"Please! Show me the way to the NKVD."

Without thinking of it as a conscious assumption of his duty Fomin knew he must follow the man in the Homburg hat, just as he would normally have done a week ago had the wearer then appeared in Kharkiv.

Fomin raised his arm, pointing. The man in the Homburg hat walked off in the direction indicated. Fomin followed him.

Presently they were in the street known as the Chernyshevskaya.

Fomin knew that the Germans had taken possession of the NKVD, but his imagination had not prepared him for what he now saw. Outside the building there was a sentry box painted in black-white-and-red stripes. A sentry was stamping up and down. At a second-floor window an officer in a black uniform was smoking a cigarette in a long ivory holder.

Fomin felt his world, momentarily rebuilt, falling away. More than anything he had seen that morning the sight of this foreign officer in nonchalant possession of the NKVD struck at the very roots of the Party and State authority.

The man in the Homburg hat entered the NKVD.

Freely translated, *Narodny Kommissariat Vnutrennikh Djel* (more often referred to by its initials) means People's Commissariat of Internal Affairs. Grander buildings there were in Kharkiv, but none so well suited to administrative supervision. Here were facilities for monitoring all channels of communication and movement, both civil and military. Here the population was registered and every branch of the bureaucracy—that is the total fabric of life in city and country—charted.

Those Kharkivanians who had led the Germans to the NKVD a few days before, believing the Germans to be the liberators of the Ukraine, had erred in thinking that the Germans would immediately destroy the hated records. In this firm triple-façaded building within easy reach of the main centres of government SS *Einsatzgruppe* C, as it had been led to expect from its experience in the cities behind it, had found quarters fashioned to its exact requirements. The Soviet cadres, having received no order from Moscow (not knowing that another German Army was at that moment at the western suburbs of Moscow, continuing to believe implicitly in the wisdom and paramountcy of Moscow, themselves not daring, nor even thinking, to act without the authority of Moscow), had quietly withdrawn. Thus the *Einsatz Kommandos* had at their disposal a modern system of prisons, isolators and interrogation rooms; more important to their immediate purpose were the massive archives.

Entering the archives section of the NKVD the man in the Homburg hat paused to look around. A single electric bulb burned weakly. By its light he saw tier after tier of filing cabinets, smooth unscalable cliffs of wood and brass, reaching into the gloomy recesses of the room. In dark canyons between the filing cabinets uniformed clerks, working by candle or flashlight, were turning out innumerable drawers.

Presently the man in the Homburg hat recognised a young officer he knew slightly. Catching the officer's eye he removed his Homburg hat, made the short continental bow. The officer greeted him.

"Herr Doktor Karandash."

"My dear Oberleutnant Soedermann, this is the real thing. The records of a whole country."

"For each and every individual," said Oberleutnant Soedermann, "a dossier."

Oberleutnant Soedermann inclined his plump, good-natured face towards Dr. Karandash.

"As far as the *Wehrmacht* is concerned the work is practically at an end. Should I tell you that from information gathered in this room we have been able to identify every unit of the Russian Army, their order of battle in fact?"

Together they walked across the room. At a nest of tables at the centre of the room officers and translators were working over a mass of documents by the light of battery lamps. A young officer in a black uniform turned towards them.

"Untersturmführer Doktor Gruber, *Vorkommando Kharkiv,*" said Oberleutnant Soedermann.

Dr. Karandash bowed. The officer was hatless, evidently very busy and impatient of the interruption. Through thick-lensed spectacles he stared owlishly at Dr. Karandash.

"I remember you," he said. "You were in Kiev."

"Yes," said Dr. Karandash.

"You are too early."

"In Kiev I was too late," said Dr. Karandash.

The officer slowly relaxed his severe expression, slowly began to smile. Oberleutnant Soedermann laughed outright.

"Here you are," said Untersturmführer Gruber.

With a sudden careless movement he gathered several large dossiers from among those heaped on the desks and put them in Dr. Karandash's arms.

"Thank you," said Dr. Karandash.

"Many, many dossiers," said Untersturmführer Gruber, with a wave of his hand.

It was a very good joke and all the translators and all the junior officers laughed.

Dr. Karandash did not laugh. With the dossiers in his grasp he felt again the urgency which had gripped him while standing in the Sumskaya.

In a far corner by a window he found an empty desk, put down the dossiers, took off his Homburg hat. From his overcoat pocket he took a leather-encased flask with a silver top and set it beside his hat. He took a cigarette from a large silver case, tapped it on the case, lit it. Drawing deeply on the cigarette he stood looking through the window at the city.

Faintly, through the window, he heard the sound of a machine-pistol.

He turned away from the window, troubled by a recurrent image. He had been surprised, standing in the Sumskaya, by the size of the human tongue, so often, in those swaying cadavers, thrust into a rude protuberance; how deceptive in life that collop of prehensile and empurpled flesh!

Dr. Karandash reached for his leather flask. Into the silver top which acted as a small cup he poured a full measure of cognac. He held it for a moment, savouring its fragrance, then tossed it down.

The largest of the dossiers bore the name Shevchenko.

"Shevchenko," said Dr. Karandash, repeating to himself the lines of the poet:

"Bury me, be done with me,
Rise and break your chains. . . ."

He emptied the contents of the dossier on the desk. The papers, some old, some new, some bound together with tape, fell out in unprecedented confusion. Among them was a photograph.

Dr. Karandash picked up the photograph and was suddenly looking across thirty years of unbridgeable time.

It was a portrait of a man with a high domed forehead and a bush of fine black hair falling almost to his collar. He wore a pince-nez secured to the lapel of his coat by a black ribbon. The lenses of the pince-nez were no bigger than the finger holes of a pair of scissors. From the high broad forehead the face tapered to a small sharp chin.

Spaced through the mass of documents were a number of papers written in the same fine hand. These were the subject's own depositions made at intervals over a long period. Dr. Karandash knew this to be an obligation of Russian Party members. He took up the earliest of the autobiographical papers, a yellowed folio at least twenty years old.

The fine, educated calligraphy, written in a precise and almost forgotten Ukrainian, the musty smell of the old paper, sent a tide of reminiscence to flood in Dr. Karandash.

Like Dr. Karandash the subject of the dossier had been born in the period of great reforms. Alas, the emancipation of the serfs, the abridgement of the Pale and the pogrom, land revision and the Code of Laws, provoking autocratic reaction on one hand, tsaricide on the other, had led to disillusionment, drift, humiliating defeat in the war, an abortive revolution. That was their youth; for their maturity, more sharply to mind, was the struggle of the liberals (in their hundred variations) for constitutional government. It was the period of the forcible dissolution of parliaments, summary arrest, secret police, strikes, Marxism, mutiny and a World War. The Revolution of April 1917 had seemed to bring Ukrainian independence closer; but it was not until Bolshevik seizure of power in November that the Ukrainians, after two hundred years of Russian domination, reforming their old parliament, the *Rada,* had proclaimed the First People's Republic of the Ukraine. But the Bolsheviks, in their desperate need for ending the war with Germany, had signed the treaty of Brest-Litovsk, and the Germans had flooded into the Ukraine, setting up their militarist government, their false Hetman. With the collapse of the Central Powers, had come the rise of Simon Petluria and the formation of the second People's Republic of the Ukraine; only to be dissolved by the White General Denikin. Civil War and the time of peasant leaders: Maryusa, that strange, cruel woman who had raised her own army, held men to ransom; the wonderful Makhno who had screwed machine-guns on to *britchkas* and thus provided himself with a galloping artillery of a formidable kind; Hryhoryev, conqueror of Odessa. The Reds, the Whites and the Greens, in that village of Shevchenko's birth fourteen regimes in three years! But the Bolsheviks had triumphed.

Suddenly Dr. Karandash threw down the paper. With his hands clasped behind his back he began striding backwards and forwards in front of his desk.

"It is 1924," he said, almost audibly, "and he is talking about the beauties of the cultural life. He is a philologist at Kharkiv University and all he can think about is how wonderful it is to teach and to write in the Ukrainian language!"

The anger Dr. Karandash was feeling was stimulated by his own memories of the period following the Civil War: the *moujik* soviets, the liquidation of the *kulaks,* the rounding-up and summary execution of the Social Revolutionaries, the Mensheviks, the Anarchists and the militant peasants; he remembered the incalculably devastating famine, the crop seizures, the revolt of the peasants and the mass deportations, the beginning of that steady stream of land-loving, gay, fruitful, unbroken Ukrainians entrained eastwards.

But now, pausing in his stride, resting his chin in the cup of his closed fist, he began to think that in those years there had, indeed, been a warm swift flowering of the long-dormant Ukrainian literature, already dying as it opened to the light, but undoubtedly, for one working in the cultural conservatory, a matter of wonder and excitement. It was not the last time, thought Dr. Karandash, that intellectuals were to be so misled.

"The test," said Dr. Karandash, "is not 1924, but the period of the collectivisations. He was a Ukrainian nationalist, yes? Then how did he survive that period?"

Now, fully absorbed in his subject, Dr. Karandash sat down at the desk, began shuffling the papers. He was not long in finding an answer to his question. In 1930 Professor Shevchenko had been among the accused in the famous "Trial of the 45."

In Kharkiv Opera House, under the Kleig lights, they had had a splendid trial, those forty-five professors, doctors, writers, artists, poets, schoolmasters, editors. Efremiv of the Academy and the obscure Shevchenko, all answering to the charge of having belonged to a society for the liberation of the Ukraine, all, a trifle unsteadily to be sure, making a full and ready confession. And they had all been found guilty in the most dramatic and exciting manner, condemned to exile and imprisonment without the right of communication which, in GPU jargon, had meant death by shooting. And shot they undoubtedly had been, all except Professor Shevchenko.

But how had Professor Shevchenko become involved in the great trial?

Gathered together in his dossier was most of the evidence against him. Here were a score of affidavits signed by his pupils, each affidavit identical in language, the work of some zealous GPU operative. Dr. Karandash turned them aside for a statement written in an educated hand, a long confession of association by a colleague of the Professor.

A colleague? As he read Dr. Karandash realized that the writer was a woman. It was evident that she had been the Professor's mistress. Perhaps mistress was a misleading word. They had lived together, certainly without benefit of clergy, perhaps without benefit of document, a companionate marriage after the manner of the times. The language of the statement was subdued, the expungement of a deeply-felt guilt. Now she was saying, with great sincerity, that she had committed a grave error against the Party; Professor Shevchenko, in the intimacy of their relationship, had revealed "bourgeois nationalist tendencies."

Dr. Karandash laid his large hands over the dossier, feeling that he held a life there. What keen and far-reaching intelligence had devised this system of personally-written biographies, affidavits, reports and confessions? It had been accidental, of course. In those early days there had been few clerks, few even on the Party committees who were literate; in those horny hands a pistol had been more easily grasped than a pen. So the intellectuals had set the pattern. Willingly and with enthusiasm they had written their own private histories. And what they had written had been so much more real, so much more self-committing, than any collection of second-hand evidence, any number of dutifully-filled-in forms. Whatever one wrote the next year, one's first account was always there in its fresh and original meaning. And the cross-references! Here, when you came to think of it—and Dr. Karandash let his gaze wander over the wide room—was recorded the emotional life of the country.

Dr. Karandash looked at the signature on the denunciation. The name was Zeta Yarmoslansky.

He half-rose out of his chair, fell back into it.

He had known Zeta Yarmoslansky. Now, overtaken by

remembrance, he saw again her eager mouth, the expression of intelligent provocation. He had known her as a student. For a time they had been intimates.

On a sudden impulse Dr. Karandash left his desk and began to search among the filing cabinets for that one which would contain the dossier of Zeta Yarmoslansky. He was helped by a gray-uniformed clerk with a little hand-generated flashlight which made a whirring sound.

The clerk, a stout man, watched Dr. Karandash remove the file.

"What," said Dr. Karandash, "you begrudge me this *one!*"

The clerk smiled obsequiously.

Back at his desk Dr. Karandash regretted his impulse. The weight of the dossier disheartened him. He had no desire to examine the Party history of Zeta Yarmoslansky. Not now. Not here.

He poured himself another cognac, swallowed it quickly.

After the trial Professor Shevchenko had found some small employment at the Korolenko State Library. This did not surprise Dr. Karandash. Such survivals were often a part of the larger Bolshevik tactic. Who knew but that the Bolsheviks themselves, for political reasons, might not, at some future date, need to stage a national revival? Against such an eventuality Professor Shevchenko had been preserved.

The professors who had been sent from Moscow to take the place of those engulfed in the "Trial of the 45" had produced various works, including a dictionary of the language, which the Party had launched with conclusive solemnity. Parallel with these official productions Professor Shevchenko, working in some crevice of the Korolenko State Library, had been preparing his own dictionary. He had been given no official encouragement, but, to judge from his reports, there had been a great deal of official interest in his work.

Dr. Karandash visualised the quietly-contained passion gripping that serene head, the pince-nez shaking a little as he penned his attacks on the official dictionary, listing its inaccuracies, evasions, fearlessly promoting his pure Ukrainian. Thus, all the time they had been pushing the official work, the Soviet cadres had been provided with a clear view of its value.

In the vast purge of 1937 the professors from Moscow had disappeared. In the hours of their interrogation they had no doubt been surprised by the Soviet cadres' expert knowledge of their philological sabotage. But there was no triumph in Professor Shevchenko's writings during this period. The reports were brief, episodic, wandering into research, reminiscence, finally into incomprehensibility. The great purge had concluded with the liquidation of the old Soviet cadres, the GPU, and their replacement by a new generation, the NKVD. Under pressure the Professor had written reports about other people, but they were people who had had no existence.

Dr. Karandash took up the last paper. He read: "Adopting the attitude of the utmost Party vigilance I have now to report the defection of my brother Ivan. This occurred in the trenches during a heavy bombardment by the enemy. Suddenly there was an explosion. I looked down and saw that my head was in my hands, bloody, but cleanly decapitated. And then my mouth smiled at me and my head spoke to me and the language was Ukrainian. But when the dust settled I saw that it was not my own head that had been torn off and fallen in my arms, but the head of my brother Ivan."

Dr. Karandash thought he understood the parable. Mad the Professor might seem to the unimaginative men of the NKVD, but Dr. Karandash knew that he had found what he had been looking for: here together, Professor Shevchenko and the Library, living in consort, each fertilising the other, was perhaps the last pregnable seed of Ukrainian independence, the secret, indefinable, fecund seed of language.

Echoing across the great archives room came the words: *Achtung! Achtung!* Immersed in his dossier Dr. Karandash failed to hear the order. A shadow fell across his desk. He looked up. Standing before him was the figure of an SS General.

Dr. Karandash rose, stepped to the side of his desk, holding himself erect in the official manner.

The SS General was looking at the dossiers on the desk.

"You are a specialist of traitors?" he asked.

"Of patriots," said Dr. Karandash.

The SS General gave him a quick, appreciative look.

Dr. Karandash saw that he wore the oak leaves and star of a full SS Obergruppenführer, and on the left sleeve of his jacket the insignia of the SD. The tailored uniform, upswept black-visored cap and large round spectacles gave him the appearance of a stock theatrical figure.

"They are Communists you have here?" the Obergruppenführer asked.

"We look for people who have learned the lesson of Stalinism."

"You mean the Opposition?"

"Elements of opposition."

"You are perhaps a former Communist?" the Obergruppenführer asked with excessive politeness.

Dr. Karandash inclined his head and smiled, as at demonstrable absurdity. "I have never been a member of the Communist Party," he said.

"What did you say the name was?"

"Karandash."

The Obergruppenführer repeated the name: "Karandash, Karandash. An improbable name. You should have thought of something better than that," he said.

"My papers . . ." began Dr. Karandash.

The Obergruppenführer waved a hand in the direction of the filing cabinets.

"Have you looked to see if your dossier is here?"

Dr. Karandash was chilled. It was an idea which had not occurred to him.

"Anyway, not under the name of Karandash, eh?"

Dr. Karandash had always relied upon his appearance to carry him through his association with officials of one kind or another. His round head with its cropped white hair, the small eyes and short nose, the wide mouth full of irregular teeth, all this had hitherto served as an unchallengeable camouflage. Now, for the first time, he felt his disguise had been penetrated. Standing there in his black coat and waistcoat and his dark striped trousers, he began to sweat.

The Obergruppenführer shuffled the dossiers about.

"What are they?"

"Dissidents," said Dr. Karandash.

"I mean, are they Jews?"

The Obergruppenführer began reading the names, pronouncing the Cryllic script without effort.

"Yarmoslansky, what kind of a name is that?" he asked.

"Nothing," said Dr. Karandash.

The Obergruppenführer stood back from the desk.

"I think," said the Obergruppenführer, "that we must go into this question of Communist usefulness. Come with me tomorrow at noon and I will show you what I mean."

The Obergruppenführer turned lazily. His mouth assumed an expression of stern and contemptuous boredom. The SS clerks sprang stiffly to attention as he sauntered, jauntily erect, out of the archives room.

If Dr. Karandash had been younger, and easily frightened, he would have been trembling. He was able to control the outward expression of being hopelessly trapped. But he could not repress the agitation in his heart.

Putting the flask to his lips he drained it dry.

He put on his Homburg hat. Then he stood for a moment, overcome by a sense of shame.

Turning back to his desk he gathered together the papers of Professor Shevchenko's dossier, put them back in the large envelope. The act of doing this gave him new determination. He took the dossier of Professor Shevchenko and that of Zeta Yarmoslansky and put them securely under his arm.

As he walked out of the archives room he heard hasty footsteps behind him. He quickened his pace, but Oberleutnant Soedermann caught him by the sleeve.

"You spoke with Obergruppenführer Rauch?" said Oberleutnant Soedermann.

"He spoke to me."

"It is very good for you," said the Oberleutnant. "It is a big success. He is a big man. A friend of Heydrich."

"We have an appointment for tomorrow at noon," said Dr. Karandash.

Watching Dr. Karandash depart, Oberleutnant Soedermann did not notice the bulky dossiers under his arm.

In the street Dr. Karandash took a deep breath. There were several children gaping at the German sentry. A hundred paces distant, loitering in a doorway, he saw Fomin.

Dr. Karandash did not waste time hailing Fomin. He walked quickly over to him.

"Boy," he said, "take me to the Korolenko State Library."

As though he had been waiting for exactly this request Fomin turned, without speaking, and led the way out of the street.

They had walked a couple of blocks when Fomin halted and pointed.

"The Street-of-the-First-of-May," he said.

Dr. Karandash took him firmly by the arm.

"Take me to the Library," he said.

The Street-of-the-First-of-May was in bad shape. Clearly through this street had passed the traffic of an army. The walls of the adjacent buildings had been splashed with mud to the eaves. In the gutters there were holes where great wheels had spun.

At the corner of a small side street the soldiers who had been pushing and hauling their vehicles, the limbers and the cannon and the troop carriers, had endeavoured to pack the soft gripless mud with ballast sufficient to hold the wheels, and for this purpose had found, somewhere near by, numberless books. The mud holes were now frozen, but congealed in the frozen mud there were books.

Looking down the Street-of-the-First-of-May, which he now recognised as the old Moscow Road, Dr. Karandash saw that the soldiers had repeated their improvisation its entire length. In some places the pages of books had spun out from beneath the wheels like confetti and now lay over the surface of the road, held tight by frost.

Following Fomin, Dr. Karandash stepped across the frozen mud and entered a side street. Down this street the books had been brought in armfuls. Where books had fallen they had been left. Soon Dr. Karandash was standing before the Library from which the books had been taken. On the steps of the Library there was a cascade of books, most of them expanded accordionwise by damp, before being frozen.

Now that he was here before the Library he remembered it. The street in which he was standing had been called Petrovsky Street. How many hundred times had he entered the old Public Library in Petrovsky Street?

Stepping over the fallen books Dr. Karandash entered the foyer. In the little hall in the middle of the building he paused.

The quiet that lay over Kharkiv was accentuated by the acoustics of the high closed room. He could have heard a clock tick, a rat scuffle, but there was no sound. As his eyes became accustomed to the faint light filtering down from the tiny high windows he remembered the little hall. Chamber music concerts had been held in this hall. It had been popularly said that it was here, and not in St. Petersburg or Vienna, that Count Razoumovsky had permitted the first performance of the Quartet in C. And there, over there by the table, had sat the young woman to whom they had all been so indebted, the lady librarian, daughter of a noble and liberal family, who had organised and conducted the clandestine library of revolutionary works. It was from her, he remembered, that he had obtained Plekhanov and Bukunin and, later, Kautsky and Luxemburg. Ah, those fervid clandestine readings under the very noses of the *Okhrana!* A thin rod of sunlight lanced down from a small high window. In its aura Dr. Karandash saw a confusion of books and broken chairs on the floor of the hall. A company of soldiers had recently camped there. Empty cognac and vermouth bottles lay about. The odour of tobacco and boot leather and sweaty underclothes hung in the air.

Dr. Karandash felt that he had no more time to waste. He began making a search of the Library building. He looked briefly into the main reading room without much expectancy. He then went to the stacks rooms, wading through heaps of books to peer into every corner. The rooms were cold, damp, empty.

In the hall Dr. Karandash shouted:

"Shevchenko!"

Echo answered with a long drawn out o-o-o-o.

Going out into the street Dr. Karandash saw something he had not noticed before: hanging by the neck from an upper window, hugging the wall, was the body of a man. Dr. Karandash turned to Fomin.

"Is that him?"

"No."

The body of the man appeared to move slightly and Dr. Karandash was sure that he saw the man's tongue fall out.

He could bear no more. The afternoon was waning and there was already a night chill in the air. He remembered his warm room in the Krasnaya Hotel.

Standing in front of the Korolenko State Library, Fomin watched the man in the Homburg hat walk swiftly away.

An unconsidered consequence of German methodism (in the effort to achieve a permanent solution to the Communist problem) was now the number of parentless children in Kharkiv. It having been the custom of the Party generally to enroll man and wife, not the one without the other, so the *Einsatzgruppen* generally had been taking both parents. There were at once thousands of orphans in Kharkiv. Some children went immediately to friends and relatives. But for many there were no longer friends or relatives and for these, and for the very young, the streets spelled an unnameable terror. So they stayed in their empty homes until the intolerable tedium of confinement, hunger, and the irreducible need to repair the routine of their lives sent them, finally, to school. Most schools were closed. But at one schoolhouse, the old wooden schoolhouse in the Sadovo-Kulikovskaya, some children found the schoolteacher Maryusa Selova.

Maryusa Selova was not one of those Ukrainians who had met the Germans with bread and salt, as the saying is. On the day that the *Wehrmacht* arrived in Kharkiv she had remained at her schoolhouse. There had been few pupils that day, but she had kept the schoolhouse open.

Now, three days later, the attendance was nearer normal. The classrooms had filled up and Maryusa was planning to give the children a course of self-study. But then she saw that the children sat very quietly at their desks and that their behaviour was not like that of normal boys and girls. And suddenly she was aware that the school had silently filled with scores of young children who ordinarily had no place there. As she left the quiet classrooms she saw children crouching in the hallway and corridors. Everywhere she was met by grave childish eyes. Some of the children had brought infant brothers and sisters. In the hush that lay over the schoolhouse she heard a baby cry.

The sound stirred Maryusa Selova. A serious Ukrainian woman of peasant origin, the cry produced in her, as never before, and never to be allayed, an overwhelming sense of responsibility. She knew suddenly her role in these days of loathing.

She at once threw wide open the doors of the schoolhouse. The school was situated in the district of the Party organisations and was attended mostly by the children of Party members. Maryusa welcomed all.

Mostly they were children who came seeking shelter, but there was one other. He stood inside the entrance. When Maryusa saw him she mistook him for a soldier and was afraid. He was so gaunt, hard, expressionless. On his cheekbone there was a blue gash. He brought into the schoolhouse a breath of the city. Maryusa sensed what it must be like out there in the streets. He looked at her with agate eyes. She felt a weakening under that gaze.

"You may come," Maryusa said.

Fomin did not reply. He was studying the schoolhouse.

"This is a Normal school," Maryusa said, "for young children, but you may come in."

"This was my school," Fomin said. "I was here a Link leader of Pioneers."

"Yes. Many who were Pioneers are here."

"Yes?" Fomin said. "Then there is an organisation?"

"There is no organisation."

"But it is a place to wait," Fomin said, entering.

Inside the schoolhouse that evening there was warmth. Outside the night wind brought a faint animation to the balconies; for then the elongated, wooden-limbed, foot-slack figures with their pale brush-drawn faces would stir and commune like monstrous puppets in a puppet theatre which the puppet master has closed for the night.

In the morning the hoarfrost sparkled in the sun, but Dr. Karandash, stepping out of his hotel later than usual, somewhat hungover, was filled with revulsion for the fresh, sharp air which stung his nose and made his eyes water.

The dark sunglasses offered a grateful relief from the cloudless blue sky. As his vision adjusted itself he saw Fomin.

The youth came immediately over to him.

"Come," Fomin said.

Dr. Karandash sensed an involvement.

"Come with me," Fomin said.

As they walked through the streets Dr. Karandash tried to rationalise his action. He is a serious boy, he thought. He is leading me to something of importance. He is obviously a Party product, otherwise he could not command. I must act cautiously.

They were very soon at the schoolhouse in the Sadovo-Kulikovskaya. Fomin led Dr. Karandash into the building.

It was dark inside the school and Dr. Karandash had to remove his sunglasses in order to see about him. He was taken aback by the number of small children and would have retreated but that Fomin took him by the elbow and led him firmly into a small inside room.

"Wait," said Fomin.

Dr. Karandash looked about the room. The window had been blacked-out with sheets of newspaper. There was a truckle bed in one corner, a small bureau in another. The floor was bare.

The door opened and a slight, stooped figure entered, not quite propelled or pushed, but diffidently a half-pace ahead of Fomin. Fomin closed the door.

"This is him," Fomin said.

"Who?"

"The one you were looking for. The Shevchenko."

"I am Professor Shevchenko, certainly," the figure said.

Dr. Karandash bent to look closely at the source of the voice. He was moved to see how much resemblance there was to the photograph in the dossier. The bush of hair was thin and dank and streaked with grey like candle grease. The broad forehead was hollowed at the temples. The jaw tapered to a feline chin, but under the chin there was a deep recess, so that the chin seemed as sharp as a chisel. A ribbonless pince-nez was balanced on the straight nose, but the lenses were so thick and so clouded with greasy thumbmarks that they looked like moonstones.

The old man wore a high starched collar and a thin white linen tie tinily knotted. His coat was of the kind that used to be called a Norfolk jacket. The narrow lapels met together above the breastbone. The jacket was belted and the skirts of the jacket hung wide and low, showing the flaps of very large pockets. There was a fob pocket. The trousers of the suit were knickerbockers, but instead of stockings and shoes the Professor wore a pair of patched peasant *valinki,* or felt boots.

Professor Shevchenko saw that Dr. Karandash was observing his dress. His smile was one of childish pleasure.

"You should congratulate me, yes?"

"I do," said Dr. Karandash. "Really, I have not seen anything like it. Truly 1900."

"Very practical," said Professor Shevchenko. "For bicycling."

"Yes, yes. I remember. The sportive style."

"It can be done if one is careful," said Professor Shevchenko.

"Well, it will soon be over. Then you will have a coat like this one."

"It is a very beautiful coat," said Professor Shevchenko, looking with admiration at the black worsted with the sable collar. "But it not for such as I."

"Why not? You are a professor of philology, are you not? An esteemed calling."

"It would be superior. Such coats are for responsible workers."

"I looked for you at the Library," Dr. Karandash said.

"Ah!" The expression on Professor Shevchenko's face might have been mistaken for merriment.

"You understand that the Germans have conquered the Ukraine?"

"So?"

Dr. Karandash looked solemnly at Professor Shevchenko.

"Can it be," he said, "that you did not notice this?"

They were looking at each other. And then Dr. Karandash saw himself in Professor Shevchenko's eyes. He began laughing, his round frost-pinked face splitting open like a half-ripe pomegranate to show red gums and white teeth.

"You take me for a provocateur?" he said. "A GPU man, eh?"

"Not you." The words, spoken swiftly and softly in German, shocked Dr. Karandash into instant sobriety.

The Professor was staring at him through the misty orbs of his pince-nez.

Dr. Karandash looked at Fomin. The boy had not taken his eyes off them since entering the room.

"Of course," said Dr. Karandash. "Let us go outside. Let us walk."

The sun, moving towards its zenith, now gave welcome warmth. Dr. Karandash lit a cigarette. In the act of doing so he observed Professor Shevchenko's frame assume a birdlike tension.

"Pardon me," said Dr. Karandash, "you will have a cigarette?"

With delicacy Professor Shevchenko extracted a cigarette from the large silver case. For a moment he held the cigarette in his fingers and then suddenly it disappeared. Dr. Karandash stared as one who sees, but cannot fathom, a conjuring trick. There was a bench near by. They sat down.

Dr. Karandash did not quite know how to begin the conversation he had planned the day before.

"You know the Library is ruined?" he said.

"So."

"Hitler exaggerates," Dr. Karandash said. "That is why in the end the Germans always fail. Hitler will fail too." Dr. Karandash looked at Professor Shevchenko meaningly. "That will be to our advantage," he said.

"Naturally."

"Yes," said Dr. Karandash. "You agree?"

Professor Shevchenko smiled. His small mouth widened into a smile of appalling innocence and candour.

"Here," he said, "Ukrainian is an approved language."

"The approved language, but not the spoken language. I understand that Russian is spoken everywhere now. There are many Russians in Kharkiv, yes?"

"In the villages everyone speaks the Ukrainian."

"In the villages, yes, and in Siberia."

"A big place, Siberia."

"Big enough to hold the Left Opposition, the Workers' Opposition, the Bundists, Trotskyists, Bukharinites and the rest."

"Ah, yes, so big."

"Professor Shevchenko, let us not waste words. Have you heard anything of Kussivizsky?"

"I do not remember."

"In Kiev," said Dr. Karandash, heavily, "there were many who did not have the opportunity of remembering. That is why I hurried here. I thought to get here before they could begin liquidating the Party members. I am afraid that I am too late. You understand me?"

Dr. Karandash waited, then he said:

"What of Stalin?"

"It is a name often heard, the great Stalin."

Dr. Karandash stood up. He clasped his hands behind his back and took a step to one side of the bench, turned and paced back.

"Do not imagine," said Dr. Karandash, "that I do not know what you are thinking. Or that I do not understand the moral problem."

He looked searchingly at Professor Shevchenko.

"You are asking why I am in alliance with the forces of reaction."

He raised a white forefinger.

"Because," he whispered hoarsely, "there is no other alternative. There is only Stalin and the forces opposed to Stalin. There is nothing else. It has taken the world a long time, but the world has learned that at last. Until Stalin is destroyed there is nothing else, nothing!"

Dr. Karandash's voice took on the authority of a lecturer.

"Of what practical use is it to discuss questions of principle or method? Parliaments? Legal opposition? Socialism? Bureaucracy? Democracy? It is academic. Stalin has answered us with his twenty years of history! The Workers' State has disappeared under his personal dictatorship. Before there can be any progress *he* must be destroyed. If we do not destroy him, he will destroy us. I mean all of us. Look at what has happened in Germany! And Spain! Think for a moment what would happen if he should win this war. We Ukrainians know what would happen. Russian chauvinism, inflated as it never was under the Czars, running wild, with Europe, the whole world, before it! In the face of this menace you take allies where you find them."

Dr. Karandash stood back from the bench.

"There," he said. "You have my position in a few words."

"When you make a speech the language is much better," said Professor Shevchenko.

"It will be necessary to make speeches."

"Yes, they are permitting speeches?"

"We must act now while the situation is still flexible and they are happy about their victories."

"The situation is flexible?"

"There is a faction in Berlin which is in favour of a *cordon sanitaire*. They talk vaguely about the Ostland, about colonising. But they have no firm plans. Indeed they have not the slightest understanding of the political situation here."

"The Ostland? A German expression."

"That hurts you, eh?" Dr. Karandash became confidential. "You know, we could have Ukrainian accepted as an official language—after German, of course."

Professor Shevchenko smiled.

"At every crisis in the history of our country," Dr. Karandash continued, "an attempt has been made to suppress the Ukrainian language. Why? Because our language is the expression of our independence. Our country is fragmented, but language binds us together. We cling to language to preserve our national identity."

Dr. Karandash paused.

"We shall have Ukrainian taught in the schools. We will make it the vehicle of our communication with the masses of workers and peasants. Then, as we grow, we shall strengthen the language with literary works, with drama and poetry, papers of scholarship and political economy. In a few years we shall have an intelligentsia. The intelligentsia will grow out of the masses and it will defend and inspire the masses."

Dr. Karandash looked at Professor Shevchenko. An expression of innocent guile curtained his round face.

"Of course," he said, "I shall not put it like that. I shall say that the encouragement of the Ukrainian language is the strongest bulwark against communism. We might even prohibit the Russian language. Yes, they would like that."

Dr. Karandash glanced at his watch.

"When I see the Obergruppenführer today I shall broach the subject."

Professor Shevchenko, wet-lipped, his mouth bracketed between creases of incredible youthfulness, his pince-nez shaking, his eyes small and blue and mirthful, was regarding his visitor with superb good humour as though he had just heard and was savouring an anecdote of incomparable and undiminishing irony.

"How's that, eh!" said Dr. Karandash. "Who would have thought of Ukraina that her liberation lay in the lap of a grammarian?"

For a moment Dr. Karandash had an irrepressible urge to laugh. But he did not laugh. He overlaid the impulse to laugh with an earnestness and a heavy gravity, the continental gravity.

"We shall proceed with the utmost caution," he said. "In Lviv they hung out signs, the old signs, 'As the People Think, the People Will.' The Germans killed them all. Here we shall wait."

Dr. Karandash became ever more grave.

"But there is much work to be done. We must prepare."

"Yes, yes," said Professor Shevchenko.

"And we will need you," said Dr. Karandash. "I shall be quite frank. What we need is the name. The glorious name of Shevchenko!"

"A common name."

"It is a name around which a national movement could be rallied."

"I think not."

In the silence, imperceptibly, the good humour faded out of Professor Shevchenko's countenance giving place to an expression of detachment. It was as though Dr. Karandash were no longer there, as though, indeed, the world were nonexistent, particularly the world of Kharkiv.

"Remember," said Dr. Karandash, "what I am offering you may be nothing less than the Presidency of the Republic."

"The time for republics," said Professor Shevchenko, "is over."

Dr. Karandash drew on his gloves.

"Last April Alfred Rosenberg was made commissioner for the central control of all questions pertaining to the Eastern Territory. Rosenberg hates us. But he knows our economic value. Through him we might save ourselves."

Dr. Karandash brushed out the creases of his black worsted overcoat with the sable collar.

"Let me ask you a question," he said. "What has happened to Zeta Yarmoslansky?"

Professor Shevchenko did not answer. Dr. Karandash saw that he was shuddering.

"I am sorry," said Dr. Karandash, "it is a painful subject."

"It is nothing," said Professor Shevchenko, "just that it is cold here."

"How stupid of me. Let us go indoors."

Dr. Karandash looked again at his watch.

"But I must be going," he said. "I shall call again. Meanwhile goodbye."

At Dr. Karandash's request the Obergruppenführer ordered the driver to halt the Mercédès at the war memorial in Teveleva Place. The memorial was a tank anchored in a bed of concrete. Rust peeled from its rivetted boiler-plated sides and the sawn-off six-pound naval guns protruding through the sponsons were green with verdigris.

Together the Obergruppenführer and Dr. Karandash viewed the memorial.

"A Medium Mark A," said Dr. Karandash. "On the Somme they were a failure. You observe the great length, ten metres or more. It was not sufficient to bridge the shell craters, the engines stalled. . . ."

The Obergruppenführer looked around Teveleva Place.

"The British sent a squadron of A Mediums to Denikin. We invented a technique for stopping them: the gasoline bottle. . . ."

"You are an expert, eh?"

"In my book, *The Steel Fist,* I predicted that German armour would turn the French flank at Sedan."

"It has not escaped attention."

"I am not surprised. Their dossiers contain everything."

"Their dossiers! In the *Sicherheitsdienst* we have our own information service. I seem to remember that you fought then on the side of the Communists."

"That was long ago. There were no Communists then; no such thing as a Communist. We were a great working class movement. Either we belonged to the majority or minority factions of the Russian Social Democratic Party, or we were Social Revolutionaries, liberals with ideas of social justice, or we were even more idealistic . . . pure . . ."

"You were of the pure?"

Dr. Karandash hesitated. "Yes," he said.

The Mercédès was a military convertible with glass

windows protecting the rear as well as the front seat. In the shelter of the rear windshield the sun was warm. The Obergruppenführer removed his peaked cap, took off his spectacles, began wiping them with a handkerchief.

Looking out from the corners of his dark glasses Dr. Karandash studied the Obergruppenführer.

He was a man of about thirty-five, slightly bald, with a broad forehead and a well-buttressed jaw. His nose was short and straight, his chin slightly cleft. His mouth was held tight, thin-lipped against emotion. His eyes were deepset and shadowed, probably a dark blue, but steady in their gaze as though permanently focussed, like a falcon's, into great distances.

"My father was an old National Liberal," he said. "He used to talk like that. He had a farm near Hanover. I myself, at sixteen, was a youth director of the German National People's Party."

"The tradition of German liberalism was a fine one."

"Liberalism rationalised his unending struggle with debt without destroying his sense of belonging to the traditional bourgeoisie. Already I was of another generation. I no longer had a stake in the class system."

"Yes," said Dr. Karandash, slightly astonished.

"Yet, when I looked at the life in our village, the moral and religious life, the family life, the good German life, I could not become a Marxist. I did not know then, as I learned later, when taking my law degree at Leipzig and Goettingen, that the international aspect of Bolshevism derives from the character of Marx, from the eastern Bund, from Trotsky and his like."

"Why do you tell me this?"

"Because it is possible to have made a mistake, especially for those of the cities who had not had the benefit of the communal life of our villages. The disillusioned Communist may be of value to us. I do not speak of the bureaucrats."

"If you speak of the present," said Dr. Karandash, savagely, "I will say that when a Stalinist becomes an ex-Stalinist his methods do not change. He merely employs them in reverse."

"It is not, then, a matter of principle?"

"They embrace the principle because it justifies the method. It is the method which attracts."

"Our methods," said Obergruppenführer Rauch, "are dictated by the Bolsheviks. In the strategy and tactics of the Bolshevik world revolution no rules preside other than those which further and promote its aims: the extermination of class enemies, the deportation of whole populations, the liquidation of every vestige of political opposition."

"Alas, we of the Ukraine . . ."

"In total war the weapons of the enemy become your weapons. We need men practised in the enemy's weapons."

"You are not afraid of spies?"

"We are aware of that danger. It is a difficult problem. There are several ways. I am thinking now that a man's true disposition may be brought out in normal conversation, in his own jargon, especially on first principles."

Dr. Karandash suddenly understood.

"You wish me to talk to such men on first principles? What first principles?"

"For example, that peoples are independent organisms which must solve their own problems."

"What! I should talk about the Rosenberg Plan!"

"The Rosenberg Plan?" The Obergruppenführer's voice expressed innocent puzzlement. "The Rosenberg Plan is simply an aspect of the method. Like the Bolsheviks we have to maintain face with a weak and sentimental world. You understand that."

"But the economy," said Dr. Karandash.

"We of the *Einsatzgruppen* are all economists."

The Obergruppenführer put on his spectacles, settled his high upturned cap with its oak-leafed visor and tiny death's head insignia.

He had spoken without a trace of humour or irony.

They had driven out through the factory district to the southeast of Kharkiv. Now, as they approached the famous tractor factory, the road skirted a large barbed-wire compound in which there were upward of a thousand Soviet prison labourers. The compound was an expanse of trodden mud, frozen hard. There was a group of rough barracklike buildings at its center. High guard towers, log cabins on stilts, commanded every side of the compound. In the guard towers there were guards.

The Obergruppenführer told the driver to halt. There were a number of prisoners within call. They wore shapeless mud-coloured clothes. Dr. Karandash called to the nearest prisoner in Ukrainian. The prisoner came over to the wire. A hundred prisoners turned towards Dr. Karandash and suddenly they were moving together towards him. Dr. Karandash had the brief ineradicable sensation of being on another, older planet; standing looking across the cold silent landscape of exhausted aeons and then seeing this movement that was like an outlasted crustacean life, formless, earth-coloured, merging from the earth itself as soldier crabs emerge from the muddy tidal sands and move together, at no discernible signal, yet out of some residual intelligence, perfectly regimented, in one direction, at one pace, with quiet aimless menace.

"Bread," the prisoners cried, "give us bread."

In the guard towers the guards were shouting, working the bolts of their rifles.

"They are starving," said Dr. Karandash.

"They will not have long to wait," said Obergruppenführer Rauch.

The Mercédès began moving and Dr. Karandash fell back into his seat.

"How is it," said Dr. Karandash, "that they were not able to break out before you arrived?"

"The guard, the *militsia,* have come over to us. We have screened out the best of them. We have even some German ex-Communists."

"I see," said Dr. Karandash. "Now I see."

Close by the tractor factory there were several large barracklike buildings, workers' dwellings, not very different from the hutments inside the compound, except that they had heating systems. Here a *Teilkommando* of *Einsatzgruppe C* was quartered.

An SS officer led Obergruppenführer Rauch and Dr. Karandash into one of the buildings. An SS officer was seated at a table on which there was a notebook. Lined up before him were eight prisoners.

They were like wolves in a famine year, but young, pale-eyed, shifty wolves. They were clothed in quilted jackets and padded trousers of incomparable filth. Their feet were bound in rags cemented together by mud and frost. In the heat of the room the poultice bindings were thawing. The stench, beginning now faintly, gave promise of becoming soon unendurable. The prisoners did not appear to notice their own smell. They wore straggling beards. Beneath their beards the skin was creased in grime. The flesh of their necks was wasted. Several were toothless. One wore a pair of cracked spectacles.

But they stood erect, stood in line like soldiers and did not waver. The SS officer had given them cigarettes. They were smoking the cigarettes carefully. They sheltered the cigarettes in black calloused hands.

"You observe," said Obergruppenführer Rauch, aside to Dr. Karandash, "the military stance. They have all done service at some time or other."

"The *Rote Front,"* said Dr. Karandash.

The SS interrogation officer took up a bundle of eight Soviet passport cards and passed them to Obergruppenführer Rauch. Rauch selected one and gave it to Dr. Karandash.

The passport was made out in the name of Albert Müller and had been issued by the Administration of the *Glavnoye Upravleyne Lageri,* called *Gulag* for short, or Department of Prison Management, fourth department of the NKVD.

"Müller!"

The prisoner called Müller stepped forward. He was a thin man of about thirty-eight years. He was the prisoner wearing spectacles.

"You were among those Party members who went to Russia in 1933?" Dr. Karandash asked Müller.

"Yes."

"Imprisoned at the time of the Russo-German pact, yes?"

"Yes."

Dr. Karandash could think of nothing to say. "What are you going to do now?" he asked.

"What do you think?" one of the prisoners said. "We have joined the *Waffen* SS."

The prisoners had broken their line and they were now grouped around Dr. Karandash, standing around him at arm's length, not looking him in the face, but, doglike, throwing a look now and then at his figure. Glancing over his shoulder Dr. Karandash saw that the Obergruppenführer and his interrogation officer had withdrawn. Through the window Dr. Karandash caught sight of the Obergruppenführer's back.

"Are you a Russian?" one of the prisoners asked.

"No. I am a Ukrainian."

"It is the same."

"In the prison camps you cannot trust the Russians," one of the prisoners said. "They hate all foreigners and spy on them."

"They spy on one another," a prisoner said.

"All they understand is spying," another said.

The man Müller spoke: "The Russians deliberately sabotaged the German revolution and destroyed the German leadership."

Dr. Karandash was startled.

"Take no notice of Müller," one of the prisoners said.

"No doubt you have had many opportunities for observing the rebirth of Russian chauvinism," Dr. Karandash said.

"Only *we* know!" said a prisoner.

"Have you ever been in a Russian prison camp?" said another.

"No," said Dr. Karandash.

"Then you know nothing."

The prisoner called Müller had pinched cheeks and a prominent bony chin. His mouth was small, the shape of the lips still discernible, and surprisingly tender.

He did not look Dr. Karandash in the eyes, but kept looking at the sable collar of his overcoat. Behind the cracked spectacles there was an expression of sly, mocking, venomous humour.

Müller waved his hand in the direction of the tractor factory compound. "Out there in that rabble there are doctors and professors, peasants and workers, architects and engineers," he said.

"But very few Party members," said Dr. Karandash.

"That is true," one of the prisoners said.

"Except yourselves. You eight."

"Yes," one of the prisoners said. "We Germans."

"How do you explain it?"

"They were going to exchange us for Russian Party members imprisoned in Germany, but it was already too late." The voice laughed. "Hitler attacked."

"Yet, since the Germans attacked Russia, many German Communists are heard again on the Moscow radio," said Dr. Karandash.

"Why not? It is better than dying of hunger. Besides they are Communists. A Communist is the instrument of history. It is not personal."

"Besides," Müller said, "they may be right."

"Take no notice of Müller," a prisoner said, quickly.

"Müller is a brain monkey," another said.

"You have been a prisoner for a long time, Müller," Dr. Karandash said. "You no longer have the ability to think clearly. It has become an obsession."

"The Russian Revolution was a revolution of a bourgeoisie seeking to establish itself in the wake of a declining feudal aristocracy," Müller said.

"Rosa Luxemburg once said something of the kind."

Immediately Dr. Karandash regretted his remark. He saw that Müller was grinning at him as though he had expected such an answer. Dr. Karandash felt that he had been trapped into a disclosure of his own political position.

Before he could say anything Müller had seized the lapels of his overcoat, a lapel in each hand, and was addressing him in a whisper.

"Luxemburg! Liebknecht! Whoever heard of them? Foreign names to men in leather jackets with pistols and to peasants with reaping hooks."

Dr. Karandash did not try to detach himself. He felt that Müller was not very strong.

The other prisoners bore grimaces of acute interior amusement. They were laughing; but their laughter was a kind of tittering, like young dogs panting.

"Is it not obvious?" Müller was saying, "Brest-Litovsk the NEP, Rapallo? They kept saying to us Germans, 'Versailles, Versailles,' but what had the Entente to do with us, the revolutionary proletariat? Now we can see that it was the new Russian bourgeoisie addressing itself to the German bourgeoisie, already aiming at that alliance which came only in 1939."

Dr. Karandash stepped back. His Homburg hat had been shaken to a curiously rakish angle. He was alarmed to notice that something of Müller's *Gulag* odour had been transferred to his person.

"So," said Dr. Karandash, "this is the outcome of all these hours of solitary thinking."

"But you cannot understand what has happened to the revolutionary bourgeoisie of Russia," Müller said. "There they are, millions of them, out there in the camps of *Gulag*, digging canals, cutting lumber. And still believers! Yes, how could it be otherwise? They love their *country*."

"The Old Bolsheviks," Dr. Karandash said. He was smoothing down the ruffled fur of his lapels. "We know something about it. Much has come out regarding the trials."

An expression of smugness appeared on Müller's face. It was as though Dr. Karandash had exposed a vulnerable ignorance which delighted Müller.

"If I were to tell you," Müller said, "that ten million people disappeared in the great purge would you believe me? If I said seven million, or even five million, would you believe that?"

One of the prisoners gave a sharp raucous laugh.

"We will probably never know the whole truth," Dr. Karandash said. "But ten millions! Or even seven millions! It is an enormous figure."

"In Russia everything is done in a big way," one of the prisoners said.

"It was a whole class," said Müller. "They had made the Dictator for their own purposes. To secure their ruling class position. And then they were afraid of him. Afraid he was ruining them. Some would have liked to depose him. Others would have liked him to be more reasonable. Less crude. It is the classical reaction of the bourgeoisie to dictatorship."

Müller put out a hand and touched Dr. Karandash. Dr. Karandash avoided shrinking from the touch.

"But can you fail to admire such a man? This Stalin! Such tenacity! Such endurance! And the masses upon which he operates with such contempt—are they not comtemptible?"

"The masses may be weak," said Dr. Karandash, "they may be even corrupted, but they are not contemptible. In the end they will destroy Stalin."

"You believe in the indestructible excellence of the working class, yes?"

"Yes."

"I believe in natural selection," Müller said, grinning.

"Food, pleasure, you will have your fill in the SS?"

"No! The need to kill Russians!"

Müller's face was suddenly distorted. Dr. Karandash was startled to see so swift a change from the sly mocking expression he had been wearing. Grasping Dr. Karandash's coat collar Müller began thumping the broad chest with his skinny fists.

"It is not good what you say," Dr. Karandash said. "Anywhere else it would be theatrical, striking an attitude. But here, now! Do not say it!"

"But look what they have done to us," a prisoner said. "This filth!"

"The Russian is a barbarian."

"The Russian is a beast!"

"Russische Scheisse!"

The prisoners panted, laughed noiselessly. Dr. Karandash felt like a bear who is being baited by dogs.

"There is a time in the lives of such men as we," Müller whispered, "when we can endure no more. Smug bourgeois! Do you not understand?"

Dr. Karandash took Müller's wrists, but there was power in his grip.

"This is the time when nothing will end the unendurable except to kill. Then a man must kill. Kill . . . kill . . ."

With the last phrase Müller gave Dr. Karandash a prodigious push so that the round head bobbed on the broad shoulders and the Homburg hat went spinning to the ground.

Müller immediately let go, emitting a shout of joy. The prisoners stood back watching the black hat roll in a circle in the dirt and seepage of their feet. There was delight in their eyes.

Dr. Karandash was looking at Müller. The round white

head on the broad shoulders was suddenly all Ukrainian. The eyes were small and the whites of the eyes could not be seen. He was steadily watching Müller. He was waiting for Müller to stamp on the hat. He saw the intention in Müller's expression and he was waiting. He was ready to take the German's neck in his hands and break it.

Then Müller sighed. He picked up the hat and attempted to brush off the dirt. The sooty blackness of the Homburg was ruined.

"I fear it will never be the same again," Müller said, "not even as a disguise."

The Obergruppenführer had gone. Dr. Karandash was driven back to Kharkiv in a *Kübelwagen.*

In those first days Kharkiv was like a city of pestilence.

But soon there was a stealthy movement; it was the movement one may detect in a deserted lot; gazing at the refuse long enough one presently comes to believe, with a prickling of the skin, that the wasteland is *alive.* The rats of Kharkiv were *feldgrau* in colour and moved leisurely; or they were dun-coloured and moved sharply from light to dark. But they were suddenly everywhere. The city was lithe with their movement.

The rifles of the *Feldgendarmerie* crackled over the wasteland like summer lightning, yet the movement waxed. The fallen body was lying, and then it was gone, dragged swiftly, surreptitiously into the refuse-haven. Around the commissaries, flour mills and sugar factories small clawing battles were being fought among scurrying hordes.

And then order was restored. General von Paulus arrived. The apartments in the new buildings were requisitioned for his staff. Teveleva Place, the former Nikolaevskaya, was renamed the Paulus Platz. The dead were cut down and carried away in wagons.

Because of their ideological and administrative functions members of the Communist Party had enjoyed a priority with the SS. But now that the great majority of

Communists had been disposed of the SS was turning to other matters. The city was entering a new period.

In Soviet countries, as is well known, each citizen above the age of twelve is required to carry an identification card, or passport. If you are a Jew it says so on this card, the Revolution in its bounty having conferred upon Jewry a cultural autonomy. Therefore, as most people had forgotten, the Germans had merely to ask a citizen for his, or her, passport in order to establish cultural origin, or, as they would have it, race; and (the request for documents being a commonplace of Soviet life) most citizens were readily bowing to authority and producing their passports and some were then astonished at what happened.

Every day people were being driven through the streets of the city like cattle on the way to market. The citizens of Kharkiv had not yet learned the meaning of the word *razzia;* but they were learning. A squad of black-coated soldiers would appear. All exits to the street would be blocked. Those identified as Jews would be separated, herded together, and driven away to a place outside the city whence they did not return.

These herdings were the more pitiful for the children who followed their parents, as foals run beside the mares in a corralling of horses, the mothers trying desperately to disown their children, to drive them off, slapping them for disobedience, then seizing them in their arms with hopeless inconsolable grief, and then putting them down and thrusting them out of the herd; for it happened that the *Sonderkommandos,* having come many kilometres through many towns were here careless of numbers, were diverted by the confusion of the children, letting many go.

Some of these children found their way to the schoolhouse in the Sadovo-Kulikovskaya. Maryusa Selova did not turn them away. But they presented her with an insurmountable problem: how to feed so many mouths.

The problem was met by Fomin. He sent the children into the city where they took part in the pillaging of the commissaries. Sometimes Fomin took quite young children with him on these forays. Maryusa knew that the young children were required for entrances which could not be made by the older children. She waited in anguish for their return.

Such food as the children brought back to the schoolhouse Maryusa carefully distributed among all there. The big girl called Olympia brought back the best food. The old man, the Professor, tended the stove.

The children who went into the city brought back stories of a great activity. They had stood in the streets and watched the spluttering motorcycles, the thundering troop carriers and the heavy cannon; and they had listened with curiosity to the guttural shouting of orders and the laughter of young soldiers. They had seen prisoners of war, Red Army men, being transported to the West; they had stood beside the railroad tracks and heard the prisoners, endless carloads of them, singing; they told of gangs of peasants, under guard, picking up the rails of the railroad bed and moving the rails closer together to suit the gauges of the German rolling stock. They had seen box cars bearing strange names in strange letters: Stettin, Breslau, Frankfurt. They had seen the big Junkers airplanes taxiing in and off Kharkiv airport. Never in the time of the Communists had there been so much to see, so much display.

There was a dynamism in this movement of great forces which stilled grief; it was felt by many in Kharkiv that however deep their private sorrows the sufferings of the day would soon be ameliorated by the war's ending. But this feeling was not shared in the schoolhouse in the Sadovo-Kulikovskaya. There none dared speak of the coming German victory for fear of Fomin.

Maryusa could not but admire the way Fomin quietly dominated the schoolhouse. He said very little, neither tendered advice, nor distributed praise. Neither did he admonish. But he told the children what to do. That was very important. In his company the children ceased to be afraid. It seemed to Maryusa that Fomin was a youth without fear and that others borrowed from his fearlessness.

Fomin's value in the small community of the schoolhouse was settled beyond question one day about a month after the arrival of the Germans.

It was a cold day. There was snow on the ground. The children were in the schoolhouse, huddled together in the largest room around the small stove.

A large closed wagon drew up outside the schoolhouse.

Six men in black greatcoats leaped out. They carried machine-pistols slung across their shoulders.

"This is the place," the Sturmführer said.

He kicked open the door of the school. Four of the SS men went in behind him. Two remained by the wagon.

Inside the school it was half-light. The SS men stumbled through the entry into the big room. There they paused.

The room was submerged in gloom except for a faint glow from the small stove. As their eyes became accustomed to the gloom the SS men saw that the room was filled with children. The children sat or lay close together on the floor, some were on benches, others lay covered with the rags of blankets. Their faces, pale triangles of lesser gloom in which hung round staring eyes, were turned towards the intruders. Their faces were empty. There was no movement. No sound.

"Which are Jews?" the Sturmführer said.

"They are all Jews," an SS man said.

"Take four," the Sturmführer said.

One of the SS men sniffed the air. The atmosphere was close with the smell of living. The sound of the SS man sniffing was heard clearly through the room. A child somewhere gasped. At the same time the fire in the stove crackled and sparked and a sudden influx of light made the wide staring eyes of the children gleam whitely. It was as though the whole room were hung with pairs of ghostly eyes.

"Which are Jews?" the Sturmführer said.

Maryusa who had come into the room from the rear was as though frozen. She could not speak.

"They are all Jews," an SS man said. "Look at them. They are all Jews. It is a Jewish cave."

The SS man spoke in German, but his meaning was clear. He unslung his machine-pistol. A second SS man unslung his machine-pistol. A third SS man unslung his machine-pistol. In the silence there was the sound of the drawing back of the safety catches.

"Leave four," said the Sturmführer.

In the weighted second of that awful moment there was a stirring among the children. The boy Fomin came forward. He stood in the middle of the room facing the SS men, direct-gazing over his high cheekbones, his rawboned figure squarely set, his big hands hanging loosely. His Ukrainian origin was terribly obvious.

He turned away from the SS men towards the children.

"These are Jews," he said.

Deliberately, without haste or hesitation, he pointed, one after the other, at four children in the room.

The four children indicated began to weep. The sound of their weeping appeared to anger the SS men. They seized the children and bore them away.

Obergruppenführer Rauch liked large rooms. He had been impressed by the office of the former All-Ukraine director of the NKVD.

The room had double doors, one door of panelled hardwood, a second covered with green baize. The doors had been recently oiled and opened noiselessly. When the green baize door was closed all outside sound was cut off. The walls were thick and the floor had been laid with a soft soundless substance. Down the length of the room there was a long committee table with chairs. The committee table and the chairs were factory-new and did not look as if they had ever been used. Beyond the table the room stretched away into deep gloomy recess. At the far end were two tall windows like refectory windows. Between the windows there was a rectangle of light wall space where, until very recently, a large portrait had hung. Below this space there was a large leather chair and a wide desk.

Obergruppenführer Rauch moved into the room. A month later he had not quite possessed it.

The big room was profoundly quiet. When Obergruppenführer Rauch strode up and down its twelve metres, as he liked often to do, his boots fell silently on the floor. The sensation of movement, progression, action, was absent. When he shouted, as he did very occasionally, his voice, instead of ringing the ceiling, fell dully on his ears. He had the lighting arrangements increased by many thousands of watts. He had portraits of the Party leaders brought in and hung on the walls. On one wall he set up a *Wehrmacht* staff map of the area under his control, adding coloured marker pins to show the front. On another wall he hung his most prized possession, a huge Party flag with a gold fringe and tassels and the precious legend *München* in one corner. But colour does not create sound harmonics. The room was still without echo, as quiet as the recording studio which, in one sense, it had been. Obergruppenführer Rauch was a very busy man. He did not allow what he felt to be the room's racial inheritance, so to speak, its sinister quietism, to unduly disturb him. But there were occasions when he noted the effect of the room on others, in subdued talk and excessively guarded movement. This disturbed him.

Thus, this day his officer aide ushered in the quartet of old Jews Obergruppenführer Rauch felt his sensitivity in regard to the room to be quiveringly touched. For the old people moved into the room with the utmost quiet, stepping in awe, with exaggerated care, out of respect for the high officer. One of the old people bowed low to him. And then they stood there, bearded, stooped, as though hardly daring to breathe.

Obergruppenführer Rauch called to his aide.

"Take them away!"

"Herr Obergruppenführer, the recruits are ready."

"Take them away!"

"Yes. Herr Obergruppenführer."

The aide began hustling the old Jews out of the room.

"Wait!"

The aide stood to attention.

"Bring young ones."

"Yes, Herr Obergruppenführer."

The green baize door of the room closed noiselessly behind the officer aide and the old Jews. Obergruppenführer Rauch stood up. He took a deep breath and looked out of the tall window.

He was still standing there when the eight recruits from the tractor factory compound marched in. The Obergruppenführer did not hear the door open, but the tramp of sixteen heavy feet, even on cork, and the resounding click of their ironshod heels, were ecstasy. He looked them over.

The eight recruits in the *Waffen* SS were in long black

uniforms, long black coats which reached below the tops of their shining high boots, new black belts with shining nickel buckles, new black pistol holsters fitting snugly to their waists at the left side, long collar lapels with piped edges, black painted helmets on which the insignia of the winged swastika and small death's head were mounted. They looked very different from the broken, lice-ridden, bearded men of the tractor factory compound. Their faces had lost the sallow begrimed look, new dentures made their jaws firmer and longer, the stoop had been lifted from their shoulders, their backs were straighter, their heads up. The man Müller wore new spectacles. Whereas a month ago they had been a fragment of the unidentifiable Siberian mass, today they were recognisably what the world had come to know as German.

"Attention!"

Obergruppenführer Rauch looked them over. They were an uneven group, some shorter, some older than the prescribed standard, but that did not matter in this moment of need. What mattered was that they were all (he was almost sure) of Nordic-Phalian-Germanic blood.

Obergruppenführer Rauch had a carefully rehearsed address for this occasion.

"You are entering a service," he began, "the difficulties and satisfactions of which you cannot yet know. . . . The SS is a completely realistic organisation. . . . We are the products of natural selection. . . ."

Obergruppenführer Rauch made the speech now in the quiet room standing before the recruits, taking a step up or down the room, his hands behind his back, his voice hardly raised above a whisper. All the recruits could see of his face was the terrier's nose, for the rest of his visible head, below the visor of his high up-turned cap, was taken up by his large spectacles, each lens a perfect steel-rimmed circle with an outward curvature which so caught and reflected light that the Obergruppenführer's eyes were seldom seen.

The speech went on for some time.

"I have mentioned the very difficult tasks that have to be performed by the SS men," he was saying. "The worthy German at home says, 'Yes, there are many disagreeable tasks to be performed, the extermination of the Jews, for example, and this is what the SS is for, and this is what the SS is doing.' But this worthy German, who may have seen some Jews taken away in a wagon, has no conception of the task. Not one of the millions who talk this way has seen it done."

The green baize door of the big room opened. A child stepped into the room—two, three, four children, one after the other, thrust forward by SS men, made to stand in line against the wall, their faces to the wall opposite the line of recruits, below the portrait of *Der Führer*. Obergruppenführer Rauch did not pause in his address.

"Perhaps you think it easy to be an SS man. Perhaps you think it easier than being a *Luftwaffe* pilot, for example? Let us take the case of the *Luftwaffe* pilot who pulls a lever and drops his bombs and kills a thousand of the enemy. Now let us take this same man, this *Luftwaffe* pilot, and let us provide him with a machine-pistol and a case of ammunition, and let us put him before a thousand men and women and, yes, children. Let us see whether he has the moral stamina to perform his task the SS way. No doubt as bombs get bigger and the means of their delivery are dispersed among greater numbers of people the individual responsibility will be diffused. This is one of the interesting problems of war. For the SS maintains that there must be responsibility. General devastation may shelter the consciences of the weak by making responsibility collective, but, to be effective, damage done to the enemy *must* be discriminatory. The SS man cannot fly away into the clouds. He must examine the target. He must look at the results. That is why the SS man must be the highest human type. He must be realistic, materialistic. He must be strong. He must have character. That is why the SS man is, always, an individualist. His is the ultimate of individualism."

During the last part of his address Obergruppenführer Rauch had taken his pistol from its holster. He now held it before him, having cocked it with a casual and practised movement of his thumb and wrist like shooting his cuff. He stepped over to the nearest of the children facing the wall, put the pistol to the child's ear, pressed the trigger. The sound of the report was sharp but echoless.

"To be an SS man you must be able to do this," said Obergruppenführer Rauch. "Is there any one of you who feels he cannot do this?"

The Obergruppenführer waited. A minute of silence went by in which the only sound was the sniffling of one of the three remaining children. The Obergruppenführer was looking at the eight recruits, but none could see his eyes.

"You," he said.

The man indicated stepped forward. His ironshod boots clamped down in three paces as he crossed the room. Still at attention, in regulation movements, he drew his pistol and, holding it steadily, put it to the head of the second child, fired. The sound gave no harmonics. As the child fell the German ex-Stalinist about-faced and, with three even paces, marched back to his position in the line of recruits, stamped out the one-two of the about-face, stood to attention.

Obergruppenführer Rauch was pleased.

"You," he pointed to another man.

The man indicated was less certain than the other. He crossed the room, halted for a full thirty seconds behind the third child, withdrew his pistol, fired quickly, swung round and stepped back into line.

Obergruppenführer Rauch waited. The wait was a long one for the six recruits who had not yet crossed that room. They felt an intense scrutiny bearing on each one of them. Obergruppenführer Rauch looked along the line of faces. One face was paper white. He looked steadily at this face for a whole minute.

"You," he said.

Müller stepped forward. He marched unsteadily across the room and stood behind the surviving child. The surviving child was a girl. It happened that this girl, randomly pointed to by Fomin, was not of Jewish origin, but this point did not occur to her, if it mattered, for she would not have been able to protest it, not understanding it, and being racked with weeping. The SS man Müller paused a long time behind this little girl. His back shielded his face from the eyes of the other recruits and from Obergruppenführer Rauch. For a moment the rigidity of his black uniform appeared to unbend. Then it straightened. He had withdrawn his pistol. There was another pause. In this moment the little girl turned and began desperately to claw at Müller. There was an instant of unseemly scuffling and then there was the sound of a pistol shot. The SS man Müller stood above the body of the girl for a halting second before turning and marching back to his position. As he took his place in the line he bumped against the man next to him.

The room was deadly quiet.

When Obergruppenführer Rauch at last spoke his voice was very soft.

"What is your name?" he said.

"Müller," the spectacled ex-Stalinist said.

"Re-holster your pistol!"

Müller looked quickly at his hand and saw that it was still holding the pistol. For a few slow seconds he continued to look at the weapon. Then slowly he put the weapon back in its place.

"Sieg Heil!"

"Sieg Heil!"

The eight new members of the *Waffen* SS marched out of the quiet room. The green baize door closed silently behind them.

Obergruppenführer Rauch walked over to the tall window and stood there. On his face there was a faint, sardonic smile, an expression of personal satisfaction. He suspected that the German ex-Communist was a Jew.

Everyone agreed that it was the heaviest winter in memory. At the front the *Wehrmacht* thermometers often registered temperatures of forty degrees below zero. The city of Kharkiv lay under a metre of snow. Gangs of women worked to keep the main thoroughfares clear, but there was no attempt to open the side streets.

The wooden schoolhouse in the Sadovo-Kulikovskaya was buried in deep drifts. Those inside felt that the schoolhouse was unlocateable and this made them feel comfortable. There was always a small fire burning in the stove in the big room. There was some food. They felt inaccessible, secure. And then the *sound* began again. It was a faint sound, almost inaudible, but it destroyed immediately the sense of isolation.

The sound was an unemphatic, continuous threat to those inside the schoolhouse. It unsettled the children. Some of the younger children whimpered when they heard it. But it also affected those who were not, strictly speaking, children.

"I do not like it," Olympia said.

Olympia was a big, good-natured girl, about sixteen years of age. Peasant born, she owed her fine Greek name to the chance that she had been named for a relative who had herself been named, as often happened in the Ukraine, by a village *pope,* in a time when there were *popes.* On the morning of the second day of the occupation she had come to the schoolhouse bringing by the hand a younger child, Olympia herself staggering a little, laughing.

"I do not like it," she said now.

"It is nothing," Fomin said.

"I shall go away," Olympia said.

"Where will you go?" Fomin said.

"It will not end well," Olympia said. "It will bring the SS."

"Do not leave us," Maryusa said.

"You are needed," Fomin said. "You have brought food."

"*Wehrmacht* food," Olympia said.

"It is good food," Fomin said. "It is not possible to steal such food."

"You are strong. You will help us," Maryusa said.

"That damned sound makes the children cry," Olympia said. "I do not like to hear the children cry."

"Nor I," Maryusa said. "I do not like to hear the children cry. But one must bear it."

"I am not like that," Olympia said. "I am not motherly. Besides when I go there will be room for another."

"That would be stupid," Fomin said. "I shall tell the old man to go. He is a useless mouth. I have always said it."

"Who is to say what is a useless mouth!" Maryusa said. "Are we not all useless mouths?"

Maryusa did not like to oppose Fomin. But she had come to hate and fear this latter-day Party phrase, "useless mouth."

"All right," Fomin said, "he can sell matches. He will be good for selling matches because he is old and they will not notice him."

"What have you got against him?" Olympia said.

"He says that he has a useless mouth," Maryusa said. "He should not say it."

"He has a better *mouth* than I have," Olympia said. "Listen!"

"He is always talking," Fomin said.

"When he talks the children stop crying," Maryusa said.

"Where will you go?" Fomin asked Olympia.

"Listen to the old man!" Olympia said.

Squatting among the children, his head no taller than those about him, Professor Shevchenko was talking in a low even voice. Around him there was a spell of quiet which spread each moment to bind more and more children.

"I prefer kasha," Professor Shevchenko was saying. "I eat much kasha. Several bowls of kasha every day. Huge kasha, mountains of kasha. I also eat bread, white bread, big loaves of white bread still warm from the bakery, yes, and honey, bottles of honey, and honey in the comb. And potatoes fried in oil. Every night when it is cold and I cannot sleep I have this to eat."

"What else do you eat?" a boy asked.

"I eat melons with sugar and sweetcake that is in the shape of a *pope's* crown with cream like ermine laid around it and aniseed and raisins set in it like pearls and garnets. I also eat tartlets, huge tartlets like the top of a Cossack's hat, all red with cherry juice. And tangerines like the poufs in a Turk's harem. And ginger and spice. And grapes blue and frosty like cannon balls. And oranges, and lemons."

"I do not like lemons," a girl said.

"Who cares about you!"

"Let the *Deda* talk."

In the rear of the room the older ones looked across to the old man. The children were crowded close to him. They were absorbed in him. Maryusa listened with shining eyes. The fear that had been in her a moment ago was quenched. She no longer heard the sound outside.

"He talks about food," she said.

"It is not good to talk about what you cannot get," Fomin said.

"He talks about things I have never heard of," Olympia said. "He uses words I have never heard before."

"But look!" Maryusa said. "The children! They love him!"

Professor Shevchenko spoke very quietly. There was in his enunciation nothing of the sonority of the Great Russian tongue. Instead there was humour and self-mockery. His voice, pitched high, fluting, had the filmy irony of primitive woodwinds. It was a voice of high cultivation, yet of a culture and a civilisation hard to identify, because already lost. The children had never heard such a voice. Their own voices were harsh and gruff, colloquial and profane. When the children spoke it was the way adults, today, spoke. In the education, in the minds of adults, as of the children, there was nothing any longer which could easily shape tongue and lip, much less define, many of the words and phrases uttered by Professor Shevchenko, yet some inherent memory cell, some connection of etymology with a life lived, was stirred, imparting to the old man's images an unfathomable excitement.

Fomin listened. In his grave direct-staring eyes there was puzzlement. He turned away from Professor Shevchenko. He turned to Olympia.

"Are you going to live with an officer?" he said.

Olympia laughed: "With a regiment," she said.

"Yes? It is not difficult?"

"It is nothing," Olympia said. "After the first night it is nothing."

"The first night," Fomin said.

"The first night, *that* first night there were thirty-six," Olympia said.

"That is many."

"Many is nothing."

"Nevertheless you counted them."

"You're a smart one, Fomin."

"They are rich. They have food," Fomin said.

"They have long woolen trousers under their breeches," Olympia said.

"They are good to you?"

"They are all the same. They are quick. They are ashamed it is quick. They do not like it to be quick. For myself I am glad it is quick. A company, a regiment, it is nothing."

"You should go with the SS," Fomin said. "They have more food than the others."

"The SS are not good."

"They are good for executions. They are also quick in that."

"That is easy."

"True, it is not difficult."

"The SS have chocolate and tobacco. Wine too. But they give nothing," Olympia said.

"They give vodka. A litre for a denunciation."

"It is already too much."

"A litre of vodka buys much food."

"Listen, Fomin. I do not know the SS. I know only soldiers."

"I wanted to see what answer you would give. It is a good answer."

"I said you were a smart one."

"Soldiers steal and give easily," Fomin said.

"I too have seen it."

"You are too young for soldiers. You will be for officers."

"So, officers or soldiers. I shall bring you a pair of long woolen trousers and you can wear them under your breeches."

"No, but there is another thing you can bring."

"What is it? I knew there was something."

"You could bring a pistol."

"A pistol!"

"Yes."

"Do you think I am mad? Do you think I want to be shot?"

"A man needs a pistol."

Professor Shevchenko's audience now took in the whole room. It was quiet. None noticed the sound outside.

"Do you have fish, too?" a boy asked.

"I have a large salmon fish like a Roman galley, all silver with the silver of the sea, and yet when I lay him open he is all pink like the dawn over the Hellespont. And all around my salmon there are little magenta-tinted flowers which are but cunningly-cut radishes and green leaves that are cucumber pickles. And lemons! For it is with the salmon, as well as with tea, that I eat lemon, slivers of lemon shaved as fine as fairy windowpanes. But this is not all the fish I have on my table. For there is the noble sturgeon, baked in sunflower oil, rich to the nostril, thick and meaty like the mud of the Volga. And there is sturgeon's roe, the precious *ekra,* fresh from Astrakhan, a million little grey eyes soft with unspent tears, there to be eaten from the blade of a steel knife. I have also the red caviar from Kamchatka. And herring from the Baltic, salt, salt, herring that needs to be slaked with vodka."

Fomin turned to Maryusa.

"There is no vodka, but there is herring for tonight," he said.

"Yes," Maryusa said. "You have found herring?"

"Last night," Fomin said, "there was a provision train. We climbed aboard while it was moving and threw off two barrels."

Fomin was stating fact. That was no pride in his voice.

"The herrings are from Norway," he said. "They are not like Russian herrings."

"It is good to have herrings," Maryusa whispered.

Professor Shevchenko, seated among the children, was talking of banquets.

"That is how the Communists eat," a boy said.

"That is not how *we* ate," a girl said.

"That is the way they eat in Moscow."

"How do they eat in Moscow, *Deda?*"

"Ah, in Moscow," said Professor Shevchenko. "There in the great marble hall there are long tables. The light shines down from the crystal chandeliers. The tables are covered with the whitest cloths you have ever seen. And on the cloth the plates and the knives and the forks are all made of gold and inlaid with pearls and rubies. And at every place at that table there are eight glasses, not less than eight ruby-stained goblets with stems encrusted with precious stones, one glass for each of the different kinds of wine and vodka that will be drunk this night. And on the table there are all kinds of delicacies, little fish in aspic jelly, cheese shaped like buttons, forcemeat like flowers, and all the different kinds of caviar, the cold eggs sliced like fields of buttercups. And then the guests arrive. The beautiful officers in their red-and-gold uniforms, their chests covered with orders, the foreigners in the black-and-white silk clothes, and some from the oriental countries in rich brocade, wearing turbans set with sapphires, and the lovely dark-eyed women, they come in and they take their seats. As the waiters in their white uniforms bring in the hot rich soups and the roasted sturgeons and great roasted goose and suckling pigs there is the toast, the toast that is shouted so that the voices echo high in the vaulted ceiling. Ah, Moscow! Moscow!"

Fomin stood staring at the old man. He was gripped by a strange sensation. A power of seeing had been awakened within him. In his mind he had suddenly *seen*. He had seen the large hall, the table laden with food, the throng of guests.

"Moscow!" Fomin said to himself.

Professor Shevchenko had ceased speaking. Fomin was looking at him, at the soiled shabby figure in the old cycling suit, at the pale pointed face, the cloudy pince-nez. Fomin looked and it was as though he had put out his arm and had grasped Professor Shevchenko.

In the silence that had fallen on the room the *sound* was heard again.

The sound came from outside the schoolhouse. For, of course, it had become known in Kharkiv that there was food and shelter at the schoolhouse and, with the snows, many came seeking both. In the city and populous suburbs there were still countless lost and straying children. There were those children who had been absorbed into other families; there were those who died eating excrement, or of exposure, small frozen bodies so much resembling refuse that they lay often long unnoticed in the final huddled position in the deserted basement or ground hole; and those, somewhat stronger, who led a macerating existence divided between a lone banditry and mendicancy, of whom some came regularly to the schoolhouse seeking that refuge which they heard could be obtained there. So that any day or night there were always three or four or half-a-dozen figures standing in the snow outside the schoolhouse. They stood so still, crouched in their grey rags, in the purplish light of day or the luminous gloom of night, that it was possible not to see them, as for example, one does not see a tree in an avenue of trees. One heard the *sound* before seeing. The sound was the faint click of a spoon on the side of a tin plate or can. The sound, soft and faintly melodic, like a constantly shifting arrangement of three or four minor notes played flatly, was so close as to be sourceless, unlocateable, until one's eyes, drawn involuntarily, looked close upon another pair of eyes, dark in their hollows, dumbly supplicate, yet remote, of that other world outside. The *sound* tore at the heartstrings of Maryusa Selova.

It would be close to her, under her feet, beneath her window, and it would pursue her all day long. But there was nothing she could do. What could she do? Her impulse was to throw open the doors of the schoolhouse to all, as she had done in the first days. But to do that now would be to jeopardise the existence of all who were already there. It was Fomin who acted. It was Fomin who decided which of the suppliants should be admitted to the school. And which of those in the school should be sent out to take their chance in the villages. His authority was not questioned, neither by those inside the school, nor the tinkling shadows outside. Those he passed over went away knowing that their supplication was ended.

Fomin went now to the door of the schoolhouse. He let himself out of the door and he stood there before the building where the beggars had made tracks in the snow. His bony frame loomed large. He made no gesture. Presently the beggars who had been there went away. Fomin came back again.

Maryusa looked at him. She could not but wonder about him at these moments. She did not ask herself how he could do it. Was it loyalty to herself, or to the school? She did not ask. She was grateful. Because her gratitude was profound she loved him at this moment.

She went over to him and she put her hand on his arm. Through the thickness of the cloth of his coat she felt the steel-like biceps. The sense of his strength overpowered her.

Had Maryusa asked Fomin on what basis he selected some and not others to share the shelter of the schoolhouse and the provender largely of his foraging he would have answered simply that it was on the basis of their usefulness. But that was not the question in her mind.

The winter was already in decline when the SS paid its next visit to the schoolhouse. This time they came less hurriedly. There was a Sturmführer and an SS man. Both carried weapons, but neither made any effort to ready them. They came into the school, their heavy boots thrashing the wooden floor, their voices loud and brassy, their painted helmets set squarely over their pink faces.

"Attention!" cried the Sturmführer. "Tell them to stand," he said to the SS man.

The SS man was older than the Sturmführer and wore glasses. Speaking in Russian he told the children to stand.

The children, awestruck, wide-eyed, shuffled to their feet. Pale, thin, smelling mustily, they made an unattractive picture. The Sturmführer looked at them and then withdrew his interest. Maryusa knew suddenly that they had not come to kill anybody. She felt that he must be a reasonable man.

He stood very straight in his black coat which he was careful not to bring into contact with anything around him. Maryusa heard him say to the SS man that there was most certainly typhus in the school.

"*Nein,*" Maryusa said.

"You speak German?" the Sturmführer said.

"*Nein,*" Maryusa said.

"A pity," the Sturmführer said. "The necessity for bringing in another teacher for the German lessons would have been obviated."

He then ignored Maryusa and announced in a loud military voice that juvenile banditry in Kharkiv was being stamped out. The children were more alarmed by his voice than by what he had to say. But Maryusa, listening first to the German and then to the translation made by the SS man, felt her heart sink.

In future children found looting would be shot. Children found on the roads outside the city would be shot. Children begging from soldiers would be shot. Children caught stealing *Wehrmacht* property would be shot. Ten children would be shot for every child found spying for the enemy.

The Sturmführer paused. In a different voice, turning to Maryusa, he made what seemed to be a personal statement.

"It is known," he said, "that the Russians are employing children as spies."

The SS man translated. The Sturmführer continued with his official announcement.

A food rationing system was being organised. The ration would be eleven ounces of millet bread per day. The ration would be issued only to those with Labour Front work cards and to children. The ration would be denied to Jewish children. There would be a special home for Jewish children.

"There are no Jewish children here," Maryusa said quietly, "only Ukrainians."

The translator heard her. But the Sturmführer did not notice her remark. He continued with his announcement.

Teachers would no longer instruct in the Russian language or use Russian textbooks.

The SS man translated.

"You have textbooks in Ukrainian?" he asked.

"Yes," Maryusa said.

"Collect them for me."

The first and second grade readers in Ukrainian were brought out. The SS man took one. He passed it to the Sturmführer. The Sturmführer took the book in his gloved hand and opened at a page. The SS man pointed out certain things in the text. The Sturmführer was but faintly interested. The contempt was in his gloved finger tips.

The SS man turned to Maryusa.

"Until new textbooks are printed you will use these. However, it will be necessary to make certain excisions." He looked hard at Maryusa. "You agree that it will be necessary to make certain excisions, *Tovarishka Uchitelka?*"

Maryusa looked down. Her face was tinged with red. The last words, uttered in a familiar diction, made the fear rise in her breast.

"I do not know," she said.

The SS man laughed. "You are Ukrainian?" he said.

"Yes."

"Then I think perhaps you agree?"

Maryusa said nothing. The SS man took up the books.

"You will have them back soon," he said. "And then you may resume your classes."

The SS man marched out of the school behind the Sturmführer. Maryusa sat down.

"We are to have rations," she said.

Fomin had watched the SS men closely.

"What do they find wrong with our books?" he now asked Maryusa.

Maryusa looked quickly at Fomin. Until that moment she had not realised that *she* knew, had always known, what was wrong with the books.

PART 2

The big room was brilliantly alive. The red flag with the gold fringe gave a dramatic note to the gathering; the large *Wehrmacht* map with its hundreds of marker pins was the expression of its superb confidence, the portraits of the Party leaders peering down from the walls the seal of its purpose.

From his desk beneath the windows Obergruppenführer Rauch looked over the long conference table where military officers of general rank sat beside SS leaders and civilians of eminence. The austere black uniforms of the SS contrasted well with the grey of the *Wehrmacht*, the epaulettes, the ribbons of the military orders.

It was a conference of delegations and committees. Behind the leader or chairman of each delegation or committee sat or stood junior officers, clerks, secretaries, technical experts, all of them supremely correct, obedient to the whispered instruction, constantly taking notes, assembling papers, passing in and out of the green baize door.

The bright lights dazzled Dr. Karandash. He took off his dark spectacles, wiped them vigorously, put them back on his nose.

A civilian approached him, a tall aristocratic gentleman of well-preserved age whose clipped moustache failed to give firmness to a quivering underlip.

"I heard you were here, Karandash," the gentleman said. "I am Prince Dolov."

Dr. Karandash muttered an acknowledgement.

"Quite a gathering," said Prince Dolov.

He waved a hand towards a group of liaison officers of the allied armies: Rumanians in conical sheepskin hats, wide-skirted coats and foolish swords, Hungarians, Spaniards, Finns, an Italian.

"I have been talking to Fallaparte, over there." Prince Dolov indicated a handsome spade-bearded man in the uniform of an Italian war correspondent. "He has just come from Warsaw, the guest of Gauleiter Frank, you know. Wonderfully witty fellow."

Dr. Karandash found himself the centre of a small group.

Advancing towards him now was a man wearing a hat made of karakul fur with a blue crown, a Cossack cape complete with white cartridge cylinders, and a uniform with polished buttons and red-striped riding breeches. Looking into this astonishing dress Dr. Karandash saw an aged and shrunken face from which a pair of white moustaches protruded like tusks.

Prince Dolov introduced Hetman Horopadsky.

"I hear you are an old Bolshevik," said Hetman Horopadsky in a high squeaky voice.

"I have never been a member of the Communist Party," said Dr. Karandash.

"Killed a lot of them in my time," said Hetman Horopadsky. "Never bothered to ask what Party they belonged to."

To his right Dr. Karandash heard another voice.

"I don't think we have ever met before. I am Father Wròbel."

"Glad to meet you," said Dr. Karandash.

"I really have no business at this conference," said Father Wròbel, "but they insisted that I come. I expect that you will be very busy here."

The air of the big room was blue with tobacco smoke. The subdued murmur of voices was continuous. Sometimes one voice would rise above the others as the spokesman of a delegation or committee rose to make his report. The room would quiet for the moment it took to catch the drift of the speaker's remarks and then the hum of voices would rise in volume to drown the speaker's words.

"If it is not impertinent," said Dr. Karandash, turning to Prince Dolov, "may I ask why you are here?"

"I cannot say I wanted to come," said Prince Dolov. "I was most reluctant. But Baron Hoffenstein insisted. You know, even in the former times I hardly ever visited the country."

"Prince Dolov's family is very famous," said Father Wròbel.

"A rather large property," Prince Dolov said, "somewhere to the north. Twenty-five villages if I remember correctly. It never paid. Our managers were rather corrupt, I think."

"You hope to recover the property?"

"Oh hardly. One of the villages is now a city, I believe. But they insist that it is a matter of principle."

"What we need is an army," said Hetman Horopadsky, his moustaches feathering like sculls.

There was a cackle of laughter behind Dr. Karandash.

"That," said Prince Dolov, "is the new Obermeister of Kharkiv, Mr. Stetsenko."

"Take no notice of Stetsenko," said a serious young man who now came up to Dr. Karandash. "He is always the life of the party. It is a habit with him. In Kharkiv he goes to all the card parties. The ladies love his jokes. He is very popular. But he is not a fool. Under the Communists he had many good jobs. Each job was easier than the previous job."

The serious young man spoke with bitterness.

"I am Murkulov, the editor of the new *Kharkivanian,*" he said.

"Happy to meet you," said Dr. Karandash.

"They will kill me for this, but I have to do it," the young man said. "Before they kill me I shall say everything."

"What is it you are so anxious to say?" Dr. Karandash asked, with interest.

"The Voice of the Inner Temple commands the Corridors of the Pyramid," the young man said.

"Ah," said Father Wròbel, "it is the expression of a tortured spirit."

"You have a Polish name, Father Wròbel?" Dr. Karandash said.

"Yes, yes. I am just a poor Polish priest. From the villages. I am here to perform God's work. I am not, like you, political."

"Everybody is political," said Dr. Karandash. "Everybody here is political."

"To love God is not political," said Father Wròbel.

"It depends where," said Dr. Karandash.

"Ah, yes, I understand you. But it is no longer so here."

"What do you think of tanks?" Hetman Horopadsky said.

"There is that one of Denikin's in the Paulus Platz," said Dr. Karandash.

"That's what I say," said Hetman Horopadsky, "you can't beat cavalry in the Ukraine."

"Pay special attention to Arbeitsführer Müssfeld," Prince Dolov said, aside to Dr. Karandash. He pointed to a short square man with close-cropped hair and round blue eyes wearing a mud-coloured uniform with yellow collar tabs bearing ear-of-wheat insignia. "He has a special mission," said Prince Dolov, "and almost as much power as the Obergruppenführer."

Baron Hoffenstein stood before the conference with his broad heavy fingers resting fanwise on the edge of the table. His beautifully-shaved cheeks with their fringe of white beard were flushed and winy. His fleshy forehead below the short hedge of hair was heavily corrugated. The baleful old eyes were held from watering completely away by red gutters. He spoke in slow measured sentences. The substance of his remarks was that the titles of the former estates had been discovered complete as they were at the moment of the Bolshevik seizure. It was the proposal of the *Landesführer,* whom he had the honour to represent, that these titles should be the basis of the new ownership. Surrogate titles would be issued on the basis of the old boundaries. Hereditary rights would be dealt with in the proper legal manner after the war. There would, of course, be a statute of limitations in regard to such litigation. Meanwhile all traces of national ownership would have disappeared.

Major Wreckl, representing the *Wehrmacht,* said that officers of the supply organisation had examined the position of the collective farms and were of the opinion that any effort to reorganise them would interfere with the collection of grain and the forthcoming harvest.

At this moment, without seeking the permission of the chairman, Arbeitsführer Müssfeld rose to his feet. The Labour Front, he said brusquely, would retain possession of those documents relating to the entire collective farm organisation. These documents, he said, listed the names of peasant families, all workers, male and female, of brigade leaders, section leaders, and officials of the workers' and peasants' inspection. This information would be the basis of the redivision of labour forces. Therefore the collective farm system would, for the present, remain.

"There you have it," said Dr. Karandash, "the central problem. How is it possible to restore the estates?"

"Indeed. I am greatly relieved," said Prince Dolov.

"You would have been embarrassed?" inquired Dr. Karandash. "After all, it is not everybody who has the opportunity to establish title to a city."

"I was thinking," said Prince Dolov, "of the lawyers." His refined face puckered with a passing annoyance. "Good God," he said, "under Hoffenstein's scheme I would have been delivered completely into their hands!"

"The collectives must go," said Hetman Horopadsky. "It must be the first point of our policy."

"How do you replace them?"

"No one has mentioned co-operatives," said Father Wròbel.

"I am afraid the peasants no longer believe anything they are promised," said Prince Dolov.

"If the peasants could be persuaded," said Father Wròbel, "of the good *faith* of their rulers."

"Why not simply say, 'Peasants of Russia, the land is yours, come and take it,' " said Dr. Karandash. "The Red Army would disintegrate overnight." His remark was not heard.

The little group of civilians standing somewhat apart from the main conference meeting was now joined by a newcomer, a large, soft, white man of unquestionable worth and substance.

"Herr Doktor Kloppmann," the newcomer said, introducing himself, "of the enterprise Helfrich Sadet."

The name Helfrich Sadet was familiar to Dr. Karandash.

"Agricultural implements?" he said.

"Yes," said Herr Dr. Kloppmann.

"I remember," said Dr. Karandash, "your factory was in the Koriskovskaya."

"It is still there," said Dr. Kloppmann. "However, it is not my factory. I am an attorney. I am representing a few people who bought the Ukrainian assets of Helfrich Sadet for a small sum many years ago."

"Against such a contingency as this?" said Prince Dolov. "What an excellent idea."

"My clients were fortunate in making their purchase in the pre-inflationary period," said Herr Dr. Kloppmann.

Dr. Karandash was remembering a large red flag flown proudly from the top of the factory Helfrich Sadet in the Koriskovskaya. The red flag was by way of announcing to the world that the 2,500 workers in the agricultural machinery plant had formed the first workers' soviet in Kharkiv. They had renamed the factory the "Sickle & Hammer" factory. So this improbable experiment had been made, one of the first of its kind in a factory which boasted methods of mass production. Would it have endured? Can the workers own and control their own production? The questions had never been answered. The issue of democratic centralism had been quickly settled by the Bolsheviks. In a very short time the workers' soviet in the Sickle & Hammer factory had been liquidated as an independent organisation and the factory incorporated in the vast Union-wide Commissariat of Light Metals.

"And how is the factory now?" Dr. Karandash asked. "Much enlarged, I suppose."

"No," said Dr. Kloppmann, "on the contrary it is somewhat smaller than I was given to understand. It is clear that efforts have been made to enlarge it. There is much capital equipment lying about, some of it from America, most of it now valueless as the result of exposure."

"You expect to resume operations?"

The attorney looked uncomfortable. "As a matter of fact," he said, "I had not supposed that there were so many Communists there. The workers' delegation which met the incoming soldiers was thus not fully representative."

"The management was missing, eh?"

"I found them," said Dr. Kloppmann, "suspended from the rafters."

"Ha, ha," squeaked Hetman Horopadsky.

"It seems that in every factory the Communists have

seen to it that the senior workers are members of the Party."

"Naturally," said Dr. Karandash, "for control, discipline."

"Our *Sonderkommandos* acted with great promptitude on the information given to them by the workers. Of course," added Dr. Kloppmann hurriedly, "I do not mean to question the efficiency of the SS. Indeed not. Naturally Communists cannot be tolerated. Experience shows that there is no compromise with them. It is, therefore, our policy to, er, dispose of them. We must dispose of them. We are disposing of them. Yes, well . . . in time it will no doubt repair itself."

"You will bring engineers and foremen from Germany?"

"I have been told that the Labour Front is controlling all useful labour. The Ostland is to be considered an agricultural and pastoral region for the time being. However, my clients were curious. I do wish I could get a train. May I ask if you are having transport trouble also?"

A spokesman of the delegation representing the Medical and Sanitary Corps announced that the medical facilities of the city had been taken over by the *Wehrmacht* to cope with the frostbite emergency. The system of free medical attention had been stopped and all public clinics and crèches had been closed. Local doctors had been ordered to practise privately, charging ten rubles a visit. Emphasis was being laid on the restoration of family life. The failure of the water supply in some districts had led to local outbreaks of typhoid, necessitating areas of quarantine.

"Father Wròbel," said Dr. Karandash, "you are in favour of the restoration of family life?"

"Yes, yes," said Father Wròbel, "the family is sacred. The State must not interfere."

An SS officer was reading from a report in hand. The system of higher education was so impregnated with Bolshevik ideology as to be beyond rehabilitation. Teachers of Ukrainian origin only were being selected. The official languages would be German and Ukrainian. Indiscipline was rampant among schoolchildren necessitating reintroduction of the system of corporal punishment. . . .

"My only hope is that something will be done about the children in the streets," said Dr. Karandash.

"I have always felt," said Prince Dolov, "that we have an obligation to the poor."

"It is not a matter of helping the poor," said Dr. Karandash, "it is a matter of life or death. We must open soup kitchens."

"I had thought of something of the kind," said Prince Dolov, "but you know what they said? They said that it was collectivism. I suppose they are right. After all, if you start with a State soup kitchen, where do you end?"

"It is better to leave people alone," said Father Wròbel. "With God's help there is always a way."

"Besides," said Obermeister Stetsenko, "how do you make soup without potatoes? How do you make bread without flour?"

He laughed loudly.

Dr. Karandash walked a few paces away from the little group of civilians. Presently he felt a touch at his elbow. Hetman Horopadsky had joined him.

"I have been watching you, Karandash," said Hetman Horopadsky. "You are losing your nerve."

Dr. Karandash saw that Hetman Horopadsky was a little man. Beneath the enveloping Cossack costume there burned some kind of indomitable purpose. His feet, encased in delicate black riding boots, were no larger than those of a woman.

"This is all nonsense they are talking," said Hetman Horopadsky. "Rauch is stalling for time."

"Time for what?"

"Why, time to finish off the Jews, of course. For us there is only one important question. That is the army. The National Ukrainian Army." The old man looked fiercely at Dr. Karandash. "You know that as well as I, yes? We begin with the army."

Dr. Karandash noticed that they were standing together directly under a large portrait of *Der Führer*.

"Let me tell you something," Hetman Horopadsky went on. "Schmidt is with us. That means the General Staff approves of a National Army. If they do not have a National Army they will recruit men straight into the *Wehrmacht*. They need men. The Russians are not stupid. All this time they are not idle. There will soon be big battles. That is why, for the moment, the General Staff overrides the Party. But they will have to act quickly or that damned Labour Front will have taken every able-bodied man and woman to Germany."

Dr. Karandash was examining the wall of the big room beneath the portrait of *Der Führer*. He had discovered what he thought to be minute bloodstains, even in one place a few fair long hairs and a particle of viscera.

"You will never be President of the Republic without an army," said Hetman Horopadsky.

"The time for republics is over," Dr. Karandash said, absently.

"Let me ask you this: How do you expect to create an independent Republic when there is no national consciousness? How do you create national consciousness? With an army, of course."

Dr. Karandash was sure that the bloodstains were recent.

He looked at Hetman Horopadsky as though he had only just observed him.

"What's the matter? You look ill."

"I do not feel well," said Dr. Karandash.

"Take a pill," said Hetman Horopadsky.

Outside in the street Dr. Karandash immediately felt better. The sky was blue. The sun shone brightly on the snow-packed roofs of the city. He breathed deeply of the sharp frosty air. It bore the fresh smell of woodsmoke and paint.

Dr. Karandash walked towards his hotel in the Paulus Platz. Everywhere there was an agreeable activity. Immigrants with their wives and families and plumbing had been arriving in great numbers in recent weeks and this central section of Kharkiv was already beginning to take on a neat German appearance. The loudspeakers had been taken down. Street signs in German gave a respectable aldermanic character to the city. Everywhere small shops were opening, their names uniformly painted in large Gothic letters on a white ground. In the hotels there were many gay parties as officers, on short leave from the front, met wives and relatives who had made the journey from the Reich. Cinemas were open and German companies were appearing at the principal theatres. A symphony orchestra was billed to give a Beethoven cycle. A multilingual *militsia* patrolled the streets.

Dr. Karandash began to think of the life he had led in Prague before the occupation. With pleasure he remembered the cafés in the Václavskej náměšté. Ah, the clever, witty, cynical talk with the coffee! The international political gossip! He remembered also the quiet library, the good books, his work on the little pieces of translation that had kept him going, the paper for the learned society, the newspaper articles (often returned with thanks, but with *thanks),* the periodical that had gone to five issues, the growing nausea with which he had followed the official literature of the Soviet Union. And, of course, the serious work, the keeping-in-touch, the meetings with those just out of Kiev, the balanced picture, the estimates of morale, the solemn weighing of tendencies, the contacts with the intermediaries of foreign chancellories, the grave assurances, the confident half-promises, all that which had been the justification of his self-exile, the involvement which had given purpose to his life.

Or was it? Wasn't his pleasure in the thought of Prague merely remembrance of the enjoyment of living: the long walks beside the river, the barges and the steamboats on the river, the bridges at twilight, the old palaces, the Opera House, the lighted shops at night, shops full of good things, sausages and pastry, also shoes, articles of leather and cloth, miracles of handicraftsmanship as well as of mass production, and the students talking wildly in the cafés, the neatly-dressed women, the plump housewives, and workers wearing leather shoes?

Kind, warm recollections. Ah, bourgeois democracy! How delightful! How disarming!

He had taken to reading military literature in the idle years. But how limited were these military writers! It had only been necessary to re-read the Marx-Engels correspondence on the American Civil War to see what a political mind could make out of a battle. He had tried it for himself. In a lightly ironical mood he had written of this and that event; there was no dearth of subject matter, always a war somewhere. He had played with the military style, cultivated a ponderous authority. He had taken his old pamphleteering pseudonym, added a sound German prefix, became Dr. Karl Karandash, military expert. Soon his articles had been appearing in a score of newspapers. A publisher had offered him a contract to write a book about tank warfare. With the notes of Guderian and De Gaulle before him and his own memory of Denikin's Trojan horses, it had not been difficult. *The Steel Fist* had had immediate success. Too much success!

Appalling misfortune! It had been taken up by Goebbels, sold a million copies.

Nevertheless *The Steel Fist* had soon dropped out of sight. When the *Wehrmacht* began to march he had been remembered sufficiently to gain a rare immunity, even to exercise some influence on behalf of friends. But with the invasion of France he had achieved an inescapable celebrity. Guderian's tanks, driving through the Ardennes, turning the Maginot Line at Sedan, had performed a manoeuvre which Dr. Karandash had lightly sketched in his book.

This coincidence no one had forgiven or forgotten. Foreign military planners had begun to study *The Steel Fist* under the impression that the author enjoyed the confidence of the German High Command. The Reichs Security Office had wanted to know about his sources. They had begun looking into his origins.

Suddenly, he had wanted to run, to run, run, run.

The war with Russia had been his reprieve. Someone in Berlin (in another branch of the administration) had remembered his specialisation in Ukrainian matters, his anti-Stalinist record. There had been this proposal, at first hinted at, then made directly, that he make certain semi-official reports, recommendations in line with the general idea of the Plan Rosenberg.

It was a terrible decision to have to make. He had begun to rationalise: the idea of a German-controlled autonomous Ukraine offered opportunities. What he had needed all these years, he said to himself, were roots. Here was a chance for action! He had begun to think of the Ukraine as an escape.

Here Dr. Karandash's meditations were interrupted. He

was within a few paces of the Paulus Platz. Looking about he found himself the centre of a throng of people. The *militsia* was suddenly all around them, jostling them, driving them forward. A *razzia,* thought Dr. Karandash. He felt at once for the security of those papers which would release him if he were questioned.

But it was not a *razzia*. The *militsia* was in good temper, laughing, joking in their variously accented Ukrainian, and pushing the throng forward until it was grouped before the building which, some months earlier, had been the Communist Hall, situated at the northern end of the Paulus Platz. Here there were a number of SS officers.

Dr. Karandash did not attempt to leave the throng of people, but stood there with them. They were mostly women in black shawls and drab dresses, a few men, a score or more children. They looked towards what was to be presented to them with dull, expectant faces, iron faces, thought Dr. Karandash, feeling his own face take on the inexpressive moulding that he recognised around him.

What the SS had for them was a hanging; a double hanging. Two pale young men, their arms bound loosely behind them, were standing on a stack of empty ammunition boxes before the wide entrance of the former Communist Hall. At that moment they were being roped by the neck to the balustrade of the balcony above the entrance. The young men appeared to be resigned to their position. Presently, without ceremony, one of the SS men thrust with his boot at the stack of ammunition boxes which tumbled over so that the two young men fell as far as the rope would allow which was no more than fifty centimetres but enough so that they died jerking.

The people in the street, the old black-shawled women, the ragged children, the few men, Dr. Karandash among them, looked on without any apparent emotion in their faces. The demonstration over, they were allowed to move on. A couple of young *Wehrmacht* officers were photographing the dead men. One had a Leica and the other an automatic Rolleiflex. The SS officers regarded them tolerantly. One of the SS men laughed and shouted a jest to the photographers. But the photographers were absorbed in their hobby.

Dr. Karandash walked on to his hotel.

The eighteenth century windows of the building of the former All-Ukraine Central Executive Committee (formerly the Club of the Nobility) afforded an excellent view of the northern end of the Paulus Platz. The tall windows were made up of small panes of glass framed in oak. Behind the windows, inside the old building, there was a pleasant lofty room with an ornate ceiling, a carved overmantel, a parquet floor. This was now the operations room of the General Officer Commanding the Sixth Army. There were a number of desks in the room at which staff officers worked quietly. A Feldwebel guarded a curtained map. Field telephone wires lay across the floor. When a telephone rang the buzz was subdued. It was not possible to hear the voice of the non-commissioned officer answering it. A number of aerial photographs, all uniformly white, lay on the desk of the Commanding General.

From time to time Colonel General von Paulus would leave his desk and step over to the window. He would stand at the tall window looking out over the plaza which had been named for him. He was not conscious of looking out of the window. Like most tactical generals his mind was full of minutiae.

He was a tall thin man of fifty-two years, a "young" general, having but recently succeeded to the command of the Sixth Army upon the illness of General von Reichenau. His appearance was one of forbidding austerity. He had a thin hooked nose and the corners of his mouth were permanently downturned. He never smiled. His grey eyes, which might have seemed melancholy to some, were quite unsentimental, merciless and cold.

As he stood now at the window he was joined by a bulky, fresh-faced young man, his Adjutant, Colonel Adam.

"Our Black Friends are busy again," Colonel Adam said.

It was his careless way of referring to the SS. There was no resentment in his voice, merely that slight humorous disdain which a military man may have for a corps of superior distinction and parallel duties outside his command.

Colonel General von Paulus spoke quietly:

"What we would do without them *I* do not know."

While Colonel Adam was puzzling over this ambiguity the Colonel General had noticed the crowd gathered before the Communist Hall.

"Our Black Friends make a demonstration," Colonel Adam said.

"I am looking at the people," Colonel General von Paulus said. "Among them I count ten men of military age. Yes?"

Colonel Adam counted.

"Ten," he said, "but can they fight?"

"A German officer," said Colonel General von Paulus, "can make any man fight."

It was one of those remarks, made from time to time, which filled Colonel Adam with love for the Colonel General.

"Many things have changed in the Ukraine since I was here in the last war," said Colonel General von Paulus. "For one thing the machine age has arrived. There used to be many horses in the Ukraine. Their cavalry was among the best in the world. But now there are only broken-down tractors. Nevertheless there are still men. For a kilo of bread and a herring a day the Ukrainian will do the work of a horse."

"The recruiting begins today," said Colonel Adam.

"What is that they are doing now?" the Colonel General asked.

"They are affixing notices to the dead men," Colonel Adam said. "The notices say they are parachutists."

"Parachutists! Why do I not know about this?"

"They have just begun."

Colonel General von Paulus turned his cold grey eyes on Colonel Adam.

"Who is our liaison?"

"Oberleutnant Soedermann."

"I do not have the slightest doubt, Adam, but that you have sent them the stupidest officer on our staff."

Colonel Adam smiled.

"Be more careful," Colonel General von Paulus said.

The smile faded from Colonel Adam's face.

"Tell Soedermann to bring an appreciation."

The men hanging from the balcony of the former Communist Hall were Nikolai Pavlovich Tikhonov, 19, a former collective farm worker from the Chilyabinsk region, and Ivan Alexandrovich Kolovin, 21, a former MTS worker from Tambov. Both had been members of the Komsomol organisation. In 1939 they had paid their first visit to Moscow where they had participated in the spectacular parachute drop which had marked the May celebrations of that year. A few months later they had been drafted into the Red Army and sent to a school for political officers in the Ilyinka district where they were to have become junior political officers, or *polytruks,* as they are sometimes called. But this year they had been suddenly withdrawn from the political school and sent to a large training organisation for partizans which had just started at Smolny. After three weeks' instruction in guerilla tactics they had been dropped near the village of Podvorki, about thirty kilometres from Kharkiv.

Landing easily in the snow Tikhonov and Kolovin quickly made contact with one another. The night was luminous with the reflection from the snow which bound the whole countryside. They heard the plane which had borne them fade away out of earshot. There was no sign of a third descending parachute. In the first light of day they searched every fold of the landscape for a trace of the coloured cloth parachute and the canister of arms, ammunition and demolition equipment which, they had been told, would be dropped with them. Except for the knives which they carried at their belts they were defenceless. They spent the next night in a small wood, huddled together beneath the snow, their folded parachutes hung over their heads to break the frost. The cold was impracticable.

The next day they saw the village of Podvorki. It was small as Ukrainian villages go, no more than a hamlet at a road junction. Tikhonov went in first. The village appeared to be deserted. The door of every cabin was barred and such windows as the houses had were boarded up. Tikhonov made a fair imitation of the Ukrainian form of greeting and hammered on the nearest door. As the door opened slightly he thrust his boot in the opening and then his shoulder. He was joined by Kolovin. Inside the house they were greeted with abuse, profanity and threats by an old peasant and his wife. This did not surprise them. They warmed themselves in the cabin. They found their bearings. They stayed there, sleeping, one whole day.

On the next day two German soldiers came to the village. They were riding in a droshky driven by a very old peasant. They wore blankets over their heads and they had a bearskin rug over their knees. Beneath the rug several empty bottles rolled about. They were very merry. It was a routine patrol. The villages were giving no trouble. At Podvorki they descended from the droshky and began stamping their feet on the ground and beating their arms across their chests. A few villagers watched them from the shelter of their cabin doors. Some children came out to look. The German soldiers talked to the children. In their few words of Russian and by signs they indicated that they wanted vodka. The children shouted this intelligence to their parents. The parents shook their heads.

Presently the parents came out and stood around the droshky. The old peasant shouted at them to stand back from his horse which was steaming like a small locomotive. The soldiers offered sugar for vodka. Soon there was a group of a dozen or more villagers standing around the soldiers. The soldiers were red in the face. They were thin men with thin red faces. Tikhonov and Kolovin joined the people standing around the soldiers. They worked their way towards the front of the group. One of the soldiers was already looking suspiciously at Kolovin when Tikhonov nodded. They sprang on the Germans, taking them around the head with one arm, at the same time drawing their knives. It was not a minute before there were two

German soldiers lying on the roadway at the village of Podvori with their throats cut.

Except for Tikhonov and Kolovin not another person was in sight. The droshky, the aged peasant whipping his horse madly, was a dark blur in the distance. The villagers had vanished. Every house was again barricaded.

Tikhonov and Kolovin looked at their trophies: a German infantryman's rifle, a sub-machine-gun of Belgian make, a Mauser pistol, several hundred rounds of ammunition. They took their trophies back into the woods whence they had come. Here, not later than the next day, on the information of a villager, they were surprised, overcome, and brought into Kharkiv.

The report which Oberleutnant Soedermann was writing was rather drier than the above account. But the facts, obtained from Tikhonov and Kolovin under duress of a not very original but nevertheless well-tried and effective kind, were there. The facts, commonplace in themselves, were all that was necessary to obtain a clear picture of the fate of Tikhonov and Kolovin.

Oberleutnant Soedermann's report supplemented a report he had prepared only the day before on the Podvorki incident. An SS detail had found the bodies of the two soldiers lying in the centre of the roadway. In accordance with the Jurisdiction Order (May, 1941) of the Barbarossa Decree (December, 1940), abrogating courts-martial for civilian offenders against martial law (or for German soldiers committing offenses against civilians), specifically Part 1, Subsection 4, dealing with "collective coercive measures" against "localities," a *Teilkommando* of *Einsatzgruppe C* had battered down the doors of every house in the village, assembled the population, selected at random twenty persons, the nature of the crime meriting the recommended ten lives for each German life, and shot them. (There had been one slight departure from this procedure, not mentioned in the report. Among the twenty hostages lined up for execution had been a peasant of middle age, a heavy, thickset man with a broad face and small squinting eyes. As the SS guards were pushing the hostages into line this man had stepped backwards, and, bending low, had raced away towards the woods. One of the guards had fired a prolonged burst after him. The man was seen to stumble and fall. The SS guards did not bother to look at the body, nor, for that matter, at the bodies of the other nineteen. The peasant's name is Alexi Ivanovich Kharko.)

During the preceding week Oberleutnant Soedermann had had occasion to write six reports of incidents like that which had occurred at the village of Podvorki. But it was not until he had completed this seventh report that he was struck with the similarity of the incidents.

Now, standing rigidly at attention in the presence of the Colonel General and Colonel Adam, he trembled to make his point.

The tall thin Colonel General, his shoulders hunched like a roosting hawk, stood looking out of the high window. Each of the many small square panes of glass was edged with snow. The afternoon sun slanted in through the window. The Colonel General, listening, did not glance in the direction of Oberleutnant Soedermann.

"Well, well, what do you make of it?" said Colonel Adam.

It was with pride that the Oberleutnant answered:

"Herr Colonel, *Melde gehorsamst,* a certain pattern . . ."

"How do the villages react? Do they run away now when German soldiers come? Or do they still welcome us as liberators?"

Oberleutnant Soedermann paused. He was confused.

"Very well, tell us about your pattern."

"Herr Colonel, *Melde gehorsamst,* the pattern is this: With one exception, and that exception was on the occasion when, in contradiction to our orders, the parachutists were shot while still in the air, and so we had no opportunity of extracting confirmatory information, with that one exception on all these occasions the parachutists, all of them, Herr Colonel, have been dropped *without arms.*"

Oberleutnant Soedermann waited for Colonel Adam to digest this information. He saw that the Colonel General had also heard him, although the Colonel General was still looking through the window.

"Then you assume . . ." said Colonel Adam.

"Herr Colonel, *Melde gehorsamst,* the Russians are without arms!"

"At least," said Colonel Adam, very calmly, "they are

so undersupplied with arms that they have none for their parachutists."

"Herr Colonel, *Melde gehorsamst,* exactly."

"They must be desperate."

"Moscow is *kaputt!*" said Oberleutnant Soedermann.

Colonel General von Paulus turned slowly from the window and looked at Oberleutnant Soedermann. It was a cold regard.

"Trottel!" said Colonel General von Paulus.

He made the remark casually, but its casualness was more chilling than a word uttered in anger. There was a ripple of laughter from several officers who, Oberleutnant Soedermann realised with surprise, had been within hearing distance. The face of Colonel Adam was buckled with laughter, though the red mouth was shut and bound. Colonel Adam dismissed the Oberleutnant with a wave of his hand.

Oberleutnant Soedermann saluted and in long heavily-planted strides marched out of the room.

That evening Oberleutnant Soedermann told his SS friend, Sturmführer Doktor Gruber, about his reception by the Colonel General. Sturmführer Gruber, having completed his appraisal of the NKVD records, had been recently transferred to the personal staff of Obergruppenführer Rauch. Here he was in close touch with the latest events. Sturmführer Gruber was able to comfort Oberleutnant Soedermann with some confidential information about Colonel General von Paulus and other high officers. The faraway look in the Colonel General's eye was not due to any grave contemplation of tactical problems, but to changes that were about to take place in the staff of Army Group Command South, nothing less indeed than the recall of Marshal Rundstedt, the Colonel General's immediate superior. Thus the Colonel General had not been able fully to consider the significance of a handful of unarmed parachutists from the Smolny school. But the really momentous news which Sturmführer Gruber had to tell his friend that evening was this: *Der Führer* was about to assume personal command of all military operations.

Oberleutnant Soedermann and Sturmführer Gruber found the implications of this move a stimulating topic of conversation. It took them through a bottle of the very best French cognac and brought them, the very best of good friends, together to the Officers' Establishment where, each bowing to the other, behaving in the most chivalrous manner, Soedermann insisted on Gruber, and Gruber insisted on Soedermann, being the first that evening to enjoy the favours of a young lady of their singular preference called, appropriately enough (how jocose they were about it), Olympia.

That spring the demonstrations at the former Communist Hall were a feature of the Paulus Platz.

It is true, as Dr. Karandash observed, that the peoples east of the Carpathians are not commonly impressed by the aspect of death, and this is due not to any special characteristic of race or inheritance, but to an intimacy with an old familiar of eastern life. So much of a familiar in these late years that a good peasant may live through the winter with his, or her, dead, the beaten one, the executed one, the starved one, the ill-fortuned one, the rarely sickness-consumed one, seeing the dead every day if there are not boards enough for the humble coffin, waiting for the time when the thaw will permit a proper interment in the black earth. Nor are they easily affected by the visceral. The exquisite horror which the sight, or surrogate image, of exposed organs and entrails inspires in urban man is unknown to a people living close to and upon the birth, life and cutting of animals into whose viscera, being without the impersonal meat-rending machine, they may of necessity not infrequently have been, stripped naked to the waist for the economy of clothing, shoulder-deep. As with surgeons touch diminishes the power of self-identification: the advantage? death may have other and truer meaning.

Thus the attention paid to the demonstrations in the Paulus Platz had a meaning different from that accepted by the gratified entrepreneurs.

While none, except children, paused long to stare at

the dead it was noted that all who passed that way raised their eyes as they came abreast of the former Communist Hall and made a full, if brief, scrutiny of the hanged. Did those pale, sunken-eyed faces implant terror? Was there an increased respect for the ruthless will of the conquerors? Those who may have thought so could hardly have understood that in this eastern world, in a long time, power had been measured not by the banal demonstration of the readiness to destroy life, but by the willingness with which life was submitted for destruction. And the message the people of the Ukraine read in the Paulus Platz, as well as in innumerable and roadside places as the months went by, was that there was life to spare, still Communist lives to be abundantly expended. The message was not without authorship.

Therefore, it was not terror, or respect for terror, which registered in those faces turned sharply towards the former Communist Hall and then turned away, but dread; not dread as a particular identity, but rather dread of a condition. It was a feeling that that which they had secretly known was inevitable was about to happen. It was the foreboding of the rebirth of a struggle in which they had been immersed all their lives, but of which their present powerful but ignorant conquerors, or for that matter any of the West, knew little. It was the resubmission of the living body of the Ukraine to this struggle and the reconditioning of the physique of survival; it was a sense of unutterable weariness.

There was also in those swift glances at the hanged a practical purpose. Each onlooker was prepared for the light of recognition. The dead, though distorted by the manner of their death and often disfigured by cigarette burns and other memorabilia of their last hours, were not yet unrecognisable. But none, yet, was recognised. They were mostly men from the remote Siberias, not so far as anybody knew Ukrainians, and this was confirmed by those who had spoken with them while they were still free in the woods or in the villages. But there would be Ukrainians. Of that most people were now sure. The Germans had slain thousands of Ukrainian Communists in those first days after their arrival, but they had not, contrary to their own belief at the time, slain all. The cadres of the NKVD and the *Gosudarstvo,* together often referred to as the *Active*, were not among those whose lives had ended at the rope's end in Karl Liebknecht Street. The return of the *Active* was now awaited with a hushed and hardly bearable expectancy.

The news of the day was brought back to Maryusa Selova by her children, but she herself saw nothing of the demonstrations. The passage of winter and the promise of spring and summer were more in her mind. The routine of the school was keeping the children together. The promise of rations had not yet materialised, but there was still hope. She was making an effort to organise classes.

Their subsistence was now largely dependent upon the free market, an enlargement of the former white market, which, under semi-official encouragement, was having a vigorous life in Kharkiv. Many of the children had, by this time, paid furtive visits to their former homes. Some of the children had been allowed by the German occupants to repossess certain of their family belongings, insignificant as they were. Fomin sent them back to beg objects of barterable value, clocks, spoons, salt, matches. Some of the children did not ask the occupants, but took what was theirs by stealth; in time, the identity of their homes, never profound, being lost, they took whatever they found wherever they found it.

With this stock-in-trade, Fomin bartered for food. As soon as the roads were clear he planned to make better bargains by going direct to the peasants in the villages within walking distance of Kharkiv. Life in the villages was poor, but the peasants, remembering former occupations, had certainly buried food in readiness for the expropriations of the soldiery. Bullets would not induce the peasants to divulge these hiding places, but they would surely yield to the pleasurable exercise of hitherto illegal tendencies, the immemorial aptitude for bargaining, the inexterminable process of seeing, coveting, buying, hoarding.

Maryusa accepted what came to hand with gratitude.

She was already planning to set aside a small store against the coming months. She did not know what the coming months would bring. She did not hope for the victory of this side or that side. There was no room in her mind for general considerations. She had no political sense, as they say.

Thus it was with an expression of genuine surprise not unmixed with pleasure that she found, one evening, Lydia Artemova sitting waiting for her in the small room in which she stored her few rations and in which she slept. Lydia Artemova had been her old instructor at the Pedagogical Institute. She was an elderly woman with grey hair covered by an old black beret. Her face was wise and sad, but so long disciplined against emotion that her mouth had been reduced to a groove and there were small bitter lines at its corners. She looked steadily at Maryusa and there was no trace of a smile reciprocating that of the young schoolteacher. But Maryusa did not feel repulsed; it was the face that most people wore nowadays and it was not easily unbent.

"Well," said Lydia Artemova.

"It has been difficult," Maryusa said, "but the children have been wonderful. There are some very young ones, babies. The older children look after them. Everybody works. We could wish only that there was more food, but perhaps it will be better in summer. I am afraid of typhus. We have learned how to live on very little. At first there was a little flour and mushrooms, but latterly there has been only potatoes. Potatoes are good."

"You maintain Party vigilance? Yes?"

A cold flush spread over Maryusa's brow as she heard these words.

"The children are good," Maryusa said. "They have much discipline. It has been like that from the first day."

"You have carried on Party work?"

"No."

"A Pioneer group?"

"No."

"Why?"

"The Germans would not permit it."

"The *Germans!*"

"They watch us. If I should carry on Party work they

would hear of it. They would stop the school. What would happen to the children?"

"The Germans have informers among the children, yes?"

"No."

"You speak with too much certainty."

"I am sure there are no informers among the children. There cannot be."

"Perhaps you like the Germans. Perhaps you are happier now."

"No."

"Perhaps you are one of those Ukrainians who think the Germans are their liberators."

"You would not say that if you had been with us all this time."

"How do you know I have not been with you?"

"Because you say that. You would not say that if you knew how these children came here. You would not say that."

"I know well enough. They are the children of Communists."

"That is true," Maryusa said. "I had not thought of it that way."

"I think," said Lydia Artemova, observing Maryusa's flushed and passionate face, "that you would feel the same way if they were the children of Fascists."

"I do not know. I am not sure." Into Maryusa's broad face and blue eyes now came an expression of trenchant obstinacy. "Perhaps I would," she said.

Lydia Artemova smiled. It was a hard bitter smile.

"No doubt," she said, "that is why you expose them to Fascist propaganda."

"No. There is no politics here."

"No politics! What are you saying!"

"It is true. It is for their own protection."

"No politics?"

Lydia Artemova opened an old string bag she carried and brought forth a book which she put before Maryusa. It was one of the school textbooks in Ukrainian. It was one of the books which the SS man had taken away and then later returned to the school. Maryusa's heart became like stone. She did not need to open the textbook.

If you have seen a Soviet textbook, particularly those

of the younger grades, you will remember that the first lesson concerns the Party Lenin-Stalin and that this theme, with illustrations, is recurrent. The SS Sturmführer who had supervised the new educational arrangements in Kharkiv, in the absence of new primers, had had his assistants carefully and methodically paste strips of paper over all mention of the Party Lenin-Stalin and the illustrations thereof, so that the primers, though truncated and somewhat abrupt in form, nevertheless were still adequate, indeed rather more useful than before, being simpler.

"I have to maintain classes," said Maryusa.

"It is necessary, therefore, to teach German propaganda?"

"There is no word of German or German propaganda."

A fanatical light came into Lydia Artemova's eyes. The light animated and gave life to her embittered and drooping face. It was the radiating force of her commonplace and disciplined life. It frightened Maryusa. It did not overcome the stubbornness in Maryusa's heart. But it moved her to speak defensively.

"The children know everything that is under those strips of paper," she said. "The Germans are so stupid that they do not think that the children are provoked to know what is concealed."

The fanatical light did not leave Lydia Artemova's eyes.

"You allow the children to discover that the Fascists have the power to blot out the name of Our Leader and Teacher, Comrade Stalin," she said.

Maryusa said nothing for a moment. Then she looked at Lydia Artemova and said quietly:

"What would you have us do? Would you have us tear off these strips of paper and be shot?"

"It is not too much."

"It is not necessary," said Maryusa, "the children are loyal."

"How is it possible for the children to be loyal?" Lydia Artemova said. "How is it possible in the absence of proper political orientation? Loyal to what? Loyal to whom?"

"To me," Maryusa said. But even before saying it she knew how inept and trivial her words were. Yet it was the truth and somehow, even though she could not explain it in the terms used by Lydia Artemova, a very important truth. Maryusa was in despair.

Lydia Artemova pretended not to notice the small remark.

"We are fighting," said Lydia Artemova, "the great Patriotic War of the Soviet Fatherland in which thousands of heroes and heroines are ready to die for the freedom of their country. . . ."

"You have heard from Moscow!" Maryusa said. The intelligence, only now dawning on her, made her gasp.

"Nine months ago," continued Lydia Artemova, not noticing Maryusa's interjection, her mind retracted as though bearing upon her memory, "nine months ago Fascist Germany perfidiously fell upon our country, grossly and basely violating the non-aggression pact. The enemy calculated that after the very first blow the Red Army would break up and would lose its power of resistance. But the enemy sadly miscalculated. . . ."

Maryusa stared at Lydia Artemova whose voice was growing louder with the force of her declamation. Her eyes blazed with an inward fire, looking not at Maryusa, but at some point suspended above Maryusa's head.

She went on to speak of desperate battles near Moscow in which the German-Fascist troops had been routed.

"In the Moscow and Tula regions dozens of towns and hundreds of villages temporarily captured by the enemy have been completely cleared of the German invaders."

There was exaltation in the final sentences. Lydia Artemova's voice had risen to such a pitch that it could be heard beyond the walls of Maryusa Selova's room. For some moments after she had ceased talking the tension was still in her prim face and spare figure. Then, gradually, she became aware once more of Maryusa. She looked at Maryusa and her eyes became cold.

"Do not be so much afraid of the Fascist Germans," she said, "and take heed of this warning."

Closing her string bag tightly she rose and went away without a word of farewell.

Maryusa Selova lay down on her bed. She tried to think of what had been said. The complexity of her feelings made it difficult for her, a simple woman, to be rational. Her heart was consumed with an anger which she had not been able to express and which she could not now express.

It had begun from the instant of first seeing Lydia Artemova and it had been established with Lydia Artemova's calm assumption that she once more exercised authority over Maryusa. Almost from Maryusa's infancy she had been her political mentor. In those years long ago when Maryusa herself had been a Pioneer, a small girl in a red beret and kerchief, singing the songs and listening to the big talks and being fired with ambition, Lydia Artemova had been a serious Party member with an eye for the brighter than average child. Maryusa remembered her as an austere woman, but one who could laugh, who was younger than her years, one who could answer a child's questions, and she had reverenced Lydia Artemova and had believed everything she said. Then Maryusa had become a Komsomolka and had entered the University. At the Pedagogical Institute where she had studied to be a teacher she had listened, obeyed, and been enthusiastic for Lydia Artemova as she went through her course in Leninism. But Maryusa had not passed from the Komsomols into the Communist Party. She had never become a Party member.

It was only now, lying on her truckle bed, hours after Lydia Artemova's departure, that she remembered this. She was *not* a Party member! Therefore, Lydia Artemova had no authority over her!

Her heart leapt. But it was only for a moment. In the end it made no difference. Lydia Artemova had treated her, as always, as if she were a Party member, expected as much from her, and would pinion her in the same responsibilities. Thinking of this, Maryusa remembered other matters during that terrible period, 1936-37; remembered the day that one of her comrades had denounced her at a meeting of the Komsomol District Committee, as the daughter of a *kulak,* and Maryusa had protested that her father had fought in the Red Cavalry in the Civil War. The meeting had passed on to charges against other members. Nothing had come of it. Such things were happening every day then and it was not something to be resented. But this slur had been enough to prevent her normal passage from the Komsomols to the Party. Who would have ventured to sign an affidavit of one who had been accused of being the daughter of a *kulak?*

And now Maryusa remembered how Lydia Artemova, surviving that period, had attained a stature she had not had before, and was paid a commensurate deference, and how this accretion of authority had made her somehow more severe, more withdrawn and disciplined. And, thinking this, Maryusa now remembered many things she had heard about Lydia Artemova then and had chosen not to consider. How Lydia Artemova was almost the only survivor of all the Party functionaries of that other period. How this circumstance had invested her name and her presence with an aura of respect akin to dread, and how Lydia Artemova, though commanding the utmost obedience, never was admired, or ever spoken to or laughed with or made love to in the way it had been before that time, this being more true of the new young men who had come from Moscow for the Government and who, it seemed, saw and identified her, her type, at once. Yes, thought Maryusa, everyone looks twice at an old Party member. And you, one says with one's eyes, how many lives did you deliver that you are here? Perhaps that was why, after the period 1936-37, Lydia Artemova had paid so much attention to the young, even when, like Maryusa, they were not Party members, or (Maryusa thought with a sudden illumination) *because* they were not Party members.

Then why was she not more reasonable?

Asking this now, Maryusa knew that Lydia Artemova would not have understood. In her ears such a question would have sounded foreign, something out of the past, bookish, unreal, and she would have used a Party word to describe the character of one who uttered such a phrase. Lydia Artemova had spoken as she had because there was no other way she could speak. She was not, in a way, herself, as for example Maryusa was *herself*. She was not a person. She was a part of something outside herself, a system, a ritual, a creed, no, far more than that, a force, a dynamic of her time. It was not something she merely lived, or put on, or could escape from, it was something she *was*, something very rare and perhaps beautiful—for her.

Maryusa had always obeyed Lydia Artemova. But in the time between the last time she had seen Lydia Artemova and now something had occurred which had changed Maryusa's character. It was the taking of a decision. An infant's cry and the decision, made on Maryusa's own volition, to take upon herself, without direction, a personal and solitary responsibility. A decision which led immediately to other decisions, to the creation of dependency and the establishment of a system, to the examination and resolvement of unprecedented problems, to an affirmation of values and, no matter that it was inarticulate, a philosophy of life.

The decision had been made. She had deviated from a rule of conduct. She was in opposition to Lydia Artemova. She was in opposition to the Party. Therefore, she was in alliance with the enemies of the Party.

Arriving at this conclusion Maryusa for the first time became fully conscious of her position. Her heart filled with fear.

There was the war and there were the Germans and the SS and torture and execution, and these things were horrifying, but they were impersonal, they were what could happen to one, to flesh and nerve, but they were accident. There was not in them such terror as there was in the knowledge that one was now an Enemy of the People.

Lying now on her bed, hours after Lydia Artemova's departure, she could hear again the high declamatory voice exulting over the failure of the Germans to capture Moscow. What Lydia Artemova had said Maryusa knew to be the truth, not because such information had reached her before, but because it had been in the background of her mind, as in the minds of all other Ukrainians, from the moment that the *Wehrmacht* armies, encumbered in snow and ice, had come to a halt in the Kursk steppe.

But Lydia Artemova had brought it into her consciousness. What had been vague was now real, portentous. It was the whole focus of her fear. The great Patriotic War of the Soviet Fatherland! The words were still ringing in her ears. Strange words. The *patriotic* war, the *Fatherland.* She could not remember ever having encountered such words in utterance. Yet they were deeply moving words. Because they moved her she knew that they would move others more. Thus she gauged, accurately, the power that was gathering like a vast hurricane in the East. It was not the hurricane that she feared, though she stood directly in its path, but the eddies of the hurricane. Behind the great battles that would be fought, cruel and bitter furies would ply. The crimes that would be committed! The vengeance that would be taken!

At this moment Maryusa remembered the textbook in the Ukrainian language which Lydia Artemova had taken out of her string bag. How had Lydia Artemova obtained the book? Who had given the book to Lydia Artemova?

Suddenly, upon impulse, Maryusa got up from her bed and went over to the place where Lydia Artemova had been sitting. She felt with her hand, but she could not find the book. Then, still under the command of her impulse, she went into the big room where the children lay asleep. It was very quiet. Too quiet. The children lay under their rag blankets, huddled close to one another. The light from the little stove had died down, but occasionally an ember would break and then the room would gather to itself a momentary golden radiance.

In one of these moments Maryusa caught sight of an unfamiliar whiteness by one wall. She went immediately there. She took down from the wall a small poster which had been pinned there. She brought the small poster closer to the light of the fire and looked at it.

It was a copy, reduced in size for the purpose of illegal distribution, of a poster which could be seen on many walls in Moscow that year. It was a poster without words. It consisted of three drawings. The first drawing showed a Russian child being given a hand grenade by a Russian partizan. The second drawing showed the same child standing before a German commandant in what was clearly a German field headquarters. The third picture showed the child launching the hand grenade into the middle of a group of German officers in the headquarters.

Maryusa looked at the small poster, the work of a master draughtsman, so cunningly did the drawing appropriate an adolescent style, the primitive, compelling, childish line. Then slowly she tore the poster into tiny pieces. Carefully she dropped the pieces into the tiny stove. The stove flared upwards for a moment, but none of the children stirred.

The traps and the snares and the pitfalls that were all about her seemed very real to Maryusa. Her fear plumbed deepest at this moment. She considered denouncing Lydia Artemova to the Germans.

Then as she went back to her bed she grew chill with the knowledge that she could have such a thought. She dismissed the thought. The dismissal made her feel more in control of herself. It made her feel calmer. She began to feel that it had been childish of her to give way to alarm. It was true that the books had been defaced in a way that the Party could not overlook and would certainly inquire into. But the books had been defaced by the Germans. The responsibility was clear. She was not to blame. Lydia Artemova had been angry this evening because she had failed to reassert her former influence, that was all. Thus Maryusa arrived back at the astonishing conclusion that what she had done was right.

As though seeking a confirmation she listened for a few moments to the children sleeping, to the light breathing, the coughing, the stirrings which told her that her family had gone back to sleep. Then she sighed and went to sleep herself.

Not all the children in the schoolhouse were asleep that night. There was one little girl, Sophia by name, who crept back into her pallet, long after Lydia Artemova had gone, and then lay awake, her eyes wide open in the dark, thinking of what she should do.

Sophia was eleven years of age. Her parents had been among those Party members killed by the Germans in the first week of the occupation. Her parents had been good parents, factory workers, Party members since the Civil War, but never functionaries, solid people not bright enough to have held office in those bright early days and then, because of those early days, ineligible for office, a circumstance they had held in their innermost thoughts to be of great good fortune. No longer young when Sophia appeared they had loved her more than children are normally loved, or they had loved her differently.

It was the decade when people's affections were being withdrawn from externals, from institutions and propositions, and were being centred, so far as it was possible, upon the felicitous and real. Thus the three Samoilovs, father, mother and Sophia, had lived so much together, the child becoming so much a part of the parents, that they were a kind of trinity, so compacted in sensibility that what one thought was already in the minds of the others, even, without the precedent of experience or consciousness, in the mind of Sophia. Thus Sophia, without being aware of it, knew many things, had, by transference, many feelings the origin and rationality of which she would never know. That is not to say she was precocious, or supersensitive, or a dreamy girl; on the contrary, as became the offspring of Ukrainian workers, she was sturdy of limb, hardy of mind, and without timidity.

Like many other children she had been present when the Germans had come for her parents and she had heard the brief interrogation which had established their identity. Her parents had been taken away in a large van and she had not seen them again. Some hours later the room had been broken into by neighbours who in a few minutes had stripped it of such meagre articles of food and clothing as the Samoilovs had possessed. It was the neighbours who had told Sophia that her parents had been shot. All the Party members were being shot, they had said. There was malice in the way they had flung the intelligence at her; but if they had expected her to quail they had been unrewarded. She had already accepted the fact that her parents had been killed because they were Party members.

Sophia's parents had often feared this. They had feared

it most in the period when Sophia was six or seven years old. It is impossible to exaggerate how deeply this fear had possessed them, or how helpless they had felt, not knowing of what crime they were guilty, yet feeling guilty, being unable to measure or to understand what was happening. Night after night, for months, the Samoilovs had sat up, silently waiting for the knock on the door and the man or men who would take them away, as thousands were being taken away all over the country that year, and disposed of, they knew not exactly how, except that it would be final, their souls' end, for some infraction of a Party rule, some lack of vigilance, or some trumped-up charge that would be unanswerable, because so improbable, but, in truth, for one certain reason: because they were Party members, Communists. The child lying awake in her cot had been deeply impressed.

The relationship of the three Samoilovs was such that the very fact of their fear being guarded from expression had imparted to the child an equal sense of apprehension; indeed because of her childish lucidity, her naïveté, gave her a clearer, sharper enlargement of the emotion, so that it had remained with her and had not, as in her parents, been diminished by time and circumstance. Out of terror had been born a hatred so overpowering, yet so quiet and subdued, a deafness of the mind, that all Sophia's later life had been like a dream.

That day Sophia felt that the expected had happened: they had come for her parents and had taken them away and killed them.

Since there was no expectancy of her parents returning, and nothing in the room to eat, Sophia had gone out into the street. There she had found herself in the company of men and women moving about the streets and lanes and debauched buildings of the city, scattering before the grey-uniformed patrols, or staring at them, enjoying, for the first time in the lives of most of them, the sensation of lawlessness, of being utterly and unbelievably free. That night a man robbed Sophia of her boots and, as an afterthought, raped her. In the morning she was hungry. She was noticed by a large laughing girl who staggered out of an alleyway full of soldiers and took Sophia by the hand. She had been among the many small dishevelled creatures taken in, fed and bedded by Maryusa Selova that day.

Lying now, some months afterwards, in her bed of straw in the old schoolhouse, a sturdy worker for Maryusa, a quiet almost secretive child, Sophia held her eyes wide open in the dark, thinking. This evening all the children had heard Lydia Artemova declaiming. The sharp voice had gone beyond the walls of Maryusa's room. The children had sensed the threat in Lydia Artemova's speech. But only Sophia Samoilov knew exactly its meaning. Towards morning she knew exactly what to do about it.

Very early, therefore, she left the schoolhouse and walked down the hill towards a section of the city not far from the former Communist Hall. In the Chernyshevskaya before the unobtrusive building which had housed the NKVD and was now the headquarters of the SS she paused. The doors were closed. A soldier sat nodding inside a striped sentry box outside the doors. Sophia did not wake the soldier. She waited standing close to the wall of the building. In a little while the soldier stepped out of the sentry box and stamped his feet and hugged his mittened hands. Shortly afterwards a guard detail came by and another sentry stepped into his place. The doors of the building were unbolted. The sentry exchanged words with someone inside the building. People began to arrive and depart from the building. Some were in *Wehrmacht* uniform, some in the black uniform of the SS, a number wore ordinary civilian dress. Sophia Samoilov waited for the SS Obergruppenführer whom everybody knew was the most important man in Kharkiv.

He arrived late. Sophia heard first and was startled by the clatter of the sentry as he stepped out of his box and stamped to attention, at the same time throwing and holding a large salute. A black Mercédès drew up before the door. A porter ran down the steps and opened the door of the Mercédès. The Obergruppenführer stepped out. He wore shining black boots and a long creaseless black coat. Against the background of thawing ice, the paintless building, the campaign-worn uniforms of the sentry and the porter, the Obergruppenführer was immaculate.

For a minute he stood there, unhurried, commanding. Then he felt a jerking at his coat sleeve.

Obergruppenführer Rauch looked down. He saw a small ragged girl tugging at his sleeve. The porter already had his hand on the small girl's shoulder, the sentry had already brought his rifle to the port, when Obergruppenführer Rauch smiled. The porter sentry stood back.

"Please, please," Sophia said. "You speak Ukrainian?"

Obergruppenführer Rauch did not answer. Instead he looked at the porter and the sentry with a kind of delight in his face.

He reached down and took the small hand in his black glove. Leading Sophia by the hand he entered the building and walked, making sure he did not step too fast or too long for the small girl, to the office of his aide, Sturmführer Gruber.

The building occupied by the *SS Einsatzgruppen* had the atmosphere of efficiency one associates with a smoothly-running bureaucracy. It was a relaxed atmosphere. Visitors waited in the anterooms while officers carefully occupied themselves at desks. Clerks sauntered down the corridors. In the cellars guards crashed the steel doors of the isolators and waited, motionless in time, listening to the inmates listening to them.

The conferences in the big room were no longer fully attended. The little group of civilian collaborators (responding to invitations it would have been unwise for them to reject) now occupied a small section of the main conference table. The young man who had said he was editor of the *Kharkivanian* had made one more appearance and then, to Dr. Karandash's regret, vanished. Obermeister Stetsenko was at every conference, but much changed. He was now a very serious man, deeply concerned with the money market.

The official exchange, fixed at ten rubles to the mark, had for a time remained uncomprehended by a people accustomed to accept paper money, in all its uses, at arbitrarily determined values. And then, suddenly, it had dawned upon many citizens that there were advantages to be obtained from dealing in money at the unofficial fluctuating rates of exchange. A frantic trade sprang up. Foremost among the speculators was Obermeister Stetsenko whose pockets were now jammed with dirty wads of ruble notes and whose blunt grin-broadened face was sapped by anxiety of a kind quite new to him.

The behaviour of Obermeister Stetsenko diverted Dr. Karandash and Prince Dolov.

"In 1938," said Prince Dolov, "I had a very unhappy experience with francs."

"I was never able to master the intricacies of the trade," said Dr. Karandash, "but in Switzerland on one occasion I was able to dispose of some zlotys at an encouraging figure."

"It was never the same," said Prince Dolov, "after England went off the gold standard."

"Ah, the pound," said Dr. Karandash, "the pound and the franc, bulwarks of the bourgeoisie."

Obermeister Stetsenko, who had been listening closely to this conversation, now asked a question:

"Is it true," he said, "that there is a money market in other parts of the world?"

"Indeed," said Prince Dolov.

"In all countries there is such speculation?"

"Yes, naturally; you did not know?"

"How could he know?" said Dr. Karandash. "They don't mention it in their home propaganda. For good reasons."

Obermeister Stetsenko's face widened. He was clearly a man beset by a Vista.

"But is it legal?"

"Of course."

"Tell me," said Obermeister Stetsenko, "how many marks to the dollar?"

"You see," said Prince Dolov, "he has heard of them too."

All at once Dr. Karandash had a distaste for the conversation. He felt an unreasonable, perverse anger growing in his heart.

"In former times," Prince Dolov was saying, "I remember there used to be a very big business in foreign exchange in Russia."

"It was conducted by the Jews," said Hetman Horopadsky.

"That was all you ever let them do," said Dr. Karandash.

"That was too much," said Hetman Horopadsky.

"The Jews have their own community," said Father Wròbel.

"The Jews have always been the petit bourgeoisie of the Ukraine," said Dr. Karandash. "Not being permitted to own or work the land they became tradesmen and shopkeepers and speculators."

"The Jewish Bund was a Bolshevist organisation," said Hetman Horopadsky.

"On the contrary," said Dr. Karandash, "it was Menshevist in colour."

"What's the difference," said Hetman Horopadsky, "they were all Marxists. Judaeo-Marxism is a dream of world domination."

"In 1917 the Jews supported the Bolsheviks," said Father Wròbel.

"They have always supported extra-national movements," said Dr. Karandash, "knowing well what to expect from nationalism."

"I am not so sure," said Prince Dolov, "whether it wasn't from a sense of cultural superiority to the life around them, an appreciation of the ruling class. You know we used to say: 'It takes a Jew to manage a Ukrainian peasant.' "

"Thousands of Jews joined the Communist Party," said Father Wròbel.

"Many more were enemies of the Communists," said Dr. Karandash. "How many *kulaks,* for example, proved to be Jews."

"The *kulaks,"* said Hetman Horopadsky. "They said *I* was a *kulak."*

"True," said Dr. Karandash, "the Bolsheviks were not particular. The agitation against the *kulaks* was a device to activate the peasants. To make them class conscious. To bring them on the side of the Bolsheviks. If you can arouse and direct the hatred of a community against a specific object you can control that community. *Kulak,* bourgeois, capitalist, Jew, Trotskyite, what does it matter so long as you have a focus for hatred?"

Dr. Karandash was aware that the big room had become very quiet.

"It is a technique Hitler learned from the Bolsheviks," he said.

He said the phrase, against his will, knowing it to be explosive, not wanting to make it, foreseeing the trouble it could make him, yet nevertheless saying it with more passion than he intended or believed he felt for the subject.

The silence of the big room was broken.

"It is possible," said Obermeister Stetsenko, looking up from some calculations on a piece of paper, "I could make a million dollars."

There was an undertone of hushed laughter among the visitors. The Germans did not laugh.

Obergruppenführer Rauch, at the top of the conference table, spoke:

"You were saying, Dr. Karandash, something about the Jews? Please address us in German."

"There are a million people in this city," said Dr. Karandash, "twenty percent of them Jews. You need these people. They constitute the class of artisans and mechanics."

None spoke. Then, as though he had not heard Dr. Karandash, Arbeitsführer Müssfeld resumed the conference at the point which had provoked this irrelevant interruption.

"We have here," he said, "a communication from General of the Infantry Thomas, Chief of the Armament Department, OKW. He is in need—urgently in need—of skilled labour. It is his suggestion that the Jewish problem in the Ukraine should be solved by the extensive labour utilisation of the Jews. In our position as directors of the Reichs Labour Front we have ordered that all Jews between the ages of sixteen and sixty shall in future be screened for labour utilisation and those acceptable shall be marked with a yellow star affixed to the breast and back of their clothes and prepared for transportation."

Having made this announcement Arbeitsführer Müssfeld and his party snapped shut their briefcases and walked out of the conference room.

"Have you other suggestions to offer?" Rauch said.

"Yes," said Dr. Karandash. "The *Gulag* prisoners.

Why not use them? There are thousands of them. In the compound at the tractor factory at least two thousand."

"Ah, the tractor factory," said Obergruppenführer Rauch.

"We will enlist them in the Ukrainian National Army," said Hetman Horopadsky.

"You could perhaps do this," said Obergruppenführer Rauch.

"It is necessary to do something," said Dr. Karandash. "Otherwise you will alienate the whole country."

"Indeed?" said Obergruppenführer Rauch.

He beckoned to Sturmführer Gruber.

"Bring the little girl in."

Hetman Horopadsky had not ceased to glare at Dr. Karandash. He now came around the table to his side.

"Are you crazy?" he whispered, hoarsely. "Do you wish to upset all our plans?"

"Your plans will come to nothing unless they stop killing people." Dr. Karandash spoke loudly.

"The whole country is with us," said Hetman Horopadsky. "In an hour we go to the first meeting of volunteers for the Ukrainian Army of Liberation. You will see. They will flock to our standard."

"The white-and-gold standard?"

"No," said Hetman Horopadsky, "for the time being they will wear *Wehrmacht* uniform."

"There is no shortage of those uniforms."

"It is a good uniform. Very practical."

"And they will be given rifles also?"

"Ah, they will be given rifles. And ammunition. You do not know them. They *want* to kill Russians. There is a whole generation waiting for vengeance."

"Vengeance! They must want more than vengeance. They must want freedom, liberty, independence."

"Words, words," said Hetman Horopadsky. "There is

no harm in those words. But you do not understand. What they want *now* is to kill some Russians."

Hetman Horopadsky patted Dr. Karandash on the shoulder as one comforting an emotional child.

"Do not be disturbed by this." Hetman Horopadsky waved his hand around the conference room. "This is nothing. In a month we will have an army in training. In three months there will be a Ukrainian National Army welded together by battle, tried and tested, already comrades in arms, proud, victorious!" Hetman Horopadsky leaned close to Dr. Karandash. "And then," he said, "we will see about a Provisional Government and, who knows, a President of the Republic."

"You are being absurd," said Dr. Karandash. "I shall not go to your meeting."

"But you must. It is an order. The Obergruppenführer has put you down for a speech."

The beginning of an idea entered Dr. Karandash's head. But its proper development was interrupted by the appearance of Sophia Samoilov.

Obergruppenführer Rauch had risen from his place at the head of the committee table and he had walked across the room and taken Sophia by the hand. He now led her to a place beside his chair. Sophia stood there, her head and shoulders at the level of those of the people sitting around the table. She looked at everybody, directly, without confusion.

"This little girl," said Obergruppenführer Rauch, speaking in Russian, "came to see me this morning. All by herself. Isn't that so?"

"Yes," Sophia said.

"You have eaten well?"

"Oh, yes," Sophia said, "such kasha!"

"Now will you tell the gentlemen here your name, please?"

"My name is Sophia Markovna Samoilov and I am eleven years."

Obergruppenführer Rauch spoke gravely.

"Do you like it here, Sophia?" he said.

"Oh yes, I did not know it was such a big room," Sophia said. "I thought it would be a small room. Why is it such a big room?"

"For meetings like this one," said Obergruppenführer Rauch.

"I am sure that there were not meetings like this before," Sophia said.

The remark made Dr. Karandash smile. He was touched by Sophia's appearance: her ragged coat, far too small for her, the sleeves ending just below the elbows, the man-size boots, the old cloth cap, the red chapped hands and the thin white face with the big brown eyes.

"What did you think of the people who were here before?" Obergruppenführer Rauch said.

"You mean the Communists?"

"Yes."

"Communists are bad."

"Why are they bad?"

"They are just bad."

"And Stalin?"

"Stalin is bad too."

As Sophia said the words the men at the conference table were aware that she was seized by a deeper emotion. For a fractional instant the expression in her face was that of a child who is about to have a convulsion.

"I hate Stalin," Sophia said.

The relief that came with the words was like the relief that comes with the passing of the mounting convulsion.

"An extraordinary demonstration," said Prince Dolov.

"You would like a drink of tea?" Obergruppenführer Rauch asked.

Sophia looked at him. "Yes," she said.

"It proves something," said Prince Dolov.

"Child, may I ask you a question?" It was Father Wròbel speaking. Many at the conference table glanced in his direction. His person was more familiar than his voice. "Child, do you believe in God?"

"No," Sophia said.

Father Wròbel sat back in his chair, nodding his head. "She does not know God," he said.

"It does not matter," said Dr. Karandash.

"Alas," said Father Wròbel, "she has been brought up in atheistic surroundings."

"Yet she knows what is good or, more precisely, what is bad," said Dr. Karandash. "She knows that Stalin is bad. You and I, we could produce many arguments to prove that Stalin is bad. But I do not think that we could improve on the child's simple statement. What is so wonderful is that she has arrived at this conclusion without argument."

"She has merely to look about her," said Prince Dolov.

"On the contrary she has no standards of comparison. She is too young ever to have known how people in other countries live. Nor is it likely that she has been exposed to any system of ethics or morals. No, this little girl is truly the child of Stalinism. Nevertheless she has an adverse opinion of Stalin. One assumes that she has arrived at that opinion on the evidence of her senses, through human feelings that are *instinct*. She has not needed religious instruction in order to understand that Stalin is bad. The fact that she has not had religious instruction makes her testimony more valuable."

"Without knowledge of God," said Father Wròbel, "the feelings you speak of will consume the child's mind."

"I would say," said Dr. Karandash, "that those instinctive human feelings are acceptable evidence of the existence of God. Of God in man. I would say the only evidence."

"Decency," said Prince Dolov.

Sturmführer Gruber had brought Sophia a glass of tea and now she had drunk the tea and put the glass down.

"I am sure," said Rauch, "that this little girl has not come to the SS merely to tell us that the Communists are bad. Remember, the SS has not yet asked her any questions. The SS is not heartless. It is understanding. But the SS expects that she has something of importance to tell us." Rauch turned to Sophia. "Now," he said, "will you tell us what you know?"

"I came to tell you that the Communists are here," Sophia said.

"The Communists are here?"

"They have come back."

"How do you know this?"

"Last night in the street," Sophia said, looking at Obergruppenführer Rauch, "I saw Lydia Artemova. I followed her. She went to a house, number ninety-eight in the Klochkovskaya, where there was a meeting. I saw them enter."

Obergruppenführer Rauch stood up. He stood very

erect. He looked very severe. He made a signal to Sturmführer Gruber who left the big room.

"Who is Lydia Artemova?"

"She is a Communist."

"How do you know?"

"Everybody knows Lydia Artemova. She is a specialist of Komsomols."

"What is she doing here?"

"She would make Party vigilance."

"How do you know this, Sophia?"

"I know it."

"But you saw her in the street. How do you know that she is here to make Party vigilance? Did you speak with her?"

"No," Sophia said.

"Then how do you know?"

"I heard her speaking," Sophia said.

"Where?"

Sophia looked at Obergruppenführer Rauch. She shrugged her shoulders.

"Oh, at this meeting," she said. "She made a speech."

"What did she say?"

"She said that the German Army had been driven back from Moscow."

"Who was at this meeting?"

"There were others. I do not know. I do not care about them."

"Yet you know them to be Communists?"

"Oh yes, I think they were here."

"Here?"

"Yes here." Sophia swept her arm around the room.

"Ah, so. *Here.*"

"NKVD."

"You know about the NKVD?"

"Naturally. They killed many people here too."

"Ah," said Dr. Karandash, "now I begin to understand."

"I don't think we need you any longer," said Obergruppenführer Rauch. "But tell me one thing, Sophia, are there any more little girls like you. Little girls or boys who think the Communists are bad? Little girls or boys who would come to see me?"

"I think Gasha would," Sophia said. "Mia would too if

I spoke to her. And perhaps Losha, because he is so quiet."

"You will speak to them and bring them to me?"

"Perhaps."

"There will be much to eat."

"They will come," Sophia said.

"But you will not say one word to anyone else. Remember it is a secret between us."

"Oh yes. And when I see Lydia Artemova again I shall come myself to tell you."

Rauch shook his head slowly. "You will not see Lydia Artemova again," he said.

"I hope not," Sophia said. "I hope she is soon dead."

"Now, Sophia, you will go with Sturmführer Gruber. He will show you to a door in the next street which you will use when you come next time. You will ask for him, Sturmführer Gruber. Let me hear you say his name."

"Sturmführer Gruber."

"Correct. Goodbye, Sophia."

"Goodbye. And thank you for the kasha. It was good."

Dr. Karandash watched the padded green baize door close behind Sophia. The soundless closing of the door was final, a severance sharper even than the slamming of a steel-barred gate.

The conference ended and Dr. Karandash rose to light a cigarette.

The voice and appearance of Sophia Samoilov had cast him into a mood of deepest nostalgia. What he needed to deliver him from the terrible tedium of official confinement to Kharkiv was the company of children. He could perhaps find children. There was the school he had visited. But even more comforting would be the companionship of a woman. What woman? Perhaps among those grey-shawled heads one saw in the streets of Kharkiv there were comely women who disguised themselves from the soldiery. But that was not what he needed. His need was for a woman of sense. Sadly he thought of Zeta Yarmoslansky, whom he had known so well, so long ago. She must be alive somewhere, otherwise her dossier would not have been in the active files of the NKVD. Nor would the SS have caught up with her, since the dossier lay undisturbed in the bottom of the clothes closet in his hotel room. He had not looked at the dossier. He still feared its bulk. That great mass of hideous Party history could not be bridged by sentiment. But where was she?

A hard hand gripped Dr. Karandash's arm above the elbow. It was Obergruppenführer Rauch.

"Sit down," said Obergruppenführer Rauch.

Dr. Karandash took a chair in front of the long desk under the refectory windows.

"Your remarks interested me. You are so much like our good Germans, full of humanism and misunderstanding."

"The *Einsatzgruppen* leave little room for misunderstanding."

"You should know that the purpose of the *Einsatzgruppen* is not merely to secure the rear of our armies, but to provide *permanent* security."

Dr. Karandash said nothing.

"It is like the class enemy for the Bolsheviks," the Obergruppenführer said. "Even if it were not an ideological problem it would still have to be done."

The Obergruppenführer paused.

"The Jews know us now. Therefore, every Jew, at this moment or in the future, is our potential enemy. Even as they weep you should hear them crying, 'Long live Stalin!' "

"And the gypsies?"

"In war the gypsies are traditional carriers of information."

"And the Krimchaks and the Karims? Do those persecuted minorities also cry, 'Long live Stalin'?"

The Obergruppenführer was hatless. He now removed his large circular spectacles and began slowly to wipe them with a clean handkerchief. There was a slight gill-like movement in the heavy bosses of his jaws, but the firm thin mouth and the cleft chin belied nervousness. Below the broad bridge of his forehead the deeply recessed eyes were as still as blue stones.

"I see," he said, "that you make the common mistake of thinking us sadists. Nothing could be further from the truth."

Dr. Karandash sat silent.

"It is sometimes necessary for me to be present at executions," said the Obergruppenführer, "but I usually try to avoid it. The scope of our operation, of course, leads to inevitable excesses, but we take every precaution against them. Our *Kommandos* are not chosen from volunteers, but are selected by rotation. Only that number of victims are brought to the place of execution as each particular squad can handle. No squad is in action for more than an hour at a time. The *Kommandos* shoot in a military manner and upon orders. Individual action by individual men is forbidden. There are no *Genickschussspezialisten.* It is strictly ordered to avoid maltreatment. Undressing at the graveside is forbidden. Publicity is not permitted. Wherever possible a physician is present. And the very moment it is noted that a man has experienced joy in carrying out executions it is ordered that this man shall never participate in any more executions."

The Obergruppenführer took a bottle and a glass out of a cabinet, set them on his desk.

"You wish to drink?" he said.

Dr. Karandash was surprised. The bottle answered an urgent need in his mind. Without hesitation he poured himself a drink. Obergruppenführer Rauch made no move towards the bottle.

"Don't you ever get drunk?" Dr. Karandash asked.

The Obergruppenführer gave no sign that he had heard the question. He adjusted his spectacles on his nose. The deepset eyes retreated from sight.

"Why do you tell me this?" Dr. Karandash said, suddenly suspicious.

"You are a writer, yes? I have in mind that you should write a book."

"A book! What kind of a book?"

"A book about our work here in the *Einsatzgruppen,* a scientific work."

"To give credit where credit is due, yes?"

"A book to correct many misunderstandings."

"I cannot do it."

"Give some thought to the matter," Rauch said. "Such

an occupation may prove more sustaining than this adventure in provincial nationalism. Incidentally I see you are programmed to speak at a meeting of the Ukrainian National Army."

"I have not been told about it."

Obergruppenführer Rauch made a signal with his hand. From the rear of the large, now emptied, room Hetman Horopadsky came running forward, his white moustaches waving.

"Here is your Dr. Karandash," said Rauch. "I have no doubt he will lend colour to your meeting."

"He is a specialist in Bolshevik crimes and will speak persuasively," said Hetman Horopadsky.

Dr. Karandash stood up.

"Later we will discuss the book," Rauch said. "But I feel you cannot begin your researches too soon. For such a book, of course, you will have to observe every aspect of our work, not only the work of the *Einsatzgruppen*, but also the splendid *Waffen* SS, the fighting branch of the service, the battle leaders."

"No!" said Dr. Karandash.

"By the way," said Rauch, "I must ask you to tell me about yourself sometime. How you came by this curious name, for example."

"Come," said Hetman Horopadsky, "the Liberation Army awaits us."

The meeting was already in progress when Dr. Karandash and Hetman Horopadsky arrived. There were a number of people on the platform.

It was not a very large hall, one built for private rather than public gatherings. Yet it held several hundred men. The men were being addressed by an officer in the *Wehrmacht* uniform with white sleeve-markings. The officer, his face turned towards the audience, was unknown to Dr. Karandash. He spoke the Ukrainian language. He was talking about the liberation of the Ukraine and the duty of Ukrainians to maintain that liberty by fighting the Bolshevik armies. The chairman of the meeting was General Schmidt, sitting very straight in his stiff uniform, the ribbon of the Iron Cross, First Class, tucked into his tunic front, visored cap bridging solemn oyster eyes, heavy jowls resting on collar tabs, epaulettes like omelettes. Beside him sat a younger officer. It was evident that neither understood the Ukrainian language, but they sat there, very correct, looking out over the gathering towards the back wall of the hall, creating a very strong impression to judge from the glances of the audience which wavered constantly in their direction.

The Ukrainian in *Wehrmacht* uniform resumed his seat and Hetman Horopadsky was speaking.

Dr. Karandash had an irrepressible urge to laugh. To laugh in the Ukrainian style, lightly, without bitterness, perceiving the irrepressible comicality of life, the comic urgency of one's own strivings for what, as one has been able to see, is after all nothing. This impulse Dr. Karandash recognised, with alarm, as a recrudescence of an older, irresponsible, and therefore to be deprecated, attitude towards serious matters. It was the first time since returning from exile that Dr. Karandash had come close to penetrating and joining the recessed spirit of his country.

And then suddenly, the act ended. Hetman Horopadsky sat down and Dr. Karandash heard his own name announced as the next to speak. He did not now laugh. Instead the emotion of laughter became something else.

He took a few paces towards the centre of the platform.

For the first time he looked down into the faces of the audience. Round peasant faces, red unshaven soldiers' faces, pale student faces, grim workers' faces, stolid, unmoving, worn, resistant, hard Ukrainian faces stared at him without any sign of understanding. They stood still, listening for his first words. They did not shift their feet or their heads, nor did they speak to one another, but looked with intent, unlighted eyes towards the platform, towards him. They were poorly dressed. Some wore quilted jackets, some wore old leather jackets, some were in stained cloth coats. Here and there among them was a fragment of Red Army uniform, a grimy fleece-lined cap, a pair of breeches, leather jackboots. They looked hungry. They were hungry. The collective expression was one of hardness, unimpressionability, as though they had been moulded of iron, but Dr. Karandash knew that beneath that surface-hardness there was a childish credulity. He knew that he was expected to engage that credulity.

He stood there before this assemblage of his countrymen, in European clothes, in the black worsted overcoat with the sable collar, and battered Homburg hat. His age was perhaps twice the average age of those before him. But the broad fleshy head set thickly and firmly on heavy shoulders, the thick strong arms and the wide wrists, proclaimed his origin. He spoke now with the harsh emphasis of Ukrainian speech. His language, though corrupted by foreign usage and unleavened by the colloquial idioms of this last score of years, by profanity or the new irony, was the language of the Ukraine. His sense of humour had departed the moment he had risen to his feet.

Instead he now felt himself being overtaken by a passionate feeling. He began speaking with passion. He spoke briefly of the history of Ukrainian independence. Suddenly in the fury of speech-making he lost himself. The caution, the commonsense, that had led him to seek the guarded minimum, was forgotten. The emotion that had guided his life from the earliest years took command.

It was an emotion compounded of many feelings; of the simple, direct feeling he had experienced as a boy upon seeing his father, an old house servant, born a serf, beaten with rods on the orders of his Russian master, a titled lout from St. Petersburg; of the bitter handicaps that were fastened upon the intelligent son of a former serf; of the elated feelings he had had upon discovering the Kievan literature, that heady stuff of resistance and revolt; of the new wisdom dawning out of books; of the feelings aroused by the poetry of the disbanded and wandering representatives of the *Narodnya Vola;* of the sudden, immense and expanding universe of socialism; of feelings of respect, even adoration for the early social revolutionaries; of feelings of distrust for Cossacks and Kirghiz, for Tartars and Georgians; feelings of distaste for all the peoples of the East and the odour of thawing ordure; of his own love of the black Ukrainian soil and its strong, loving women, the singing, the dancing, and the fresh, sweet riches of wheat and sunflowers and honey-cake; and feelings, more recent, of despair for the condition of this country, its impoverishment, defilement and ravishment by alien hordes. All this feeling, long dammed in foreign walls, now burst out in his first speech in twenty years to his kind. His voice rose to that pitch most favoured by the Slavic peoples in their speech-making. It was the declamatory style. He spoke of Russian crop seizures, expropriation of the peasant land, the organised famines, class liquidations and mass deportations. He spoke of the promises of the Communists to recognise Ukrainian autonomy and how those promises were betrayed. He spoke of Communist methods of infiltration by agreement and compromise and concession and the gradual seizure of power. He spoke of the error of attempting to come to terms with the Bolsheviks. Of the fate of those who had tried. Where now was Shumsky? What of Chubar, and Kossior, and Petrovsky and Lubchenko? And Hrushevsky dying in exile in the Caucasus! He spoke of the long succession of presidents of the Soviet Ukrainian Republic, each deposed to make way for another more ruthless in the pursuit of Moscow's aim. He spoke of the rule of terror. He spoke of his friend Myola Khvilovy, the writer, who was forced to confess publicly that he erred in his works and who then committed suicide. Of Skrypnyk who killed himself the following year. He spoke of the tradition of struggle, of the heritage established through centuries, of freedom. Then, lowering his voice, he spoke the words of the Great Poet:

"Bury me, be done with me,
Rise and break your chains
Water your new liberty
With blood for rain.
Then in the mighty family
Of all men that are free
Maybe sometimes very softly
You will speak of me."

Dr. Karandash paused in his speech. The great emotion was ebbing away as fast as it had come. Like one awakening from sleep, from an intense dream, he began to look at real things, to adjust his vision to actuality. He was looking at the audience. The audience did not stir. No expression crossed those iron faces. By no sign had they shown the most fleeting interest in what had been said. In twenty years of speech-making, of Party harangue, of Stakhanovite promotion, of *Pravda*-reading, of loudspeakers endlessly trumpeting, of *agitats* and *polytruks,* they were familiar with the declamatory style, and immune to it, as men who live by a mountain torrent do not, in time, hear the sound of the waters or, in the hard core of their indifference, care much about what debris is borne thereupon. Dr. Karandash noticed that the men nearest to him were looking at his shoes.

All this, all this which I have been saying, is romanticism, Dr. Karandash said to himself.

The pause in Dr. Karandash's speech had become an interval. In the corner of his eye he saw that General Schmidt was about to interrupt. Suddenly Dr. Karandash spoke quietly, dryly, briefly:

"You will be given rifles. When the time comes take your rifles and go into the woods."

Dr. Karandash sat down. He saw the Ukrainian-speaking officer whispering to General Schmidt.

The audience stirred. A young man in the audience stepped forward and made a short impassioned speech about the death of a cow which, he said, was his mother's cow, although this had been disputed by the *kolkhose* committee, and they had come to take the cow, so that there was a struggle during which the cow had been killed, thus it was you could neither live nor die on a *kolkhose*. Another man was speaking from the centre of the hall, a thin man, drooling with hunger, and he spoke words that nobody understood. Then another was shouting, and another, until the meeting was bedlam.

"*Achtung!*"

General Schmidt, pop-eyed with anger, bellowed the order in parade-ground style. The room was hushed. The men in the hall looked towards General Schmidt. They saw that he had risen to his feet. General Schmidt, glaring at them, began speaking in military-school Russian. He ordered all men volunteering for service in the *Wehrmacht* to step to the rear of the hall.

"You have ruined everything," Hetman Horopadsky hissed in Dr. Karandash's ear.

"Old fool, they were merely using you as a decoy."
"They will kill you for this."
"So they may, but I have delivered my message.'"
Doors in the rear of the hall opened revealing a number of armed *Wehrmacht* Feldwebel.
"This way, this way," shouted the Feldwebel.
There was a moment's hesitation in the audience. Then, with a shrug of his body, the young man who had spoken passionately about his mother's cow walked towards the doors. Others followed. Some of the heavier, peasant-faced men waited until the number in the hall diminished and then quietly got up and joined those already departing. In the end all the men in the hall, except one, went.

It was never known what happened to them, for none ever returned. It is possible that some were among those Dr. Karandash later saw in a shallow trench on ground recaptured by the Germans at Stalingrad, the high-waisted *Wehrmacht* uniform failing to disguise the broad Ukrainian trunk, their shaven heads and their preference for old patched *valinki* testifying, even more than their sleeve markings, their origin, if the smoke-black bullet hole in the back of each head was not enough. And it is more than probable that others, for the recruitment went on, were among those men Dr. Karandash saw, some years later in that war, in an American prison cage in Bavaria, waiting patiently in the rain to be turned over to the NKVD, along with General Vlasov, their most recent commander, for prompt and, everybody agreed, just execution.

But on this day in Kharkiv there was one man who did not leave the meeting hall. He sat alone on a bench at one side of the hall. Dr. Karandash had not left the platform with the other speakers, being under a profound and unreasonable compulsion not to move, not to leave the hall, a fear as strong as agoraphobia. He did not at first notice this man. Then, as they were finally alone together, he looked at him and recognition came.

"You!" he said.

Professor Shevchenko smiled. He rose now and the two men met in the middle of the hall. Professor Shevchenko still wore his outmoded cycling costume, topped by a round sealskin cap from which the fur had mostly disappeared.

"A very interesting speech," said Professor Shevchenko. "The language was much improved."

"But, I am curious, how do you come here?"

"Oh, we were all in the street and they pushed us in here."

"You are surely too old for the *Wehrmacht.*"

"One does not argue with the *militsia.*"

"What do you do?"

"I am in business."

"Good God, what business?"

"I have this."

Professor Shevchenko touched a small tray that was suspended from his neck. He drew back a cloth covering the tray displaying a number of crudely-made match boxes.

"The work of Professor Kornechenko," he said. "Are they not cleverly made? He was Professor of Organic Chemistry at the Kharkiv University. Now he is in hiding and makes matches."

"These are evil times for Ukrainians," said Dr. Karandash.

" 'More lowly than the grass, more silent than the water,' " said Professor Shevchenko. "It is a proverb from the time after Catherine."

"Yes, that too was a time of foreign Hetmans."

They sat down together in the empty hall and Dr. Karandash took out his flask, unscrewed the top and took a short swig. Glancing at Professor Shevchenko he was astonished at the expression of longing behind the cloudy pince-nez.

"Here, drink," he said.

Professor Shevchenko took the flask and put it to his lips, taking the spirits in deep pumping gulps of his Adam's apple.

"We celebrate a notable bi-centenary," he said.

"Somewhat more than two hundred years, I think, since the breaking up of the *Kazak* host," said Dr. Karandash.

"I refer to the bi-centenary of General Keith."

"General Keith!"

"During the reign of the Empress Anna," said Professor Shevchenko, "the Tartars of the Krim swept through our country, razing this city, and there was none to fight them. Then it was that General Münnich, on the advice of the Duke of Courland, brought in this brave soldier."

"I seem to remember that he was an Englishman, yes?" said Dr. Karandash.

"Such is the irony of history. He was a Scotsman, a brother of the last Lord Marischal of Scotland. He organised our foot soldiers and our Cossack horse and he led them into the battle of Ochakiv between the estuaries of the Bug and the Dneiper, defeating the Tartars and driving them from the Ukraine, himself suffering a deep wound. The coarse and amiable Anna was pleased with her *Hospidar General* and gave him five thousand rubles, but General Keith did not fare well at court. A man of great quietness, this Scotsman. Russians, as for Ukrainians, he must have presented an unusual sight, the dark hair and the dark blue eyes, the long straight nose and the thin lips, on all occasions *dour*. A word not in the language. Wherever he went he was accompanied by a Negro valet, one Mocho, a prize of the Spanish wars. And at Ochakiv he captured a Muslim girl, the dark and beautiful Eretulla or Eremete, the daughter of a captain of janissaries, with whom he fell deeply in love. He had also in his retinue an aide de camp, a man of his own country, a captain who wore a skirt and could make stirring sounds by blowing into the belly-skin of a sheep, sometimes dancing with great discipline and sternness over crossed swords. The General was very popular and Anna made him governor of all the Ukraine. Her advisers imagined that one who had but the rudiments of the native speech, who was moreover a soldier and therefore stupid, would not notice the depredations, the crushing of Ukrainian culture, the dispersal of the communes, the crowded prisons, the gallows at every cross-roads. But they were wrong. Shall I tell you our Scotsman's secret? He was a Jacobite. He was like ourselves, if I may say it, an uncompromising separatist. General Keith had become a soldier by fighting, as a very young man, to drive the English out of Scotland, learning in those high Scottish lands how to wheel cavalry and deploy infantry. Nor was this because he came of a great family which was in alliance with the Catholic King of Scotland—for General Keith was a Protestant whose austere Calvinism later prevented him from rising in the service of Spain—but because he loved Scotland. He knew what it was to be dominated by a country close to and like, yet not like, one's own. He knew the meaning of cultural oppression. Thus he understood the Ukraine. Where he found Ukrainians held to account for political crimes, he had them released. He forbade torture. He reduced the authority of the Russian military officers. He liberalised the laws. So it was that, after invasion and devastation, in a period of rigorous suppression, humiliation and pain, there came to the Ukraine this moment of peace."

Dr. Karandash could not quite name the unusual feeling which he now experienced, and it was some seconds before he realised it was hope. He looked at Professor Shevchenko, wondering how it was done.

"I shall not ask you what happened to General Keith," he said.

"Naturally they intrigued against him and, fearing that he would be sent to Siberia, he left Russia for the service of Frederick the Great who understood him. He died in battle, many years later, of an Austrian bullet."

"And where is all this to be found?"

"In the books of a vanished library."

"And the English still occupy Scotland?"

"Yes."

"Let us drink to General Keith."

Together they emptied the flask.

"And now," said Professor Shevchenko, rising to his feet. "You could perhaps help me . . ."

Dr. Karandash was alarmed.

"Please do not go!"

Professor Shevchenko adjusted his tray of matches.

"Are you still at the school? May I visit you there?"

"There is food at the school. But now if you would be so good?"

"Whatever you ask."

"To find my passport. At the door they took all our passports, and so I have no identification. But you, with your great influence, could perhaps request that it be returned to me."

They walked together to the entrance of the hall. Here on a table they found a heap of several hundred passport cards. Very quickly, in a sleight-of-hand which reminded Dr. Karandash of the occasion he had given Professor Shevchenko a cigarette, the Professor now shuffled through the cards. In a few moments he had found his card. Or was it someone else's? Or had he taken several cards? Dr. Karandash did not know. While he was still wondering, Professor Shevchenko had bowed and, smiling benignly, was gone.

The fear of leaving the building that had agitated Dr. Karandash a few minutes previously now returned. He knew that he must leave. Yet he wished to delay leaving. He wished to delay it for all time. He did not wish to go out through that doorway. Yet he must.

He took the step. He stood at the entrance to the hall, noticing, for the first time, that it was, in fact, the Communist Hall. Standing there he saw what he had expected to see. The dark uniform of an SS man was silhouetted against the entrance.

As Dr. Karandash came out the SS man pointed to a large grey van that was standing beside the curb.

"Get in," said the SS man, "in front."

Sturmführer Gruber escorted Sophia to the small side door and let her out into the street.

Sophia felt very happy. Her happiness proceeded from her stomach. Her stomach was slightly distended. She put her hands on her stomach and she thought about the meal she had just eaten. She could not remember ever having eaten so much kasha at any one time before. She skipped a few steps. But she soon gave that up and began walking seriously. The Klochkovskaya was some distance.

It was not necessary to go by the circuitous route over which she had followed Lydia Artemova the night before. There was a shorter, more direct way. But she would have to hurry to get there in time to see what was happening.

The Klochkovskaya was empty when Sophia entered it. The appearance of an SS car a few minutes earlier had sent everybody out of the street or into their houses. Sophia dawdled along the street. The SS car was drawn up before number 98. Sophia crossed to the opposite side of the street so that she could see better. The driver of the SS car sat behind the steering wheel. He did not notice the small girl. The door of the house was open and an SS soldier stood within the entrance. He held a machine-pistol in his hands. There was nothing else to be seen.

A few minutes later a second car drew up behind the first. Eight black-uniformed members of the Ukrainian *militsia* jumped out of the car. They did not enter the house. An SS Sturmführer came out of the house and gave orders to the *militsia.* The *militsia* divided and went to either end of the Klochkovskaya. Presently they began bringing people out of their houses and from neighbouring streets driving them from the further ends of the street down towards the house which was number 98 Klochkovskaya. The people stood there, silent, unmoved. There were old women with black shawls tied around their heads. There were old men in padded jackets. There were few children. There were no young people. They stood looking at number 98. Then one said: "It is the house of Anastasy Kononenko." This was repeated. Another said: "The Kononenkos were a Party family. Look, a whole house to themselves." Yet another said: "It is not true that the Kononenkos were among those hanged." An old man said: "The Kononenkos went to Moscow." An old woman said: "May the children of the Kononenkos die with their tongues choking them." A *militsia* man who heard the muttering, and misunderstood it, said loudly in accented Ukrainian: "You will see what happens to those who harbour Communists."

There was a shattering of glass. A windowpane fell to pieces under the butt of a rifle. The SS man in his shiny black helmet could be seen moving behind the broken window. Some feathers floated out of the window. Another window was broken. The sound of splintering woodwork was heard. Plaster was being ripped from the walls. Little clouds of white dust floated out into the street. Through the open doorway the onlookers could see that the floorboards had been torn up in some places. There was a growing heap of papers in the hallway.

The SS worked unhurriedly. Presently an SS man brought out a sack which he threw into the car. The SS man did not go back into the house. He stood by the car talking with the driver. It was like this for more than an hour. Sophia began to get bored. Some of the people pleaded with the *militsia* to be allowed to go home. The *militsia* did not answer them, but spat on the ground.

Sophia gave up looking at the house and began looking at the people. The people were herded together. They stood patiently. But they kept looking at the house, number 98, the house of the Kononenko family. It was while she was looking at the people that Sophia saw an extraordinary thing. At first she could not believe what she saw. It was so improbable. It was the wrong way round. Then she looked harder and she was sure. Not more than four paces away stood Lydia Artemova. It was the same Lydia Artemova even though she wore a black shawl over her head and was pretending to be an old woman. She was clutching a string bag to her midriff like an old woman. But that did not deceive Sophia. It was the same string bag that she had carried the night before. Sophia was staring at Lydia Artemova, but Lydia Artemova did not see her. Lydia Artemova was looking at the house, as well she might, since only last night, defying the curfew, she had gone into the house, Sophia presumed, to sleep. Lydia Artemova's eyes did not move from the house. Her eyes were hard. What made her almost unrecognisable was the bitterness and the hatred in her eyes. It made her so much like the other women. Like an old woman she was muttering to herself. Watching this, the muttering lips, Sophia saw that Lydia Artemova was also listening. Her head was held like one who is slightly deaf, still and slightly bent, intently concentrated. Then Sophia saw that there was a man standing behind Lydia Artemova and that this man was also watching the house and that his lips were also moving. Sophia saw at once that Lydia Artemova and the man were talking to one another. Sophia suddenly knew the identity of the man talking to Lydia Artemova.

This was the man whom Losha, the son of a former high official of the Central Committee, had recognised in the street the day before. Losha had boasted about him to the other children in the schoolhouse. He was one of the big bosses of the NKVD, Losha said. He knew everything that happened. He could kill you if he wanted to, just like that. Sophia now looked at this man and did not think Losha's description very good. But that was probably because this man was pretending like Lydia Artemova. He wore an old leather jacket with holes in it, an old fleece-lined cap, dirty padded trousers stuck into old boots. His face was white and his beard, for he had not shaved for some time, was black. He looked like anybody you might meet on the Sumskaya. Only, it was true, his eyes were not full of bitterness or hatred, and he did not look frightened. That was how anyone who wanted to could identify him. He had not lived the poor life long enough to keep his shoulders bent and his eyes on the ground and to look sometimes quickly over his shoulder. This man looked tense. The way he was looking now at number 98 was to see everything and to make sense of it.

Sophia was proud and excited. She watched Lydia Artemova and this man and she saw that their slight lip movements corresponded to an exchange of words though nobody who was less curious than Sophia would have detected any relationship. Sophia decided that she would try to overhear what they were saying. She quietly withdrew to the rear of the throng of people and then slowly worked her way to a position immediately beside Lydia Artemova.

What Lydia Artemova and this man were saying concerned Sophia though, of course, they were not aware of it. They were attempting, as well as they could in the circumstances, to review every likely step leading to the betrayal. The descent of the SS men had followed so quickly upon their first meeting that the information must have been first hand. It had been immature to meet together in this house. Yet it had been necessary to have an address and there were so few addresses remaining. Had they been spied upon? Or was it information from within? The man who was with Lydia Artemova went over in his mind, as he was experienced in doing, holding the characters of others always in this light: those who had known this address. Apart from himself there were three. Of these three had one talked? Was there a careless one? It was unlikely. Was there an overzealous one?

He was assessing the risk that was Lydia Artemova. Lydia Artemova undertood that she was being assessed. She therefore listened with care and answered all she knew and she knew that she would never know the decision arrived at. At this moment she had a perfectly clear conscience.

Having assessed the risks the man made a decision and now issued an order.

"Send them out of the city. The city is premature. There is nothing for us in the city. Send them to Pilchuk. They will work as partizans."

"And me?"

"You are not wanted."

It was only this part of the exchange that Sophia heard. Perhaps that was because the man spoke more clearly than he had done previously. But then she forgot to listen to the man for her attention was drawn to what was happening at number 98.

The SS men came out of the house. Their black uniforms were powdered with dust. They laughed and began dusting each other. Another SS man came out of the house carrying a gasolene drum. From the easy way he held the drum it was evident it was now empty. The sharp smell of gasolene drifted out of the house. The Sturmführer and another SS man came out of the house with a civilian. They held the civilian between them. The civilian was hatless and his clothes were awry. He was pale. He was dazed. The SS men held him roughly and roughly thrust him into the car.

"Nikolai Andreyvich!"

Sophia heard Artemova whisper the name.

"He knows all our names!" Lydia Artemova said.

The man beside her said nothing. He was looking at the prisoner. He was looking at him as a physician looks at an ailing man, differently afflicted, but as inevitably dying.

"At dawn tomorrow," the man with Lydia Artemova said almost to himself. "There is time."

"Oh!"

Sophia heard the gasp. It was a woman's gasp. It was not despair, but emotion.

Sophia looked at Lydia Artemova. Lydia Artemova looked at Sophia. Lydia Artemova's look was sharp and piercing. Then gradually her face was transported with a terrible enlightenment.

Sophia knew that Lydia Artemova knew everything.

There was a sharp splintering explosion. The corridor of number 98 burst into a large rolling flame. One of the SS men took the pin out of another egg-shaped grenade and unhurriedly threw it through one of the broken windows. It was like looking through a furnace door.

The SS men climbed into the wagon and drove away with their prisoner.

The fire was crackling through the old wooden house. Gusts of smoke flew up into the air. As soon as the SS had gone the *militsia* relaxed their guard. The people did not stay to watch the fire. They dispersed. When Sophia looked again Lydia Artemova and the man who had been with her had gone. She did not try to find them. She was not interested in them. She was more interested in the fire. She was delighted with the fire. *Her* fire.

When the roof caved-in the winter-old snow fell hissing into the flames and clouds of steamy vapour were added to the picture. When the walls collapsed a shaft of sparks and burning embers shot skywards. Sophia had never seen anything so beautiful.

When the fire began to lose its vehemency the *militsia* went away and Sophia Samoilov was the only person in the Klochkovskaya. She was very pleased with herself. She had forgotten all about Lydia Artemova. At least for the moment.

The large grey van rolled down the Paulus Platz, turned left at the former Street-of-the-First-of-May and went out towards the southeastern factory district.

It was some minutes before Dr. Karandash ventured to glance at his escort.

"Müller!" he said.

"Yes. You did not recognise me in this uniform?"

Dr. Karandash wanted to ask where they were going, but an unwillingness yet to hear the worst made him hesitate.

"I am under arrest, yes?" he said.

Müller laughed. "You really expected arrest?"

"Yes."

"Now why could that be?"

"For what I said."

"It was not a speech to die for."

"You heard it then?"

"You played the Obergruppenführer's game. By proposing that the volunteers desert with their rifles, you discredited the nationalists."

"Can he be so subtle?"

"Take our meeting like this. Do you imagine it to be a coincidence?"

"You mean he arranged it?"

But the van at that moment slewed into a snowdrift and Dr. Karandash lost the reply.

"What have you been doing in the interval?" Dr. Karandash asked.

"I have been very fortunate. It is having the language. There are not so many who are literate in the language. For a time I revised schoolbooks. Took statistics on schools."

"Counted the children."

Müller did not answer.

"Today," he said, after they had driven some distance, "I was given the task of driving this wagon."

Once more Dr. Karandash wanted to ask where they were going.

"Have you listened to the Russian propaganda?" Müller said. "The anguish about the Jews, and the concern for the freedom-loving libertarian countries of Europe?"

"Stalin has allies to placate."

"Always," said Müller, "*he* takes the superior moral position."

"The Russians feel moral about everything," said Dr.

Karandash. "They must. A Russian who feels immoral is like to die. The moral feeling of the Russians has no connection with their acts. Indeed it enables them to commit any act."

"The Germans know what has to be done. They are too sincere to make moral claims."

"You mean," said Dr. Karandash, "that the Germans are conscious of immorality. And because they do not conceal their immorality they feel inherently moral. Yes? Clearly, to be transported by high moral feeling, the Germans must first savour guilt."

"Morality is survival," Müller said. "We expiate our guilt by surviving."

Dr. Karandash sighed.

"Isn't it rather silly," he said, "for you and me, for *us,* to be taking nationalism seriously. Great States have no territorial borders, nor are they ethnic regions. We are no longer Germans or Russians by birth or culture. We are fragments of Great States bearing those names and we partake of the nature of those States whether we like it or not."

Müller began to laugh loudly. Dr. Karandash understood that Müller had been playing some kind of game. It was not a game pleasant to himself. The bright intelligent eyes shone with a perversity which troubled Dr. Karandash more than if they had been filled with violence. He knew at once that nothing Müller had said had been said sincerely. Müller was, in a way, not living in his mind, but using his mind, like the taut skin of a drum, upon which to beat out the rhythm of retribution.

"Do you know what this van is?" Müller said.

"No."

"It is well known in Kharkiv. The people call it the *Dushegubky* van."

"Dushegubky?" repeated Dr. Karandash. "It means literally 'soul-destroyer.' "

"Literally that is what it is. The body of the van is airtight. The engine exhaust empties into the body of the van."

Dr. Karandash was conscious of the movement of the van. The motion of the van was firm, as though it were heavily loaded.

"Where are you taking me?" Dr. Karandash asked.

"To the tractor factory. Do not you already recognise it?"

Dr. Karandash looked.

"The *Gulag* prison compound," he said. "But where are the prisoners?"

"You imagine them to be still alive?"

"But there were hundreds . . . thousands. . . ."

"Ah, Herr Doktor Karandash, how delightful you are! How unrelievedly serious and sound! How innocent!"

PART 3

The friendship of Sturmführer Gruber and Oberleutnant Soedermann had progressed under the strain, that is to say the boredom, of life in Kharkiv. The colonial atmosphere was not suited to the tastes of these young men. Such entertainments as were available were of a formal character, as became conquerors, or they were provincial, after the style of the German county families which were now settling in the region. The conversation like the beer was of a prescribed density. Gruber who had taken part in the conquest of France spoke nostalgically of that country, of French wit, French wine, French women. Soedermann could not match this, never having been further west than the Wuppertal, but he spoke nevertheless of the excitements of Budapest. Together Gruber and Soedermann found solace, more and more often, at the Officers' Establishment. Here, out of respect for Gruber's position (after all it is something to be an aide to an SS general), they were able to obtain for themselves a private room in which, several times a week, so often as they cared, they could eat and drink and indulge in such amusements as they craved.

Nothing enhances pleasure so much as good company and so they brought to these gatherings chosen guests. There was often a young officer of the *Luftwaffe* photo-reconnaissance section (Soedermann, an enthusiastic amateur photographer, made use of the darkroom) and a certain Major Wreckl. Major Wreckl was much older than Gruber or Soedermann. He was short, fat, baldheaded, middle aged. But his head was shaved, he wore a fierce moustache, a very good decoration from the first war, a monocle, a hint of rouge, a long duelling scar, and he told excellent stories. He was also from Berlin. And he did not hesitate to make jokes about higher officers or to indulge in gossip. He achieved that delicate balance of savagery and cynicism to which the younger men aspired. His greatest attraction, however, was that he could produce food and wine from sources unavailable to the others. On his second visit he brought a set of very beautiful silver goblets which he said had been contributed out of the magnanimity of a Polish nobleman. The goblets were large and exquisitely wrought. Thereafter, to fill the goblets, Major Wreckl brought always a case of French champagne and often cognac. Gruber and Soedermann found the parties very agreeable.

The parties began in the strictest etiquette, with a meticulous observance of rank. There were formal toasts and brief exchanges of words, veiled insults, and a calculated iciness of demeanour, the secret joy of which was the knowledge that it would soon dissolve into delightful debauchery, the jests would become broader, tunic collars would be undone, wine would be spilt, compliments passed, friendship mended and wind broken. In all this Major Wreckl maintained perfect poise. The younger officers, even the young *Luftwaffe* officer who had received an education, watched and copied his style.

The delight of the evening (because it happened exactly as they imagined it would happen) was the moment the girls were brought in. At first the girls were shy before so many men together. With so many men it was uncultured, they said. In Major Wreckl, however, they immediately recognised a friend. Major Wreckl put them at their ease among the young men and was soon their favourite. They sat on his fat knees and kissed his bald pate. He brought them little gifts of soap and eau de Cologne. On one occasion when he discovered that the eau was being sold as a beverage he insisted that the spirit be immediately rubbed into their persons, a task he elected to do himself, all of which led to behaviour of the most boisterous kind. The eau, however, noticeably overcame the ever-present smell of *mahorka* which the young women brought into the room and from which, indeed, there seemed no moment of escape in all Russia.

There was also entertainment to be had at the expense of the girls' ignorance of the finer things of life. They were as uncultured as young savages, Major Wreckl said (though they were quick to pick up the rudiments of German speech). They refused, at first, to touch the champagne, but, when persuaded to do so, their behaviour provoked great merriment. They were fascinated by elegant wrist watches and fountain pens and other unfamiliar objects. Olympia, for example, who was admired by all, never would believe that the shining silver goblets were made for drinking. There was much amusement that night when Major Wreckl very solemnly persuaded her to tip first one, and then the other, of her firm young breasts into goblets he proffered her, so that she was standing there, her full white body glowing with youth, her round thighs touching, her small stomach, with the child's navel, not yet flesh-embedded, flattened, the high wide cage of her ribs, fleshed and powerful, easily lifting, standing there, her elbows out, holding in her fingers a large shining goblet over each breast, and looking down at the goblets and then at the men with half-delight and curiosity and wonder in her curved red mouth and dark eyes. The old silver clung to her white flesh. For a brief moment none spoke or moved.

Then with a shout Sturmführer Gruber leaped up, drained his own goblet, and set it, stem upwards, on the head of Olympia, on the fair loose hair (fairer than it had been three months before), so that Olympia was suddenly absurdly crowned.

"Brünnhilde!" cried Sturmführer Gruber.

"A perfect Brünnhilde," said Oberleutnant Soedermann.

Olympia put the goblets down. The rims of the goblets had left a pink halo around each breast. Olympia was now self-conscious. She giggled.

"How old are you?" Major Wreckl asked.

"Seventeen."

"A child," Major Wreckl said.

"The SS loves children," said Sturmführer Gruber.

Sturmfüherer Gruber had put his arm around Olympia's waist. His black uniform enfolded her white body like a shroud.

The gesture made Oberleutnant Soedermann suddenly angry. He stood up a little unsteadily, heavily, and he pushed Sturmführer Gruber away from Olympia's side.

The rude action might have led to serious consequences, except that the appearance of Oberleutnant Soedermann at that moment made everybody in the room laugh. His face was as softly flushed as a baby's. In his baby-blue eyes there was such porcine longing, so much adolescent sentimentality, that Sturmführer Gruber could not but feel his superior.

"A toast to Brünnhilde!" cried Major Wreckl.

Major Wreckl filled the goblets. They drank a toast to Olympia.

"All the Brünnhildes I have known would require saucepans," said Major Wreckl.

They drank to all the Brünnhildes. It was necessary now to restore something of the military character of the party. They began to talk like the military men they were.

"Wäre nicht schlecht zu wissen wieviel Divisionen der Russki an die Bielgorod-Kursk Front bringen kann."

"Verdammt noch mal. Es müssen eine Million Mann sein."

"Ohne Zweifel eine Unzahl von Divisionen. Letzte Woche haben wir Gefangene eingebracht, deren Divisionsnummern uns unbekannt waren."

When they spoke like this Olympia did not understand. But when their language broke down into the simpler, personal forms she was able to follow what was said.

"Good, good," said Major Wreckl, "so many more to be killed."

"He is such an optimist," said Oberleutnant Soedermann.

"Soon we shall have all the information," said Sturmführer Gruber. "The SS is acting. The SS is sending spies into all the villages. The SS will soon have spies even in Moscow."

"To be caught as a spy in Russia, that would not be good," said Oberleutnant Soedermann.

"Our spies will not be caught," said Sturmführer Gruber.

"Then you must train them well," said Major Wreckl. "In France we were all the time shooting spies. It was easy."

"Our spies are being well trained."

"They must have the language," said Major Wreckl.

"Our spies have the language."

"Ah," said Oberleutnant Soedermann, "then they are Russians."

"How can you trust them?" said the *Luftwaffe* lieutenant.

"We are first trying them in the villages. In the rear of the front. To protect our rear from attack by guerillas."

"And then you send them through the lines? It will not be easy. They will be recognised. The Russians are not fools."

"These will not be recognised."

"What are they then? Women?"

"No. Children."

Sturmführer Gruber drew back from the table. He was smiling, satisfied with the effect of his remark.

"What children?" Olympia said.

"Some," said Sturmführer Gruber, not noticing Olympia, but looking at the men, at Major Wreckl, and Oberleutnant Soedermann, and the *Luftwaffe* photographer, "some may be Jewish children!"

It was an occasion that made necessary the filling of the silver goblets.

"Gentlemen!" said Major Wreckl. "We speak of war. We speak of the coming offensive. We speak of the shape of things to come when all around us we have the most delightful fronts and rears. Gentlemen, drink to the ladies. Yes, it is time for the ladies."

"The Ladies!"

It was a toast which Major Wreckl knew well how to make and made now with a leer of such theatricality that the young men accepted him enthusiastically for a man of realism and experience; it was one of the advantages Major Wreckl enjoyed from having worked so long under Stanislavsky.

Olympia's greatest concern on such occasions was over being parted, for an hour or two, from her leopard-skin coat. She worried about the coat being stolen from her room. It was not a beautiful coat. It had been worn by a decade of Polish women before being given to her by Oberleutnant Soedermann. But it was the most beautiful thing Olympia had ever touched. At night it was never far from her reach and in the morning she slept with it under her body. Her keenest pleasure was to go out walking in the coat.

On this next morning the sun fell warmly on the yellow coat and on her yellow hair, and Olympia was pleased with the attention she attracted as she walked down the Paulus Platz. She looked at everyone who passed and everyone looked at Olympia. It was very rewarding. Even the frozen faces of the German women were, in a way, a tribute; while the soldiers who grinned and the officers who smiled, the corners of their mouths held downwards, confirmed the opinion she had about her elegance. When she caught the glance of an officer whom she knew she looked away, smiling a little to herself.

She walked nonchalantly as a woman in a leopardskin coat should walk. She put one foot precisely in front of the other and she swung her handbag that was full of delicacies she was bringing to her former teacher at the schoolhouse in the Sadovo-Kulikovskaya. She paused to look in the window of the Krasnaya Hotel where there was a manicurist at work on the hands of a plump German woman. She wondered, gravely, with complete absorption, what the manicurist would ask for painting her nails: a little vodka, a piece of soap? It was a matter which fully occupied her mind.

At the schoolhouse she was received with awe. Most of the children were sitting in the sun behind the schoolhouse. Some of the children were combing the hair of other children. Small boys were playing the game of Fascists and Communists. They all stopped to stare at the beautiful woman who had come to visit them. Then some of the older children, with astonishment, recognised Olympia. They clustered around Olympia. They asked her questions, looking at her with expressions of wonder. Some stroked the leopardskin coat. Olympia opened her handbag and took out a bar of chocolate which she broke into pieces and gave to the children. Then as this was not enough to go around she took out a second bar of chocolate.

She would have distributed all the treasures she had brought, such largesse being in the character of a grand lady in a leopardskin coat, but Maryusa Selova came out of the schoolhouse and protested vigorously. She took the handbag away from Olympia and bore it into the schoolhouse. When she reappeared a few minutes later the bag was empty. It was not until Maryusa kissed Olympia that she saw Olympia fully in her new magnificence. Maryusa then stood back and looked at Olympia, and there was such disingenuous admiration in her gaze, even enthrallment, that Olympia experienced intense pleasure and at this moment loved Maryusa more than she had ever loved anybody in her life.

Even as she felt this she was looking beyond Maryusa's shoulder. The man staring at her was not, as she was suddenly conscious, a man at all, but Fomin. He was big enough for a man, of man's height, broad but not yet of such depth of chest and shoulder as he gave promise of being. Fomin had grown. His hair was cropped close to his uneven skull. His eyes below the drawn brows were like the eyes of a cat. The whites of the eyes were almost unseen. He stood erect. He nodded without smiling.

They sat down on the wooden bench behind the school, Olympia, Maryusa, Fomin.

As Olympia spread the folds of her leopardskin coat on the bench she stroked it, looking quickly at Fomin, and said:

"Do you like it?"

But it was Maryusa who answered.

"It is very beautiful. I have never seen such a coat."

"It was given to me," Olympia said.

"The bourgeoisie have many beautiful things," Fomin said.

"I am also to have new shoes," Olympia said.

"Shoes from the tractor factory?"

"No, these will be from Lublin," Olympia said.

"The shoes made in capitalist countries are unpractical," Fomin said.

"Nevertheless they are very pretty," Olympia said.

"They are not made for workers," Fomin said. "They are made for the bourgeoisie who exploit the workers."

The sound of the old words was suddenly delightful to Olympia. It was something she had almost forgotten. It was like hearing again the loud voice of her father.

"And how much could you sell this coat for on the free market?" Olympia asked.

Fomin looked at the coat very gravely.

"Maybe a thousand marks," he said.

"So much!"

"Perhaps more."

"You are now much experienced on the market, yes?"

"Yes. It is the foreign capitalist evil."

"Yet you practise it."

"Speculation is a normal condition of the foreign capitalist occupation. It is necessary to bring that condition into prominence."

Olympia laughed. "You are so serious," she said. At the same time she was thinking that Fomin had got this from someone recently.

"When do you go?" Fomin said.

"Go? I do not go," Olympia said.

"Many are going. Every day the trains are filled with people going to Poland and Germany."

"Oh, those are the workers," Olympia said.

She looked at Fomin, at his new breadth and sinewy hardness, at his obvious labour capacity.

"Are you not afraid they will take you?" she said.

"They have first to find me," Fomin said.

"Take care of yourself," Olympia said.

"And you?" said Fomin. "Do you take care of yourself?"

"What do you mean?"

"Have you been sick?"

"No."

"It is bad for you to be sick," Fomin said. "You should take care not to get sick."

"Two girls were sick last week," Olympia said. "They sent them away."

"Where?" said Fomin.

"I do not know. They were taken away in a wagon."

"They were taken to the tractor factory," Fomin said. "They take them all to the tractor factory."

"You have been to the tractor factory?"

"Yes."

"Is it bad to work at the tractor factory?"

"There is no work at the tractor factory," Fomin said.

"Ah, I have heard," Olympia said. "The tractor factory is a prison."

"Yes," Fomin said. "Some are held there, but mostly they are killed. They kill all the sick."

"Why do they kill the sick?"

"It is simpler for them."

"I would not like to be killed," Olympia said.

"There is no sense being killed if you have work to do," Fomin said.

"There is one thing to be said," Olympia said, "when there are fewer people there is more to eat."

"There are fewer children in the school, but there is not more to eat," Maryusa said.

"Some children have gone?" Olympia said. "Which children?"

"Mia and Losha and the one called Sophia. Others also."

"I remember Sophia. I brought her here."

"Ah, this war," Maryusa said.

"War," said Olympia.

"How long will it last?" Maryusa said. "It cannot go on forever."

"Listen," Fomin said, "you can hear the sound of cannon."

Faintly, borne to them on the soft wind, there was the far distant sound of artillery.

"Each day it gets closer," Fomin said. "Soon it will be here."

"No," Olympia said.

"What will happen then?" Maryusa said.

"I know what I shall do," Olympia said.

"I asked you," Fomin said, "when do you go?"

"Not yet," Olympia said. "In the Crimea there are victories."

"Yes?" Fomin said. "You hear that?"

"I hear everything," Olympia said. "I have all the informations."

"So?" said Fomin.

"This," Olympia said, waving her hand in the direction of the artillery, "this is nothing. Besides they have spies everywhere."

"That is normal."

"You know that?" said Olympia.

Fomin looked at Olympia. "Naturally," he said, "there are always spies."

"Ah yes," Olympia said, "but there are all kinds of spies."

"Sometimes," said Fomin, "they come in leopardskin coats."

Olympia was shocked. It was not the shock of accusation. It was the shock that Fomin could be so wrong. She had been about to tell Fomin of Sturmführer Gruber's child spies, but now she refrained.

"If they," Maryusa inclined her head in the direction of the artillery, "if they should come close it would be terrible."

"The artillery of the Red Army is very accurate," Fomin said.

"I am not thinking of the shells," Maryusa said. "I am thinking of the Germans. I am thinking of what they would do."

"You would do better to think of the Communists," Fomin said.

"I think of them all the time," Maryusa said.

"I do not think of any such things," Olympia said. "It is not practical to think of such things. If they come, I shall go. Yes, that is evident."

A flight of geese flew overhead. To the distant rumble of artillery was added the lofty sound of honking geese.

"Look," Maryusa said. "It is spring."

"In the *kolkhoses,*" Fomin said, "the wheat is rising, but there are few peasants and there is no oil in the tractors."

"The old people will make the harvest," Maryusa said. "It will be as it was in the other war."

"The Fascists will not get the harvest," Fomin said.

"You mean no one will get it," Olympia said.

Olympia saw that Fomin's seriousness had been oppressing Maryusa. Olympia saw that Maryusa was thin and pale. She saw that the children playing in the sun were thin and pale and did not yet show the sun in their faces. She saw that the winter had been hard. Seeing this she was angry about the propaganda.

While they were sitting there Professor Shevchenko came out of the schoolhouse. The old man was so small and so thin and so quiet that Olympia did not notice him.

Then she recognised him, remembering with pleasure his storytelling in the schoolroom during the time she had spent there. In the bright light of day his old clothes were miserably shabby, but there was a fineness about his pointed white face, the foggy pince-nez balanced on his nose, the long dank hair, that made Olympia feel pleased to know him. It was not often in these times that one saw such an obvious *intelegant.*

Professor Shevchenko made a little bow that included Olympia as well as Maryusa and squatted down in the sun beside the bench. He held a tin bowl of soup and a piece of millet bread in his hands. He began eating his bread and soup. He ate with feline delicacy, motionlessly lapping the soup, bolting his bread with little jerks of his neck, as careful of crumbs as a cat of feathers. Maryusa watched him with the same expression of pained devotion that she had for the children.

Occasionally Professor Shevchenko peered at Olympia and Fomin. It was comfortable in the sun and they continued idly to talk.

"Last week," Olympia said, "I went to church."

"Yes," said Maryusa, "was it interesting?"

"It was the old Church of the Assumption which has been a museum. The *Nemtsy* have caused it to open."

"How many *popes* were there?" Fomin said.

"There were no *popes,*" Olympia said. "This is a *Nemetski* church. There was a priest from Poland."

"Under the Communists," Fomin said, "the churches have real *popes.*"

"Why did you go?" Maryusa asked.

"It was something to do," Olympia said. "One of the girls went to pray."

"Did you pray?"

"I do not know how to pray," Olympia said. "My parents were militants of the League of Godless. Besides it is uncultured to pray."

"I do not know how to pray either," Maryusa said.

Professor Shevchenko spoke: "I know how to pray," he said. His voice was light and childlike.

"What do you say when you pray?" Olympia said.

"You say anything," Professor Shevchenko said, "anything."

"You cannot say anything," Olympia said. "There must be something secret to say like this girl said."

"Anything," Professor Shevchenko said.

"I do not believe in God," Maryusa said. "My parents also were atheists. They were atheists by conviction. But that is not why I disbelieve in God. How can you believe in God when you see what is about us?"

"That is when people believe most in God," Professor Shevchenko said.

"You believe in God?" Fomin said.

"No."

"Then why do you pray?"

"It is something to do. It is good to do. And easy."

"It is superstition," Fomin said.

"I pray to the old gods," said Professor Shevchenko. "Sometimes I pray to Svarog and his son the mighty Svarozhich, for all gods have sons. Or I pray to Perun or Khors and Dazhd, to Veles and Volos. Sometimes I talk to the little people they call the Bisey."

"You are very old," Fomin said.

"The old gods were cruel gods," Maryusa said. "It says so in the books."

"It is necessary that God should be feared in order that He should be believed," said Professor Shevchenko. "Therefore God must excel man in everything. It is more and more difficult for God."

"It is better when you talk of Moscow," Fomin said.

"Ah, but one does not pray to Moscow," said Professor Shevchenko.

"But one can be afraid of Moscow," Olympia said.

"Old man, are you afraid of the Communists?" Fomin said.

"The Communists?" said Professor Shevchenko. "Who is afraid of the Communists? The Communists are reasonable men. Always they have reasons."

"The Communists are logical," Fomin said.

"It was said by Homer: 'Zeus gazed afar on the land of the lordly Hippemolgi who live on milk, and the Abii, the most just of men.' "

"The old man is crazy," Fomin said.

"It was an illusion which bemused Hrushevsky," Professor Shevchenko said.

"*I* am afraid of the Communists," Maryusa said.

"That is because you are kind," Professor Shevchenko said.

"I would like to be reasonable," Maryusa said.

"Kindness and righteousness are like oil and water. It is a proverb," said Professor Shevchenko.

"But I am sure I am reasonable," Maryusa said. "It is right what I am doing. It is wrong for us to do that which will certainly bring about our deaths. It is only that I cannot find the words. If only I could explain what I feel."

"It is possible," said Professor Shevchenko, "that humanism needs a new dialectic."

"The former people had no dialectic. Only the Communists have the dialectic," Fomin said.

"True," Professor Shevchenko said.

"What is the use of their propaganda?" Maryusa said. "What can it do here now? How can it have any bearing on the minds of these children?"

"How can we know?" Fomin said. "It is too big for us to know. Only Stalin knows."

"You are a Communist?" Professor Shevchenko asked. He was smiling at Fomin, a smile of infinite gentleness.

"No," said Fomin.

"No?" said Professor Shevchenko. "But you are nevertheless reasonable and not without certitude."

"How the old man talks," Fomin said. "Like a child."

"The old often share the presentiments of the young," Professor Shevchenko said. "I sit here and listen to the children playing in the sun. . . ."

"It is good for them to play," Maryusa said.

"They play the game of some against others," Professor Shevchenko said; "yes, it is a game children have always played. But I notice that today it is the smaller children who are the *Nemtsy*."

"I do not know," Maryusa said. "I do not know what games they play, only they must not put Iron Crosses on their clothes."

"The big children are now the Communists," said Professor Shevchenko.

"It is natural," Fomin said.

"It is just."

"How you all go on," Olympia said; "but it is true that Moscow has not fallen."

Maryusa said: "Listen to the cannon!"

The talk ceased as they sat in the sunshine and listened to the far distant rumble of artillery. At intervals the sound would rise in volume giving the momentary illusion of an unbearable proximity and then it would almost die away.

"It is the guns which frighten our teacher," Fomin said.

"Always they are there," Maryusa said. "At night you can see the flashes."

"I am sorry that our teacher is afraid," Olympia said. "Do not be afraid, Marusinka."

"It is not the guns," Maryusa said.

"There is no need to be afraid while Fomin is here," Olympia said. She was watching Fomin.

Fomin said nothing.

But the remark gave Maryusa a feeling of pleasure and joy. The expression in her face showed quite plainly that she wanted love. She wanted Fomin to love her. Clearly if Fomin loved her everything would be much simpler. He would, loving her, understand her and there would not be the necessity to explain and justify herself. For Maryusa love was the solution to everything. She had never understood why people did not love one another.

Fomin stood up. He called to the bigger children to desist from bullying the younger children. The children obeyed. But then some of the children spied Professor Shevchenko. They came running over to him, demanding he tell them a tale, and they bore him away.

"Look," Maryusa said, "how high the geese fly."

"In the country," Fomin said, "there are swans on the lakes. The birch is already in leaf and the willows have catkins."

"It is so beautiful in the spring," Maryusa said.

"It is true," Olympia said. "Everything is different in the spring. Men are different too."

"How are men different?" Fomin said.

"They are *different,*" Olympia said.

"Everybody is different," Maruysa said. "It is the sun and the air. Everywhere the sap is rising."

"But how are men different?" Fomin said.

"There are more of them," Olympia said.

Maryusa looked at Olympia. She saw the white-gold of her skin and the soft hands. She took in, for the first time, the perfume which she could not have identified as eau de Cologne, but which, to her sensibilities, was infinitely delicious and provoking. She put out her hand and touched the softness of the leopardskin coat.

Maryusa could not endure it any longer. She jumped up and hurried inside the schoolhouse.

Olympia looked at Fomin. She knew that she could have Fomin at any time. She knew that Maryusa could not.

"So, you are going away," Olympia said. "Tonight, yes?"

"How do you know?" Fomin said. He was poised, tense like an animal.

"Oh, that's easy," Olympia said, a little thrilled by Fomin's animalism. "If you were not going away you would be afraid that I would denounce you to the SS."

"Right."

"You've been waiting for this?"

"Yes."

"Have you told Maryusa? Will you tell Maryusa?"

"No."

"You don't care about any of this. The school. Maryusa."

"No."

"But you organised it for them. Made discipline."

"Yes."

"I think you are funny people, you Communists. Even when you are not working for the Party you have to be ordering something. If it's not other people it's yourselves."

"Don't talk about the Party, you!"

"I think you're a damn son-of-a-bitch," Olympia said.

This was the spring, so long ago, so soon forgotten, that the Red Army counter-attacked. The Siberians and the deep winter had saved Moscow. Artillery held it. A force of thirty Russian divisions was now bearing down on the city of Kharkiv. From Voronesh and Tambov they marched across the Kursk steppe to meet the German Army at the line of the Donetz. They would force the Donetz and they would take the city of Kharkiv, their general with the Ukrainian name was told, and from Kharkiv they would cross the Dnieper and so down to the Black Sea, cutting the long German arm that had already reached out to Sevastopol and Rostov and threatened to go beyond into the lands of the Don and Volga. The bony-faced boys who had survived the great retreat and the dark men from the central plains, each in his shabby fleece-lined cap and his long unhemmed greatcoat, splashed through the spring rains and lay nights in thickets of hazel and oleander. Or they dug holes in the ground where the ground was defrosted and dry under the ashes of the burned-down dwellings of the steppe villages. They ate black bread and herring and they knew where, in the abandoned collectives, the turnips were heaped, the grain buried and the honey hidden. In the water meadows of the great rivers their sharpshooters could stalk the homing geese, but the ordinary soldier wasted no ammunition, hugged close his short-range machine-pistol and his hand grenades like ketchup bottles. There were some with mortars and heavy machine-guns. Some had the long-barrelled anti-tank rifles which they carried shoulder-to-shoulder like the poles of a Sedan chair. Their sappers were carpenters who built corduroy roads and trim nailless bridges with hatchet, adze and auger. Their supply was a fleet of aged Ford trucks and a multitude of low-wheeled pony carts driven by old bewhiskered peasants. The soldiers listened attentively as their political officers read from *Krasnia Svesda* the lists of atrocities committed upon the body of their country. They were beginning to hate the enemy who had brought this much more into their already austere and impoverished lives. They were beginning to fight well, that is to say, their patrols were returning with prisoners and they were using their native steppe-craft to infiltrate and surround the forward positions of the enemy. In pressing these attacks in the face of enemy fire they were showing resolution. But the artillery was mostly around Moscow.

Except for the lack of artillery and anti-aircraft guns and the absence of air cover, it was a well-planned offensive. The general staff had provided for every other kind of harassment of the enemy forces. In the woods and on the lonely roads behind his forward lines the enemy was to know no security, the staff propagandists said. They advertised, for the comfort of their own soldiers, as well as for the disquiet of the enemy, a widespread uprising of guerillas. And it is true that many brave men and women went through the enemy lines, or were dropped by parachute in the enemy rear, where they performed the tasks of provocation and diversion before being themselves destroyed. In the spring it was easier for the diversionists to escape capture and to hide in the woods where the work of earlier comrades having had its effect, they found a company of men and women who had fled their farms and villages to evade enemy reprisals and a peasantry everywhere in terror of the foreign soldiers. With what weapons were at hand the diversionists attacked the enemy where he was isolated and unguarded, adding the enemy's arms to their own. Among the diversionists there were now men trained in the use of all arms, demolitions and communications. There were also Party functionaries and officers of the NKVD.

In the wooded country to the north of Kharkiv there was such a group, one of whose members was a man named Alexi Ivanovich Kharko from the village of Podvorki which is on the highway between Kharkiv and Volchansk. One day the Germans had come to Podvorki and had taken Kharko and his wife and a number of others and assembled them for execution. While they were doing this Kharko had run away. That night Kharko had taken a young pig and had set out for a place he knew deep in the woods. He remembered this place from many years before when it had been the abode of a family of horse traders who, correctly denounced as speculators in the period after the NEP, had been transported to Tashkent. This place, at a confluence of streams, comprising a couple of log cabins and the ruins of a small barn in the shelter of a high bluff, like many relics of the collectivisations, had been so long abandoned that few remembered its existence. But when Kharko got there he found it already occupied.

Kharko stepped into the small clearing. Around the clearing the tall leafless birches rose like giant organ-pipes. In the centre of the clearing a spiral of blue smoke drifted softly upwards. There was no other movement. The three men in the clearing were as still as startled cranes. They were looking at Kharko Kharko saw that they were in the rags of what had been Red Army uniforms. He saw that they were unarmed. Kharko let the pig fall from his shoulder into the snow where it lay emitting cavernous grunts through its bound snout.

"The pig is mine," Kharko said.

The men did not reply. They did not move. A fourth man stepped out of one of the log cabins. His head was muffled in rags.

"I will share the pig," Kharko said.

"Here," said one of the men, "we share everything, including the killing of spies and informers."

"And Germans?"

"And Germans."

"I also would share in that," Kharko said.

The four men in ragged uniforms stood around Kharko. This Kharko was a short squat man with a head that appeared to be wider than it was high. His mouth was full of flat yellow teeth that looked as though they had been filed down. His eyes were like shiny black spiders in a web of fine wrinkles. He had a pronounced squint. Thus he wore the fixed, unalterable expression of being at once crafty, obsequious, cunning, cruel, avaricious, humorous and strong. The four ragged soldiers saw that he was a peasant. They accepted him.

Kharko learned that the four men were a remnant of the massacre of the 176th Corps at Gomel. The man with his head swathed in rags had been a captain. He had been wounded and he now wore a bandage across his face below the eyes. The eyes were fine blue eyes, but cold. Below the eyes the bandage lay flatly on his face as though there were no nose beneath it. His mouth and jaws were concealed by a greying beard which had not yet lost bristle-stiffness. When he spoke Kharko saw that he wore a complete set of stainless steel dentures. His language, in his speech with his comrades and with Kharko, was that rarest of all speech, grammatical Ukrainian. But speaking appeared to give him pain. After he had spoken to Kharko he removed the dentures and Kharko did not again hear him speak.

One of the soldiers told Kharko that they had belonged to a division that had been in tactical reserve to the east of Kiev on the upper Dnieper. The men of the division had received no word of the approach of the enemy. They had been surrounded by German columns moving in their rear. Their general had negotiated with the Germans. The soldiers had been disarmed and they were held in large enclosures outside the town of Gomel. They had waited to see what the Germans would do. Some had said that the Germans were already in Moscow. Some old soldiers said that in the last war the Germans had sent prisoners to work on the farms in Poland. Others said that there would be no prisoners because Stalin had made a new pact with Hitler and the war was over.

On the second day a detachment of *SS Einsatz Kommandos* relieved the *Wehrmacht* guards. The *Einsatz Kommandos* set up machine-gun posts around the enclosures and early next morning they commenced shooting. At first there was only one machine-gun and there was a moment of suspended motion before the closely-packed mass of men understood they were being fired upon. Then, as a man, they dropped to the prone position. They lay there, huddled close to the ground, while the SS, with carefully-directed machine-gun fire now from all sides, blanketed the wide enclosure. There were some men who jumped up, and one young platoon leader who called upon his platoon to rise and charge the wire, and these men ran leaping across the backs of their comrades, but none reached the wire. Other men crept beneath the bodies of the dead and wounded, but these movements, detected by the machine-gunners, attracted the intensest fire. There were pauses as the machine-gunners cooled their weapons, and during these pauses the wounded could be heard. It was not until midday that a lull in the firing drew silence. Where there was still movement, where a body turned slowly, or arched, where an arm fell back and grasped the wet earth, there the SS threw a small grenade. Finally the SS advanced among the fallen, walking cautiously, through fear and on account of their boots, stopping occasionally to snap a fresh clip into their pistols, leaning over, here and there, like leisurely field workers, to put a bullet through the heads of those who seemed still to breathe. There were, nonetheless, many hidden among the fallen who were still whole or but slightly hurt, and these were routed out and set to work to dig with their hands long trenches into which they eased the dead. And when this task was completed the SS prepared to kill them, the survivors, but at this stage many fled, the SS being too weary to fire effectively upon them. How many died at Gomel? The soldier said that there had been three divisions. That would be above thirty thousand men. But many had escaped.

"In the region of Starobielsk in the woods there is such a place," Kharko said, "but that was two years ago and they were Poles."

"There is much death," the soldier said.

Kharko lived with the four soldiers. He was useful. He knew where to get food. He went often secretly to the village of Podvorki. In the spring there had been much activity on the highway. While the ground was still frozen German tanks and heavy artillery had gone through the village. Then as the season of *rasputitsa* arrived, horse-drawn limbers and wagons had been driven by at a pace which slicked the cabins with mud as high as the roof-trees. Old peasant women patiently washed the mud off their houses with pails of water drawn from a well in the centre of the village. Then there were warmer days and the mud had turned to dust. Columns of soldiers were constantly passing through the village. They walked at the side of the road making way for wheeled traffic. Many of the passing wagons were driven by Rumanians wearing wide-skirted coats and sheepskin hats. The wagons raised clouds of dust and the foot soldiers cursed the Rumanian drivers. When there was a traffic block the soldiers would halt and they would squat at the side of the road looking at the village or at the staff cars in which the generals sat like wooden men. There were airplanes in the sky, but they were not Russian airplanes.

On his visits to the village Kharko went secretly to the house of an uncle where his son, a boy of ten, was living. Kharko's uncle, and other elders of the village, were in fear of the Germans. They were too close to the front and the Germans did not trust them. At either end of the village there were new signposts in German and Rumanian letters. The German signs were in black letters on a white ground. The Rumanian signs were on plain wood. There were also signs in code and numbers. Telephone wires lay loosely at the side of the road or were drawn together and festooned over cabin roofs. An old peasant who cut two metres of wire for himself was shot. The wire had been identified as binding around his ragged *valinki.* After that printed occupation notices signed by the commanding general were pasted on the wall of the village meeting house.

A *Wehrmacht* unit took up quarters in the meeting house. The soldiers behaved correctly. After they had put out a guard they liked to sit at the door of the meeting house in the twilight and to sing and play the accordion. The whole village listened to their music and presently the meeting house was a gathering place for village children. The German soldiers encouraged the children to sing their songs and were pleased with the pure young Ukrainian voices that were so quick to pick up a melody. Sometimes they gave food to the children. The *Wehrmacht* unit moved on leaving a mess of refuse in the meeting house, straw palliasses, bottles and cans.

Then two SS men driving a *Kübelwagen* came to the village. One of the SS men spoke Ukrainian. He asked if there were any Communists in the village. The same day a number of villagers followed Kharko into the woods. There were now a dozen men living in the abandoned settlement at the confluence of streams.

A troop of Rumanian Army horse drivers set up a corral near the village and camped there. They were mostly peasants from the northern Carpathians and their speech was understood by the Ukrainians. They told the villagers that a big battle was in preparation. The men from the village who were hiding in the woods wanted to bring out their wives. Kharko worried about his son. Along the highway to the north of the village where the highway entered the woods German engineers were unloading material and stacking it in the cover of the trees. A German guard detail was camped at this place. Constantly patrolling guards made it difficult to enter or leave the village. In the first days of June there was the sound of guns. Sometimes the guns sounded very close to the village.

When Kharko heard the guns he left the forest and came at night to the village. In the house of his uncle he learned that there was fighting to the west of the Donetz. That was already close to the village. Next morning in the house of his uncle Kharko saw the man they called the Kohut. When Kharko saw the Kohut he remembered that he had intended to denounce him. That had been one of the first things it had been in his mind to do after the Germans had come, but there had been many obstructions, the strange manner of the Germans, the reprisals, and the circumstance that the Kohut, by absenting himself at this time, had avoided reminding anybody that the moment for his removal had arrived.

Now, as Kharko looked at the Kohut with the former intention clearly in his eyes, in the black spiderlike eyes in the web of wrinkles in the squat round face, Kharko knew that it was already too late. He saw that there was in the Kohut's bearing the confidence that Kharko could do nothing. The Kohut, which in Ukrainian means Cock, wore that expression of vicarious triumph which had long ago earned him his nickname. He was a tall stringy man with a long upthrust neck in which the Adam's apple floated like a crop, a pointed nose and beady bright eyes full of baseless challenge. He was no fool, yet he was not wise, being vain without caution and, in any company, disreputable. The Party Workers who had come to create enthusiasm for the *kolkhose* had been pleased by the Kohut's endorsement of their slogans and encouraged by his irrepressible, if incoherent, speech-making at the *kolkhose* meetings, until, realising that their whole effort was in danger of ridicule, they had, with menace in their voices, begun shouting him down. It required shouting. From the first the Kohut had embraced the system of Soviets as his own. None in the village spoke of it with more enthusiasm, more often, or more inaccurately. And then, as Party Workers followed one another into that strange limbo reserved for superseded Soviet bureaucrats, and those villagers who had been strong had been sent to Siberia or the arctic colonies, so that only those were left in Podvorki who had known no other condition or, like the uncle of Alexi Ivanovich Kharko, and Kharko himself, knew how to submit and be silent and wait, though it be a century, then the power of that village had devolved upon the Kohut. For though the Kohut, no matter how much he might wish it, canvass it, talk of it, was not, and never could be, a Party member, being without respectability, honesty, or the capacity for work, or those attributes which could enable him to endow the slogans of the moment with an acceptable sense, being anyway now too old, yet it was nevertheless clear, since none of the Kohut's enemies or even those who failed to pay some homage to his vanity had survived, that at some stage in the more recent history of the village he had acceded to other funtions than the merely functional. He was, finally, though without official position, the master of the village. In the end the structure of non-elective government rests upon such.

Why was the Kohut here? What did the Kohut want?

Kharko looked at his uncle, asking the questions with his eyes. But the old man looked away. Then Kharko looked again at the Kohut. There was calculation in his regard. The Kohut, seeing this, cocked his chin and there came into his face an expression of boldness and challenge.

"Listen to the guns of the Red Army!" said the Kohut.

The guns sounded very close. Flakes of distemper floated down from the ceiling of the cabin. Cracks between the trimmed log walls emitted a faint effluvium of dust.

"You say they are Russian guns?" the uncle said.

"We are about to be liberated by the victorious Red Army," the Kohut said.

"Is that what they say?" the uncle said.

Kharko went to the small window of the cabin that looked out on the highway. He could see his son playing with other children.

"I came for Mitya," Kharko said.

"It is better," the uncle said.

"Who is that with him? Is she of this village?"

"She is from Kharkiv. They come now for food."

"We will go tonight," the Kohut said.

Kharko looked at the Kohut, but did not answer.

"You should come too, old man," Kharko said to his uncle.

"If all go," the Kohut said, "the Germans will be suspicious. They will follow. Then all will be lost."

"He is right," the uncle said.

"There is no danger here," the Kohut said. "The Red Army will be here tomorrow. Or the day after."

"They say that?" Kharko's uncle said.

"Here is your Red Army," Kharko said.

He was looking through the small window of the cabin. The uncle and the Kohut peered over his shoulder. Except for the children the little village was empty. A breeze fluttered the occupational notices and penalty lists which had been pasted on the wall of the meeting house. But now, down the highway into the village, escorted by guards, came a column of Russian prisoners. Some were without caps. The uniforms of many were caked with earth. Their eyes, enlarged and distraught, or half-closed, were turned inward against the bewilderment of compounding and intolerable events. As they passed through the village some of the men saw the children in the street. One soldier made the motion of drinking water. A guard shouted and crashed the bolt of his rifle. The children did not move but looked at the soldiers. At the rear of the column there were wounded. The blood of the wounded had not yet hardened in the cloth of their uniforms. Some wounded wore rough bandages, some already staggered, draining the effort of each step from their hearts. As the end of the column went past the cabin of Kharko's uncle the last man in the column missed his step and fell at the very door of the cabin. The man lay as though dead. One of the guards, a sturdy sunburned man with his tunic open at the throat and his sleeves rolled, turned the Russian soldier over with his boot. The soldier's head rolled back. The eyelids fell back and where there should have been eyes there was a pair of white sickles. The guard went on behind the column.

The Kohut drew back from the window. He took several long steps around the room. He made a clucking noise with his mouth.

"They are taking prisoners," Kharko said.

"They are unworthy," the Kohut said. "No Red Army man should be taken alive."

"Is that what they are saying?" Kharko's uncle said.

A group of village children stood about the dead soldier.

"We will all go tonight," Kharko said.

"Yes, tonight," the Kohut said, "soon."

"Tonight," Kharko said.

"But not all tonight," the Kohut said.

"Tonight," Kharko said.

"You would leave everything? All this for the Germans to take?"

"He is right," the uncle said.

"Tonight," the Kohut said, "we will take food. And there are some who will meet us."

"So?" Kharko said.

"Tomorrow we will take other things. In a few days the Red Army will be here and everything will be good."

"Tonight I shall take my son," Kharko said.

Kharko opened the door of the cabin cautiously. He now made a quick sortie and seized his son by the collar, much as a cat picks up a kitten, and brought him swiftly into the cabin. He began to thrash his son.

"Why do you stand there looking at the dead man?" Kharko said. "Is it something you have not seen before?"

The boy began weeping.

"Get ready," Kharko said."We go tonight. Already it is late."

"She wants to come too," the boy said.

"Who?"

"She is from Kharkiv. She has come to visit her aunt, but her aunt was among those killed during the reprisals. She wants to come with us into the forest."

"Mitya! What have you said?"

The boy shook the tears from his eyes and looked at his father.

"Everybody knows you are a partizan," he said. "Everybody knows you have a hiding place in the woods with soldiers and men. Everybody knows that you have come for me. They want to come too. Nobody wants to stay here."

"Why would he give us guns?" Kharko said.

"It is ordered by Stalin."

"Yes?" Kharko said. "Since when has Comrade Stalin been arming the Ukrainian peasants?"

"Comrade Stalin is a true friend of the peasants."

It was an unfamiliar voice. The company turned in the direction of the speaker. They saw a man in a worn leather jacket and cloth cap. He looked like a worker from the Donbas. He had a narrow face with large brown imaginative eyes and curling eyelashes, a large mouth and an unshaven blue-black jaw. The expression on his face was that of calculated audacity and at the same time reserve. None there had seen him before, but they recognised the type.

"An *Activist,"* Kharko said.

"I come from the Partizan Commander," the stranger said. "There are guns for those who will help in the glorious task of liberation."

"There are too many in this room," the uncle said. "Meetings are forbidden." He went to the door and bolted it.

"What happens if the Red Army does not come?" Kharko said.

"Yes," another said, "if the Germans remain?"

The problem lay heavily on the humble minds in that cabin. There was dislike of the Kohut and distrust of the stranger. But there was also the knowledge, born of recent experience, that the enemy was a merciless enemy. There were caution and slowness of thought, the limitations of illiteracy, and there were long memories. The *Activist,* whose name was Pilchuk, measuring the factors that were weighing against him in that room, placed remembrance of the past first among them, but did not despair. He knew, had been trained to know, that among people whose grasp on life is firm, memory is an isolated incident in the past whose connection with the present diminishes with the enlargement of events and that it is a rare and unusual mind that may abstract a past experience into a rule or line or precept of conduct in the future. It was an unusual mind that could presume to estimate the Party's conduct in this war on the basis of Leninist-Stalinist methods of collectivising the land. An unusual mind is often an influential mind, and so the *Activist,* Pilchuk, took note of Kharko.

There was, at that fortuitous moment, the unbearable

splintering detonation of an incoming shell. The seams in the log walls of the cabin puffed a silent exhalation of white dust.

"The guns of the Red Army!" Pilchuk said.

"I heard only one shell," Kharko said.

"The Germans prepare to die. Look!"

A portion of the company peered through the small window in the direction indicated by Pilchuk. In front of the village meeting house there was a square of village common ground. Here children played and here on summer evenings old folk came to sit and gossip. In this square a German soldier was working.

"They are digging trenches in the square!"

"They are digging graves," Pilchuk said.

Now, carefully watching the German soldier, they saw that he was indeed digging graves. The holes were narrow rectangles set in line close to one another. The black earth was piled up in orderly heaps at the foot of each hole. At this moment the gravedigger was working strongly. The earth was flying from his shovel and presently only his old grey head could be seen.

"They will put their crooked crosses above the graves," Pilchuk said.

The woman made the Greek sign of the cross.

"Why should they bury their dead in our square?"

"They have done it in every village. They are people of the cities."

There was a murmur of assent.

"I have seen them," a man said. "They know not a horse."

"It is also," Pilchuk said, "to remind you that Podvorki is a German village and, therefore, a proper place for German heroes to be buried. Afterwards they will erect a monument in your square."

"Afterwards," the Kohut said, "we will dig them out and feed them to the pigs."

"Who is for the partizans?" Pilchuk said.

As the question was asked, as the problem, momentarily diverted, lay once more before them, there was a heavy banging on the door. The woman glanced swiftly out of the window.

"The SS!" she said.

"I knew," the uncle said, "there are too many here."

The banging on the door was renewed. The noise was made by a heavy boot. The eight men and the two children in the cabin drew back from the doorway. The men stood with their backs pressed against the walls.

"Open!" The command was uttered in German-accented Ukrainian.

"Be quiet!"

It was a childish voice. It called to those outside to be quiet. It was the little girl called Sophia speaking. She went across the room and unbolted the door. She opened the door just enough to put her head out.

She looked directly into the face of the Ukrainian-speaking SS man.

"You cannot come in," Sophia said. "My mother is sick."

Those inside the cabin could hear the Germans talking between themselves. They heard the word typhus.

None in the cabin spoke or moved. In the hush there was a slight sound. The eyes of all were turned in the direction of the sound. They were looking at Pilchuk. Unnoticed he had drawn a pistol. The slight sound had been the cocking of the pistol hammer. He now held it pointing at that place by the door jamb where the SS man's shoulder would come thrusting forward. Pilchuk's unshaven blue-black jaw gave emphasis to the now-pallid face. But the large eyes were wide open and steady. It was a German pistol. The sight of the sleekly-finished gunmetal deeply moved the peasants. Part of this feeling arose from being on the right side of a gun, any gun. Another part was cupidity. In all the men and women in the room there had been this moment of nerve-tied frozen fear. They saw that Pilchuk was also afraid. They looked at the Kohut and they saw that he was yellow with fear. There was kinship in this experience.

Müller was surprised to see Sophia at the door of the cabin. Only the day before he had brought her to Podvorki in the *Kübelwagen*. He had set her down at a deserted part of the road about a kilometre from the village. He had driven on into the village, found Scharführer Schewe, tossed his kit into the cottage beside that of Schewe, and prepared himself for his new job as courier and interpreter without any further thought of Fräulein Sophia. He had been amused to call her Fräulein Sophia because of her curious gravity. They had had a conversation on the way out from Kharkiv. Her function had been explained to him. It was not unusual. There were many such children. But he had not expected to find one of such firm and passionate views.

He had forgotten her, put her down and put her out of mind, and now here she was looking at him from the doorway of this peasant cottage, the thin face with the big eyes and the wispy braids of hair, holding the door open just enough to frame her face, and looking at him gravely and saying this about her mother.

"She says her mother is sick," Müller said in German.

"Typhus!" Scharführer Schewe said.

Schewe made a movement as though to thrust past Sophia into the cottage. Müller restrained him.

"She is the spy I brought from Kharkiv," he whispered.

"So?" Schewe said.

He had not liked Müller's restraining arm. It was with obvious reluctance that he now forewent the experience which his instinct had told him lay beyond the partly-open door.

"Typhus must be stamped out," he said.

"There is no disease. She wants us to go away," Müller said. "Later she will bring us the information."

They stepped back from the doorway and Schewe called to the dogs which had led them to the cottage.

Since his illness Müller had been subject to curious fits of imagination. There was a great fogginess in his mind about all matters past, especially the cause of his illness, but when he remembered something, he remembered it vividly. Only yesterday he had brought Fräulein Sophia out from Kharkiv, and he might never have thought of that ride again but for seeing her face at this door. Now his mind went back over every word of their conversation.

"I hate talk," she had said, finally.

"You mean," Müller had said, "you hate lies."

"Yes."

"I have the same feelings. I had forgotten about it. But now I have it again."

"All talk is lies."

"It is difficult for the human tongue to utter truth."

Sophia looked at Müller. "You know?" she said.

"Words are for something else," Müller said. "For poetry, for feeling, but not for truth."

"I often *feel* what is true," Sophia said.

"One should never lose that feeling."

"I shall always feel what is true."

"So sure?"

"Oh, I feel so *much!*"

Müller looked at the small girl again, her wispy braids of hair, her thin frame, her skimpy legs in the big boots, her small bundle held tightly in her lap. For some unaccountable reason he was reminded of a time when he must have been like that, only somewhat older, a thin, skinny youth, a fledgling schoolteacher, an intellectual, large-eyed, immaculately sincere, sick with cynicism. He had *felt* so much.

"No words can express it, can they?" he said.

"Words are weakness," Sophia said.

"Words lie, yes. Therefore make words lie for you."

"What a good idea!" Sophia said. "I must remember that."

"But remember to make yourself big lies. Prove your superiority by the magnitude of your lies. When you are on the side of truth, when you *possess* truth, the lie is a tactic."

"You are a Communist, yes?"

"Yes," Müller said, half-absently.

"It is the way a Communist would think. Even though you are in the SS you are a Communist."

"What have I been saying? I am not a Communist. No Communist would talk like that."

"Then you are religious," Sophia said.

A tremor of fear went through Müller.

They were driving in the *Kübelwagen* along a sunny road, passing an occasional military vehicle, a convoy of horse-drawn wagons, a file of soldiers resting, and none of this had meaning. The real thing was the fear which had been like a dog at his heels ever since his experience in the hospital. He was afraid, but he did not know what made him afraid. But the fear was a thing. It was tangible. And it never left his side. Looking at Sophia he had a sharp, inexplicable hatred and aversion for the small girl, as though the fear, the thing, that was by his side *were* Sophia.

"It is really self-pity," Müller said.

"Are you a Christian?" Sophia asked.

"No," Müller said.

"A lot of people in Kharkiv are religious now," Sophia said.

"The war brings it out."

"No. It is the church being open. There was no church before. Now there is a church."

"Indeed? So you have been to church, Fräulein Sophia?"

"Yes. I went to see what it was like."

"What is it like?"

"It is like you said. All words."

"Some poetry too, perhaps."

"I do not know. The priest talks all the time about love. I cannot help it. I do not love God. Once he asked me if I believed in God and I said, 'No,' just like that."

"What are you, Sophia?"

"I cannot pretend."

"Sophia, why do you do this? Why are you a spy?"

"Because I want to."

"Are you not afraid?"

"Some day it is possible I shall be killed."

"Why do you do it?"

"It is very simple. I hate Communists."

"I suppose you know the priest hates Communists too."

"Oh no, he doesn't. He says he loves Communists and will take them to his bosom. He says he only hates communism."

"Yes! What an intelligent idea for a priest."

"I hate Communists," Sophia said.

"You really hate them, don't you?"

"I would burn them all up."

Sophia spoke with a soft vehemence which startled Müller. He glanced at her. Her thin face was distorted in a way that made him think for a moment that she was in the course of one of those fits children are sometimes subject to. But then the expression subsided and he saw that it had been simply passion of an insupportable kind.

"Hate is bad for us, Sophia."

"You should pray," Sophia said.

"Pray? What a strange thing for a young atheist to say. Tell me, how is it done?"

"The old man at our school knows how to pray. He is not religious, but he prays. Often I have heard him praying quietly. He prays to Svarog and the Svarozhich and sometimes to the Bizy."

"And if I prayed, Sophia, what should I pray for?"

"You could pray for yourself."

"That would be a good idea, except that I don't like myself."

"Then you could pray for those you have killed. You have killed someone, haven't you?"

The fear leaned on him with the weight of a struggling child.

"For whom do you pray, Sophia?"

"For little girls like myself who get shot."

That was where he had put Sophia down. They were less than a kilometre from the village. The roadway was deserted. As soon as he had put Sophia down he had completely forgotten her.

For nearly three months Müller had been a patient in the SS infirmary. He had been well looked after. It was an infirmary devoted exclusively to the care of members of the SS. It had been a surprise to Müller to learn that he was in such a place, or that such a place existed. He had been unconscious when brought there. He had been suffering from a congestion of the lungs, brought on, it seemed certain, by shock and exposure, but there were complications. Those two years in *Gulag* prison camps, half-starved, worked to a standstill, marched here to there, had weakened his constitution in a way that a few months of good food and cleanliness had not yet repaired. The strange thing had been that as he had recovered consciousness he had been able to remember the *Gulag* compound at the Kharkiv tractor factory, and all that had happened before that, but nothing of what happened afterwards.

The experience of awakening had been extraordinary.

At first he had not been able to separate the real from the unreal. Once he raised himself in his bed and looked at the man in the next bed. The man was a big man with a sunburned neck, corded, throbbing. The big man was strapped down on his bed. This was real. Müller lay back and tried to think about it. While he was thinking he had the feeling that someone was looking at him. He raised himself and looked across the ward. There was another man there, half-sitting in his bed, with his eyes held steadily away from Müller. Yet Müller knew that this man had been looking at him. Müller dropped his own eyes and felt the man's gaze return to him. Then he looked quickly again at the man and the man's eyes were looking away from him although Müller was sure that there had been a slight movement in the man's eyes. The man was quite still, simian in his expression of sharp, tricky detachment. Müller asked himself: is this real? In the night when the ward was darkened he saw many such eyes, eyes bearing on him, resting on his face like moths' wings. Sometimes he arrested a look and then the stare was unwavering, went right through him like the steady unblinking gaze of a mandrill.

One night there were not only eyes staring at him, but there were people in the ward he had not seen before. There was a man who crawled about the ward on all fours barking like a dog. There was another man who sat up in a position of utmost dejection, his head fallen on his chest, his hands hanging laxly between his knees. And there was an old woman, naked, skinny, whose long breasts hung like ribbons from her bony chest, crouching on the floor, slowly smearing the floor, he could now see, with human excreta. This was not real. It could not be real. Yet it was vivid in a way that the surgeon-doctor and the orderly were not. This was something he *saw*. Just as the smell was something he smelled. And the sounds something he heard. He could not invent such sounds. His imagination could not reproduce the high-pitched toneless voice endlessly reciting the Ukrainian poets. There were many Ukrainian words he had never heard before, for he was not a scholar, though he had studied the language. Or was it merely that he had the *impression* that he was hearing a learned Ukrainian voice?

During his convalescence, sitting on the balcony of the SS infirmary, he was able to study his comrades at leisure.

At first he was puzzled by the argot. They spoke a new German of words and phrases chosen for impact. They were constantly profane, but the number of their profanities was limited. They employed inflexion and emphasis to convey variations of meaning. They despised all other branches of military service. They were proud of their exploits and often spoke of them. In all such narratives the aim was to establish the quality of their experience. When they spoke of sexual adventures the aim was the bizarre. They liked pictures of nearly-naked girls, especially if they were of the theatre or cinema and could be entreated in public by name. In their pocketbooks they carried photographs of a more scabrous kind. There were also photographs that supported their claims to experience. And family snapshots. If they had ever loved they knew that those whom they had loved were now unfaithful. They knew that personal comradeship was fortuitous, impermanent. They drank. They whored. They gambled. They spoke freely of loot. They were cynical about their officers, about their political leaders, about war aims, about themselves. In short, they were soldiers.

Indeed, by far the greater number of men at the infirmary were members of the *Waffen* SS, the fighting arm of the service. If the men of the *Waffen* SS differed from other soldiers it was because they had no expectancy of survival. Their special characteristics, Müller thought, arose from this condition. They were careless of death, for others as for themselves. They had only contempt for those who feared death. If they had an ideal it was the ideal of dying well. They were merciless towards those among themselves who failed in this ideal. At the hospital Müller heard about the Hook, a method of punishment administered to SS men who showed hesitation or cowardice in the face of the enemy, in particular, a punishment for deserters, those who once having put on the SS uniform attempted to evade its responsibilities. The Hook was a butcher's meat hook upon which the erring SS man was hanged by the throat until he died. They liked to describe executions of this kind. Such descriptions provoked laughter. They were young, strong men, thought Müller, sitting with them on the balcony of the infirmary, proud of their toughness, making toughness an article of faith.

At the same time they were tolerant of the defects of character arising, not out of fear, but from the rigours of their day-to-day work. It was work which produced many breakdowns. Convalescing in this nearly-secret infirmary Müller began slowly to understand this. Almost every night the hospital ambulance brought its case of dementia, paralysis, melancholia, paranoia, or other mental disorder, more often than not accompanied by violence, so that the patient arrived gagged and strapped in a straitjacket. The afflicted were the subject of much joking among the recovering patients. They had names for each variety of aberration. It amused them that the *Sonderkommandos* supplied most of these patients. Yet there was also, on account of this, a respect for this service.

Müller had expected to find his SS comrades firm, undeviating members of the NSDAP, the Nazi Party, bigoted mouthpieces of Party ideology. Instead he found them, by comparison with his own training, apolitical. There were many SS men who had not been members of the Nazi Party before joining the SS. There was no intellectual discipline. No thought control. No fear of spies among themselves. The operations of the *Sicherheitsdienst* which was the supervisory political organisation within the SS were much different from the operations of the NKVD. These men were not afraid to talk. At the same time there were some subjects about which they could not be induced to talk. They would not talk on abstract subjects.

Müller felt that he understood them. They were young men, just as he had been, hating and distrusting words, but unlike him they had not been deceived by the attractions of dogma. There was vanity and self-interest, and there was perversity, but there was no pretension. There was no edifice of words to justify the acts. They acted without talking. Between his time and theirs there had been a vast dissolution. In his own youth he had thought that there was nothing any longer to believe in, yet he had found belief, even faith. But these believed in nothing. They were the truly disillusioned, the lost generation. They were that youth which, having seen all possible ideals corrupted, made muck of, had accepted the necessity for an undivided leadership, whatever that leadership might be, and were dedicated to the everlasting struggle, reaching far beyond their own lives, of continuing and sporadic wars, counter-revolution, extermination and waste, preliminary to the establishment of that single unequivocal leadership without which humanity as a whole was doomed to destroy itself.

As he thought this he knew it was another effort by his tempestuously facile mind to find escape: he knew that the SS was not an ideal, or even an idea, but a void.

Scharführer Schewe (to whose *Teilkommando* Müller had been assigned after leaving the hospital) was a tall young man, almost two metres in height, with a fair skin, fair hair and red lips. He had a small fair moustache and grey eyes. He would have been the very picture of the SS man shown in the Party illustrations except for deep excoriations in the ridges of his cheeks like the scars of an old eczema which had been physically scrubbed out.

Schewe had arrived in Podvorki a week before with an old bloodhound bitch and her yearling puppy. He kept the dogs in a large kennel, painted in black-white-and-red stripes like a sentry box, outside the cottage in which he had his quarters. He fed the dogs with his own hands and the first thing he had said to Müller on his arrival was that Müller should not attempt to pet the dogs.

"The bitch will bay softly if there is a stranger in the village," Schewe said.

At the sound of Schewe's voice the hound looked at

him expectantly out of eyes hidden deep in fleshy folds of hide.

Together Schewe and Müller walked through the village. Podvorki was no more than a score of dusty dwellings around a road junction. Where the two roads met there was a little square of common ground. On one side of the square there was an old clapboard building with an onion-shaped dome which might once have been a church, but was now both schoolhouse and village meeting place. On the opposite side of the square were three cottages of superior carpentry. No paint had been used in the village. There were no made streets or sidewalks. On the crest of a hill overlooking the village there were the ruins of a great house. In the fields around the village huge sunflowers grew in profusion, their yellow-and-black faces turned to the sun. Beyond the fields the birch woods began. A few kilometres distant there was a collective farm, a vast swathe of unfenced wheatland.

"You would think the place was deserted," Schewe said, "but there are forty-five people here, including eleven children."

They walked across to the little square where the old Feldwebel was digging the graves. There were seven graves. They had been dug to a depth of about one metre, all except one. In this grave the head of the old Feldwebel was below the lip of the grave.

"Feldwebel! What are you doing?" Scharführer Schewe called to him.

"Splittergräben!" shouted the old man.

"Come out of it, old fool. No one is going to attack the village."

When the old man had scrambled out, saluted, and marched off with his shovel over his shoulder, Müller said, cautiously, feeling that there was something here that was hidden from him:

"Then you expect casualties?"

"Casualties?" Schewe said. "You will see. There will be dead enough to fill the graves of a hundred villages."

In his tall black coat and shining black helmet, his dogs squatting behind him, the young Scharführer stood silently above the empty graves.

"How old are you, papa?" Schewe spoke quietly.

"Thirty-nine. Why do you ask?"

"They are combing the prison camps and the slums and the hospitals."

Schewe lifted his head so that he looked over the rooftops of the little village.

"They may find a million," he said, "but history will show that *we* were few. We! The SS *Verfügungstruppe!* The *Waffen* SS! The battle leaders! It is we who have made the victories!"

That afternoon Müller had a message to take to a neighbouring village. He did not return until evening.

He found Schewe lying fully dressed on a bed in their quarters in the cottage facing the village square. There was food cooking in the room and Müller ate. Schewe had a bottle of cognac by his side and he was thumbing through a magazine. He offered Müller a drink.

Müller saw that there was a portable phonograph on a small table beside the bed.

"Let us have music," Müller said.

"No. I would rather talk. It is just this hour of suspense the night before the attack." Schewe lit a cigarette. "Do you hunt?" he asked Müller.

"No," Müller said.

"In my youth I hunted all the time. In the Böhmerwald."

"There is nothing to compare with the great pine forests of the mountains," Müller said. He was remembering a walking tour organised by the League of Communist Youth.

"In the summer and autumn it is best," Schewe said. "Often in the summer I would be in the forest for many days at a time, sleeping on the pine needles, sharing cold bacon with the dogs."

"You hunted with dogs?"

"I am a dog man. I worked always with dogs. It is the best way to hunt. If you live and work with dogs there is a relationship between you and the dog. It is a good relationship. It is purer than the relationship between men. If you work close with dogs you can always tell how old the scent is. Yes, even to a day. It was always better for me when the scent was old. For the true joy of hunting is not to come too quickly upon the quarry, but to outwit the quarry, to exhaust all its resources."

"I see you are a sportsman."

"Do you know that whatever is hunted, even if it is a deer, even a bear, it develops an instinct for you? The quarry may never see you. You may never see it. But there develops between you this feeling of an interlinked fate. It is also a feeling of respect."

"That was before this war?"

"Yes. There was peace then. In the great forests and on the high mountains one had the feeling of peace. Sometimes the trail would lead above the snowline. For the hunter this is the finest of sensations, the breaking-out of the deep forest through the gnarled frost-killed timber of the stony summit and then the blinding white light of the snow. Sometimes the trail would lead above the snow-line into the high wind-swept ridges. I do not know why. The sense of being hunted, perhaps, for there is no escape across a mountaintop. Sometimes I would have to abandon the trail and come back to an inn or a village to get food. And then I would commence again. I was always patient. Once you have this relation between yourself and the quarry, of which I have spoken, there is no conclusion except what we hunters call the gift of death. In those days I carried a Mannlicher, one with a cheek-fitted stock, a precise and beautiful weapon. But even with the telescopic sight it was difficult to bring down a man, except at close range, and man is like a bear at close range: he is then most dangerous."

"Man?"

"*Jawohl.* I was in the *Verfügungstruppen* border guard. If you have once hunted man you will never hunt anything else. There is no quarry to match him. Even as you close in on him and the dogs are leaping with excitement, he will try to ambush you, trap you, fall on you out of a tree, roll stones on you, bury you under an avalanche."

"What kind of men?"

"Fugitives. The Communists were the most resourceful. It was a pleasure to hunt Communists."

Schewe poured a tumbler half full of cognac for Müller. He swallowed a gulp of the spirits from his own glass. Müller said nothing.

Schewe picked up the magazine he had been reading and tossed it to Müller.

"That is what I was talking about today," he said.

Müller took up the magazine. He saw that it was not a

magazine of entertainment but a Party publication called the "Roll Call of Honour." This was the magazine which celebrated each month the death in combat of officers of the various services. The pages of the magazine carried row after row of pictures, each a little larger than a postage stamp, of smiling young men. Below each picture there was a brief note of the officer's name, rank, service, orders, origin, end.

Müller fingered the magazine's several hundred pages. The feeling of death hung heavily on its smooth print.

"In the SS you must be able to look on death," Schewe said. "I will show you."

Schewe took from his pocket a wallet of snapshots. One by one he handed the photographs to Müller.

"That was Cracow," he said.

Müller saw a picture of a number of people hanging from trees. Beneath the trees was the recognisable Schewe, dog on leash.

"It is not a good picture," Schewe said. "Here is Przemysl."

Once more the recognisable Schewe, this time one of a group of long-coated officers in a snowy field facing a line of men and women standing above a trench. An accompanying photograph showed the same scene apparently a few minutes later, the men and women recumbent.

"Here is something," Schewe said.

This was a picture of Schewe, one of a group of laughing officers looking into the camera from a position in a circle around a man held down over a barrel and in the act of being flogged. The man being flogged was in *Wehrmacht* uniform. The ferocious expression on the face of the soldier with the whip seemed, like the laughter on the face of the spectators, to be arranged for the camera. The expression on the face of the man being flogged did not.

The picture, provoking some curious recollection, made Schewe laugh.

"Kraft durch Freude," he said.

As he laughed the clean-washed spongelike cheeks opened.

Other pictures followed. This was Tarnopol. This Lvov. This Czernowitz. This Jitomar, Kiev, Odessa, Nikolaev. Schewe was in a mood of reminiscence.

"Now, here is what I mean," he said.

The picture showed a huge pit in which there were an uncountable number of bodies. The bodies had been flung into the pit in every condition. Some were naked. Some partially clothed. There was the body of a woman clad, like the girl in the photograph on the wall by Schewe's bed, in nothing but a pair of black panties. There were children.

Müller's face went suddenly as white as paper. His lips were blue. He stood up.

"Yes," Schewe said, "it gets boring. *Verflucht!* Let us have music."

"I think I shall go outside for a moment," Müller said.

"This is the Quartet in C Major," Schewe said.

"I shall listen to it outside."

Outside it was very dark. The new moon had slipped over the western horizon. He could see nothing. But the night air was cool and fresh with the smell of earth and leaves and sunflowers. He lit a cigarette with shaking fingers. There was a slight movement in the kennel beside the door and the wet slap of the chops of the old bitch as she laid her head down where she could watch him.

As he began to recover his nerve he heard the music inside the cottage. He took no notice of the music. And then it began to take hold of him. There would be a pause as Schewe changed the records and then the music would go on. It was many years since Müller had heard music, but he knew this for the music of Mozart. The understanding that this which he was hearing had been created by a man came to him slowly and he was incredulous. When the quartet had finished Schewe began to play it again. An exquisite dissonance brought to Müller the revelation he had been seeking.

He knew now that evil was real, also created.

The afternoon of June 12 a battalion of the division Viking of the *Waffen* SS went through the village of Podvorki. It came swiftly in clouds of dust. The troop carriers thundered over the rutted highway. The faces of the soldiers were as black as their helmets. Only their eyes were alive, blue-white like the eyes painted on age-darkened Roman statuary. With each lurch of the big vehicles the soldiers swayed to one side, swayed back, stone-like in their private immobility, while the drivers, their lips drawn, the sweat in damp patches at the armholes of their uniforms, swung on the wide steering wheels. Then, as swiftly as it had come, the cavalcade ended. The dust silently settled on Podvorki. The sun sank gently into the birches. Two children came out to look at the road where the great wheels had so recently plunged. The voices of the children were the only sounds in the evening stillness.

At dawn of June 13 the 1st Battalion of the division Viking of the *Waffen* SS attacked a narrow sector of the bridgehead held by the Red Army on the western bank of the Donetz River. The sector had been chosen by the *Wehrmacht* command because of its open terrain. From a sparsely-wooded ridge the earth sloped gently downward over a distance of a thousand metres to the level marshland bordering the river's multiple course. The Germans held the ridge. The Russians had redoubts sunk among the rush and claybanks at the marsh's edge.

The Russians had been recently driven off the ridge by artillery fire, but shelling had failed to dislodge them from their entrenchments in the marsh. Their redoubts had roofs of crossed birch logs covered with earth. In the redoubts there were machine-guns and anti-tank rifles. The communication saps and shelter pits had been dug deep down into the soft earth, ingeniously drained, their sides saved from engulfment by a wickerwork of osiers. The land between the ridge and the first line of redoubts was close-cropped grassland. It had been shallowly pitted, here and there, by mortar shells. The swollen carcass of a black-and-white cow lay in one place.

On this dewy morning while the earth was still and quiet and the Russian watch was thinking sleepily of the black bread that would soon be its fill the German soldiers began their advance. Without artillery preparation, without a single shot, they came out of the night-shrouded ridgetop and began to march down the grassy slope towards the Russian positions. Down in the grey misty rush of the river flat a machine-gun began firing. It was irregularly joined by small arms fire. Then the firing, haltingly, ceased. The Russian soldiers had stopped firing to stare agape at what they saw. The 1st Battalion of the division Viking of the *Waffen* SS was advancing in close order, column of platoon, that is, they were shoulder to shoulder in ranks that were fifty men wide, and behind each rank there was another rank and then another, back to the dark treeline. They were marching in step. The sun, striking out its first rays, flashed on the black dew-wet boots as the boots lifted together and were set down, silently, in unison. The little dark men from the central plains of Asia stared with frozen ovate eyes and the bony-faced youths who had survived the great retreat had stirrings of an old panic. "The SS! It is the SS!"

The first rank of the 1st Battalion of the division Viking had advanced a third of the distance between the ridge and the river flat before the Russian soldiers recovered from their surprise.

The brigade commissar, the company political instructors, the colonel, the major, the captains and the junior officers, risen out of cramped sleep, began shouting at the soldiers. The soldiers fell to their guns. The loopholes in the log redoubts blazed with their fire. The *Waffen* SS did not waver. There was no hesitation in the step of the heavy dew-wet boots. Nor did they return the Russian fire. They carried sub-machine-guns at the ready, but no man of them pressed a trigger. There were grenades hanging from their belts and poking out of their boot-tops and they remained there. In silence they marched forward. It seemed to some Russian soldiers that the Germans were immune from their fire. But that was largely because many Russian machine-gunners, in their excitement, had omitted to correct the sights of their machine-guns and their bullets were now flying a few centimetres above the heads of the Germans. It was also due to the way the division Viking accepted the fire, closing ranks as men fell, the rearward ranks stepping over the bodies of the fallen, and, even as the first rank melted, those of it who were left falling into the second rank, picking up step and marching forward.

In the Moscow communiqué, a few days later, this was referred to as "a psychological attack." It was a phrase which had appeared a number of times in the communiqués that spring. The psychological attack, the propagandists hinted, was done with drugs and vodka. But the soldiers who faced the attack that early morning on the Donetz knew what it took.

The constantly re-formed first rank of Germans was now halfway from the ridge to the forward redoubts. There had been no discernible diminution in their numbers. The Russian soldiers could now distinguish the faces of their enemy. They could see the dark narrow jaws under the black helmets. Sometimes they could see the gleam of a man's teeth. This was the moment that the Russian soldiers, cooling their redhot machine-guns, remembered to correct the sights, the moment that the mortar crews found their trajectory, the moment that the riflemen reached for new clips, the moment that the news of the attack was telephoned back to division, to corps, to army, to Moscow. But what made this moment critical was the measure being taken by each Russian soldier of the strength of the enemy's determination: there was no man in that tract of marshland who did not, at this moment, understand that, though the distance separating him from the enemy might yet be piled high with dead, the dark mass of the *Waffen* SS would soon be upon him. He was able to measure the fury that would then ensue for, as a soldier, he knew that there is no savagery of mind comparable with that of the soldier who, under pain of his own will, exposes himself to open fire, and no soldiers so calculating and merciless in the satisfaction of that savagery as those who, in the midst of slaughter, have survived such fire. There would be no prisoners.

Like all front-line soldiers the Russians were aware that, in staff estimates, in the event of a large-scale attack, they were a calculated expenditure. In the minds of the Russian soldiers there was, at this moment, a conflict difficult to resolve: whether to face the enemy and die, or whether to flee. It was the moment for the political officers and the commissars to draw their pistols.

As though to assist in the resolution of this conflict in the Russian soldiers the German artillery began. The shells were falling behind the line of redoubts, in the area from which support for the forward positions might conceivably come. But the Russian soldiers, feeling the air-riven detonations close to them, having but recently learned how to endure such shelling, forgot their learning, hugged the wet earth. The machine-gun fire faltered. The mortars ceased. With the commencement of the shelling the forward ranks of the 1st Battalion of the division Viking began loping forward. Suddenly the whole slope was a curtain of soldiers as the *Wehrmacht*, flanked by light tanks, went in behind the SS. A young Russian political officer leaped to the top of a redoubt calling on his men to fight. An old commissar shot two soldiers who were cowering beneath their gun and himself calmly took over the gun. The Russian fire picked up. But the SS was already among them.

The Russian soldiers' estimate of the quality of the fighting in redoubt, sap and trench, among the rush and willows of the marshland, was fully borne out. There were no prisoners. Nor were there any who escaped.

The battle was carried on across the marsh to the river's edge by the *Wehrmacht*. The 1st Battalion of the division Viking re-formed at the first line of redoubts. They could now look back over the grassy meadow over which they had recently marched. The meadow was no longer green, but black with their numbers. The medical corps with jars of plasma moved slowly among the wounded.

It was at this moment that the Commanding Officer received, over his newly-extended communications, a message to the effect that Russian guerillas threatened a village in his immediate rear. For their relaxation, as a kind of reward perhaps, he sent back, to deal with the threat as they felt, the seventeen survivors of the three forward ranks of his battalion.

The peasants who had followed Kharko to the abandoned settlement at the confluence of streams were impressed by the appearance of the Partizan Commander.

He was a man of middle age, thickset, short-necked,

strongly built. He wore a peaked cap from which insignia had been removed leaving a little star of unbleached cloth above the brim. The cloth of the cap was shapeless, sun-bleached, and rested loosely on his head. His face, beneath the brim, might have been, at one time, like that of the men now before him, rounded, heavy, expressionlessly concentrated, but experience had changed that. It was a face not of lard, but of granite. The pig eyes were not eyes that were any longer bemused by events, but saw clearly and could calculate, native cunning had become intelligence, suspicion cynicism, obduracy ruthlessness, sentience insentience. He wore a grey padded jacket like that of a collective farm worker. Strapped around this was a regulation leather belt. A Mauser automatic of the kind that has a wooden holster which can be fitted as a stock was slung from his right shoulder to his left side. A map case on a thin strap hung from his left shoulder to his right buttock. He wore the breeches and the heavy black boots of the Russian infantryman. It was clear that he was a Red Army officer of rank.

The Partizan Commander said that the purpose of the two SS men in the village was to destroy the village and to kill everybody in it as the German Army retreated. By liquidating the SS men the peasants would save their village.

The Kohut, standing beside the Partizan Commander, said that the plan was simple: four men, four men from the village, would be required. That night they would enter the village by stealth. They would break into the cottage occupied by the two SS men and they would kill them. They would be armed with rifles. If the SS men offered resistance they would set fire to the cottage and burn them alive. The village would then wait the coming of the Red Army. If there was trouble with the Germans the whole village would take to the woods, proceeding by various routes to this abandoned settlement.

The men from the village listened in silence. Their faces were set in the heavy expressionless mould of an indigenous suspicion.

"What if the SS should know?" Kharko said.

"They will not know," the Kohut said.

"They will not know unless you tell them," the Partizan Commander said.

Kharko looked at the Partizan Commander. He did not resent the Partizan Commander's remark. He was puzzled only by the certainty of mind, as exhibited by the Kohut and the Partizan Commander, that there would be no betrayal. Such certainty seemed to show inexperience. He could not believe that the Partizan Commander was inexperienced.

The peasants squatted on the ground or leaned against the log walls of the crumbling cabin in attitudes of grave attention. The Captain with the bandaged face and the three soldiers whose place of refuge the settlement had been before the arrival of Kharko sat beyond the circle of the peasants. They also listened. The soldiers had a bottle of vodka which they passed to one another. The peasants did not drink. The afternoon was quiet. The village was many kilometres distant. None there heard the sound of the troop carriers at that moment passing through the village.

The plan of attack which had just been outlined by the Kohut bore heavily on the mind of Kharko. He was searching, though he could not have put it that way, for the imponderables. The sun was warm. A cloud of midges which came out of the forest and descended upon the men in the clearing, causing them to slap frequently at their necks, at the backs of their hands, their foreheads, did not trouble Kharko, so concentrated was his thought. He did not look again at the Partizan Commander, but glanced about him. He looked quickly at the Captain. Above the dirty bandage that was bound flatly across the Captain's face the cold blue eyes, it seemed to Kharko, were full of mockery. Quickly Kharko looked away as one who, not wishing to be implicated in the guilt of another, makes the act of disassociation. Nothing could have been more shifty than his appearance at that moment.

Then Kharko looked away across the clearing to where his son was playing with the little girl called Sophia. Each time he saw Mitya he was pleased. His mind steadied. Now, looking again at the Partizan Commander, he began to say what was in his mind.

"On the highway, six hundred metres to the north of the village," Kharko said, "there is much German matériel hidden. Much."

"Military matériel is a trophy of war," the Partizan Commander said. "Such matériel belongs to those who capture it."

"It will be ours," the Kohut said.

"The matériel is guarded by a number of German soldiers," Kharko said. "They have machine-guns and one heavy machine-gun."

"Well?" said the Partizan Commander.

"If there is the sound of shooting in the village," Kharko said, "the soldiers will come to the aid of their comrades."

"There must be no shooting," the Kohut said. "It must be done by stealth."

"There may be shooting in the village," the Partizan Commander said. "There probably will be shooting."

"Then we will be overwhelmed," Kharko said.

"No," the Partizan Commander said. "Between the village and the soldiers there will be guerillas."

Kharko said nothing more. The aroma of the forest was heavy. All around the clearing the birch trees, their roots watered by the converging streams, their white trunks as thick as a man's waist, rose like a high mysterious stockade. The sound of the river was muted. In the high blue sky there was borne to them the trumpet call of the copper-tongued crane. The children played happily.

"How do we know there will be guerillas?" a peasant asked.

"You will see. Soon they will be here."

"They bring arms," the Kohut said.

"Why do not the guerillas kill the SS men in the village?" the peasant said.

"Fool!" the Kohut said, "Petlurian scum! Bastard of Makhno! Do you not understand that only those who are familiar with the village can undertake this work? Would strangers know which house to attack?"

"True," the peasant said. "I had not thought of that."

"We will take the Kohut with us," Kharko said.

"Certainly," the Partizan Commander said, "we are all guerillas here."

"I am a guerilla," one of the soldiers said.

"Comrade Partizan Commander," a second soldier said. "I ask you a big privilege. Permit me personally to kill the SS."

"Give us guns," the third soldier said. "We are Red Army men."

The first soldier held up the bottle which had contained vodka. He looked at it sadly and then tossed it into the trees. A peasant got up from the group and went to retrieve the bottle. The group broke up.

In the evening the guerillas arrived. They were led by the man called Pilchuk. They resembled Pilchuk, that is they were dressed more like workers than peasants, but they were younger than Pilchuk. Two of them were women, except for short ragged skirts, indistinguishable from the men; the rest were gaunt gamey boys, the youngest of whom was seventeen.

"Komsomols," Kharko said, dispassionately but with distaste. There was nothing in his experience which would have enabled him to see them as pathetic.

They carried rifles, pistols and several sub-machine-guns. They also brought a can of gasolene and a case of prepared demolitions. Under the supervision of the blue-chinned Pilchuk they stacked the weapons and matériel in the disused cabin.

The peasants shared their food with the soldiers and the guerillas wolfed the black bread and the pork fat. During the night the guerillas took turn to stand guard over the cabin. They patrolled the clearing. Each hour they counted heads.

Kharko and the Captain sheltered in the ruin that had been a barn. They lay within hearing of one another. During the night the Captain spoke to Kharko.

"Kharko," the Captain said.

Kharko knew what the Captain wanted to say. Kharko was reluctant to listen to the Captain. His native caution forbade him intimate speech with a stranger, one of another class.

"Kharko!"

"Yes," Kharko said.

"The dump on the highway, of what does it consist?"

"Rubber boats. Pontoons."

Half an hour later the Captain again spoke.

"Then it is not for nothing that we are visited by a high officer of the Red Army."

"So?"

"This Partizan Commander, is he concerned for the liberation of your village?"

"Less than nothing."

"He arranges to divert the enemy?"

"It is possible."

"What will you do?"

"In war all depends upon arms. It is necessary first to obtain arms."

As the night advanced it became cooler. The nuisance of insects diminished. The restlessness of men did not.

"Kharko."

"Yes."

"Do you believe the Red Army will liberate your village?"

"Not tomorrow."

"But some day?"

"It is probable."

"It is a factor to be considered?"

"So."

Those who slept that night were awakened by the sound of artillery. It was barely light. The morning birds had not yet made their first calls. In the moist still air the guns sounded closer than they were. Some men bounded to their feet.

The Partizan Commander was already standing outside the cabin in the attitude of a man who listens for a recognition signal.

The guns were stomping. There were many batteries. The sound was sometimes loud, sometimes faint, but continuous. It was the sound of a barrage.

The Kohut was awake and nervous.

"The Red Army!" he cried. "The Red Army comes!"

The blue-chinned Pilchuk and the Partizan Commander walked away from the guerillas and the soldiers and the peasants. The Partizan Commander took a map from his map case. Together they studied the map. Presently they came back and Pilchuk called out three of the guerillas. Pilchuk spread the map on the ground, kneeling over it. The three guerillas crouched beside him. The Partizan Commander stood above them, granitelike. Then the three guerillas left the clearing.

Presently the arillery ceased, not suddenly, but in a series of separated bursts. The Partizan Commander looked at the large leather-cased watch on his wrist. The barrage had lasted forty minutes.

As soon as the artillery ceased the sun came into the clearing, touching the treetops with gold, and clearing the moist night air. The strong odour of the forest came back. The day was a day like another.

The peasants again shared their food with the guerillas and soldiers. Afterwards the children began to play.

But Sophia soon tired of play. She wanted to sleep.

"Why do you want to sleep?" Mitya said.

"Because."

"Because why?"

"Because I'm sleepy."

"I know that. But why are you sleepy?"

"Because I want to sleep."

"Why do you want to sleep?"

"Oh stop, boy."

"I will tell you why you are sleepy. It is because you were out last night."

Sophia looked at Mitya with large eyes. "How silly you are," she said.

"It is true."

"How would you know? You were sleeping beside your father."

"You were away a long time last night. That is why you are sleepy."

"If I tell you why I want to go to sleep you will tell everybody."

"Tell me."

"You must promise not to tell."

"Yes."

"I am going with the guerillas tonight."

"You cannot. They won't let you."

"I will go by myself. I shall follow them."

"Oh Sophiana, is it true?"

"Yes."

"May I come too?"

"Perhaps. We shall see. But now I want to sleep."

At midday there were others there who found surcease in sleep. The sun was warm and it wrapped the sleepers more closely than a blanket. At midafternoon, however, all were awakened. Two of the guerilla scouts had returned.

What they had to tell Pilchuk and the Partizan Commander was reassuring. Pilchuk called the peasants, soldiers and guerillas together and began distributing arms. Kharko drew a Russian Army rifle of an early make. Though the rifling was pitted with rust he was deeply pleased. There had been a time when he had lived by such a rifle and had learned that it could be relied upon. Pilchuk sought to instruct the peasants in the use of the variously assorted arms, but, like Kharko, few needed instruction, for there was not one among them who had not borne arms, at one time or another, in some cause or other allying itself with the interest which now exercised them.

There were eighteen armed men and two armed women assembled in the clearing. The blue-chinned Pilchuk now stood before them and began addressing them. The address was a paraphrase of that made a few weeks previously by the People's Commissar of Defence. It concerned an order of the day, May 1, 1942, the fifth paragraph of which incited men and women guerillas to intensify partizan warfare in the rear of the German invader, to destroy his communications, transport facilities, headquarters and equipment. "Stint no bullets against the oppressors of our Fatherland," concluded Pilchuk in his practised Party Worker voice. "Under the victorious banner of the great Lenin—forward to Victory!"

"Long live the Red Army and Navy!" cried one of the guerillas.

"Long live the Bolshevik Party which is leading us to Victory!" cried a girl's voice.

"Long live our Glorious Native Land, its Freedom and its Independence!" cried Pilchuk.

These were slogans which had been printed, along with many others, in *Pravda* in connection with the address of the Commissar of Defence.

"Long live Comrade Stalin!" the Kohut said.

The peasants and soldiers heard. Except for one of the soldiers who cheered, and then was immediately taken aback by the sound of his voice, there was no enthusiasm.

The Partizan Commander divided his forces. Kharko and three other peasants from the village comprised one group. The leader of this group was Pilchuk. Taking his group to one side Pilchuk explained that their task was, as outlined the previous day, to infiltrate the village and to kill the two SS men. They would strike at midnight. The other group would deal with the Germans guarding the bridging equipment at the roadside. Kharko noticed that Pilchuk now carried a sub-machine-gun of German make. Kharko drew attention to the fact that he had not been issued ammunition for his rifle. Pilchuk gave him one clip. When he asked Pilchuk for a spare clip Pilchuk said there was no more ammunition. "With five bullets, Comrade, you can kill five Germans." Kharko said nothing. He took the clip and thrust it into the magazine. He worked the bolt of the rifle to bring a cartridge into the breech.

His son Mitya touched his sleeve.

"You go?" Mitya said.

For answer Kharko took his son firmly in his arms and hugged him to his breast. He kissed the boy tenderly on both cheeks and on the mouth.

"Father, may I come also?" Mitya said.

Kharko put his son down and began immediately shouting at him:

"Fool, blockhead, calf," he shouted. "You will stay here."

"Yes, father," Mitya said.

The Partizan Commander waited until dusk for the return of the third scout. When the third scout did not return he ordered the groups to move towards their objectives by different routes at well-spaced intervals.

The scout who had not returned was Fomin Andrenko.

Pilchuk had chosen Fomin to reconnoitre the village because his youth was its own disguise. Without cap, bootless, Fomin had entered the village by way of an old ditch that had, in some forgotten age of landowning visionaries, been part of the waterworks at the village. He had made his way along the ditch and had entered the village unobserved. He had joined a group of children playing in the village square in front of the old meeting house. The children were playing at war. The newly-dug graves made fine trenches.

The barrage had ceased some time before. In the distance there was the sound of lesser gunfire, but this too soon ceased. A dispatch rider on a motorcycle came through the village. Then everything was quiet. The children played in a subdued way and as soon as the SS men appeared they went indoors. Fomin saw the two SS men, the tall one and the old one wearing spectacles, leave the house where they were quartered. He saw the tall one unleash the dogs, saw the dogs bound forward and then come to heel. Fomin watched the SS men and the dogs make the round of the village. They went from cabin to cabin. At each cabin the dogs would pause and then go quickly on to the next cabin. Fomin watched the men turn at the end of the village and casually saunter towards him. Fomin waited for the dogs to take his scent. He saw the old dog stop and point. She lifted her head and bayed softly. Then with her nose skating the ground she came straight to him until her old eyes were suddenly on him. Less than a metre from him she stood tense, her flanks quivering. Fomin did not move. He did not take his eyes off the bitch.

"I do not remember that one," Scharführer Schewe said.

"A beggar," Müller said. "That bony face."

"A village idiot," Schewe said. "Otherwise he would run. Look how he stares at the bitch."

"He has no boots. In Russia they say that a child without boots is a child close to God."

"Yes, you believe in God?"

"It is a proverb."

"Come, there may be news of the attack."

Schewe called to the bitch and she came to heel. The two walked the thirty yards to the house across the square where they were quartered. Schewe put the dogs back on leash.

Fomin had not moved. He was looking at the dogs tethered to their black-white-and-red striped kennel outside the house. The dogs were something he had not calculated upon. Neither Pilchuk not the Partizan Commander knew of the dogs.

About midday a convoy of ambulances passed through Podvorki coming from the direction of the front. They moved slowly breathing the heavy breath of chloroform. A little later a procession of staff cars led by a light armoured vehicle drove through the village towards the front. The generals who sat in open cars wore dust visors over their eyes. They bent stiffly over maps laid out on a table fitted between the front and rear seats of the car. Among the officers Fomin recognised the man in the Homburg hat, now, however, wearing a *Wehrmacht* cap and uniform without markings of rank. After that, for a long time, there was no activity. The children came out and resumed their playing. The quiet of late afternoon fell upon the village.

About five o'clock in a fury of dust, a troop carrier from the front arrived in Podvorki. Even as the brakes squealed there were dark-uniformed men leaping from the vehicle with lithe weapons in their hands. Within the space of a few moments they had effectively encircled the village. At one moment all was quiet and the next moment there were light machine-guns at each tactical corner of the village. Fomin saw one machine-gun set up to enfilade the ditch by which he had entered the village and by which, in six or eight hours, a party of guerillas or peasants would follow him. Fomin saw that there was no longer any possibility of leaving the village to warn the Partizan Commander.

Fomin did not move from his position by the newly-dug graves in the village square. He saw the tall SS Scharführer welcome the commanding officer of the newly-arrived detachment of SS men and humorously congratulate the officer upon the dispatch with which the operation had been performed. Fomin saw this in their actions. Then he saw the two SS officers walk towards him. He slipped gently down into one of the graves and lay flat against the earthy bottom. The sensation was stupendous.

The graves dug in the village square by Scharführer Schewe's orderly were, like those thousands of others in Ukrainian villages, about a metre in depth, except this one grave which the old orderly, under the stimulus of the second (and last) shell to fall in the vicinity of Podvorki, had dug into a deep fox-hole. Dropping suddenly to the bottom of this hole and lying there was like falling through the earth. The village of Podvorki, the day, the hour, vanished. There was such silence that Fomin could hear the beating of his heart, and nothing more. A runnel of earth pouring into the hole from the side of his entry was like a landslide upon him. The rectangle of sky which hung above was as unreal as a mirror. It was like looking into a pool of still water and seeing the sky and the clouds reflected there. He waited, expecting to see the upside-down head, like the reflection of his own head, float in from the edge of the pool, and then to see the pistol, foreshortened, remote, and not even to hear its report, but to be already dead, and so conveniently that they would have only to kick the earth in upon him. The thought was comical, the sensation unbearable.

He drew his own pistol and crouched below the level of the grave. And then, as he peered over the edge, the world swung back on its normal orbit. The two SS officers had passed the square. They were thrusting open the door of the meeting house. The sound of their voices diminished suddenly as they went inside. They came out again and Fomin saw them go back to the quarters of the tall SS man in the house on the opposite side of the square. The tall SS man unleashed his dogs; then they went from cabin to cabin bringing the peasants out of their cabins into the roadway. The first SS man was already driving the peasants before him, directing them around the square to the meeting house, and into the building. Fomin lowered his head. He heard the peasants talking among themselves. He heard women calling to the children. The voices came loudly across the square and then dropped as the peasants entered the meeting house. Each cabin in the village was aroused, the doors flung open, the inhabitants driven out and escorted to the meeting house. The doors of the meeting house were then slammed shut. Guards stood outside the doors.

Fomin understood that the SS men had been warned of the impending attack of the guerillas. He understood that the SS suspected the peasants of co-operating with the guerillas. The SS was taking precautions to see that no one in the village warned the guerillas that a trap had been set. That was why they had come so swiftly.

Listening, his head just below the level of the ground, Fomin followed in his mind the movements in the village.

He could hear the thick young German voices. He could hear the heavy iron-shod boots. There was the sound of splintering wood. Suddenly there was a short burst of a machine-pistol, muffled, reverberant. The SS was looting the village, forcing doors, tearing up floorboards. They knew that in the dry earth under the wooden floors of their cabins the peasants hid what was most precious to them: bags of wholewheat flour, sunflower seeds, pork fat, honey in wax, cutlery, harness, boots, vodka. It would be the vodka that the SS sought, the grey wheat vodka sealed down in thick glass bottles. Already Fomin heard shouts and singing. In the same moment he considered whether they would leave the food. Now there came to him on the evening air the smell of cooking, the smell of white bread and sausage, of frying fat and tea and sweet canned milk. The smell made him light in the head.

Slowly Fomin sank into the grave. This time the shutting-off of the world was welcome, though, on account of his strained hearing, not so complete as before. The sky, that water-mirror above him, was already darkening in tones of deepening violet. Above, in the village the long twilight of the steppe lingered, but soon night would provide cover enough for him to crawl under the German machine-guns. Then, as Fomin thought of his escape, he thought of Pilchuk.

How would Pilchuk accept the news he would bring? Would he be waiting in the abandoned settlement? What if the guerillas were no longer there? What if he should fail to reach them, fail to escape?

The night air was so still and so clear that even at the bottom of his hole Fomin could hear sounds in the village. From the meeting house there was nothing. The peasants, peasantlike, were already asleep. But he could hear other sounds. There was laughter, faint, recognisable. There was another burst from a machine-pistol, as the SS, drilling through the floorboards with gunfire, went on looting. The looting was leisurely. They too, then, knew that the guerillas had planned to attack after the midnight hour and before dawn. Clearly they had means of detecting any movement other than their own in or near the village.

Lying on his back in the cool earth Fomin looked up at the sky. The sky was a rectangle of faintly-luminous dark pricked with stars. Fomin counted the stars over and over, but the count was never the same. He was happy counting the stars. The stars were pretty and wonderfully dissimulating. There was one star which shone boldly and there were other stars which were there and then, no matter how hard you looked, were not there. All the time the pattern of the stars was changing. The bold star had been at the bottom of the rectangle and it had gradually moved until it was now at the top of the rectangle immediately over his head. Fomin was not sure whether this meant that he was lying east to west, the way the Tartars buried their dead, or north to south. He could find out. For Fomin there was no mystery about the stars. His world was superbly finite.

Every so often as he filled in the hours he would finger the grip of the heavy German automatic pistol at his side. It was not the lethal power of the weapon which made Fomin feel that the world was firm and his place in it secure. Indeed there was doubt about the weapon's effectiveness. It was a service pistol of the former war, made, according to its maker's stamp, in 1915. The cartridge chamber in the pistol grip was filled from the top through the breech. There was no way of unloading except by breaking the weapon down and no way of calculating the number of rounds unfired. Pilchuk, explaining this to Fomin, had said that there was a cartridge in the breech, at least one or two in the chamber. He had told Fomin to aim the pistol below the target because the pistol was dirty and would probably kick and fire high. That the pistol might be defective did not matter to Fomin. It did not matter that it was his first gun and therefore an object of curiosity and pride. What mattered to Fomin was that the pistol was a symbol of confidence. It was recognition. It was responsibility. Passing it to him Pilchuk had smiled and Fomin had smiled back, his rare smile. He had felt a way he had never felt before. He felt it as liking for this dark-jawed man with the large liquid brown eyes and curling eyelashes. But it was more than liking; it was stronger and less personal. It was induction into a vast comradeship of Pilchuks. It was becoming part of something that was bigger and broader than oneself and incomparably more sure. It was acquiring and sharing purpose in life. It was being drawn into the current of history. At this time, in this temporary confusion, the gun was as good as a Party card.

He began to think of food. Out of his storehouse of images he saw a great banquet table, its spotless napery laden with delicacies from all the corners of Asia, little fish in aspic jelly, cheese shaped like buttons, forcemeat like flowers, all the different kinds of caviar, and cold eggs sliced and laid like fields of buttercups, and the huge dishes of salmon, all pink and silver, lying in gardens of radishes and lemon wafers, and the red bortsch smelling faintly of fennel and sour cream, and the rich baked sturgeon, and the great roasted goose, and the exotic fruit, the yellow apricots and the golden tangerines and the blue grapes. Against this background he saw himself: the hard-hard muscles within the soft black jacket and breeches and the soft leather boots, the impregnable shoulder unyielding among the guests who, brushing its steel, step aside bowing in their corruptible softness, and the austerity within the hard-hard frame burning like a flame, clear, unwavering, intense; going through the great halls of columns, and the tall buildings and the great squares, standing in the boxes of the vast gilded theatres, the amphitheatres, the immense chimneyed industrial plants, the endless factories, carrying its light in the calm, undaunted, never-to-be-clouded directness of the straight staring eyes, before which the weak lowered their own eyes but which those like himself, like Pilchuk, met evenly, impersonally, but in a bond stronger than life: all this is ours, *mine!*

The hours passed. The hunger tore at his belly. Then, at last, he heard the sound he had been waiting for: the soft baying of bloodhounds.

Fomin climbed out of his grave. The village was quiet. In some cottages there was the subdued sound of men gathered drinking. An edge of light shone in some windows. The old bloodhound bayed again, not harshly, or long, as in pursuit, but restlessly. Fomin walked slowly towards the house of the SS men, the cool dust soft between his toes, the old German pistol heavy in his hand.

The dogs saw him coming. The old bitch waited for him, having known of him all that day, having understood from the first his thought and his intention. At the moment he came within the length of her tether she made a short running leap at him, so calculated that the leash, jerking tight, with her whole weight behind it, would drag the heavy kennel those few extra centimetres needed to get her old fangs, now dry-white with her hot breath, into his throat. But Fomin stepped back. And then, at the moment the leash brought her crowding to the ground, he shot her.

Fomin was not conscious of hearing the pistol shot, the shattering explosion entered his body through his arm, paralysis for every nerve and muscle below the shoulder. But the old bitch was dead. Slowly her body unsealed itself, as, lying on her side, her skull smashed in, she went through the action of leaping as in slow motion. With his left hand Fomin took the pistol out of his numb right hand. The pup, bouncing on his shorter leash, falling over it, was harder to hit, took the second bullet, yelped, lay still.

Fomin stood back looking at the dogs, waiting, unable to move, his legs suddenly ungovernable, his strength sapped out of him.

The door of the house was flung open and the two SS men were standing there looking directly at him. Fomin realised that coming out of the lighted room into the night they could not see him.

"Licht!" shouted the tall SS man.

The spectacled SS man brought an oil lamp from the house, a yellow orb in the blue-glass night. Together they bent over the dogs. The tall SS man took up the dead bitch like a child in his arms. Fomin could see her tongue licking out between her staining teeth onto her master's cheek. He laid her down gently and then, drawing his pistol, he put it to the ear of her whimpering pup. The concussion put out the flame of the oil lamp.

Both SS men suddenly faced about, stood standing,

looking directly at Fomin, the one with his pistol still in his hand, which if it had been fired would have killed Fomin where he stood, the other shrinking back. For Fomin it was an amazing experience. Whereas he could see them distinctly, more distinctly than if there had been a moon, for there were no shadows in his star-conditioned night vision, they were like blind men. Their feet felt for the touch of earth and their heads were in that position of straining for the supersense of the blind. And Fomin stood there within spitting distance of them. The sensation of being invisible was also the sensation of being invulnerable.

The tall man began shouting.

"Alles raus! Mörder unter uns! Müller! Wachen auffstellen. Niemand darf das Dorf verlassen. Jedes Haus durchsuchen! Feldwebel, die Gräber nicht vergessen, alles anleuchten."

The foreign language was incomprehensible to Fomin. But in his new strange sense of immunity he took no notice of it. The SS men were running past him, no more than a few metres distant. He did not move. His mind and his sense, his whole being, were invaded by a more pressing urgency.

The open doorway of the house breathed warmly on him, breathed the odour of rich, rare food. Without further thought he walked to the door of the house and went inside. Stepping barefoot, silent, light as a cat, he turned left inside the door, went straight to the small kitchen, to the food.

Outside there was shouting and in the distance the sound of machine-gun fire, but Fomin, wolfing the food, felt happy, weak, sinking. He knew that the one house the SS men would not search was their own. Secure in that knowledge he fell asleep.

The four peasants crouched in the ditch which led across the field to the village. Behind the peasants was the

Activist Pilchuk. The peasants stopped in their tracks. They did not move.

"Go on," Pilchuk aid.

"You heard?" Kharko said.

"Go on."

"No."

"Go on!" Pilchuk said.

Pilchuk thrust the muzzle of his sub-machine-gun into Kharko's back.

"No," Kharko said.

"I shall shoot."

"Not here," Kharko said.

"Go on or I shall shoot."

"It would be a waste of ammunition. Listen!"

There was the sound of a pistol shot in the village.

"That is the third shot," Kharko said.

The four peasants and the *Activist* crouched in the ditch listening.

"The third shot was made by a pistol of a different calibre," Kharko said.

"There is trouble in the village," one of the peasants said.

"We will go and see the trouble," Pilchuk said.

"No, we will wait," the peasant said.

"Let us go," Pilchuk said.

"The Communists will lead the way," Kharko said.

"Think of your wives and children," Pilchuk said.

The peasants said nothing. There was shouting in the village. The men listened.

"Germans," one of the peasants said.

"The village is full of Germans," Kharko said.

Looking towards the village they could see points of light made by flashlights.

"It is a trap," one of the peasants said.

"The trap is sprung."

"Who made the trap?" Kharko said.

"Yes," one of the peasants said, "who has been leading us into a trap?"

"Leading us from behind," Kharko said.

"Quiet!" Pilchuk said.

The road through Podvorki entered a small wood about six hundred metres north of the village. Here under cover of the trees the Germans had stacked a large quantity of equipment required for bridging the Donetz River. The area surrounding the dump was heavily mined and trapped. A score of soldiers guarded the dump.

The course favoured by the Partizan Commander was a direct frontal attack down the road from the north. It had been Pilchuk's idea that they should attempt to divert a portion of the German guard by simulating a revolt in the village to the south of the dump. He had planned to enter the village with his four peasants, noisily attack the SS post, set fire to a cottage, and perform any other action calculated to draw the attention of the Germans while the guerillas were creeping towards the dump. His plan had not been greatly esteemed by the Partizan Commander.

Now, his attempt to enter the village frustrated, Pilchuk waited for the attack of the guerillas on the dump to the north.

It came in the shape of a tiny brilliant comet. At the end of its arc, above the dark line of the treetops, the flare broke silently and hung in the sky. Pilchuk saw from the trajectory of the arc that the flare had been fired in the direction away from the village and must be gently and brilliantly poised above the road and the woods where the guerillas were waiting. Even at this distance the flare shed such brilliance that its light fully illuminated one side of the ditch and shone moonishly over the village.

By its light each of the men crouching motionlessly in the ditch could see the machine-gun mounted at the village end of the ditch so that it could enfilade the entire course of the ditch.

As he lay flat and motionless against the earth Pilchuk could hear the separated bursts of a Spandau gun being fired at a target. There was also small arms fire. And there were muffled rifle shots followed by the short splintering detonation of rifle grenades. Then Pilchuk knew that the guerillas had been taken by surprise before they could close with the guards at the dump. They were pinned down on the edges of the roadway and in the woods.

The flare, soft and blooming, dropped slowly below the level of the treetops. The light faded.

The five men crouching in the ditch rose to their feet

and ran back to the shelter of the trees in the field's edge.

"Let us wait here," one of the peasants said.

"Let us go back," Pilchuk said.

"No, we will wait," the peasant said.

"It is too late," Pilchuk said.

"Why should we go?" the peasant said.

"Let the Comrade Communist go by himself."

"What are you thinking of!" Pilchuk said.

"We were thinking of our wives and families," the peasant said.

The passivity of the peasants fused a slow-raging anger in Pilchuk. It was not new to him. This blue-chinned mobile-lipped man with the large imaginative eyes and audacious bearing was from Odessa. He had a long acquaintance with the Ukraine. He was not deceived by the heavy cloddishness of mind, the obtuseness, the stupidity; he knew it for a cunning and long-lived resistance. The sullen non-recognition, that was not yet refusal but also not acceptance, of the reality that was the Party, that had been the Party for a quarter of a century, for the lifetime of most of them, was irrational and self-destructive, but it was so. It was the root of all trouble. In the mind of Pilchuk it was a canker of frustration. For, beneath the passive stupidity, there was betrayal. Always there was betrayal. In little things, in the breaking of a tractor crankshaft, in neglect of the land, in the tacit rejection of an agronomist's directions, in the failure of a threshing. In all this there was betrayal. And always impossible to isolate. Just as now his mind searched for the betrayer of the guerillas and could not find him. Among that inert mass whose was the responsibility? Who had betrayed them? Whoever was the betrayer in person, the betrayal in fact was the passivity of these peasants, of all the peasants. For how could the enemy succeed without their neutrality? Even when one calculated for betrayal there was counter-betrayal. Which of these men, if not the betrayer, knew how the guerillas had been betrayed?

In his long experience Pilchuk had learned that there were no measures that could extract that information out of the self-confused illogic and negation of their minds, nor was there any punishment that would be corrective. With the defeat and possible annihilation, the certain pursuit and dispersal of his preciously-garnered band of patriots at hand, Pilchuk sought about him in that one moment for an object upon which to wreak his fury.

The light, rosy, orange-hued, woke Fomin. He awoke with the fatigue still upon him. He felt that he could not have been asleep for more than a fleeting moment. The events that had brought him to this place were fresh in his mind, as of this night.

He remembered the half-seeing, catlike reaching for the bread and sausage, the ravening for it, the thrusting of the food into his mouth, and then, as the food appeased, the flow of saliva, the too-soon sense of fulness, accomplishment, and the not-caring and the sinking slowly to the floor, so into sleep. Here was the crust of bread still in his hand. He began eating again, steadily, fast, all the time looking at the light creeping through the windowpane, along the window's edge, the wall beyond, into the cube of this kitchen in which he lay slumped like an earth-dusted sack of grain.

Lying there he heard children talking.

"Why do we stay here?" the boy said.

"Because he told us to stay here," the girl said.

"But he is a German."

"He is a Communist too."

"He is an SS," the boy said.

"I know what he is," the girl said.

The voices came from the larger room occupied by Schewe and Müller through which Fomin had passed into the kitchen. The voices were clear, but subdued. A burst of machine-pistol fire somewhere outside the house drowned the voices for a moment.

"Why are they shooting?"

"They are shooting at the doors and windows."

"Where is everybody?"

"In there. In the old meeting house."

"It must be very hot in there."

"They will all be burned alive."

"Why?"

"Because the people in this village went with the Communists."

For some moments there was silence in the room. Outside flames crackled and timbers fell. Then the girl spoke:

"I wish Lydia Artemova was in there," the girl said.

"Who is Lydia Artemova?" the boy asked.

"She has been coming to our school and talking to the *Deda.*"

"Is she a Communist too?"

"I denounced her, but she got away. The *Deda* made me promise not to do it again."

"What is your *Deda* like?"

"He is not really my *Deda,* but he is the only one left to love."

"I don't want to see the fire any more. I want to go to my father."

"Be quiet! The fire is beautiful."

But Fomin was no longer listening. He too was looking at marble-veined flames curling upwards from the gasolene-sprayed walls of the old meeting house. Faintly, through the window he could hear the old wood combusting under heat. Around the meeting house there was a widely-spaced ring of SS men. Against the glare the squat-helmeted, high-waisted, heavy-booted shapes looked like little figures of black metal. Occasionally one would fire a burst into the crumbling building, directing his weapon at a fissure in the lower walls. But now the flames, leaping through the old onion-shaped dome of clapboards, reached the pinnacle of their height. The ring of SS men was backing slowly away from the heat. Patently life was no longer existent in the old meeting house.

The walls had collapsed and the building had been reduced to a few blazing embers when Fomin withdrew his gaze. The children had gone. Inside the small kitchen he could see nothing. He had lost his rare star-conditioned vision. Fomin went quickly out of the house into the acrid night.

When the Partizan Commander heard the three pistol shots, the two made by the old Parabellum and the one by the Luger, he knew that Pilchuk's plan had miscarried. It was not more than he had expected. The Partizan Commander, a veteran of many wars, was himself a Ukrainian and, despite a recent education at the Academy Freunze, still mostly peasant. He knew that the purpose of the peasants who had elected to go with Pilchuk was not to help simulate a revolt in the village, but to prevent any such action. He said nothing about this to Pilchuk. The Partizan Commander did not tender advice. The involvement of the village, every village, in the activities of the guerillas was a Party decision: Party decisions were final, irrevocable, right. The means of involvement was Pilchuk's responsibility. To have made a recommendation, a suggestion, would have been to infringe that responsibility. It was something the Partizan Commander had not even considered. His orders were to attack this night and he was so resolved.

The same native intuition which had made the Partizan Commander privy to peasant motives also made him sure that the plan of attack would be known to the enemy. His mind did not encompass the means by which the enemy might have secured that knowledge; he simply took it privately into account; he built on it. Like many experienced field commanders he placed no reliance upon plans which depended for their success on the element of primary surprise. He preferred the enemy to be aware of his general, and even his particular, intentions, so that he might calculate the enemy's reaction, and so redress his own movements. Having been informed, by a source the enemy believed to be reliable, that the guerillas would make a frontal attack down the narrow road the enemy might be so confident of repelling this attack, and so concentrated upon it, that he would neglect his flanks. The sound of the pistol shots in the village was, therefore, a confirmation of his judgment: they had been betrayed, the enemy was prepared. (The sound of the dog yelping, which he had heard between shots, also conveyed its message and, without thinking of it, since it had no bearing on the decision he was reviewing at this moment, the answer was given somewhere in the back of his mind to the question mark left by the boy who had been sent to reconnoitre the village and who had not returned; and at an even less conscious level, since the decision having been reviewed must be made, there was raised another question mark: police dogs?) The decision he made, immediately upon hearing the pistol shots, was to signal his guerillas to proceed down the road towards the enemy strong points. Their orders were continuously to engage the enemy fire at any cost to themselves.

Four hours later, stepping into the abandoned clearing in the first light of day, the Partizan Commander could count that cost. Of his party of sixteen five were left. It was not too much, since the objective had been partially attained. He regretted most, if he could be said to regret anything, the loss of his women guerillas, especially the big one who had smiled at him. He had chosen the two women for the task of passing through the minefield and booby traps around the dump and of setting up the demolitions and incendiaries. He had chosen the women for this work because experience had taught him that young women are more resolute than young men in the carrying out of singular operations in the face of almost certain death. He had sent them in from the flanks, barefooted, armed with long three-edged Russian bayonets with which to probe for mines, the demolitions and incendiaries strapped to their backs. He had sent them off after a brief lesson in what to look for and what to avoid, particularly how to deal with the trip wires attached to grenades hanging from trees. He had been surprised to find how quickly they absorbed this information. They were intelligent young women, Komsomolkas, probably already with seven years of education. He had told them to move slowly and with the utmost caution.

Lying on his belly in the woods behind the guerillas, the tracers lying like a quilt of fire over the roadway, the flares making the whole area more brilliant than daylight, the high shocking sound of the Spandau gun dominating the rifle and sub-machine-gun fire, the white bursts of the rifle grenades and the swiftly-diminished screaming of the young mortally-hit guerilla, all this (while he was at the same time calculating in minutes how long it would last) was subordinated in his mind to the tense attunement to the expected earth-conducted feel, rather than sound, of an exploding Teller mine. He did not feel such an explosion and (while his mind registered at some preconscious stage which he would later turn up, like a card in an index, the suspicion that in these rearward areas the Germans planted more *"Minen"* notices than mines) he now waited for the firing of the incendiaries. It came finally, not vast, but substantial, so that the shooting over the roadway immediately slackened and the moment for the withdrawal was provided.

The young women had reached their objective. They were intelligent young women, Komsomolkas, patriots. He presumed they were now both dead, because, if they had not been detected and immediately killed by the Germans, he did not think they would allow themselves to fall alive into Fascist hands.

In the clearing in the forest at the confluence of streams there was already the Partizan Commander and his five guerillas. There was Pilchuk and the four peasants, the one they called the Kohut, and the Captain with the bandaged face. Fomin watched them.

The men were eating bread. They ate silently, slowly, each man still living between the walls of his own experience. Measurelessly fatigued, they had yet the need to uncoil the wounded senses before sleep. There was no vodka.

"All the time the SS was there," a peasant said. He made the remark idly, as to himself, to appease his wonder.

"Yes," Pilchuk said.

"Before there were only two SS," another peasant said.

"The two we were going to kill," Kharko said.

"There must have been a hundred of them," the first peasant said.

"We were betrayed," the second peasant said.

"Yes, we were betrayed," Pilchuk said.

The men continued eating. The remarks did not impinge on the separate isolation of each.

"There is an informer among us," Pilchuk said.

"Who would inform on himself?" a peasant said.

"Whoever informed is not with us," Kharko said.

"Who is not with us?"

"In the roadway and in the woods lie eleven who are not with us," the guerilla said. "You could ask them."

The guerillas were thinking of the power of the enemy's fire. The peasants were thinking of the fire in the village. Pilchuk was thinking of the betrayer. The Partizan Commander was thinking of the food in his hand and how soon they could leave and how far they could travel that day.

"In the meeting house was my wife," one of the peasants said.

"In the meeting house were my children," another said.

"It was terrible to watch."

"If you had attacked the village, the meeting house would not have burned," Pilchuk said.

"The meeting house was burned because we attacked," Kharko said.

"Yes," Pilchuk said, "you know that?"

"Yes," Kharko said.

"How do you know this?"

"It was clear."

"Clear to you, yes?"

"From the first."

The peasants and the guerillas looked at Kharko. It was the first pointedly-focussed gaze they had brought themselves to make since they had come back to the clearing. Kharko looked quickly at them, one to the other, his bad eye shifting.

Suddenly Pilchuk went over to Kharko and took the rifle from his side. Kharko did not protest the disarming.

Now the Kohut spoke.

"The anti-Soviet elements are known," he said.

"Who fired the shots in the village?" Kharko said.

"Yes," one of the peasants said, "who fired the shots?"

"If there had not been shots we would have walked into the trap," Kharko said.

"Someone was killed then."

"A dog was killed," the Partizan Commander said.

"A dog?" Kharko said. "Well."

The peasants and the guerillas wondered about the Partizan Commander's remark without coming to any conclusion about it.

"I killed the dogs," Fomin said. He had come silently on his bare feet out of the forest. None except the Partizan Commander took note of him.

"It was better," the Partizan Commander said.

The Partizan Commander looked at Fomin with a certain kind of appraisal in his eyes which made Fomin more proud than he had been in his life before. By this one remark the Partizan Commander had shown that he understood precisely the decision Fomin had made. "It was better to kill the dogs than to kill the men," the Partizan Commander might have said, but he had not needed to say more than he did to make Fomin feel that he was now within the select order of partizan comrades and that his future was assured, so long as he lived.

"Are there more dogs?"

"No."

The men sat quietly eating the bread.

"Is there anyone left in the village?" one of the peasants asked.

"None," Fomin said.

The peasant began to weep. He wept without shame. The tears flowed down his face. He made no effort to brush them aside. One of the guerillas got up and struck the peasant heavily across the face. The peasant fell to the ground and lay with his face to the ground.

"All this is interesting," Pilchuk said, "but who betrayed us?" The last words were said with heat. Several men looked up.

"Who was opposed to the plan?" the Kohut said.

"Yes," Pilchuk said. "Who?"

"Opposition is betrayal," the Kohut said.

"No," Kharko said.

"The anti-Soviet elements and the Fascists, they are the same," the Kohut said. "They collaborate."

"No," Kharko said.

"In the cabin I remember you," Pilchuk said.

"I was against the plan then," Kharko said, "because I knew what would happen."

"So," Pilchuk said, "you knew what would happen."

"It was clear."

"You were opposed to us, but you went with us in order to betray us."

"No," Kharko said.

"It is as I told you," the Kohut said.

"The action was provocative," Kharko said.

"His language is the language of a spy," the Kohut said.

"It was a successful action," Kharko said. "There need be no further fear that the peasants of Podvorki will collaborate."

"What does he say?"

"The Party cannot be displeased," Kharko said.

The control that had governed Pilchuk's fury broke. He leaped to his feet, his large eyes wide open, his breath broadening his nostrils, his dark chin outthrust. All the men in the clearing were also on their feet, standing in a circle around Kharko, their eyes on him, stepping closer towards him. Pilchuk picked up his sub-machine-gun. But the Partizan Commander was quicker.

"No," he said. He laid a large hand on the gun. "Do you want to bring the SS here?"

"Let me kill the dirty son-of-a-bitch of a counter-revolutionary Fascist," Pilchuk said.

"Yes, kill him," a guerilla said.

"Kill him!"

"Why not," said the Partizan Commander, "but no shooting. There are enough of you. Make him a pair of wooden horses."

One of the guerillas laughed. The men turned away from Kharko. The tension was ended, the spring was uncoiling.

"I did not betray you," Kharko said.

"Then who did?" Pilchuk said.

Fomin said: "Where is the little girl?"

Pilchuk swung round to look at Fomin. In his eyes there was the small light dawning into certainty.

"Yes," he said, "where is the little girl?"

The question was one which had occupied Kharko ever since he had returned to the clearing but had feared to ask for thinking of his son.

"There is no time for this," the Partizan Commander said. "Let us go! Let us go!"

The guerillas took the rifles of the peasants.

"Stay with us, Kohut," Kharko said.

"No."

"You will come back to us?"

"No. I am finished with this place."

"They have made you a Party member, yes?"

"Yes," the Kohut said. He looked around to see if there was anyone within hearing. "I am a member of the Party," he lied.

"Good health," Kharko said, making his mouth grin.

The guerillas filed out of the clearing, eight men in single file, in ragged clothes, one of them, a youth with agate eyes, barefoot. They walked slowly, carrying a varied assortment of weapons. Behind them they left in the clearing at the confluence of streams a sick soldier and the four surviving inhabitants of the village of Podvorki.

"A wooden horse," said the Captain with the bandaged face. "It is something I have not heard since I was a child."

"Mitya," Kharko said. "How I shall thrash that boy!"

In his firm neat hand Dr. Karandash made the following entry in his notebook: "We are in the presence of a great victory: the Russian front has crumbled for a distance of 500 kilometres; Von Kleist's armour is galloping down the corridor between the Don and Donetz rivers; Von Hoth is driving due east; Von Paulus stands before Voronesh. In a matter of weeks the *Wehrmacht* will be on the Volga and in the Caucasus. Nevertheless in the first day of the attack there was already the element of a vast defeat. I make this observation: the first aim of a soldier must be to survive; an army is lost when its soldiers are together careless of their lives, for then they are seeking death. The first sign of a soldier seeking death occurs when his will to overwhelm the enemy becomes the desire to *exterminate*.The passion for extermination manifests itself when the soldiers, against all the evidence, in the face of victories, know in their hearts they are lost; themselves lost, as their cause is lost; for the desire to exterminate is but the effort physically to bring about at once what cannot happen: the ending. The truth about war is that it is never quite Homeric; that humanity survives. Though the villages are empty, and many dead are to be counted in the ruins, there is life in the country. In the deep forests of conifer and birch which stretch down from Briansk to the north of Kharkiv there are gathering small bands of men and women, and sometimes children. They will live, as perforce they must, as marauders, by banditry and ambuscade. I commend the wise general to study this material."

It was a sick and savage old head that Dr. Karandash raised above his insignialess *feldgrau* uniform; but in the eyes there was a stubborn, if tired, satisfaction. The notes were written in Russian.

In the huge area of conquest the German forces were indeed spread thin. Patrolling was done at section, or platoon, strength; a solitary man in German uniform was more than likely to be waylaid and done to death. There was an advantage in taking such a man because he bore arms, but there was, it must be said, often a ritualistic satisfaction in his death.

Thus it was that an SS man fell into the hands of a small group of exappropriated peasants and a wounded soldier in the forest to the north of Kharkiv that summer while the *Wehrmacht* was crossing the Don. The peasants had bound the SS man and left him with the soldier while they set about roping the top of a tall birch tree. The four peasants drew on the rope until the top of the tall tree touched the ground, securing it there, lopping its branches and feathered top until it lay fully revealed, a taut and powerful arc, the white bark gleaming like steel.

For an SS man the appearance of the prisoner was disappointing. He was not young. He was neither fair-haired, blue-eyed, nor arrogant. He appeared to be middle aged. His face was thin and deeply lined as through hardship. He wore spectacles. His bearing was that of a man whose spirit has waned.

He spoke fluent, heavily accented Russian.

"How is it you speak the Russian?" the Captain said.

"It is taught in the Army schools," the prisoner said.

"You lie. You learned it in Moscow. Yes?"

"It is true. Why should I deny it?"

"When were you in Moscow?"

"Why do you not kill me now?" the prisoner said.

"You have the Muscovite way of speaking," the Captain said.

"You also were in Moscow?" the prisoner said.

"It is not inconceivable."

"We were possibly there at the same time," the prisoner said. "I can tell by your teeth."

"Many in Russia have steel teeth."

"In the great purge of 1937 the fists and boots, yes, and the Bazum bottles, of the NKVD fell heavily on the mouths of the Party members that they might more readily confess their crimes. The Soviet dentists were never so busy."

"So, you were in Moscow in 1937," the Captain said.

"I do not deny it. At that time I was a Communist."

"So," the Captain said, "you understand 1937."

"Yes."

"For us who lived through those years the SS is nothing new. Yet you are in the SS."

"I was drafted out of the *Gulag* into the SS."

"You lie," the Captain said. "You went into the SS because there was satisfaction in it for you."

"Why do you not kill me now?"

"In the end," the Captain said, "it is the private mystical satisfactions which count."

"In the end nothing counts," the prisoner said.

"That also is true," the Captain said. "But it is irrelevant. I am surprised that a former Communist should mention it."

"I meant," the prisoner said, "that in the end one's personal needs and vanities do not count."

"I see that you are religious."

"Now you should shoot me," the prisoner said.

The Captain turned away. Through the doorway of the hut there was a view of the clearing. The sun was shining on the abandoned settlement at the confluence of streams. A flock of yellow-breasted birds descended and then rose again in hasty flight. The Captain and the prisoner could see Kharko and the three other peasants working among the birch. They were hauling on a second tree, some thirty metres from the other, which they anchored so that its lopped top, when bent, touched the top of the other tree. Together the two trees were like shining curved sabres with points lowered and touching.

"They call them wooden horses," the Captain said. "It is a *Kazak* custom."

"For the young this is a tragic time," the prisoner said.

The prisoner was looking at the two children, the small girl and the small boy, who were chasing a butterfly in the shade of the woods.

"The little girl has been with us before," the Captain said.

"I brought her here a month ago," the prisoner said.

The Captain showed his steel teeth. The prisoner realised that he had not seen the Captain, only his mask. There were the fine blue eyes, there was the dirty bandage lying flatly across the face, below the bandage there was this mouth full of steel teeth, around the mouth this straggling beard. The prisoner was looking at the Captain and, except for the eyes, there was no face. And the eyes were cold, chilling eyes.

"You seek revenge?" the prisoner asked.

"No. I seek only freedom. Absolute freedom."

"I understand. What freedom is more absolute than the freedom to kill?"

"So."

"To savour absolute freedom is to indulge the keenest pleasure of which the human soul is capable."

"You know this too?"

"The pleasure is keenest when it is at the command of

Will. Therefore, it is not in battle or struggle that absolute freedom is to be found, or in any situation in which Will may be crossed, or the objective risked, but when it is upon *you* to act or not to act. It is in the killing of the weak and the defenceless that absolute freedom is most keenly enjoyed."

"Before sacrifice, immolation."

"It is when the restrictions of civilisation seem most to bear upon man, frustrate him, cage him, that man dreams most of absolute freedom."

"It is the secret dream of modern man."

"In the modern State the organisations of political supervision, the SS and the NKVD, provide man with the opportunity, within the rules of society, to experience the pleasures of absolute freedom."

"The surrogates offered by bourgeois society finally do not satisfy."

"Thus, there are some who seek the modern State for the pleasures of absolute freedom hidden within it."

"It is interesting that we should be so much in agreement," the Captain said. "It is interesting because you have clearly quite deliberately put yourself in the position of one who is weak and defenceless."

"There is absolute freedom also for the victim."

"You *let* the little girl bring you here."

"Yes. She thinks I am a Communist."

"I see," the Captain said. He said nothing for a moment. Then he said: "There is a great self-righteousness in being a victim."

"I ask only one thing. As a former Party comrade do this for me. Do not let them do this thing. You have my pistol. Shoot me."

"You have forgotten," the Captain said, "that your pistol is unloaded. You forgot about that. And by the look of the pistol I should say it has never been fired."

"It was fired," the prisoner said, "once."

The Captain showed his teeth. Through the grey beard the steel teeth shone strangely. The blue eyes were expressionless. The soiled bandage lay flatly across his face. From the bandage there came the faint sweetish-sickly smell of gangrene, as of death.

At this instant the terror in the prisoner's breast pinnacled to ecstasy. He *knew* now that he was not in the presence of a man.

Presently the peasants came over to the hut. They took the prisoner and stripped him, dividing his clothes among themselves. They took him and shackled his feet, each foot separately by a metre-long rope, to the top of each anchored birch tree. Then they stood back and looked at him.

The SS man's body was not a good body. In the hollow chest, belly and legs there was the evidence of a rachitic childhood. Now, at the end of its life, the dark head with the balding crown was rolling backwards and forwards, the eyes were turned upwards, there was spittle on the mumbling lips. The hands, loosely bound at the wrists, were making curious signs. The sounds that were issuing from the body made the peasants angry. One of the peasants took a hatchet and with a sharp blow severed the anchor ropes holding the bent trees. The huge white sabres leaped upwards in a great sweep which halted only momentarily at the fractional instant the body was held intact in midair, the white flesh in that second drumming tightly over the dislocated joints and then bursting, as in a stiff breeze the breaking of an ensign, the body splitting in twain and the separated parts flying back in compensatory, but lessening arcs, truly like pennants the pink and bloodied entrails flapping at the tall white trunks.

The Captain took Sophia by the hand and went back to the cabin.

"What were you talking about so long?" Sophia asked.

PART 4

That year the frosts were late. Summer declined into autumn and the autumn was long and soft. The forests of birch turned yellow and the oaks slowly to red. Leaves hung firmly against the mild winds. A deep haze lay over the pasturelands. The aroma of hot green grass became the smell of wind-combed straw as quitch and goosegrass seeded and laid itself to ground. The little dry flowers of the wild verbena blew away like confetti and melon vines wrinkled and shrunk to dry crackling harrows. Convoys of military vehicles moved for days under the same column of dust. Travelling by compass they were alone. The land was empty. In the villages there were old women and children, and there were villages in which none lived, nor even a chicken pecked its way. In some villages, if there had been fighting, the foreigners left small cemeteries as though, being mostly of urban origin with urban orderliness, they were reluctant to yield their dead to the great lonely steppeland. In some villages there was sickness and outside these villages the foreigners put up notices: *"Verboten: Typhus."*

When the first sleet drove into the dry earth, but the earth still did not freeze, the military convoys ceased. Now in the vast ocean of soft earth the cities were like islands. Partaking of the nature of this time they were lonely islands. There was no smoke over these cities. The factories were silent. The pit heads were still. There were people in the streets, but there were fewer people than there had been for as long as anyone could remember. Even the foreigners were fewer in number. The military establishments had gone forward in the wake of the victories. There remained always the SS. The foreigners kept to themselves, kept to the better sections of the cities, living their own lives, supervising the thinning of the local population, but ignoring it. At the end of that year the cities of the plain lay inert, awaiting without interest and little hope the resolvement of the war in the battles that were now being fought far away in the lap of Asia.

It was at this moment, the moment of greatest inertia, that there commenced within these cities an activity of a limited yet far-reaching kind. It was an activity that energised and revitalised those whom it touched. Among those whom it touched in the city of Kharkiv, largest of the cities of the plain, was the former instructor at the Lenin Pedagogical Institute, Lydia Artemova.

All these months Lydia Artemova had waited, almost losing heart, hearing nothing, working every day unloading sacks of flour with other women at the Kharkiv railway yards, holding grimly to her false work card, receiving her ration, living on in the faith that some day word would come.

Then word had come. In the street this one had walked for a few paces beside her and without looking at him she had remembered his voice. He had told her to go to this house in the northern section of Kharkiv.

She was having trouble finding the house. The streets in this district were unnamed and the houses unnumbered. But when she knocked at the door she knew she had come to the right place.

"Typhus, typhus," a child's voice cried from within.

But there was more urgency in the young voice than the commonplace announcement warranted. Lydia Artemova knocked again.

A small boy opened the door, a small thin boy with large eyes. Lydia Artemova entered the dark damp-smelling house. It was empty. In a small back room, by a cold stove, she found an old woman sitting in a chair, perfectly immobile, but alive. She spoke to the old lady.

"She can't talk," the small boy said.

The eyes of the old lady, bright as sequins, looked at Lydia Artemova.

"What is the matter with her?"

"She's paralysed," the boy said, matter-of-factly. He did not look at the old woman.

"This is your house?"

"They took the others away," the boy said, "but they left us."

"The Germans, yes?"

"Yes," said the boy.

The boy told Lydia Artemova to wait and then went away somewhere. Alone in the house with the old woman Lydia Artemova waited. She understood that a time must elapse. She waited for several hours and then she heard footsteps quite close to her. Without her being aware of it a man had entered the house. Now, as she looked up at him, startled, he beckoned to her to follow him. He led her out of the rear of the house, across several backyards, to another house. The man looked like a worker from the Donbas. He had large brown eyes with curling eyelashes. His chin was dark with several days' growth of beard. He indicated that Lydia Artemova should enter, and went away. As he turned to leave she saw that he had a pistol loosely thrust inside the opening of his jacket.

Inside the house she looked about. It was a small dim room without furniture. As her vision adjusted itself she saw that she was in the presence of a man. He was a small man and he sat easily in a chair which he tilted back against the wall. He balanced the chair on a foot that was encased in a soft leather cavalry boot. The clothes he wore were loose and in the Party style. He wore a leather cap that was much too large for him. He wore the cap straight on his head and the visor of the cap and its pancaked crown projected out over his narrow head. He had a small white face of which nothing was visible except the black eyes. This man smoked a long *papyros* and blew the smoke out in front of his face so that his face appeared to be enveloped in a cloud of muslin.

Lydia Artemova waited for him to speak and the first words she heard seemed peculiarly inappropriate to his form. Then she understood that it was not the little man who was speaking to her, although he never took his eyes off her, but that the voice was coming from another room. She saw now that there was a door opening into an adjoining room and she understood immediately that she was being spoken to by another man.

The necessity for these precautions Lydia Artemova well understood. She was deeply excited. She knew now that she was in touch with a serious activity.

She listened to the voice in the next room and she knew that it was the voice of one who was not a mere functionary. The voice was deep (which was what had made it sound incongruous in association with the little man in the leather cap) and it was flat and unaccented. There was none of the practised exhortation or rhetoric that marked the voice of the Party Worker. It was not the voice of an Old Bolshevik, loquacious, demanding. Yet it was an educated voice. Not educated in the old sense, that is, given to fanciful embellishments of language and a class-distinguishing accent, but educated in authority. This voice had never been raised above its normal level, because it had never needed to be so raised. It was a voice which, when heard, was listened to; it was a voice which had never been contested, argued with, or disobeyed. In a way it was an old voice; but it was also a young voice, a voice trained in the essentials, trained in the minimum of personal expression. Lydia Artemova was proud of herself for having recognised the calibre of this voice: it was the voice of one high in the cadres of the NKVD.

She was no longer in an organisation of Party officials, of the *Gosudarstvo,* but in an apparatus, an *Active*.

She did not now betray her excitement. On the contrary she became more austere, more cold, more self-possessed, purposeful. The questions were the usual ones. The first questions were like those which had been asked of her many times by various control commissions and Party cleansing committees. She answered all the questions exactly as she had done many times before. The questions concerned her history from her very beginnings, even before her beginnings, reaching far back into her obscure social origin, and then going forward through her childhood and education, her earliest Party connections.

As she answered the questions she looked at the little man sitting in the chair. Sometimes he tilted the chair backwards or forwards with his foot, or he lighted another *papyros* from the butt of the old, then carefully stowed the old butt away. He had plenty of *papyros*. He must, therefore, have come recently from Moscow. Realising this Lydia Artemova was thrilled.

"Why were you not killed?"

The question, flat, unemphatic, escaped her for a moment. The Interrogator repeated it. Then Lydia Artemova understood that it was a normal inquiry: to what chance did she, of all the Party members in Kharkiv, owe her immunity from the SS bullet.

It was something she could not explain. Everybody knew that the SS had made use of the NKVD files to track down Party members. How had she escaped?

"Yet you made contact with other Party members?"

"Yes."

"With Andreev?"

"Yes."

"Why?"

Lydia Artemova did not know how to answer.

"From whom did you obtain instructions to join Andreev?"

"There were no orders," Lydia Artemova said. "We came together because we were members of the Party Lenin-Stalin."

"You planned to form an *Active?*"

"Yes."

"You expected Moscow to fall?"

"Yes. No, no!"

"You had in mind a new Party organisation?"

"We wished to work against the enemy."

"In your new Party organisation you would seek to co-operate with the collectives?"

"No," said Lydia Artemova. Now she weakened. "It was Andreev," she said. "It was his idea. He listened to the radio."

"He had literature. Where did he get the literature?"

"It was dropped from a plane."

"He said that?"

"Yes. I am sure it was true."

"Andreev was arrested."

"Yes. They burned the house down and they hanged him."

"How do you know they hanged him?"

"I saw his body," Lydia Artemova said, "hanging in front of the Communist Hall."

"You were betrayed?"

"We were immature. I know we were immature."

Looking at the little man in the leather cap Lydia Artemova wanted to explain that they had acted as they did because they had had no experience of illegal Party work. In foreign countries the Communist parties were illegal and the Party members were therefore conversant with illegal work. But here in the Soviet Union the Party had never been illegal, always legal, and so they had never had that experience. But as she looked at the little man in the leather cap she saw that, although clearly a Russian Party member, he was steeped in illegality. It confused her.

Now the questions bearing on the betrayal were coming forth. They concerned each part of her experience. They went backwards and forwards over her experience. They struck at surprising angles of her experience.

Then the Interrogator asked a curious question:

"Did you know," he said, "that you were betrayed by a child?"

It was surely an ordinary question, but it so further confused Lydia Artemova that she did not immediately answer. The Interrogator waited for her. Then she heard him stirring in the next room like a man who has finished for the day.

"Tomorrow," he said. "Tomorrow we will go into that."

He told her not to go back to her old address. He gave her a new address to go to that night.

"Tonight you will write a history of yourself. Not this one you have for functionaries, but a full history of yourself. Tomorrow, here."

Then he was very quiet for a moment. The little man in the leather cap was rigid, watching her. Something was expected of her, she did not know what.

"All right," said the little man in the cap. "Go."

It was the kind of question which made you feel that *they* knew everything. It made you admire them and feel proud that there was such efficiency in the Soviet cadres. It made you feel that it was no use concealing anything from them. It made you anxious not to *seem* to be concealing anything.

That morning when the SS had arrested Nikolai Andreyvich she had taken her eyes from the burning house for one moment. Drawn by some furtive movement she had looked downward and she had seen this small girl looking at her. The expression on the child's face had startled her. Such a concentration of hatred! It was not impersonal. The little girl had recognised her.

Lydia Artemova had guessed that she was one of the children at the school on the Sadovo-Kulikovskaya. There had been no time to think about it then. But later, in the days and months of her concealment, even as she worked unloading the heavy flour sacks at the railway yards, she had been haunted by the small face full of hate. Finally, against all caution, she had visited the schoolhouse to seek out the child.

How could the Interrogator have known about the child?

It was not easy for Lydia Artemova to write her personal history that night. At the new address where she had been received, not coldly, but not enthusiastically (she judged it to be the home of a militiaman, a Kharkiv policeman), she had obtained an old school copybook and she had begun this task which, as a Party member of long standing, she had performed many times. The last words of the Interrogator, his warning not to make the error of writing a formal history, and to write fully, she accepted with great seriousness. Yet how does one write of oneself in such a way? There are the dates. Yes, one has them always at hand for such occasions. And the documents. There are the documents to support the chronology. But taking this evidence in review it gives very little sense of the person concerned. That is to say, she did not want to invent a bourgeois personality for herself, an individuality, but the bare facts, the dates, all this had happened so long ago in what could only be described as an atmosphere, a climate, which had utterly changed, so that they could not now be easily understood.

How easy it must be to be a young Party member! All they had to do was to fill in a few lines. Yet, as she thought of this, Lydia Artemova knew that it was a wrong thought.

Now, in the confusion of writing her history, she wanted to throw down her pencil and cry out that she loved Comrade Stalin. She wanted to rise to her feet and passionately declare her loyalty to the Party Lenin-Stalin by shouting the slogans in a loud voice, by screaming the imprecations, and to repeat word for word the last speech of Comrade Stalin. She wanted to show how ruthless had been her vigilance, how deeply she hated the foreigners, and how willingly she would lay down her life for the Party. She wanted to do these things to *prove* her loyalty.

What she did not want to do at this moment was to write down names: either the names of the people who had signed the affidavits by which she had entered the Party, or that of her first and much-loved Professor, or the name of her former lover, or of any who had made love to her, or of certain of her best pupils, or of some who had considered her a friend.

And now, when it came to the last chapter of her history, she did not wish to set down this matter of Andreev's betrayal to the SS. She did not want to mention that she had visited the schoolhouse. She had acted as a Party member should act. But it had exposed her to identification by the little girl, and thus to being shadowed to Andreev's address. She was not afraid to acknowledge this error. What she was afraid of was where it would lead.

In spite of her confusion Lydia Artemova nevertheless did complete her history that night in accordance with the obligations of a normal Party membership. In the morning she brought it with her to the house in the northern suburb and once again waited for a long time before being conducted to the presence of the little man in the leather cap and the hidden Interrogator.

They did not ask her for the document, but began a new line of questioning.

"You are a Party member of long standing, yes?"

"Yes, I have written . . ."

"You are known to many old Party members?"

"Yes."

"You have known many expelled from the Party?"

"Yes."

"You were not yourself expelled?"

"No. No."

She was looking at the little man in the leather cap who returned her gaze through a haze of cigarette smoke. More and more it was as if the little man were somehow a ventriloquist's dummy, or rather as if the little man were the ventriloquist and the voice in the next room his voice, pitched there by some evil trickery. And then the Interrogator asked this question:

"Has an enemy agent approached you?"

And there was this stricken moment, because until that moment Lydia Artemova had hoped to avoid it, but now there suddenly flooded into her mind this scene which she had tried to forget.

"Yes," she said.

She saw the little man with the flat leather cap take the *papyros* out of his mouth, forgetting to blow out the smoke which now curled in faint spirals from his nostrils, and hold the *papyros* in his hand, steadily looking at her.

Lydia Artemova began to talk. She told how she had been sitting on the bench at the schoolhouse in the Sadovo-Kulikovskaya not more than a fortnight ago when this man had sat down beside her and began to talk. He had said that he wanted to help the Communist underground. That was the word he had used, *podpolnya organizatsia,* underground organisation. She had never heard the word before. She had not dared to listen further. She had gone away.

When she had said this there was silence in the little room. Lydia Artemova had told the truth, but it was not the whole truth. Now she waited, her heart thumping, thinking how much more of the truth she would have to tell. She watched the little man pinch out his lighted *pa-*

pyros, exactly as she had known he would do. She saw the small wiry fingers press hard on the lighted end of the cigarette and she watched him slowly put the butt away in a pocket of his jacket. Inside the next room there was no sound, not even the rustling of papers.

Then Lydia Artemova suddenly understood what concerned them both, this little man in the leather cap and the voice in the next room. She had just informed them that she was known to the enemy as a Communist. And she was alive. And here!

Lydia Artemova was deeply agitated. She wished with all her heart that the man in the adjoining room, the Interrogator, would come out of the room and look at her. She could not bear the scrutiny of the little silent man who was now looking at her, quite still, having crushed out his cigarette. She had to restrain an impulse to rush into the next room and to show herself to the high officer.

And then, in the middle of her distress, she remembered the history she had written the previous evening. She opened her string bag and took out the pages she had removed from the old exercise book. She tendered the pages to the little man in the leather cap.

He took them, holding them as if they contained an infection. There was an expression of incredulity on his white face.

"She actually wrote it," he said.

"Yes," said the Interrogator, "she wrote it."

The little man dropped the pages to the floor and in an instant had struck a match and set a light to the paper.

Then, only in that moment, Lydia Artemova understood that in illegal work nothing is committed to paper. They had asked her to write this history in order to test her maturity, her experience. Her innocence. She thought the little man's grin was more friendly.

"Tonight you will stay here," he said.

The Interrogator was a young man. Yet it would have

been impossible for Lydia Artemova, had she seen him, to have guessed his age. He was already ageless.

He was the son of an Orenburg peasant and he was the end product of those secret schools in the *Gosudarstvennoye Politicheskoye Upravleniye* (GPU), the State Political Directorate (not to be confused with the Comintern schools for the study of agitation, propaganda and espionage, known to foreigners), reserved for children of exceptional social origin.

It was a characteristic of institutions that were being set up in the period following the post-Revolutionary wars, that, where a proposed institution did not fall naturally within human capacity, humanity was made to fit the institution. There were, of course, inevitable breakdowns. It became apparent that the independence of the new State was being constantly threatened, not only by its enemies without, but by its enemies within, not alone by active enemies, but (since the State was all) by inactive enemies, by what appeared to be inertia, neglect and irresponsibility, all damaging to the power of the State, and (since they believed in the "word") by certain ideas in the minds of the individuals of the State, either lingering there or implanted there, which militated against the oneness of the State.

For the onerous task of guarding the State against these constant threats what was more natural than to select and train a special, and necessarily secret, cadre? And what better material was there for such a cadre than the many children of the Revolution, this youth untainted by bourgeois influences, yet full of the energy released by the Revolution?

It was a hard training, more sheltered than that of a lamasery, more crowded that that of a poor medical student, more rigidly disciplined than the severest military academy. The peculiar quality of this early training had been its intellectual and physical austerity. Self-indulgence, emotional or intellectual adventure, study for its own sake, the pursuit of pleasure, play, love, happiness, the gratification of the senses, all this was denied the future Interrogator. Had he shown a disposition towards such indulgences he would have been quickly diverted, like many who entered the schools with him, to channels of lesser trust. As it was, having little or no imagination, an ice-cold mind, a native indifference to mortifications of the flesh; and being humourless, he had graduated a triumphant example of the GPU man.

In his mind and character there was no trace of those sentimental and humanistic notions which linger in many who, without his training, might yet call themselves materialists. To his education and training there was now added a number of easily-accepted privileges, better food, better clothes, better living, the means of satisfying his physical appetites, a certain freedom of movement and speech, the profound deference of all who did not enjoy his position. It was a superiority which could not be shaken by the evidence of the misery of the mass of people, or such misery as his own acts might create, because he *was* the People, and so in his bearing, and voice, there was an innate primacy. He would never appear in any official capacity in the Party or Government, and he had only his gazetted rank, an invented name and a suitably invented biography, yet he exercised an authority more complete than any other known to man, the more so because it was a delegated authority, impersonal, abstract, moral.

The Interrogator, in fact, stood for the theory that man is morally free only when his actions conform to his real will and that his real will is the general will and the general will is embedded in the State. He stood for the principle that the freedom of the individual depends on the continued independence of the State and that, therefore, the State may impose an absolute sacrifice on the individual to maintain its independence. Thus freedom is not an absence of restraints, but a self-determination imposing restraints. The Interrogator personalised self-determination where it did not exist.

In his questioning of Lydia Artemova the Interrogator had been motivated by no other purpose than to test the quality of the material he was expected to use. The problem of Lydia Artemova herself offered no difficulty. As usual it was solved by the subject herself.

Lydia Artemova prepared to spend the night in the house where the small boy and the old paralysed woman lived. The old woman sat in a chair beside the white-tiled stove, which was stone-cold, with a rag blanket over her knees. The boy brought her tea and some bread. She watched the boy feed pieces of bread to the old woman. She wondered about the relationship of the boy to the old woman.

"Is the woman your mother?" Lydia Artemova asked.

"No," the boy said.

"She is your grandmother, then?"

"I do not know who she is," the boy said. "She was left behind."

"Do you not live here?"

"No," the boy said.

Lydia Artemova sipped her tea. It was cold in the house. The old woman drooled the bread crumbs.

"I was at the school," the boy said.

"Which school?"

"I remember you," the boy said. "You came to see the *Deda*."

"Yes," Lydia Artemova said.

"It is useless to feed the old woman," the boy said. "She will surely die."

"Why do you feed her then?" Lydia Artemova said.

"I do not know," the boy said.

"Is it something you learned at the school?"

"Yes," the boy said. "That is it."

"Is it your own food you are giving her?"

"Yes. It is irrational to feed one who is dying. I shall not feed her any more."

"Why did you leave the school?" Lydia Artemova asked.

"It is finished at the school," the boy said.

"What is finished?"

"The Germans are finished. They do not care any more about the school. They have got all the clever ones."

"They did not get you?"

"I am not clever. My father was not very clever. He

was not a Communist, but he was hanged just the same. That was not clever."

"You have told this to the Interrogator?"

"Oh yes, but he does not accept it. He is right not to accept what anyone says."

"Do the Germans still issue rations to the school?"

"Yes."

"I suppose they issue rations to all the schools."

"I do not know. But they issue rations to this school."

They thought about the school. Then Lydia Artemova said:

"How did you come to get in touch with these," she gestured, "the *Active?*"

"The same as you."

"Oh, so you know."

"No, but it is the same. Someone is watching you. Then they talk with you and you go with them. Yes?"

"Yes."

"Only I must not tell who it was."

"No."

"I like to be with them," the boy said. "They are very strong. They make you feel strong. I would like to be strong."

"Yes," said Lydia Artemova, "then you must eat your bread and not give it to the old woman who was left behind."

"That's right."

"But you may give her my bread. Yes, here is my bread. Give it to her."

There was not enough warmth in the house for comfortable sleep, but Lydia Artemova did not wish to sleep. She had much to think about. It was as the child said: you were watched and everything was known.

Haunted by the expression of hatred on Sophia's face she had returned to the schoolhouse. It was a foolish thing to have done, but she had felt compelled to do it. She had sat on the wooden bench behind the schoolhouse and watched the children at play. She had been joined by Professor Shevchenko. How could she explain the pleasure and happiness of that meeting? She had told Professor Shevchenko about the little girl, described the little girl to him, and without hesitation he had brought Sophia by the hand to Lydia Artemova's presence. It had been a fearful moment. What a strange little creature! How old in mind, yet how childish! But Sophia had clung to Professor Shevchenko's hand and it was clear that she loved him deeply. She had looked at Lydia Artemova with suspicion, but she had promised the *Deda* not to tell anyone that she had seen Lydia Artemova. The *Deda* (thereafter Lydia Artemova thought always of Professor Shevchenko as the *Deda*) had accepted Sophia's promise with simple confidence. Then Lydia Artemova understood how the children in that schoolhouse loved their *Deda*. It was a love she had been hungry to share, but hesitant to seek.

She had come back to the school many times, sitting on the wooden bench in the sun with the *Deda* while the children played. Then this day, a fortnight ago, a stranger in a black hat and an overcoat with a fur collar had appeared. The *Deda* had mumbled some words of introduction. Then the foreigner, accepting her ragged clothes and work-worn hands as evidence of Ukrainian origin, had begun to talk against the Fascists, cursing them, railing against their stupidity, their atrocities, and certain horrors of which, apparently, he had precise knowledge. Listening to this talk by one who, clearly, had come with the Fascists, Lydia Artemova had felt cynical. In her coldest tone she had addressed the stranger:

"If you feel like that why don't you do something?"

Her sharp words, perhaps her expression of contempt, had startled the stranger. With shrewd calculation he had asked:

"Lydia Artemova, you are a Party member, yes?"

"Yes."

She had been alarmed by the way he remembered her name from the mumbled introduction. At the same time she had made the admission, against all the rules, out of pride.

"In the Civil War," the stranger said, "I worked with Bolsheviks. I can do it again. Tell me how to get in touch with the Communist underground. I have much information to give. I have sources in the SS and the *Wehrmacht*. Just tell me how to get in touch with the underground."

And then, under the stress of what she had done, Lydia Artemova had jumped up from the bench and run away.

Now, to tell this to the Interrogator would raise a problem which frightened Lydia Artemova. Yet she must tell the Interrogator. If she did not tell him he would have means of knowing. But how was she to do it? All that night she thought about it.

In the morning she brought to the presence of the little man in the leather cap and the hidden Interrogator the positive intention of telling everything she knew. But the questioning quietened her: How many children were there at the school? How many such schools were there? Where did the children come from? Who were the parents of the children? Were any of the children the offspring of parents who had come from other cities? From Stalingrad? From Voronesh? From Moscow? How old were the children? What would have been the age of the eldest? Did they have relatives in any of the cities mentioned? Were there children of Red Army officers? Did the children understand military terms? Could they count? Recognise rank?

Lydia Artemova was abject. She understood now that she had gravely exaggerated her own part in the activities of the school. She understood from the nature of the questions that the Interrogator was not wasting time on a matter of casual interest. She saw that he was engaged upon an investigation that was of the widest significance.

To most of the questions asked by the Interrogator Lydia Artemova had only negative replies. Except those questions concerning the teacher of the school. Lydia Artemova was able to give the Interrogator a full account of Maryusa Selova's origin and history.

There had been few changes in the little schoolhouse in the Sadovo-Kulikovskaya. During the summer a number of children had drifted away. The babies which had been successfully kept there during the winter were adopted into other families. Several of the babies went to German families which had come to Kharkiv and Maryusa saw no harm in this. However, there were still children coming into the school. Sick or wearied of begging, abandoned or freshly orphaned, they sought out and usually found shelter there. The ration of millet bread made it possible to keep the school open.

Now, with the second winter upon them, there was again anxiety. But there was also Professor Shevchenko. Every day for an hour or two he would entertain them with a wonderful story. Professor Shevchenko made life seem worth living. Listening, as she always did, in the deep background of the gloomy closed-in room Maryusa smiled to herself. She found as much enjoyment in the fantasy as did the children. Professor Shevchenko's discourse was like a continuous fairy tale, a serial play, of which the children never tired, nor could endure to see the end of, anxiously demanding the repetition of each familiar image, avid for the new image.

This day, from her position in the background, Maryusa looked down on the large gloomy room, not with her usual buoyancy, but with love and foreboding. The faces of the children, dimly illuminated by the light from the little stove, were like pale triangles hung in space. In each face large grave eyes shone with a stilled inner pleasure. Seeing this, the pleasure in these faces, Maryusa felt, as always, a surge of affection for her children. The feeling was inclusive. It gathered to her bosom not only the waifs of this city, and such Communist orphans as remained, but also Professor Shevchenko. Squatting on the floor, his pointed white face bent over the bowl of soup, he could have been mistaken for a very young child. It was because he was so young, Maryusa thought. He *was* young. He was light. He was gay. That was the way of children.

"Tell us more, *Deda*," a boy asked.

"Tell us more. Tell us about the bear who was made of butter."

Maryusa smiled and settled herself to hear, once more, the story of the incredible bear.

"Ah, that bear!" said Professor Shevchenko. "He is all yellow, a bright light yellow, because he is made from good dairy butter. Such a big, bold bear! But you will not see him often, for he lives in the tundra and only at night, and in the winter, does he come to our part of the country. Last night he came to me and he told me his secret. And do you know what it is? His secret is that he lives in the snow. He rolls in the snow and he sleeps in it. And do you know why? Because he is made of butter. Our bear is a very great drunkard. Ah, how he drinks the vodka! Like this, *d'd na!* and then he blows on his fingers and rubs his belly. All the time he is drunk! And what things he does! Sometimes silly things. But he can pull down a birch tree with one arm and pick up a house with the other. He can take a whole town and put it in another place. Such a drunken bear! Through the snows he goes his way singing and laughing, though his laugh is often like a growl, always seeking to play jokes on people, lifting up a rooftop here and breathing down on the man and wife in bed so that they will awake crying that it is the Government come for them, and then putting down the rooftop and rolling away laughing so that the man and his wife say that it is only the thunder after all. And have I told you the secret of our bear? It is simply that he is made of butter. For, as everybody knows, if your stomach is lined with butter, you can drink as much vodka as you like and you can always be drunk, but never off your guard, so that even though people think you silly and incapable, you will all the time be aware of what is going on. You see, our bear is a cunning bear. For not only is he made of butter, but, because he lives in the snow, he is always firm and hard, and, now this is his very great secret, he keeps his vodka in the snow too. So that his vodka is always cold like ice, as vodka should be, so our bear drinks and drinks without harm to himself."

"Tell us about the wolf, *Deda*."

"Yes, the bear and the wolf, *Deda*."

"One day our bear met a wolf. This was a large grey wolf all shining because he was made of lard. Now this wolf was not a winter wolf. He was a summer wolf and he depended for his safety on the warm sun melting his hide so that he was greasy all over and when anybody tried to catch him he slipped through their hands. Ah, he was such a sly wolf! So tricky in his ways. He had a secret too. Now his secret was to drink beer, because beer is very fattening and also warm, and so every time he drank beer he added to his weight and this made up for the melting. Now it happened that this wolf came into the country one summer when it was warm and he was so slippery that nobody could catch him and so he took everything he wished and drank all the beer and was very drunk and went around boasting of his ability. And so it came to the ears of the bear that there was a wolf who said he was the biggest drunkard in the world. And this angered our bear very much. For our bear had always considered himself to be, far and away, the biggest drunkard in the world. But it was summer at this time and always in summer our bear goes away into the north where the snows still lie. But when it was winter again our bear came back and he met this wolf and he saw the wolf was no longer melting all over because it was so cold now and the wolf was afraid. So our bear laughed in his drunken way and said that he had heard that the wolf could hold his liquor better than any bear alive. So the bear challenged the wolf to a drinking contest. . . ."

Professor Shevchenko paused. The room was silent. Maryusa looked around the room and was deeply moved. The expression of rapture in each small face in that room was testimony to the capacity of each life there, the infinite worth of that life, in a way that was, for her, overwhelming. The innocent gravity of those faces was an unendurable reminder of their dependence. In this moment, the moment her heart was fullest, she also wished the end of it all.

". . . So the bear and the wolf began a drinking bout. And what do you think they were drinking?—why, vodka, of course . . ."

Professor Shevchenko began and then stopped. The room was utterly still.

Maryusa looked down into the room to find the cause for the quiet. There was no movement. Yet, she sensed an alarm, a shock. She then saw that the eyes of the children, faintly illuminated in their shadowy cavities, were turned all in the one direction. Maryusa followed the direction of their parallel gaze. She saw that a stranger had entered the room. A man.

In the gloom above the children Maryusa saw that the man's head was like the head of a statue in the corner of a darkened gallery, disembodied, separated from pose, lifelike, shining, as of a statue sleekly worn from gunmetal by abrasives of sapphire and tungsten. A modern tooling; there was nothing of this head that was not functional, no emotion, no line of superfluous expression, nothing carved there that was not, as in a good pistol, intended for action. Yet an ageless face; weathered taut, so that the nose and mouth were clearly defined without being chiselled, without softness or curvature. In the blueness and hardness of this face the eyes blazed. The colourless direct-staring eyes above the large cheekbones were as the eyes of the giant cats, wherein, it seems, the pupil floats like a fleck of mercury in a pool of topaz, in which there is no circuit of reflection or contemplation or even decision, but a liquid connection between sight and reflex.

With his silent entry the man had brought with him a current of sub-zero air and this now eddied through the room. The children stirred. The momentary stillness ended. The man looked at Maryusa, and Maryusa saw that it was Fomin.

Immediately Maryusa saw that the man who had come into the room was Fomin she understood that her troubled feelings had led her to exaggerate his appearance. What she had seen was an apparition, the material of her nightmare. Her relief was immense. She saw that Fomin had changed, but that he was still the Fomin she had known. There was now in his face an expression of pure ego, as of manhood, the face, often seen in war, that comes of having played life for life, and yet lived, and, living, found therein a special and peculiar merit far beyond trifling conceptions of fate and good fortune. She saw, as he came more fully into view, that his body was like his face, rigid with this pride of life, held as straightly as a rifle barrel, but lean, hardened into a machine of tendons and muscles. It was six months since he had gone away to fight with the guerillas. In his bearing there was all that time lived out in she knew not what experience, in struggle and risk and pain, and she could not have guessed what tasks performed, what sights seen. All she knew now was that he was thin. His peasant jacket was worn and tattered, the *valinki* were patched and bound with rags, his fleece-lined cap was encrusted with dirt. His hollow cheeks, hollow temples, the all-leanness of him, the unrested tension touched her, as though he were one of her children. She wanted to feed him.

She brought bread and potatoes.

Fomin took the bread and began eating. He crumbled the bread in his hands. It dissolved into a grey dust in which there were bright flecks of chaff.

"German bread?" he said.

"Yes," Maryusa said, "it is all we have."

Fomin ate the bread. He ate the potatoes.

"You have come back to us?" Maryusa said.

"Yes," Fomin said.

"It is good," Maryusa said. "It will be a difficult winter."

"How many are here?" Fomin said.

"Ninety," Maryusa said.

"Many who were here are no longer here?" Fomin said.

"Some went away. In the summer," Maryusa said. "But others have come."

Fomin nodded.

"Have any of those who went away come back?"

"No."

"But many still go?"

"No," Maryusa said.

"Why?"

"I don't know," Maryusa said. "I think it is because they like to hear the old man talk."

"Yes," Fomin said, "he talks?"

"It is all in the imagination," Maryusa said. "I mean it is something for them to think about."

"Something to think about."

"And you?" Maryusa said. "Where have you been?"

Fomin did not answer.

"The old man must go," he said.

"No," Maryusa said.

Fomin looked at her. "Tell him now he must go and must not come back."

Maryusa stood looking at Fomin. The hard eyes looked into hers and she could not tell what was in the mind behind the eyes. She did not think of it as a moment of decision. It was simply that, in this moment, she felt weak. She did not have the strength to resist so naked an emanation of will. She went to Professor Shevchenko and she told him to go and not to come back.

The old man smiled and bowed, as if he had understood, and he went. Seeing him go there was an instant pang in Maryusa's heart, as though she had done something wrong, but it was fleeting, already lost among innumerable other such heart-rendings, all now, she suddenly discovered, of lessening importance. She went quickly back to Fomin. In his presence there was immediate relief from such feelings. She was grateful.

Fomin did not again look at her. He examined the old schoolhouse. He looked into every room, pried open every cupboard, fingered the lesson books, counted the children, looked over the small store of food and wood fuel.

"When do the Germans come?" he asked her once.

"The Germans do not come."

"No?"

"We go to the commissary for our bread," Maryusa said.

"I mean the SS. When do the SS come?" Fomin said.

Maryusa faltered. "The SS do not come," she said.

"No?" Fomin said.

"The SS have not been here since that time. You must remember that time?"

"I do not remember," Fomin said.

In Maryusa's small room Fomin found her precious store of food, the cans of meats and fats and fish that Olympia brought her every week. Fomin ate of this store and Maryusa watched him count the cans that remained.

"This is what the SS gives?" he said. He spoke with satisfaction in his discovery.

"No," Maryusa said, "it is what Olympia brings."

"Who is Olympia?"

"She comes every week," Maryusa said.

"She is a spy, yes?"

"You must remember her," Maryusa said. "She came always when you were here before."

"Ah, yes," Fomin said, "the prostitute."

The way Fomin spoke of Olympia made Maryusa suddenly pause in her thought. She had not considered Olympia that way before.

When Olympia called at the schoolhouse the next day Maryusa saw her with new eyes. Whereas she had always regarded Olympia as the embodiment of youthful beauty, she now saw that, while Olympia's cheeks were as blooming as ever, her eyes as bright, she was no longer so youthful or so fresh as she had been a year or more ago. She saw also that Olympia was a class apart from other women, especially from Maryusa. Maryusa felt this when she saw Olympia stare at Fomin in amazement and then begin to laugh.

"He's come back," Maryusa said.

"I see," Olympia said.

"He will help us this winter as he did last winter."

"He looks more like a soldier," Olympia said.

Maryusa saw that the words were intended to please Fomin and it was at this moment that she began to distrust Olympia.

"What do you do now?" Fomin asked.

"I live," Olympia said.

"Then you spy," Fomin said.

"No."

"But you hear much?"

"Much," Olympia said.

"What do you hear?" Fomin said.

"I hear there is much fighting," Olympia said.

"Certainly."

Olympia looked with admiration at Fomin's toughened body and weathered face.

"You have been fighting?" she said.

Fomin shrugged his shoulders. It was a new gesture. It was the gesture of a much older man.

"How many have you killed?" Olympia said.

"Many are killed."

"Many SS! How is it to fight the SS?"

"They are Germans. They are fatter, that is all."

Olympia's face opened with a kind of delight. She turned to Maryusa. "He is right," she said. "The SS are fatter."

"You are fatter too," Fomin said.

"One does not starve," Olympia said.

"Spies do not starve."

"*Zum Teufel!*" Olympia said. "I do not spy."

"Why do we have to talk like this?" Maryusa said. "Why do we have to talk about spies?"

"Then let us not talk about spies," Fomin said.

Olympia looked at Fomin. The amusement had disappeared from her large round face. It was replaced by an expression of naïve cunning.

"What are you here for?" Olympia said.

"He has come back to help us," Maryusa said.

"To help in what?" Olympia said.

Olympia turned her glance to Maryusa and began to study her old friend.

"Is that what he says?" Olympia said.

"Listen," Fomin said, "go back to your Germans."

Olympia looked at Fomin.

"Aren't you afraid I may denounce you?" she said.

"You would do that?" Fomin said.

"No," Olympia said, "it is too late. It is too late to do anyone any good."

"Go!" Fomin said.

"You should wait a moment," Olympia said, "to hear the news I have to tell. I think it is news that concerns you. Yes, it concerns you, I think."

"What news have you?" Fomin said.

"It is about the fighting," Olympia said.

"Yes?" Fomin said.

"All the time I have the latest informations."

"What is the news?" Maryusa said.

"He must know it already. It is that the Red Army, since a week now, has surrounded Stalingrad."

"You must have other news," Fomin said.

"Yes," Olympia said. "Four *Wehrmacht* divisions are now grouped at Tchlamskaya to drive upon the Russian encirclement. There is among them the division Viking SS."

"How do you know these things?" Maryusa said. "How do you have the language?"

"One hears many things," Fomin said.

"But it is true," Olympia said.

"Possibly," Fomin said.

"Every day I can come here with the latest informations," Olympia said.

"Not here," Fomin said. "Do not come here again."

Olympia smiled. Folding her leopardskin coat about her ample figure, exhibiting her soft limbs, her high moulded breasts, her red mouth, her bright eyes, she made ready to go.

Looking at her, his eyes hard on her, Fomin said: "You have much tongue."

Olympia exhibited that small luscious organ.

"You should make more use of it," she said.

Then Maryusa, watching them, saw Fomin's stern face suddenly break. The new, surprising expression was a smile of puerile lubricity. Maryusa observed the expression not yet with dislike, but with a kind of evolving knowledge.

Olympia knew about the battle at Stalingrad because Oberleutnant Soedermann frequently spoke to her about it. She had been living with Oberleutnant Soedermann now for six or eight months and the relationship had become, at least in Willi Soedermann's mind, almost as settled as if Olympia were his true and lawful spouse.

Olympia's career as a *Wehrmacht* prostitute had ended in the spring when Oberleutnant Soedermann had begun to find it intolerable that his mistress' charms should be shared by others, even by his good companions. The breakthrough to the Caucasus and the consequent realignment of forces had enabled him to effect a change he had long contemplated. His companions along with the *Wehrmacht* command and ancillary services, including the military brothels, had moved forward to quarters nearer the front. Kharkiv was practically deserted. Oberleutnant Soedermann was able to instal Olympia in one of the better apartments in the Paulus Platz.

He was soon congratulating himself. The city, bypassed by the noise and pageantry of the armies, deserted by the colonists, had begun to reassert its essential character. The streets appeared to be full of dark-shawled women. The smell of *mahorka* and unwashed bodies was oppressive. The hotels were empty or they had been converted into hospitals. The entertainments had ceased long before. Oberleutnant Soedermann found solace in his private apartment. Not only was Olympia's inexhaustible good nature and healthy appetite a constant refreshment, but she proved to have unexpected domestic qualities. Of course, she operated on the black market and she distributed food among her friends, but she also cooked and kept house in a way that was altogether unlike a Slav, he believed. He had once, looking long at Olympia, come to the conclusion that she was not, could not be, of Slavic origin, but was the product of an earlier visitation of the German soldiery to the Ukraine, and this thought, with its pleasing emphasis on the selective and enduring qualities of the Nordic-Phalian blood, having once entered his head, had remained there and very soon could not have been dislodged by any consideration of fact, such as her age, or by argument. Like her qualities as a *Hausfrau,* Olympia's quick, though imperfect, grasp of the German language he accepted as evidence of the correctness of his belief. Very soon he had forgotten Olympia's origin.

Into the aura of comfort provided by Olympia, Oberleutnant Soedermann, like many an occupational officer before and after him, eased himself with an audible sigh of satisfaction. Here in his own apartment he could take off his boots. He could sip his Italian vermouth (champagne being no longer available) and read his Berlin newspapers and his home-town *Tageblatt.* It had become part of his cultivated sense of well-being to talk over the top of his newspaper, confident that Olympia was listening to him. He liked to express his views on the conduct of the war, the perfidy of the Communists, the ineptitude of the non-Party generals, the inter-service feuds, opinions that were succinct, authoritative, final, delivered without a tremor of doubt but that the good flaxen-haired woman sitting opposite him was not completely, as a good German woman should be, of his own mind and voice. Oberleutnant Soedermann's mistake was one that has been made by men even more firmly married. He had accepted the natural warmth of Olympia's embraces, all the attributes of her femininity, like her concern for his person, as the inspiration of his own grace and character. It had not occurred to him to look beyond her womanly reflexes to seek the woman stranger, the unfamiliar one, the identity of unmapped impulses, unknown thoughts, unfathomable intuition. He did not know that there could be such an existence. How could he know? There was nothing in Olympia's manner, no bitterness or sullenness, to indicate that she was not prepared fully to abide by the condition, so often proved in the history of her country, that women are the first and most valuable trophies of war.

In repeating to Fomin the *Wehrmacht* plan for the relief of Stalingrad Olympia had not intended to betray or injure her master. At the same time she was not deeply imbued with not doing so. The inequality, the profound inequality of choice in their relationship, while not producing malice had not yet bred an especial loyalty. But her instinct reached beyond this. In her wifely role she had not failed, in recent weeks, to detect changes in Oberleutnant Soedermann. The pressure of outward events had caused him to sink more deeply into domesticity. He spent every spare moment in the apartment. He ate hugely of her cooking. He spoke to her of his old parents. He brought her little presents. He gave up reading newspapers. He brought out his Rolleiflex and took photographs of her in various poses. He became tender. Certainly Olympia had no wish to hurt Soedermann when she blurted out to Fomin the plan to relieve Stalingrad. Her action was rooted rather in her appraisal of Fomin, his strength, his confidence, his obvious purpose.

What had influenced Olympia even more than this, however, was Maryusa's evident alliance with Fomin. If there was any sense of loyalty in Olympia it was towards this woman who had extended to her an act of detached kindness, perhaps the only such act in Olympia's life. It was a childish loyalty, therefore strong, indissoluble. With her woman's instinct, her whore's experience, Olympia had sensed at once that Maryusa, distraught, desperate, had grasped at Fomin, as one grasps at a lifeline, and, having Fomin in hand, meant to hold him.

Thinking of this, of Maryusa's obstinacy, her desperation, her near hysteria, knowing that she too sensed the changing fortunes of war, which could only be worse, Olympia was sure that Maryusa meant to hold Fomin by offering herself to him. When Olympia reached this conclusion she was not appalled by the naïveté of her former teacher, nor did she think it pathetic. Her reaction was that Maryusa was being impractical.

The women of Kharkiv were not pretty that year. It had become known, by a curious telepathy, that none, save those of the Germans, any longer menstruated. Thus quickly had age descended upon them. And yet, secretly, it was felt to be an honourable thing, a caste mark separating the women of the country from all others, and also a sign, a portent, of the singular determination of the women of the country each to survive. For it was not only privation which brought age down upon one, it was also, so to speak, a husbanding of strength. The spirit, too, sheltered. How much can one afford to feel? How deeply may one draw upon the well of compassion? In such a time, not to be destroyed by emotion, feeling must needs dry up, unless it rest upon and draw vitality from a system, a source, a faith, or even the unshaken conventions of a firm, if submerged society.

Maryusa had none of these things. But Fomin brought them to her. Like a young girl awakening to life she thrilled to his presence.

Because her small room, with its fastenable door and single window, offered him security, he spent the first nights of his return in this room. He crouched near the window, covering himself with a ragged blanket, but no longer attempting to conceal the pistol which he kept always at hand. At no time did Maryusa see him asleep.

Always he seemed to be awake. He said nothing, but there was a tenseness, quietness in his crouched form which did not go with relaxed slumber.

Several times Maryusa was about to break into this silence. Each time she prevented herself from doing so at the very moment she opened her mouth with the first word on her tongue. She felt she could not bear to hear her own voice. Thus she had many unspoken conversations with Fomin, imagining herself to have uttered the phrase on her tongue, and then imagining his reply, and her rejoinder thereto, and so on through the minutes, hours. In this way she achieved a state of rapport with Fomin without having uttered a word. And then it happened that Fomin himself broke the silence. Shifting his body around he observed that it was too cold for the SS this night.

So that Maryusa naturally answered with the words that were in her mind.

"Fomin," she said, "do you like women?"

"It is not a responsible question," Fomin answered out of the darkness.

Maryusa smiled to herself.

"You have been with many women?"

"So."

"It is good that you do not boast of it."

"To talk of one thing is to talk of everything."

"You are wise. I am glad that you are so wise."

"Well?"

"She is very beautiful, is she not?"

"It is of no importance."

"She is attractive to men, yes?"

"It is possible."

"I think she is very attractive."

"She is a prostitute."

"I had not thought of that," Maryusa said, "but it is true. It was you who made me think of it."

"The prostitute is a spy."

"I do not know," Maryusa said. "I do not know about that. I think she is wrong to live with a German. But I do not think she spies."

"You do not *know*?"

"I know Olympia. I have known her a long time."

"For a prostitute she has lived a long time."

"She has been visiting us since the beginning."

"It is nothing to be a prostitute. To be a prostitute for a long time is clever."

"I have never thought of it."

"To be a spy is also clever."

"But she is good. Always when she comes she brings food which I keep to feed the sick ones."

"It is clear. If she were not a spy she would sell the food on the black market."

"Now, I am not sure."

"It is obvious."

"I think," Maryusa said, "I think she does it because she likes me."

"It is not scientific to speak like that."

In the darkness Maryusa was smiling. She could not take such a rebuke seriously. She was much too pleased with her success in having provoked Fomin into making a conversation. Lying there in the room she felt that there was a community of feeling between them which could not exist in the hard light of day. There were only their voices and nothing to detract from the voices, no ugliness of dress or form, no self-consciousness of expression. Hearing his voice, the harsh plangent sound that was he, Maryusa felt the mystery of his separate existence very deeply. The strangeness of him excited her.

"What is it you know, Fomin? You know something I do not know. What is it, Fomin?"

"I know what I have learned."

"What have you learned? What did you learn in all those months you were away with the guerillas?"

Fomin did not answer.

"Is it that you have learned about dying? That is something I do not yet know about. Often I think about it, for it is something that is happening all the time, but I cannot make up my mind about it. It seems to me that if I could make up my mind about dying I would be more certain of what to do, like you."

"You will."

"What?"

"Know what it is to die."

"Can one know? I mean, can one know before one dies?"

"Yes."

"What is it like to know?"

"It is nothing. Dying is of no importance."

"What is important?"

"What goes before dying."

"That is what I want to know. What goes before dying? How does one act before dying?"

Maryusa felt that she was on the verge of discovery. Now she would know what she had always sought to know.

She waited. There was no response from Fomin.

Then Maryusa knew that there was to be no answer to her question. She understood that in answering her thus far Fomin had pursued a logical train of thought. There was no revelation in his words.

Maryusa did not feel let-down. Rather she felt a warmth towards Fomin. His rationality calmed her. She saw the foolishness of her questions.

"Fomin," she said at last, in a different voice, a warm voice, "you are very good for me."

There was a long interval of silence in the room. Except for the utter stillness, the stilled breathing, Maryusa might have thought Fomin was asleep.

At length he spoke.

"How many children have gone from the school to work for the Germans?"

The question plummeted like a stone out of the darkness.

"I do not know," Maryusa answered, before she was aware of answering. "I do not know that any have gone to work for the Germans. I do not know about that. Some children have gone away. I do not know where they have gone. Some have gone to the villages. Perhaps they are dead. How can I know?"

"But many children are gone, yes?"

"I do not know."

"You remember the names?"

"No."

"You know the names of the children?"

"Some. But we no longer keep names. There are no passports to say which are Jews. We keep no records for fear of the Germans."

"Yet the Germans do not trouble you?"

"Not lately."

"The Germans give you bread. They do not come for *Arbeiten.* They leave you in peace."

"Yes."

"Yet they make trouble everywhere else."

"Yes. I do not know."

"The records destroyed were Soviet records, yes?"

"Yes."

"But you can remember the names of the children? You can remember the names of the families, yes?"

"It is not possible to remember."

"You will remember the child Samoilov?"

"Sophia! You have seen her?"

"You must remember other names?"

"No. I do not remember," Maryusa said.

Fomin did not continue his interrogation. Maryusa found his silence more oppressive than his questions. In speech she could defend herself. She had prepared, many times, the answers she would make to such questions. Now that she had made them they sounded empty. Obstinacy made her cling to them.

At last she spoke again.

"Fomin," she said, "have you ever loved anyone?"

"Naturally. It is normal."

"No, I mean have you ever loved someone, like your mother?"

"The child loves its parents. The parents protect the child."

"Have you ever thought that you might have children of your own?"

"It is something that could happen."

"I love *my* children."

"It is an illusion. They are not your children."

"By adoption they are mine."

"That is bourgeois sentimentality."

Maryusa did not speak for some time. Then she said:

"Fomin, is it true that the Red Army makes a big victory?"

"Yes."

"Will the Red Army come this far? To Kharkiv?"

"Certainly. Stalin has said that every kilometre of Soviet land will be freed of the German Fascist invaders."

"When will they come?"

"They will come."

"Fomin, I am afraid."

There was a pause for a moment. Then Fomin spoke with a carefulness of words that was chilling to Maryusa.

"For those who are Soviet-friendly there is no need to be afraid."

Then he added, less weightily:

"There is no need to be afraid with me."

When Olympia arrived at the schoolhouse next day she was rewarded for the trouble she had taken over her appearance. She received Fomin's closest attention. But when she smiled at him there was no response. The involuntary grin which she had provoked at their last spring parting was not repeated. His scrutiny was detached and quite cold. The eyes were narrowed, watchful. He seemed to be poised, listening for sounds beyond her presence.

Olympia began to chat lightly with Maryusa about small things. She moved about the room, and even into the school corridors and back again, talking of this and that, acting indeed as if Fomin were not there. Occasionally she would throw a veiled glance in his direction. Then she would look away with a half-smile on her face. Her chatter was gay and irresponsible.

She had brought some food, a few slices of sausage, and this she distributed with the air of a grand lady and, at the same time, a comrade. Now she began to talk about Russian men. She was full of admiration for Russian men. She admired Russian men for their strength. Russian men were handsome. They made love very passionately. A woman was fortunate who had a Russian man. A woman who had a Russian man would do anything for him.

Suddenly Fomin broke in on Olympia's bright talk.

"Why do you come?" he said.

"To see you," Olympia said. She smiled at him.

"Yes. Why?"

"I like to see you."

"You have told your German I am here?"

"No."

"I think you lie. You have a trap, yes?"

"There is no trap."

"Why not?"

"I come to see a Russian. I do not denounce him."

"Well," Fomin said.

Olympia thought she saw a softening of Fomin's stern attitude. She dropped her frivolous air and became grave.

"I am your friend, Fomin," she said.

"You have left your German?"

"He is nothing."

"But you have left him?"

"He is not important to us."

"Then you plan to tell him?"

"No. But he will give me information which I shall give to you."

"It is not necessary," Fomin said. "The Red Army has all the information."

"Do not be so sure," Olympia said. "My German is a big German. He has much information."

"You do not speak the truth."

"It is true," Olympia said.

"You have another objective."

"My God," Olympia said, "how difficult he is."

"Why do we have to talk like this," Maryusa said.

"Look at me," Olympia said. "Look at me, Fomin. Do you not find me beautiful?"

"It has another objective," Fomin said. "Perhaps you are afraid the Germans will be defeated. You would like to be a Communist?"

"*Sheit ab,*" Olympia said. "What an idea!"

"It would be simpler to betray us now," Fomin said.

"Us? Who is us?"

"Why should we quarrel?" Maryusa said.

"Then it is coming sooner than I thought," Olympia said. "It is true things go badly at the front."

"Badly?" Fomin said. "Badly for you."

"Yes," Olympia said.

An expression of disdain entered Fomin's face.

"You are tired of your German?" he said quietly.

"No," Olympia said. "Yes."

"You like Germans?"

"Some are better than others."

"But now you would prefer a Russian?"

Olympia shrugged her shoulders. She was confused. The situation had not developed at all along the lines she had anticipated.

"It is clear," Fomin said, "that you are a spy."

"All the time you talk about spies," Olympia said.

"You would obtain information from me which you would give to the Germans," Fomin said.

As he said this his face assumed an expression of such lofty contempt and moral superiority that Olympia was suddenly angered.

"It is not true," Olympia said.

A flush spread over Olympia's face. It became suddenly the face of a Ukrainian peasant. Cunning rose to its surface and firmed there like the crust on a vodka mash.

"*I* know why you sent the *Deda* away," Olympia said. "They have use for him, eh?"

Fomin looked at her sharply.

"And I know now why *you* are here," Olympia added. "Why didn't I think of it? Of course, that is why they have sent you here."

"What do you say!"

Fomin had become tense. His eyes had an incalculable fury in them. The hard, weathered face was taut, the colourless catlike eyes appeared to burn.

"But you won't be able to do it," Olympia said. "Not now."

Fomin stepped swiftly towards her.

"*Predatelka!* Traitor!" he said.

Suddenly Olympia smiled. It was a smile of innocent triumph and superb good nature. She sat down and she looked at Fomin as if the phenomenon of an angry man were something that especially interested her.

"I shall not betray you," Olympia said. "But you will not be able to do it."

Now she frankly laughed and shook out the ringlets of her absurdly fair hair. She lifted a soft white hand exposing the tinted fingernails in a pose of elegance.

It was at this moment that Maryusa began to hate Olympia. There was in Olympia's smile, in her attitude, an appraisal of Fomin's character which Maryusa could not abide. It was as if Olympia invited, indeed would provoke, and with pleasure endure, the eruption of that violence which lay, well-disciplined, but nevertheless like a terrible threat, frightening Maryusa, within Fomin. Maryusa knew that Olympia's superiority to the threat grew out of her experience with men, her knowledge of the foundations of violence, its expression, and its easy expenditure. What angered Maryusa and made her hate Olympia was that Olympia's knowledge was amoral, was indifferent to the origins of violence, the mechanics of its canalisation, accepted it with candour, and this, though Maryusa sensed it now for the first time and would have been incapable of explaining it, was abhorrent to her nature. Her nature commanded that violence be only moral.

The emotion, arriving swiftly and unannounced, of hating Olympia, which faded immediately and of which Maryusa repented, had the effect of causing Maryusa to accept the violence she sensed within Fomin to be moral. She saw now that Fomin's self-control and reasonableness must proceed from an inner moral strength. She saw with a sudden illumination that Fomin had always had this moral strength, but that it was only now, since his return, that it was mature and ascertainable. She did not know from what source the morality sprang. She did not know its exact nature. Morality might be diffuse, but whatever its other aspects she could judge this one: the rejection of promiscuity.

"You must go," Maryusa said to Olympia.

"You are silly," Olympia said. "You must be in love with him."

"How can you speak of such things?" Maryusa said.

"Because I know," Olympia said.

"*You* cannot know," Maryusa said.

"Huh," Olympia said.

"Go now," Maryusa said, "and never come back."

"*Go!*" Fomin said.

She stood up and laughed in Fomin's face.

"You are here for nothing," Olympia said. "I like my German and he likes me. He has told me that the children in this school may be too valuable for the SS to leave them behind."

Suddenly the violence that Maryusa expected broke.

Fomin struck Olympia. It was a short sharp blow, not a boxer's blow, but an angled blow, swift, almost invisible to the eye, and of such hardness and force that it might have been made by a small rod flying out of a disintegrating dynamo. It took her at the base of the throat, sending her spinning backwards into her chair, paralysing the nervous system in a wave of pain that spread deep down into her sturdy trunk and feathered through her thighs and knees and strong legs down to her very toes. The pain was exquisite.

Fomin had gone.

As Olympia recovered, that was what she noticed first. Fomin had gone. She sat up and nursed her throat. She was red in the face. The pain had dispersed and there was now only the feeling of being bruised.

She tried to speak, but her tongue was like a fish in her throat. Then she said:

"The son-of-a-bitch."

The expression stirred Maryusa.

"He has gone," she said.

Olympia looked at Maryusa. Suddenly she saw that Fomin's departure was a catastrophe.

"You couldn't have kept him," Olympia said.

"He will not come back," Maryusa said.

"Don't you see," Olympia said. "Only *I* could have kept him here. I could have done it. But not you."

As though hearing her for the first time, Maryusa looked at Olympia with a strange faraway expression.

"You," Maryusa said, "you *prostitute*."

Olympia said nothing. She looked tenderly at Maryusa. She took her leopardskin coat and put it on. She came over to Maryusa and, bending close to her, spoke softly.

"Then you do love him?" Olympia said.

Maryusa's answer was inaudible.

"My poor Marshenka," Olympia said.

Olympia left the schoolhouse. She walked away holding her hand to her throat. "The son-of-a-bitch," she said to herself, smiling.

Day after day Lydia Artemova had patrolled the main streets of Kharkiv exposing herself to foreign eyes. At first she had been afraid. But nothing had happened and she had gained confidence. Finally she had been able to look the foreigners in the eye. It had been a strong thing to do, to look at the men in the black and grey uniforms and those in the good civilian clothes without dropping one's eyes. It was proof of the strength of the organisation. The organisation, so far as she had been able to observe it, was small, but every one of its members was firm. Beyond this there must be people who knew of the existence of the organisation but no longer had the impulse to betray its members. Having this now behind her, being no longer alone, Lydia Artemova felt safe. As day succeeded day she had become bolder. She walked constantly in the vicinity of the military and administrative buildings.

And then, of course, it had happened. She had seen him. She had been standing in the Paulus Platz and she had seen him come out of the Krasnaya Hotel. For a minute or two he had stood before the doors of the hotel in his black overcoat. She had seen him put up his gloved hand and press down his black hat so that the edge of the hat touched his ears. She had stood there watching him, unable to move. Then he had walked away and she had seen him turn up a small side street. Even then she had not moved. He had been out of sight for a full minute before she had been able to cross the street and hurry after him. She had gained the turning, but he had been nowhere in sight.

Her feeling had been greater than disappointment. It was again this deep sense of having committed a wrong act, for she blamed herself for not having moved more quickly to intercept him; and behind this was the unacknowledged intimation that her slowness had been deliberate. What was the matter with her? Why was she like this? There he had stood, the Fascist lackey, the provocateur, the counter-revolutionary, the Bukharinite, the Enemy of the People, the betrayer of his country, and she had failed to close with him, as she had been told to do, as she had been determined to do. She had been full of purpose, optimism, strength, and then at the moment of seeing him her mind had been clouded by an involuntary emotion.

Her emotion had been a vision (arising from sources

progressively self-censored through the years) of this man standing facing a wall, hour after hour, day after day, the muscles quivering, the veins swelling, slipping to his knees, rising again, a rifle butt thumping sharply into his kidneys, urinating in his trousers, swaying, given rest but suddenly made to stand again before his bones had time to rest; standing there while other things go on, others are interrogated behind his back and from the corridors come the shrieks of the beaten; standing there without control of his sphincter, fainting only to be brought back with a bucket of cold water, made to stand on, given warm water to drink, told to sit, told to rise; questioned now, anxious to tell all he knows, but what he knows is never enough, never what the Interrogator knows he must know, the Interrogator not yet ready to relinquish him, nor yet to end him, for he is that important mystery, a political deviation, thus needing to be probed yet deeper, to reach that which is unreachable in the soul of this man, the antithesis; so he stands facing the wall which he can no longer see, thirsty now, with the sound behind him of *Narzan* being poured into a glass, and the white smoke of *papyros* blown his way, completely soft now, malleable, but not yet penetrable, not yet understood by them, so standing on on on into infinity.

Seeing this in that fractional moment, all the secret hidden images of a lifetime of subterfuged thought, now telescoped together, blurred, imprecise, Lydia Artemova had been paralysed. And then, as she had at last moved after the stranger, she had been in a fury with herself, cursing under her breath the traitor and betrayer who had dared to talk to her, saying to herself that any fate was too good for him. But she had not caught up with him.

Returning to her address that night she received a message sending her to a new address.

Lydia Artemova realised she was at the centre of the *Active*. She did not dare look about her, or exhibit curiosity, but she sensed that there was already more activity, a greater boldness than there had been the last time she had made contact with them. A woman brought her a bowl of soup and a piece of black bread and she seated herself to eat. She saw the man with the dark blue-black jaw and large eyes with curling eyelashes, but he was the only man she had seen before. The others were unknown to her. One of them was a fattish white-faced man. They did not talk to her.

The room was warm and the atmosphere was close. Lydia Artemova felt that it must be well guarded. Feeling this protection more strongly, Lydia Artemova regained her confidence. She was ashamed for the thoughts she had had in the street. To think like that was weakness. She must guard herself against such thoughts. She felt again the need to perform some prodigious act to prove her loyalty and devotion to the Party. Tomorrow she would go to the Krasnaya Hotel, for that was clearly where the stranger lived, and she would wait for him there. She would enter the hotel, pretending to be a food vendor, and she would find him there. She would give him this message, which was no more than an address, which he would go to, and which would put him in the hands of the underground organisation, which was, after all, no more than he had asked. She would tell them now that she had failed today, but that she had found out where he had lived, and that tomorrow she would perform her task.

Having made up her mind Lydia Artemova felt immediately free to look around. She saw this young man who had been a Komsomol come in. She remembered that his name was Fomin. This young man took his soup and bread and began to eat. He looked at her without any sign of recognition, though she knew that he recognised her. Then this Fomin began to talk quietly to the fattish white-faced man. The young man spoke in a low voice and the white-faced man did not answer him.

Then the fattish white-faced man began talking to Lydia Artemova. He asked her a simple question. There was nothing unusual about the question. The language was plain enough. But it was as if the earth had opened and Lydia Artemova was falling into a bottomless abyss. She did not know which way to look. For the voice of the fattish white-faced man was the voice of the Interrogator.

Lydia Artemova was looking at him, her eyes wide open, her lips parted, looking at him as he went on speaking and still not able to reconcile the Voice which had become part of her thoughts, her life almost, with this, its human casement. She looked at the pallid face, the calm unsparkling eyes, the black hair with the quiff falling over the right temple, the short nose with the upturned nostrils, the shapeless lips, and it was as if there were inside this flesh a machine that was talking, a recording machine that was de-recording itself, not mind and matter. And then, to complete her confusion, she saw now enter the room the small man in the Russian style dress with the cavalry boots and the leather cap like a pancake on his head. He came into the room and his black eyes were immediately upon her. She looked at him and it was now already better because it was as it was before, the little man looking at her, and the other, the Voice, speaking to her unseen. It was the same voice, the cadre-trained Soviet-educated voice.

But now the Interrogator was demanding answers. The questions he was asking concerned the schoolhouse. So that in giving her answers it was necessary to look at him. She looked at him, into the dull calm eyes, into the fattish pallid face, and she answered and the answers gave her no trouble, even though they were not the whole truth.

Alone in her room Maryusa did not sleep very well. She was not thinking, but listening. Her ears were attuned to the slightest sound. This night she was aware that the children were talking more than usual. She waited for the children to quieten and when they did not she rose and went silently towards the big room. Here she listened. The children's voices were now clearly audible.

"The man has a moustache," a child said.

"It is an old man."

"It is not a German."

"Of course, it is not a German."

"Who is it?"

"I will tell *them* who it is."

"You will tell the SS, yes?"

"Yes, I will tell."

"Who is it?"

"It is a picture of Comrade Stalin."

"Who is Comrade Stalin?"

"You are too young to remember."

There were a few seconds of silence and then an infant voice chanted:

"Thank Comrade Stalin for this happy life."

The phrase, uttered parrot-fashion, was the refrain which all Soviet children, up to the time of the Germans, had been obliged to repeat in unison, standing before their desks, each morning as they began classes. The phrase coming now out of the unlighted classroom was like a stroke of lightning.

Maryusa stepped forward.

In the faint light of the flickering wood stove which kept the big room above freezing point she saw that many of the children were awake. Those that were awake were looking at a large portrait which had been hung from one wall.

Maryusa recognised the portrait as one which had formerly hung in the room of the principal of the school, a woman recently deceased, and which, shortly after the arrival of the Germans, Maryusa had taken down and hidden in a storeroom.

Maryusa moved to cross the room. A firm hand restrained her.

She turned and saw that Fomin was standing behind her. In the half-dark he looked as she remembered him looking on the evening of his return. The rigidity of his poised body made him seem statuesque. His head was a head of gun-metal. The light-coloured cat's eyes blazed.

"Listen!" he whispered.

"It is the Communist Führer," a boy said.

"Death to the Communists," a girl said.

Maryusa snatched herself away from Fomin's grip. She went across the room and took the big picture down from its place. She bore it away to another part of the school. It was some time before she came back to Fomin.

"How could you have done such a thing!" she said. "If I had not heard the children talking something terrible might have happened tomorrow."

Fomin looked at her.

"I know what you mean," Maryusa said. "I know it is bad. But it is too early to do this. Besides it is not the way to do it."

Fomin said nothing.

She went to her room and Fomin followed. She lay down on her truckle bed. She was exhausted. She heard Fomin take up his old position by the window. She heard him rub the frost off the glass with his finger so that he could see outside the schoolhouse. It was moonlight outside and the snow that lay lightly over the ground was reflected through the window. She could see him now, faintly in profile against the white window. He was looking out, but she knew that he was doing this in order calmly to govern his fury. She knew him well enough now to know that a thwarted action must be a great frustration to him. She knew that he must now be thinking how to overcome this. He would be thinking of this all the time he was looking out of the window. His mind, well-disciplined, unconfused, would be thinking how to achieve the prescribed aim. Knowing this she was a little happy. There was in this a momentary ascendancy for her. She knew him better than he knew her. Smiling to herself she fell into a light sleep.

She awoke to feel Fomin close to her.

She awoke gently, but there was a great trepidation in her heart. She smelt the heaviness of his clothes. The damp of his breath was on her cheek.

"Fomin," she said.

Fomin made no reply. She could not see him. He was stooped above her, close to her, for an interminable time.

Then she felt his hand, metallic, cold, press on her shoulder and then move across her body. She waited, inert.

Firmly, without haste, the hands broke open her jacket, parted her clothing. She felt the cold strike at her thighs. She was ashamed suddenly of the cavity that was her abdomen, the sharpness that was her hip bones.

Silently the hand possessed her. The sensation was terror.

"No!" Maryusa cried.

There was no sound now, but an exertion of strength under which she was flattened like a pelt. And then a tearing, splitting, shearing agony which could not be endured and then suddenly could be endured, a flowing, a sweetness, and then again terror.

"Fomin!"

There was only his breath.

"Say you love me, Fomin!" No sound.

"Oh, say it. Only say it."

And then swiftly, like a cloud shadow, the anxiety, the closing, the glassiness, and the going on and on, the never-ending, the wanted ending, that which promised no end, no detumescence either, the suddenly cold belly, narrowing thighs, the drying-up, the emptiness, the weariness, the about-to-happen not happening.

"Say it, Fomin. Say you love me!"

The breath hissing and then:

"I love you."

Too late for the cold.

"No, you don't love me."

"Yes, I love you."

"Do not lie, now."

"I love you."

"No, but *I* love you. Yes, I do, I do."

And then the return of strength, the clear mind, the moving, the determined predetermined movement, the obstinate clash of flesh, the harshness, the severity.

And then the end.

Truly the end with lungs dry as sand and limbs wounded and the grateful bleeding, the self-annihilation, the needed mortification, the hatefulness of self, the betrayal of self and the disbelief, and all else.

At last only sadness.

"I'm sorry," Maryusa said.

"Why?"

"I'm sorry for what I am."

"You are all right. It is always like that."

"It is being without food."

"Yes?"

And in that moment, in Maryusa, a vast and appealing sadness for Fomin, for the innocent maleness, the youth of him, the not-knowing, the never-could-knowing, the sorrow for what was not.

She put out her hand to touch him.

"I would do anything," she said.

"Tomorrow," Fomin said, "we will put up the picture."

The silence was long and heavy.

"It is not possible," Maryusa said. "The picture is destroyed."

Dr. Karandash lit a cigarette.

"So you see," he said, "I am a kind of war correspondent. It is true that, as such, I am everywhere regarded as the Obergruppenführer's personal spy."

Dr. Karandash drew heavily on his cigarette. He spoke now with careful casualness.

"Ah, that first experience! Shall I tell you about it? I think you will understand then the contest between the Obergruppenführer and myself. He had said that I should write a book celebrating the activities of the SS, and he had arranged that the reportage should begin at the tractor factory. I was driven there in the gas wagon, the *Dushegubky* van, by an SS man called Müller. I do not think that it was an accident that we were thrown together, for I believe he too was under test. At the tractor factory we were told that the Obergruppenführer had ordered that we go together to see the work that was being done. We were shown the way. It was a small ravine some distance from the factory. You have often seen such ravines, scored out of the steppe in some sudden thaw and enlarged by spring and summer rains. It was, I remember, shaped like a ship, like one of those long oil barges, tankers, you may see on the Danube or, for that matter, on the Dnieper. It began in shape like the bows of a ship. There was a drop of a few metres to the deck below the gunwales, that is, the sides of the ravine, but so much longer than a ship. Yes, the deck extended for perhaps six or seven hundred metres. It was covered with snow, just as are ships' decks in winter, and down the middle of the deck, so to speak, there was this path, like the catwalk on a big tanker, except, of course, there were no handrails, only the snow on either side of the path, for the path had been trodden down and the snow was packed tight underfoot, but at the sides of the path it was thigh-high. So we stepped down into the ravine.

"There were urine holes in the snow and the snow was

unclean, as if many people had come this way. That perhaps was the cause of our misadventure. But I remember that it was very bleak, very quiet, and we did not at all like this feeling. It is difficult to remember with accuracy. Did we really feel like that then? Or was it afterwards that we felt like that? Before a soldier goes into battle he has premonitions, yes? If he is wounded he will remember his premonitions and ascribe them to Fate, or some other mystery. But if he emerges from battle unscathed he will forget all about his premonitions. Is not that so? Yes? I think that we did have premonitions that day. We felt uncertain, almost afraid. I remember there was perhaps ground for such feelings. Because I remember now that we had not gone more than a hundred metres when we saw, both of us saw it at the same time, this leg, white and drifted with snow, but nevertheless a human leg, a bare leg, bootless, projecting out of the snow, just as if its owner had dived off the side of the ravine, which was quite steep, more than a man's height above us on either side, into the snow and had stuck there in the drift, his leg pointing upward. Although we knew that each of us had seen this leg we said nothing to each other, for the feeling of being closed in between the walls of the ravine, on the deck of this very long, very big tank ship, may have been on account of the infirmity beneath us. The sensation of being in a ship was not alone the shape and size of the ravine, but at times there was this feeling that a ship was indeed beneath us, that feeling you may have at the end of an ocean voyage when your ship is docked and there is nevertheless the expectancy and preparation for that ever-so-slight falling away and rise of the deck under your feet which your inner sense of balance tells you is there, though your eyes perceiving the ship to be firmly tied to the dock know to be not so. That was quite the strangest part of the journey, because we each felt that we had to go on to the end of the ravine, and when I say 'we' I am quite sure that the man Müller also felt it, although I never did have the opportunity of comparing notes with him afterwards, for he was taken to a different hospital and I have not seen him since that day, but I am as certain as I am sitting here that Müller also felt that we had to go on, and that it was somehow, although I know this will sound absurd, our destiny to go on down that snow-trodden path in the ravine.

"I have described this path as a catwalk on the snow-covered deck of the tanker. I think it is an exact description. For that is how we were now walking, bearing our weight subtly on one side and then on the other, but all the time stepping with the care of a cat on a rooftop. Then, of course, it happened, the inevitable happened: the ground gave way beneath us. I suppose that there had been some contraction, or expansion perhaps, as a result of the variable temperatures of the previous week, some natural phenomenon such as occurs in glaciers and other large ice formations, because what we were now walking on, even though its even white cover made it look like a huge tarpaulin-covered deck, was in actual fact ice. Our movement, or it may have been that caused by the feet preceding ours, had worked some kind of an effect on the ice, enough anyhow to start the crack, to determine where the ice mass would crack, for this it what happened, the deck, so to speak, opened under our feet, a fissure in the ice, a crevasse. We acted, I remember, as any Alpinist must act in those circumstances. In the instant of falling we flung ourselves at the edges of the crevasse, but the loose snow on the surface fell away under our clawing fingers, and then we tried to lodge our knees, toes, arms into the frozen walls. But it was not possible to hold on to the ice, even when it was so far below freezing point, as it was that day, as to be sticky to the glove. So we went sliding, grappling at the side of the crevasse, plunging finally in a metallic shower of ice to the bottom of the abyss. We had fallen, I am not sure, perhaps ten or twenty metres, for, looking up at the strip of daylight which was the top of the crevasse, as I immediately did, looking up at it and clawing involuntarily at the sides of the crevasse, as if I could still somehow scramble up them, I was blinded by the light above, the light source intensified by ice reflections, blurring the edges and promontories of the fissure making all around me dark.

"It was the behaviour of Müller which calmed me. I remember that he had screamed as the ground gave way below us. It is possible that I also screamed, although I was not conscious of having done so, and my dry and sore throat may as well have been due to the cold as to any excessive vocal effort, then or later when I shouted with effect. But it is certain that I heard Müller scream and now at the bottom of the crevasse I could hear him moaning. I presumed immediately that he had been injured by his fall, an arm, a rib, perhaps a leg broken. I must confess that it was not commiseration which caused me to look for Müller, but the sudden overwhelming feeling that I might be alone there in that crevasse. Such a sense of loneliness you cannot imagine. I moved about very cautiously looking for him, for I thought that any untoward movement might cause a further movement of the ice mass, either closing us in altogether, or bringing the mass in upon us. I found him lodged on what was the floor of the abyss, the icebed of a stream which had flowed through the ravine, quite unhurt, but much shaken, and gently moaning. I think, perhaps, that Müller had understood our situation more quickly than I had. I am willing to believe that Müller is more imaginative than I am. It may have been that his imagination enabled him to see, even before our eyes became accustomed to the gloom, even before our fall, what was about us. For, of course, as you have guessed, we had fallen into one of their disposal pits. The ravine was full of bodies. Below the snow-covered deck of that huge tank-barge there was a cargo of dead. How many? How can I guess? What does it matter? Does a mathematical symbol have reality? I have heard since that there are fifty thousand bodies there. It is not improbable. They do not themselves know. For here in the Ukraine they do not keep those records which, I have been told, are being kept in Poland, we having been assigned a category in the order of human animals, even below that of the Poles, so that the methodism which distinguishes them in other lands is unnecessary here, and numbers, in the face of the numberless hordes of Asia, do not matter.

"Do I sound bitter? I do not mean to be. How can I be bitter about this? I think now that bitterness is a form of self-indulgence, a kind of romanticism. It is also a mask of conscience. It is certainly for later when you are far away and wish to make your position clear to those who do not care."

Dr. Karandash was not satisfied with his narration. He liked the effect the story was having on his listener. He was still able to feel that what he was saying was not *exactly* his experience, but soon, he knew, his memory of the experience would be merged into the form he was now giving it, and this form would be the reality, and only occasionally, if ever, would he be troubled with an uncaptive image, an uncharted recollection. The important thing would soon be his power to move the listener, not as he himself had been moved by his experience, for that could never be, indeed must not be, but to *move* someone else, another, to create an experience, a sympathy of feeling.

"I suppose they have covered the pit since then. I suppose that was what they had intended to do, to have working parties shovel in the earth from the sides of the ravine, but they were so busy, and the earth was already frozen, the winter as you remember having come so suddenly and so severely, that they did not bother, for the bodies of the dead froze immediately into the solid mass we saw, legs and arms and bodies interlocked like the links of a sheet of chain mail, the snow sifting through the chinks of the mass, thawing and then freezing hard, joining it all into one flesh as hard as iron and as brittle as glass. For, as our eyes grew accustomed to the gloom at the bottom of the crevasse, we saw bodies all around us, some ruddy, waxlike, as you have often seen the dead in winter, others white as marble, all kinds, tall and short, old and young, people of all cultures, men, women and children. I remember that at our feet at the bottom of the crevasse there was the head of an old man. In our fall one of us had fallen on the old man's head and under the sudden weight it had snapped off, as clean as a carrot, and as raw, and now it rested at our feet, staring up at us through frosty spectacles."

Here Dr. Karandash paused. How was it possible to *tell* what then happened? How was it possible to make it credible to the listener? And yet, if he did not give it narrative form, clothe it with words, this moment would always be with him, would come back again and again to trouble him. For Müller had picked up the head and had held it before him and had begun a monologue that was all too rational, too lucid, to be sane.

"There was in this situation," Dr. Karandash went on, "all the elements of romantic horror, but that is not how

I felt. I am not a romantic, or I should say that perhaps my romanticism takes another form, certainly not the Germanic form, that cultivation of the idea of death which has made the Germans the slaves of the Baroque. I was not afraid of what was around me. I understood, of course, that it was horrible, and I hated it, in the same way that I shall hate to die, but it did not affect my reason. We made several efforts to climb out of the crevasse, trying to find footholds in this place and that, grasping whatever offered, but in the end bringing down on us a further shower of glasslike limbs. We also explored the length of the crevasse, finding that we were in its broadest part and that but a few metres on either side of us it narrowed to a bare handspace between the closely packed bodies. So I contented myself with shouting. I shouted not all at once, but at intervals, once every ten minutes perhaps, although it was impossible to guess the time. But I was sure we would be missed. I was sure that those in whom the Obergruppenführer had shown such an interest would merit a search. I was wrong. My shouting came to nothing but hollow echoes. At the top of the crevasse they could not have had more force than a whisper. Müller did not shout for help. But he talked. All the time he was talking. How can I describe it? He was talking to the dead, to those frozen bodies. The afternoon declined and it was soon night. How can I tell you of that night? For warmth we huddled together. We were, of course, warmly clad, but the frost nevertheless penetrated our clothing and our hands and feet and at length our faces became numb and feelingless. You know that sleep comes quickly to relieve those so distressed.

"I was yielding to sleep when the terrible sound brought me back to my senses. It is useless for me to attempt to describe the sound. It seemed to be coming out of that vast pack of bodies, eerie, long-drawn, fading, rising to a high scream between the ice walls. I say I am not a romantic, but at this moment I was overtaken by romantic superstition. I imagined at that moment that the sound was made by all those people there, those souls in anguish crying in the night, crying at one moment all around us so that the sound would seem to shatter the ice and then, diminishing as it rushed upwards, skywards, a long-drawn spirit wail ascending into the black frozen heaven. Nor was the sound a momentary experience, but it went on and on in a measurable period of time, and it was only after such a time that I understood what it was, for one can be romantic only for the shortest length of time in a world in which reality is thrust at you at every hand. It was the baying of hounds. That was how they found us. The dogs they keep to pursue and bring down those who attempt to run from the place of execution, either at the place of execution, or on the way there, which do this work more efficiently than man can do it, had detected our presence there at the bottom of the crevasse. Their baying brought the guard. The guard, brought to the edge of the crevasse, deciding that there was life at the bottom of it, perhaps an escapee, one who would wish the privilege of being shot before resuming his place there among those who had gone before him, as who reasonably would not, shouted down, and then my feeble shouting back, which I was careful to couch in German, at least in German tones, understood that there was more than a prisoner there, went away and presently, though it seemed a long time, came back with a lantern and a rope and others to help him.

"So we were brought back to the tractor factory and they wrapped us in blankets and put us in one of the barracks they have there, the one, the only one, they had heated, which happened to be full of strange creatures, lunatics, for they had been gathering them in from the asylums in Kharkiv and they had them there in the barracks room, the heated room, one they had heated especially for the lunatics perhaps, since many of them were those demented ones who tear the clothes off themselves, out of some strange necessity implicit in the SS mind to preserve those to be executed until the correct moment of execution. For that was to be the fate of the lunatics on the morrow, or shortly thereafter, in accordance with their hygienic practice. I remember it very well, recovering there in the barracks room, my teeth endlessly chattering, my hands and feet and face blue and swollen like sausages, blistered and putrifying, my lungs seized with the congestion that was to hold me fast for a month, recovering consciousness in that barracks room full of pitiful lunatics, naked old women, madmen chanting verses of the ancient poets, and yes, some poor palsied children who were not mad at all. I remember that Müller appeared to be deeply affected. It was the last I saw of him."

Sitting side by side on the wooden bench behind the schoolhouse in the Sadovo-Kulikovskaya Dr. Karandash and Professor Shevchenko could see the tall white building of the *Gostudastrovoi* and the spires of the Uspensky Cathedral.

"In our generation two thousand million will die," said Professor Shevchenko.

"So many!" said Dr. Karandash. "Ah, I see you mean us."

"Some die sooner than others. It is a loss of years, of experience," said Professor Shevchenko.

"It is the manner of the dying."

"The manner of the dying does not affect the dead."

"It affects the living," said Dr. Karandash. "It affects, precisely, those who determine the manner, the means, of dying. Those who assume the responsibility. One must have a good responsibility. A high moral."

"And he, the Obergruppenführer, has not?"

"He has the *Dushegubky* van," said Dr. Karandash.

"I see that you are deeply involved in your contest with the Obergruppenführer," said Professor Shevchenko.

"I know now," said Dr. Karandash, "that I returned to the Ukraine out of a profound sense of guilt. At the time I did not understand it. I felt I was acting out of other motives."

"The universal guilt."

"It is the core of our society. But the Obergruppenführer threw me into the abyss. I became one of those in the abyss. Out of the abyss I am the Obergruppenführer's implacable enemy. My guilt is absolved."

"Why does he not destroy you then?"

"He would. But he would do it in his own way. He would have me smothered in guilt, as he is. He would drive me into guilt as he has driven others. Thus he continues to thrust me into every horror on his list. I am forced to witness the executions; I see the psychological attacks; I arrive in time for the extermination of villages; I am present at those staff conferences which plan the destruction of the country and the people I was born to. Yes, I am sickened; but I do not weaken."

"Yet, rectitude is not strength."

Dr. Karandash smiled.

"As I have told you," he said, "it began over my pretensions as a military writer. The curious thing is that this experience has made me a very good military writer. For, of course, I have seen everything; I have watched their tactics in the field; I have studied their methods."

"You believe the information to be valuable."

"Of course." Dr. Karandash patted a heavy notebook in his pocket. "Not only the disposition of their armies is shown here, but their weaknesses too, their *Dushegubky* rottenness."

Professor Shevchenko said nothing for several moments. Then he spoke quietly, but with some intensity.

"I must tell you there is something worse than the *Dushegubky* van," he said. "After all, what is race? You and I know that it is nothing, an accident, that it represents the opposite of human aspiration. One is a Krimchak or a Kalmuk, and one dies before one might reasonably be expected to die. More destructive is that discrimination which singles you out because you are a Socialist or an Anarchist, a Bukharinite or a Trotskyite, a Christian or a Communist, indeed anything which they are not, which they have the means of discovering. Both in its method and in its effect the assassination of the mind is more terrible."

Dr. Karandash was astonished. Never before had Professor Shevchenko so far committed himself.

"All that is true," he said, "but it has the weakness of being an intellectual conception. It cannot move people in the way that they can be and are being moved to expiate that guilt which Hitler has thrust upon them."

"Then we are lost."

Dr. Karandash looked sharply at Professor Shevchenko. The little man was trembling. The fantasy that had wrapped itself around him like a cloak was shed. The irony had gone out of his voice which was now clear and direct.

"You think," he said, "that this information which you have obtained will be of use to the Communists? You are wrong. They will disdain it."

"Please accept my assurance," said Dr. Karandash, with sudden insight, "that I shall not betray you."

"That is what you think now. But what are you? An idealist! A man of conscience! *They* will knead your soul like dough."

"Nevertheless," said Dr. Karandash, "you must tell me how I am to get in touch with the Communist underground."

"An *underground* organisation! I have never heard of such a thing."

Professor Shevchenko was regarding his friend with that mild candour which had been the mask of their first relations.

"Then I shall make my own arrangements."

"If you will."

"You have forgotten," said Dr. Karandash, "about Zeta Yarmoslansky."

"Zeta Yarmoslansky," repeated Professor Shevchenko dreamily.

"She is still a member of the Party?"

"Alas, yes."

"And living in Kharkiv still?"

"Yes."

"Forgive me for mentioning it, but I know your relationship."

"Who dares to guess about human relationships?"

"You will tell me where she lives."

"I do not know."

"I have only to find her. As a Party member she is bound to help me."

"You should not insist."

"You see, I knew her in those early times. I am sure I shall remember her."

"Remember her? Why not? Since you have met. Here at this bench, only a fortnight ago."

Dr. Karandash's mouth was wide open, but nothing issued from it.

"Her name, of course, is no longer Zeta Yarmoslansky, but Lydia Artemova," said Professor Shevchenko.
"Lydia Artemova!"
"You pay too much attention to names," said Professor Shevchenko. "I remember how you were impressed by the name Shevchenko. Yes, you did not know that there were so many Shevchenkos."
"There are so many? I did not know it."
"At various times the Party has asked members to change their names. This was the case with Zeta Yarmoslansky. She was then a writer of children's textbooks. The Party decisions have applied especially to writers and academicians and those whose names might appear on Party works. It is not new."
"I remember the phase," said Dr. Karandash. "The Party wished to diminish the role of the Jewish intellectuals."
"Is that what they said outside?"
"It seemed a sufficient explanation."
"So Zeta Yarmoslansky took the name of Artem. You remember Artem? He is all but forgotten now. He was the Bolshevik who secured Kharkiv."
"Party members live under many names," said Dr. Karandash, "but in the Party files they have only one."
"It showed originality," said Professor Shevchenko. "There is only one Artemova. Whereas there are many Shevchenkos. So many of us now bear names connected with our illustrious history."
"Artemova," said Dr. Karandash, "and I did not recognise her."
"Nor she you, apparently."
"If I had only known."
"You terrified her with your questions."
Dr. Karandash had a twinge of conscience.
"The war brought you together again, yes?"
"An accident brought us together. The accident of a half-insane child."
"And my stupid demands drove her away again?"
"I do not think so."
"Be assured I shall not trouble you again."
"A comedy of errors, as in an old play," said Professor Shevchenko.

"And Karandash. Did it ever occur to you that Karandash might not be *my* name?"

"It occurred to me."

"Karandash. A good *nom de plume,* if you will permit the pun."

"Out of Grebojedov, yes?"

"No; there was a young Ukrainian of our generation, forgotten now, who wrote superbly under the name of 'Pero.' I was influenced."

"In Moscow," said Professor Shevchenko, "Karandash is the name of a very distinguished clown."

Lydia Artemova had been sitting in Dr. Karandash's room in the Krasnaya Hotel for several hours. She had gained the room with the help of a Ukrainian maidservant.

She had arrived in a state of great agitation. The room had made no immediate impression on her, but being alone there, and quiet, her agitation was slowly contained.

The cause of her agitation was her last interview with the Interrogator. She had lied to him. She had never before lied to the Party. But the process by which a lie was uttered was not new to her.

She had worked among Party children at their most impressionable age, when they were most susceptible to personal feeling, when the little storms of jealousy, dislike, hate, possession, love, loyalty, all the bourgeois traits, were most evident, naïve, educible; and she had taught them to discipline their feelings, to divert their feelings into the all-embracing conscience of the Party. She had hated to find children who made their little confessions, exorcisms, with difficulty or, in recent years, glibly, often prevaricating; for she had known that these were the children of bourgeois origin, or in whom there was a bourgeois influence, whose parents were jealous of the Party claim on their children, parents whose secret aim was to divert the children's education along other lines, to encourage the children to have personal feelings and individual judgments. Whenever she had traced a latent anti-Party attitude in the home of a child Lydia Artemova had always exposed it, for she had known that no good could come of it and a child was better without such parents.

Now, herself in the grip of this process, she asked (her mind suddenly accepting the accumulated, hitherto-denied evidence of years): how many children have I turned into practised liars? How deeply has our children's morality been undermined?

The Interrogator had asked her about the children.

"What kind of children are there at this school?" he had asked in his indifferent, unaccented voice.

"Party children," she had replied.

"Former Party children," he had said, correcting her.

"Yes," she had said.

"Are they Jewish children?"

"No, not Jewish children," Lydia Artemova had said, lying without hesitation, for, of course, many of them, perhaps most of them, through the circumstances of their orphaning, were of Jewish origin.

"But the Germans believe them to be Jews, yes?"

"No," Lydia Artemova had said.

She had been terrified by this deliberate lie. For the moment she had thought only how to amend this lie, how best to please and disarm the Interrogator. She could do this by performing her Party tasks with dispatch. She had set out immediately to find the foreigner and to make for him a rendezvous with the Party.

Sitting now in his room, the hours passing, she had time to control her agitation.

She began to look around the room. It was a small room, furnished with the barest essentials. There was an old-fashioned wardrobe, a heavy brassbound table, and a couple of chairs. The bed was set into a small alcove and covered with a huge eiderdown counterpane. It was an undistinguished room, but its atmosphere was distinctly that of a man, a foreign man. The tobacco smell was foreign tobacco, real tobacco, not *mahorka.* The soap smell was perfumed shaving soap. The foot smell was good leather smell and wool. On the table there were a number of newspapers, an empty vodka bottle, an ash tray, a dirty glass, a nail file. On the window sill there was a shaving brush from which the lather had not been washed. The razor, no doubt a good one, had been hidden from sight.

On the bedside table there was a book. She picked the book up. It was a book of poems. In her life poetry had been a stern chant of duty. Now, as she idly turned the pages of the book in her hand she found it hard to understand the form, even the language. But time weighing heavily she began to read. Presently she was reading the poems with attention, repeating the verses to herself, pondering the music more than the meaning.

She saw the foreigner clearly now. He was a man who read and cherished poetry. He was a man who was moved by poetry. Yes, and by horror, and by human agony! He would come into this room at any moment and he would talk to her. He would ask questions.

She must go at once!

Yet she had her task to perform. It was her duty to give him the address to which he must go this night.

She could not wait. Against all the rules she now wrote the address and the time on the corner of a piece of newspaper. She inserted the piece of newspaper in the leaves of the book of poetry. She put the book beside the bed. She looked at the book, lying there beside the fat pillow, and then she took up the book and put it underneath the pillow, smoothing the pillow with a deft, lost gesture.

Having done this she had a feeling of great relief. Before leaving she took a few steps around the room. It was faintly exciting. He was a bachelor, of course. In the wardrobe there was a single suit of clothes and some shirts. She gazed for some moments at a pair of black shoes. Nothing suggests character more than shoes, she thought. There was a hat in the wardrobe. It was the kind of hat she had not seen before. It was a Homburg hat. The hat made her feel the foreignness of the man. The feeling was nostalgia.

In the bottom of the wardrobe, under a heap of empty vodka bottles, there was a bundle of papers. They were the Shevchenko and Yarmoslansky files which Dr. Karandash had taken from the archives of the NKVD more than a year before. The files were plainly marked and their official origin was apparent. Lydia Artemova picked up the file bearing her birth name. For a moment she held it in her hands as though it were a bomb. Then she sat down and began feverishly to ruffle through the papers.

Here were all her depositions, made at regular intervals over the years, in the cool Party language. But these she did not pause to read. It was those other documents, the affidavits of former friends and acquaintances, colleagues, even pupils, which made her gasp. Forgotten names most of them, but they had written, or sworn to, monstrous allegations.

There was one, however, written in a neat scholarly hand, which Lydia Artemova removed from the file and began to read. At some time the officers of the NKVD had asked Professor Shevchenko for a statement about his mistress. Professor Shevchenko had written sincerely and with great tenderness. The honesty of the statement carried conviction; none reading it could have doubted Lydia Artemova's devotion to her cause.

Lydia Artemova began to tremble. She dropped the papers into the bottom of the wardrobe.

Hastening out of Dr. Karandash's room she was too distraught to consider how the papers had come into the foreigner's possession.

THE INTERROGATOR: You have accomplished your task?

FOMIN: Yes.

INTERROGATOR: What task was assigned to you?

FOMIN: The task of helping stamp out counter-revolutionary Fascist tendencies in the Komsomol and Party organisation.

INTERROGATOR: Where?

FOMIN: At the school in the Sadovo-Kulikovskaya.

INTERROGATOR: What was the source of the counter-revolutionary Fascist tendencies at the school in the Sadovo-Kulikovskaya?

FOMIN: I don't know. It was like that after the Germans came.

INTERROGATOR: Do you remember your Marxist-Leninist training?

FOMIN: Yes.

INTERROGATOR: Who was the source? Remember that everything has its source.

FOMIN: Some children, some Pioneers, were like that.

INTERROGATOR: Why?

FOMIN: Perhaps they were children of secret counter-revolutionary Trotskyist-Bukharinite traitors in the Party.

INTERROGATOR: Correct. Do you think the children were themselves capable of forming a spy bloc?

FOMIN: No.

INTERROGATOR: Then the bloc was organised?

FOMIN: It must have been.

INTERROGATOR: Your task was to assist in the liquidation of this bloc before it could be put to further use by the Fascist military organisation?

FOMIN: I had specific tasks assigned to me by the Party.

INTERROGATOR: What proof have you that your tasks have been accomplished?

FOMIN: Today two SS men came to the school.

INTERROGATOR: Why?

FOMIN: They had been informed by spies of anti-Fascist propaganda at the school. They had evidence of an anti-German racial movement at the school.

INTERROGATOR: What did the SS men do?

FOMIN: They collected the evidence.

INTERROGATOR: Why did they not act immediately?

FOMIN: It proves that it is not a casual problem for them. It proves that the school was important for them. They went to obtain the order of a higher authority.

INTERROGATOR: Will they come back?

FOMIN: They said they would come back.

INTERROGATOR: Therefore the task of stamping out the counter-revolutionary Fascist spy bloc is not yet complete?

FOMIN: No.

INTERROGATOR: Thus the organisers of the spy bloc have been warned in time to escape?

FOMIN: She will not go.

INTERROGATOR: Then you know who the organiser of the spy bloc is?

FOMIN: Yes.

Dr. Karandash was having difficulty finding the address. It was in a part of the city he had not previously visited. There were no street signs here. He counted the houses and he came to this old wooden house which appeared to be vacant. The windows were roughly boarded up. The snow had not been cleared away from the door.

He knocked, but there was no response. It was then that he saw the sign: *"Verboten: Typhus"* rudely painted on the door. The sign chilled him. But after a little reflection he pushed the door open and stepped inside. It was very dark and cold. But there was a moon rising somewhere and its light, filtering through the cracks in the window boards, lessened the gloom. He made out the shape of a chair. He took a few steps towards the chair and sat down.

It seemed a very likely place for a meeting with an underground organisation. It was remote, difficult to find, deserted, forbidden to strangers. Soon someone would come. He pulled out his leather flask and took a swig of vodka.

He had been deeply touched to find the message in the book of poems under his pillow. Only a woman would have done that. Would she come tonight? He would confront her with their old friendship. What kind of people would she bring? What were these latter-day *Activists* like? Should he address them as Comrades? He would certainly do so. In the desperate urgency of war it was obvious that the old revolutionary spirit had been revived. It had revived itself despite the strictures of Stalinism. Otherwise how could an underground function? Underground organisations required men of good faith, trust and comradeship. Those wonderful comrades of his youth!

In the middle of his soliloquy Dr. Karandash remembered the correct phrase to describe his thinking. He was, literally, whistling in the dark.

The idea of making contact with the Communists had not become a reality until he had found this note in his bed. The note, put there by the former Zeta Yarmoslansky, was a challenge he had felt he must accept.

Dr. Karandash took another swallow of vodka. The cold made him uncomfortable. He could no longer bear the sensation of frost in his feet and fingers since his experience at the tractor factory a year ago. The cold in this dark, deserted house was a creeping bitter cold. He could feel the ice around him.

In the disposal pit every body had been frozen through, ice-hard and dry, but there had nevertheless been a faint, at first unrecognisable smell, not of decay or putrefaction, but something more subtle than that, a smell he could only think of as death itself. On various occasions during the last year he had smelled the smell. It would come to him in some place, on a street, or in a park, and it would be overwhelming, not as odour, for that was always elusive, but for the sudden spelling-out of the accompanying images in terrible vividness. Now, sitting in this sub-zero house waiting for contact with this woman, this man or men, whom he knew must have the house under observation, taking their time to see if he had been followed, he felt that smell growing on him.

He wondered if he should light a cigarette. But to strike a match might be taken as a signal of some kind.

The old house was very still. There was no sound. Dr. Karandash could stand it no longer. It seemed to him that he had waited an interminable period. He stood up. There was a stronger moonlight outside now and his eyes were accustomed to the gloom. He *must* light a cigarette! He walked cautiously across the room, looking for a secluded place in which to strike a match so that no glimmer of light would escape.

He walked into a smaller rear room and came to a sudden halt. He remained fixed, motionless in his tracks. In the rear room there was someone sitting watching him. All the time they had been here watching him, sitting in the chair, quietly watching him.

"I am Karandash," he said, hoarsely.

There was no reply. The moonlight outside brightened and he saw clearly the figure of an old woman sitting beside a white-tiled stove. The light was reflected glassily from her eyes. There was a rag blanket over her knees, but the white-tiled stove was ice cold. Dr. Karandash touched the old woman. The cloth of her dress was starched with frost. She had been dead for a long time.

Dr. Karandash took a number of hasty steps out of the little room. He could not put his thoughts together.

As he stood there he heard an automobile. He heard the machine come slowly down the street. He heard the soft swish of snow beneath the tyres. There was the creaking of a brake and it stopped before the house. He could hear, almost below hearing, the purring of the engine.

He waited, unable to move. And then he heard the brief sound of a motor horn, the button of the horn barely touched.

He could not believe it. Could they be so bold?

There was an interval. Now there was no doubt; the sound of the horn was firm and sharp.

Dr. Karandash went to the door and opened it. He stood there on the threshold of the house looking at the large automobile standing in front of the house. He could smell the car, smell the hot engine and the polished metal. The car was a black Mercédès.

There was no movement in the car. Then a black-gloved hand reached back from the driver's seat and spun the rear door handle. The wide black door swung open.

It was an invitation that could not be refused.

Dr. Karandash walked over to the car and stepped inside. A gloved hand steadied him into the middle position of the rear seat. There were five SS men in the car. Against the fogged windscreen he could see the squat black helmets of the three in front. The dim light glinted on the muzzles of their sub-machine-guns. Those sitting either side of him he guessed to be officers.

The driver put the car in gear, at the same time snapped on the headlights. A second later the headlights of another car, a short distance behind them, came on. A vaporous glow illuminated the interior of the Mercédès. Sitting on his right Dr. Karandash recognised Obergruppenführer Rauch.

He felt a gloved hand touch his. He looked and saw that he was being offered a cigarette. He took the cigarette, lit it and inhaled deeply.

"When did you decide to do it?" Rauch said.

"Last night."

"But before that you had contact?"

"Yes, a fortnight ago."

"So there was time for them to consider you, even to check with Moscow."

"Moscow!" Dr. Karandash took the cigarette from his lips.

"We have known for some time of this *Active* in Kharkiv. It is directed from Moscow."

"I realised that there must be some kind of underground organisation," Dr. Karandash said. "But all I had was this note. She left the note for me and I kept the rendezvous."

"A woman?"

"So," said Dr. Karandash, "you have not yet arrested her."

"Your contact was at a low level, yes? It explains much."

They moved silently through the deserted streets. The headlight beam of the escort car now filled the interior of the Mercédès with light, now abruptly left it in darkness. Dr. Karandash saw mobile reflections in the large round spectacles and on the heavily sculptured jaw of the Obergruppenführer.

"Yet," Rauch said, "you had much to offer them. You explained that?"

"No."

"Why did you not ask to see their leader, this former NKVD interrogator?"

"I tell you I knew nothing of them."

"I cannot believe that he is a fool. He must have known who you were. He must have known that you have seen everything that has been done here. Even without your notebooks, which I presume you brought with you, you would have been a first source of information on *Wehrmacht* methods."

Dr. Karandash crushed out his cigarette, listening.

"It is sometimes difficult to understand the Communist mind," Rauch went on. "That is what I am trying to do, understand the Communist mind. Is it so surprising? They make a rendezvous for you and then they tell me, through an anonymous informer, that you will be there."

"They betrayed me!"

"There were several possible explanations. First, that it was a trap, an attempt to draw us into an ambush; but they know us, we are still too strong for them. Secondly, that they suspected you of being our spy and this was their way of returning you back to us."

"So soon?"

"Had you been missing for several days, instead of a few hours, I would have sent my men to pick up your dead body."

"It is possible that they expected you to kill me." Quietly Dr. Karandash added: "Will you?"

The Obergruppenführer did not answer. Then Dr. Karandash understood that Rauch was occupied with a problem transcending punishment, a mere execution. Dr. Karandash saw that in Rauch's mind, he now existed, and would continue to exist, as the symbol of a personal challenge issued by the Communist leader.

They had gone some distance before Rauch spoke again. In his voice there was now such malice that Dr. Karandash felt his heart sink.

"Can they be so confident?" Rauch said. "Can they have so much contempt for us?"

Presently the big car halted. The silent officer on Dr. Karandash's left rubbed the fogged window with a finger. It was the *Einsatzgruppen* headquarters, the former NKVD building.

"What are you going to do with me?" Dr. Karandash asked.

In the act of getting out of the car Rauch paused.

"You will continue your researches," he said, adding as if by an afterthought, "in Stalingrad."

He addressed the officer on Dr. Karandash's left. "Herr Sturmführer Doktor Gruber, see that he is flown in tomorrow." Then he turned away with the air of a man weighed down by matters more grave.

The peculiar behaviour of Obergruppenführer Rauch bore heavily on Oberleutnant Soedermann. The continuous demand for replacements in the fighting divisions of the SS had reduced Rauch's staff to a minimum. At the same time insurgency was increasing on every side. Thousands of Ukrainians who had been drafted into the *Wehrmacht* were deserting. Banditry was rife in the forest country.

But that was no reason, Soedermann considered, why the Obergruppenführer should insult him, a *Wehrmacht* officer, the only *Wehrmacht* liaison officer left in his establishment, in the presence of veterans of the SS, distinguished order-bearers and the like. Nor could it be held to account for the innumerable small errands which the Obergruppenführer, at first politely, but now more brusquely, was in the habit of demanding of Soedermann. They were small matters suitable for a servant, humiliating to an officer. Among them was the repeated request that he clean the Obergruppenführer's pistol.

Soedermann's alternative was, of course, to ask for active duty with his regiment. They had forgotten him, but a word of reminder would undoubtedly result in his recall, by air probably. His command was at this moment narrowly hedged within the Stalingrad enclave. It was a decision he wished to put off as long as possible.

In the evening he would return to his apartment in the Paulus Platz exhibiting the marks of his special martyrdom. He was pessimistic, morose. Olympia saw that a crisis was near. She knew that the time for her to act was now, not later. Would she be able to keep the apartment after he had gone? Would she be able to obtain food from the commissary? After all, Olympia pointed out, if he did decide to go to the front it would be pleasant to have a nice place to come back to, would it not? The questions plunged Soedermann into deeper gloom. But, unable to face the disruption of that peace which was still left to him, he saw to it, by some deft paper work, that, if the worst came to the worst, Olympia would retain the apartment and the commissary would feed her.

He would regret Olympia. He would regret the apartment. He would regret his neat, orderly desk with its papers carefully arranged for display. At the same time, arising out of his despair, there was scorn for this work, this place, these men. It is not fit and proper, he suddenly said to himself, for an officer of the *Wehrmacht* to look upon, or be connected with, the execution of Jews. It was not work for a military man. He remembered occasions when his sensibilities had been touched, shocked, by the SS. He had thought them thorough, efficient, at the time, and he had shrugged his shoulders. Now he knew that this feeling had been that which a fighting man experiences when he meets a gallowsman. It was not fitting to rub shoulders with a gallowsman.

In this mood Oberleutnant Soedermann answered a call from Obergruppenführer Rauch.

"You are very busy at the moment? I am disturbing your *Wehrmacht* activities, yes?"

"*Melde gehorsamst*, Herr Obergruppenführer. No."

"An assignment for you. We are very short of officers here in the SS, as you know. It should not take you long. Get some men together. Two or three will do. Take them out of the guardhouse if you can't find them elsewhere."

Rauch held out a paper to Soedermann.

"Here is your authority. A *Judenaktion* order."

Soedermann took the order.

"The school in the Sadovo-Kulikovskaya," Rauch said. "A revival of Jewish-Communist activity."

Soedermann gagged.

"I understand your *Wehrmacht* sensibilities," Rauch said. "It will not be necessary for you to unholster your own pistol. You have a pistol, yes? You have merely to be present as an officer."

"*Melde gehorsamst*, Herr Obergruppenführer, it is not my duty. . . ."

"What is your duty, Herr Oberleutnant?"

"*Melde gehorsamst*, Herr Obergruppenführer, my duty is with my command. I have to request . . ."

"But, Herr Oberleutnant, you are afraid, yes?"

"*Melde gehorsamst*, no."

"It is not interesting to see so much of a coward."

"I am not afraid to die. I am a *Wehrmacht* officer."

The Obergruppenführer made a slight movement with his hand. With a casual, disinterested gesture he held out his immaculate pistol.

Soedermann took the pistol. He stood to attention.

"I want to see you do it," Rauch said.

"Herr Obergruppenführer, this will be the seventh time."

"Not clean it, you fool! I want to see you shoot yourself."

Oberleutnant Soedermann looked into the face of the famous Obergruppenführer. The heavy brow sheltering the deepset eyes, almost unseen behind the bright spectacles, the terrier's nose, the bossed jaw and the cleft chin, this was the mask, the stylised mask, of he knew not what, nor cared, finding himself thinking, as he had thought many times before: the unbearable, humourless Prussian, an unsoldierly type, a damned intellectual and a defeatist. Behind this feeling was the thought: he is liquidating me because I know, have known for a long time, that he has arranged the documents so that the guilt is Von Reichenau's, the *Wehrmacht's.*

"*Melde gehorsamst*, Herr Obergruppenführer, I go to the front."

As he said it he thought, oafishly: it's not I who's afraid of Stalingrad, but you; then, with that rare insight sometimes vouchsafed the oafish, he saw that the Obergruppenführer's secret was that he *was* afraid.

Oberleutnant Soedermann saluted and marched out of the big room, inflated by his discovery, until, a little later, he remembered where he was going.

Part 5

The Battle of Stalingrad (wrote Dr. Karandash) is not the most important military engagement of the war in Russia; not so consequential, say, as that battle in October and November, 1941, which, after the Japanese observers had been assured of victory, yet failed to secure Moscow; nor so costly as the great battles of encirclement at Kiev and Vyasma at the beginning of the war; nor so ruinous as the siege of Leningrad. But the Battle of Stalingrad is noteworthy for one thing; it signifies a change in the heart of the Russian soldier, that is to say, since the soldiers in this battle were but a short time ago civilians, a change of heart which occurred some time ago, but less than a year ago, in the Russian people, the masses. This was a decision taken by each Russian man, the most difficult of all decisions to arrive at, that the enemy is the worst enemy, that war is the worst thing there is, and that war, unless it is stopped, won, *is* decisive, not only in a man's own life, but decisive for all time, for all that will come after, and thus for all that has gone before. To arrive at such a decision is not an intellectual feat, for it cannot be reasoned into the heart. It is made largely on the evidence, which no longer can be denied, though the mind would like to deny it, delay it, of the nature of the enemy. Through all the confusions and exaggerations of propaganda the enemy is at last clearly seen, being no further away than one's own doorstep. It is a difficult decision to arrive at for men whose lives have been narrowed by poverty and hardship, the separation between them and the State widened by the remote and harsh authority of the State, so that they do not easily identify themselves with the State or the State's interest, and know, still further, that in making this decision the power of the State, which they may have thought to hold in abeyance, will be confirmed by them, perhaps forever, and that, when the enemy is defeated, those that survive, come after, will be utterly committed to that power, its glories, but also its greed. Nevertheless they are men of a certain country and they have never heard of a better country or, up to that time, seen one, so that it may be roughly said of them that they love their country. . . .

"The decision is made and it is possible, without respite, to engage the enemy. For this decision, once made, does not express itself in terms of confidence, resolve, valour, or any of the individual virtues, which are seldom wanting in war, but rather in a competency which may come over a whole army, from top to bottom, which old officers may say with satisfaction is training, but which is not training alone, but will. In battle this will is shown not so much in deed as in wisdom, battle wisdom, and this perhaps is the hardest of all the qualities for an enemy to face, for it is implacable, appears faultless, and thus, in the enemy's view, to be relentless, unrequitable. Meanwhile, gaining pace, changing over from the defensive to the offensive, the battle-wise army whose collective will is thus composed (especially if the moral righteousness which is its core is fanned into a vociferous hatred; if the frustrations of a former condition of life are liberated in its action; if the knowledge cynically prevails that such action makes irrevocable a return to that former condition of life, if not for oneself, since the chances are that one will die, then for one's kin, those that come after), then this army, or armies, in the same way that those who have suffered much are often contemptuous of the sufferings of others, may become in the course of its momentum, given arms, numbers, a tempest of pitiless, indiscriminate and overwhelming proportions. The Battle of Stalingrad will be justly and carefully celebrated. A turning point, yes; for its sardonic exploiters a triumph!"

The Russian language, thought Dr. Karandash, runs away with you; it is made for rhetoric. But he was pleased with what he had written. In a matter of days now Von Paulus' Sixth Army, or what was left of it, would surrender to the Russians. A prisoner, he would ask to be brought before General Chuikov and he would present him with what he had written. Such a work could not be ignored, for it contained all the information he had been able to gather about the numbers, strength, movements and methods of the southern group of German armies. Being written in Russian it would be easier and quicker for them than the information which they would later piece together from the prisoner interrogations and the captured documents. (Of necessity they would read also his observations; and, although he hardly dared utter this, there was in his undespairing mind the thought that such observations, filtering into minute unsuspected cracks, like moisture in a mountainside, might later have the power, at some swift freezing, to split the granite monolith.) At the moment the satisfaction was to have survived the hell of this last month, to which Rauch had committed him, and to have grown firmer in his determination to betray the Germans to the Russians.

Outside there was an appalling din. He had heard Colonel Adam say that there was now a Russian gun for every ten metres of their encirclement. It was some weeks since the great Russian envelopment from the Don; and a few days since a division of Siberians had risen up over the river bank and thrust through the shambles of the factories to capture the Murmiah Kurgan.

Dr. Karandash had been pleased when he had discovered the Russian name for this small conical hill, marked 102 on the *Wehrmacht* maps, dominating the long straggling waterside city. It was, of course, man-made, the kurgan, or tumulus, of some unknown neolithic king, one of the many such to be found on the Eurasian plain; he remembered that in his time it had not been built upon, and the Soviet records showed it to have been a Park of Culture and Rest, one of those many, he supposed, lacking seats, dusty and windblown in summer, but fresh with peach, apricot and oleander in spring. To serve the great complex of factories along the river bank to the north of the city the Soviets had built a large concrete water reservoir on the summit of the Murmiah Kurgan.

Here, in and beneath the concrete cisterns, had been the headquarters of General Chuikov's 62nd Army until Von Paulus had driven him back through the factories to the high bank of the Volga whose lip he had held, dug in above the water's edge. Then between the huge grotesque heaps of pressed scrap metal awaiting the furnaces, beneath the smoke stacks many times perforated like gigantic flutes, and in the dim steel galleries, beneath the power grids, across the railroad beds, and through the machine shops, men had fought strange intimate battles. The great empty sheds had echoed hollowly to the hammer of machine-guns, the clang of grenades, sometimes merely to the clatter of hobnail boots on steel ladders as the German patrols had flushed out sharpshooters and artillery observers hidden among the blast chimneys and gantry tops. *Russki, Russki, burble, burrrrrble,* the German soldiers had shouted, with such mimicry that none could doubt their intention of pushing the Russians, choking, into the Volga; to which the Russians, fortified with that litre of vodka which was here their daily ration, gruff, deep-voiced, had hurled back complex, recondite, indeed unrenderable, obscenities.

All this time, with an even greater irreverence, the Russians had been digging under the battlefield into the base of the Murmiah Kurgan, burrowing through the ancient midden, disturbing the dust of the red-ochred bones of that neolithic king, his wives and retainers, breaking through to the very base of the concrete cistern at its summit, there laying enough dynamite to shift the whole emplacement. Today it had been exploded, momentarily spilling the cistern sideways, stunning the occupiers, throwing their guns and mortars out of alignment long enough so that Batyuk's Siberians, combing through the factory ruins, gained the hill. This engagement Dr. Karandash had seen from afar, thinking then that the whole hillside had become an enormous bas-relief of mud-embedded human figures.

As the Russians had closed in, the Sixth Army had been cut in two. The larger section to the south, including Von Paulus' headquarters, had been pushed back into the fallen masonry of the city's centre, that wasteland where the steel tramway stanchions were like wilted asparagus and every metre of uncovered pavement and standing wall was etched with metal splinters, where the open manholes of the sewers stank not with sewage but with the bodies of men long dead, where in the no-longer-distinguishable Square-of-the-Succumbed-Fighters-of-the-Revolution, among the litter of siege, the paper, the old letters, unexploded grenades, broken weapons, machine-gun belts, empty ammunition cases, the bodies of the recently dead had been flung out of their rat holes and now lay in gardens of their earlier excrement. Here in the city's one intact basement, that of the local NKVD building, the surviving officers of the staff and divisional commands had begun to argue, Dr. Karandash saw, the problem of capitulation.

The Russian ultimatum had been rejected. There was no longer hope of Von Mannstein breaking through to them. It was the Führer's command that they should fight to the death. There could, of course, be no finer death.

With wicked glee Dr. Karandash observed the scene: these hundred or more proud officers gathering in the plaster-strewn basement atremor with exploding shells. Commissioned to express the enduring and unique soul of the German race they seemed a little less than inspired. Where was Von Paulus? Isolated in an incommunicable melancholy, that cold austere man with the beaked nose and fluttering left eyelid had withdrawn from the main basement and was now lying, fully dressed, on a cot in an adjoining room. Could it be that in these last days, even as the rank of Field Marshal had been grandiloquently conferred upon him, he had no stomach for the task of proving by his own token death the indestructibility of the German spirit?

They still held an airstrip at Pitomak. A squadron of Junkers transports could lift them all to a place of safety. Was it honour which prevented them from abandoning their men? Were they afraid of disobeying their Führer? Or were they afraid of the SS, of Obergruppenführer Rauch and what his minions could do to them with lengths of piano wire?

The officers were coming in from all directions. Here was Schmidt in his leopardskin snow helmet; the sharp-featured hook-nosed Schlemmer; Pfeiffer; Sanne; the black-eyed bitter-mouthed Wolf; Von Daniel; Ulrich; Steeker; Von Lensky; Dubois, the sandy-haired Austrian; Von Kulowski; Lattmann; Raske; Magnus; the Rumanians Dmitriu, Bratescu, Rinaldi. Here was Walther von Seydlitz, the caricature of a Prussian general, the *Deutsche Kreuz* in gold at his throat, the long hatchet face with hair close-cropped except for a tuft forward of the crown, swaggering, insolent. Here also the elder Von Arnim, pop-eyed, fanatical, the medals clinking on his chest as he drew himself up to his full height the better to sneer.

"Das sind Diebe, das sind Halunken. So eine Schweinerei. Fight! Do you want to live forever?"

"The terms offered by the Russians are strictly honourable," said Lieutenant Moritz von Drebber. His division, the 279th, no longer existed. "It is slaughter to reject them."

It was suddenly theatrical, Von Seydlitz's monocle, Ludwig's duelling scars, Schmidt's Goering-esque belly, the high-waisted *Wehrmacht* uniforms, epaulettes, red-and-gold staff tabs, the orders and the ribbons, the Iron Crosses, high-visored caps, black boots, fur-lined coats, suddenly improbable, implausible, as though, thought Dr. Karandash, one were standing on a motion picture set instead of in a shaken basement in Stalingrad this gelid January in 1943.

The fatigue of battle was still upon them, showing curiously enough, not in drooping weariness, but in the puffy lines of dissipation, so that they looked like gamblers who had just risen from the gaming tables, not after many hours, but after months, years of play, and though now scornful and contemptuous of their luck, might at any moment, given another stake, fall back to the tables with renewed passion. The analogy, springing into Dr. Karandash's head, was suddenly illuminating. What these officers hoped for was not to preserve their men, or what was left of their men, from futile massacre, but to preserve themselves, not merely from the fate of their men as prisoners, but as officers with the possibilities and future that officers may have in the kind of world they had made. He saw them already calculating beyond this, their fox-minds exploring, on the basis of their recently-acquired knowledge of the will of Russia, the geo-political consequences of that will, their hope of exploiting that will.

This sharp insight filled Dr. Karandash with a deep fear. He knew that these men would be successful. They would go over to the Russians, and the Russians would accept them. At the same time he knew that his own hope of interesting the Russians in his notes was very faint, hardly more than fantasy. A successful graft requires like stock.

At that moment, as though to enlarge Dr. Karandash's fear beyond all bounds, there entered the basement an officer in the black SS uniform with the grey armband of the *Sicherheitsdienst*. He saluted General Schmidt and spoke to him. Dr. Karandash saw General Schmidt point in his direction. The SS officer came to Dr. Karandash.

"The compliments of Obergruppenführer Rauch," he said. "You are under arrest."

Below the thunder of the Russian guns the basement was very quiet. Every officer in that room was looking at Dr. Karandash. Von Arnim, who regarded Dr. Karandash as an SS spy, smiled bitterly.

"There is a plane at Pitomak," the SS officer said. "March!"

Some of the *Wehrmacht* officers laughed. There was relief in their laughter. Each one of them, at this moment, was qualified for SS arrest. It satisfied their sardonic sense of the humorous that the one taken should be this inconsequent, aging and ridiculous figure in the insignialess grey uniform.

The domain to which Dr. Karandash was flown back was not very well known at that time. The German soldiers themselves and the German people knew little about the clearing of the Ukraine. For the rest of the world it was a matter of curiosity to observe how those who came from that deep, silent region behind the German front behaved. Like this young German officer whom the Russian border guards brought into the presence of a party of foreign newspaper correspondents which the Red Army was entertaining in a Don village some miles to the south of encircled Stalingrad.

The prisoner was a young man. The pupils of his eyes were dilated, perhaps from the experience of having crash-landed in a gasolene-loaded plane (it had been flying into Stalingrad), perhaps from some other cause. His hands shook and he licked his lips. Yet he was well fed, a fresh-faced young man beside the lean pock-marked Russian officer, and then, because some of the foreigners had not seen such a man in a long time, there was a bridging of time, and it was as it had been years before, in Avignon or Naples, when they had seen him with his little camera and, although he was not as they were, yet there was Avignon and Naples in common with him, and they were together of another civilisation, and what had happened became the more difficult to see, the more impenetrable, for, almost as much as this young man, the foreigners (whose self-interest, like that of the Russian masses, was at this moment identified with the Russian State) were tourists in a strange land.

When the young German officer did not answer their questions the Russian officer threw a small bundle onto the table in front of the foreigners. It was the young German's identification papers, his pocketbook, which, said the guard, he had been too inexperienced, or frightened, to destroy. There were photographs among the papers. Some of the photographs were of a pornographic nature, a plump wench in various positions; others, cruder in technique, were of civilians being executed. There was nothing new about these pictures. Thousands of such pictures had been taken from prisoners. "Ehrenburg collects this stuff," said one of the foreigners, "they should send it to him." In the foreigners' eyes the pictures were obscene in a way quite different from that which had obviously, at some time or other, pleased the young officer. The pictures were like looking through a keyhole into a vast chamber of naked and bloody horror. But it was a tiny restricted view. None there but was reluctant to think how big and how vast that chamber might be. What had this young officer seen? What was behind him?

Then, for the benefit of the foreigners, defiantly, the young officer said: "They are going to shoot me. Soon they will take me out and shoot me."

The guard laughed his chuckling laugh and the foreigners, by some strange transmission of thought, began to chuckle and then to laugh. For, of course, the young man would not be shot, it not being the practice of the Russians casually to shoot people, the stroke of death, though not infrequently delivered, being less important than the authority by which the stroke is administered, an authority not to be carelessly assumed. It was the propaganda which made the young man believe that the Russians shot their prisoners. Or was it? Might it not be the young man's personal belief in shooting, in the dramatic death, the German death? And might not this belief have led him, under the influence of an almost insupportable terror, finally to compose himself for the pistol shot that would end his life? This was the undertow of misapprehension which made the Russian officer and then the foreigners laugh. For while the young man would not be shot, he clearly was not yet equipped to know how he would die. He could not know, as those before whom he stood knew, as the Russian officer knew, the future that would be his, alive. He could not foresee the cold and hunger and the work and the sickness that would be his prisoner's lot, that slow attenuation of existence until there was nothing personable, characteristic, or memorable left in him, even his name forgotten, his uniform unrecognisable or bartered away, and he, his physical person that is, had achieved anonymity, become that grey thing that could be glimpsed behind the wire stockades of Kandalashka or Kazakstan where at last typhus would unlock his poor spirit. It was the prisoner's not-knowing this, which, if he had known it, would have made him welcome, without heroic composure, the short, certain gunshot, that could not even be provoked, which made the Russian officer and the foreigners, by the completion of a circuit of hidden enlightenment, indulge the muscular action of laughter. The name of this young man was Willi Soedermann.

Kharkiv, now only a hundred kilometres from the foremost elements of the Red Army, lay under a light snowfall. When the snow stopped falling some people came out of their houses and began to sweep the sidewalks. When they saw that few citizens were engaged in this obligatory task they put away their birch brooms and went indoors. There was no traffic in the streets. It was very quiet. Across the river at the Yusnei station there was the sound of shunting railway trucks. Somewhere far away a locomotive was labouring through a snowdrift. A solitary airplane came slowly out of the blue air, the engine cut-out, coughed, and the airplane glided into silence. Soft powdery snow sliding off roof slopes was a stealthy whisper in the empty streets. In the Paulus Platz the sentries came out of the black-white-and-red sentry boxes and stamped their feet. They made much noise doing this. The *militsia*, the civil police, could be seen in their usual places, standing impassively in the shelter of overhanging eaves, snow-dusted in their dark blue greatcoats, or like statues within the double doors of official buildings.

This was the first week in February, and at the week's end the German shopkeepers began to remove the goods from their shops. They packed the goods into little carts which they pushed down to the Yusnei station at night. They went aboard trains that pulled out in the direction of Poltava. All Kharkiv knew of their going. It was observed that they had carefully locked the doors of their shops. The large black-and-white signs in Gothic lettering hung over the empty shop windows. The next morning workers at a number of small factories noticed that the German managers were no longer in their offices. The workers went home. The Ukrainian foremen who had organised the factories for the Germans did not protest the workers going, but conferred quietly together. Shortly after the departure of the managers the hospitals were evacuated. At night the sick and wounded were put aboard trains that had come empty into Kharkiv. Convoys of military vehicles came down the Bielgorod highway, but there were no tanks. The German soldiers paid no attention to the city or to the civilians.

A *Luftwaffe* photo-reconnaissance unit which had occupied a wing of the former Technological Institute made a heap of photographic material in the grounds of the Institute, set fire to it, and drove hastily out to the airport. The incident was expressive of the atmosphere that was gathering over the city. There was another. A man, surprised while attempting to break into an apartment vacated by a recently-departed colonist, was shot dead. His body was left to lie where it had fallen. None claimed the body. A number of military trains went through Kharkiv. The inhabitants of the city inside their houses heard the trains. When there were no more trains Todt labourers under guard began taking up the points and cross rails of the railroad bed, leaving only one set of rails westward from Kharkiv. They loaded the steel parts on gondolas that moved ahead of them. When there were no more trains there was no movement in the city. There was no sound of guns, as there had been the previous spring, no airplanes, no bombs. Each day the silence seemed more complete than the day before.

From the window of her apartment Olympia looked down the Sumskaya, the former Karl Liebknecht Street, but she did not step out onto the balcony.

A woman from a neighbouring apartment, also now alone, joined Olympia.

Sometimes, usually at midday, people would come out of doors, walk a few steps, speak a few words together and then return quietly. The only regular movement in the street was the *militsia* man who at intervals, as though oblivious to the atmosphere of the city, walked slowly up one side of the street and then down the other. Sometimes he would peer into a doorway, or he would pause, standing in the shelter of an overhanging roof.

"I know that one," Olympia's neighbour said. "He comes from a village on the Bielgorod Road."

"It is nothing to be a peasant."

"The peasants have gone over to the Communists."

"Only yesterday," Olympia said, "he shot a man. I heard about it."

"Today he would shoot too. But perhaps not tomorrow."

"It is easy to shoot."

"You do not understand. You are not political."

"Are you political?"

"Yes, I am political. When the Communists come I shall be political."

"I guess I am not political," Olympia said.

"I shall tell you something," the woman said. "This *militsia,* this Askar, he is political."

"Yes? How is he political?"

"Listen quietly. He is with the *Active.*"

"I do not believe in the *Active,*" Olympia said. "I have not seen any *Active.* Only an old woman who thinks she is the *Active.*"

"It is necessary for him to be with the *Active.* It is called working your passage. He does this because he is a peasant. But also because he is a peasant he does not see that in the end it will not save him."

"Are you with the *Active?*" Olympia said.

"I would have been with the *Active,*" the woman said. "I had much information to give. But I have not made the contact."

"What information have you got?" Olympia said. "I don't believe that you have any information. Your man was not in the *Wehrmacht* or the SS. He was not even an official."

"The SS! The officials! Who cares about them? Already they are gone," the woman said. "It is other information that I have."

"Yes," Olympia said, "about what?'

"My man did not wear a uniform, but he knew everything that went on."

"I see," Olympia said. "Your information is not about Germans, but about Ukrainians?"

"Yes."

"About me?"

"I shall say nothing about you."

"Why should they want to know about me?" Olympia said. "I am of no importance."

"You were born under the Soviets, yes? Your parents were Soviet citizens, yes? All your life you have been in the Soviets, yes?"

"It is true."

"It is interesting for them. It is more interesting for them than if you had been a foreigner."

"I like foreigners. I would like to be a foreigner."

"They must take into consideration that you will always be here. In the future, here. With your memories of your foreigner, foreign ways. Even if it were only your memories."

"My man," Olympia said, "promised that I should go."

"Let me tell you something. The Germans do not like us."

"How do you come to know this *militsia?*" Olympia said.

"I knew him from the first because it is useful to know such a man. Sometimes I gave him food. He is a man with a family like others."

"Is that why he stayed to work for the Germans?"

"That is why he will not go with the Germans."

"I do not like it," Olympia said.

"While he is there it is all right," the woman said. "Who knows, he may never have to go. All this may be nothing. The offensive may come to nothing."

"Then he will denounce the *Active* to the Germans."

"No, he will not do that."

"I can see why he will not do that," Olympia said.

"It is not easy," the woman said.

"What will they do when they come back?" Olympia said. "I mean the Communists."

"They will do as they did before."

"That is what I am afraid of," Olympia said.

"It is all right if you are political," the woman said. "But not too political. It is not necessary to know the Party history. But it is necessary to know who wrote the Party history."

"My father was political," Olympia said. "He was a member of the Party until they expelled him. Then he died."

"Your father was an Enemy of the People!" the woman said.

"I suppose I should not have told you this," Olympia said. "I suppose it will be something more for you to tell them. But I know it is not important. I liked my father and I was very sorry when he died. But I was never influenced by him."

The woman began to edge away from Olympia.

"I must go," the woman said.

The next day Olympia saw that the *militsia* man was no longer at his post in the street. She waited to see if he would appear. When he did not appear she resolved to leave the apartment. She put on her warmest clothing and her leopardskin coat. She made a bundle of some toilet articles and another bundle of such food as was left in the apartment. The street was deserted. She had intended to go to the *Kommandatura* and claim her right as the wife of an officer. But in the street she succumbed to the strange atmosphere that lay over the quiet snowbound city. Instead of going towards the *Kommandatura* she began to walk towards the old schoolhouse on the Sadovo-Kulikovskaya.

At the schoolhouse Olympia found Maryusa. The two women looked at one another and Maryusa's face was cold.

"I am going," Olympia said. "I have brought you food."

Maryusa took the food. She did not speak or acknowledge Olympia's presence in any other way.

"Are you going?" Olympia asked.

"No."

Olympia stood there, not speaking, waiting for the other to control her emotion. In a minute it was over. Maryusa turned to look at Olympia. Her face was hard, but no longer cold.

"They said I should go," Maryusa said. "They said that there would be room for me. But I shall not go."

"Who said that?"

"One of the teachers came. They have a place for all the teachers on the last train. You can hear it now."

"Hear what?"

"The whistle of the last train. But I shall not go."

"Is that what it is? My man said that there would be a place for me on the train. But they forgot to tell me."

"How can I leave the children?" Maryusa said.

"Where is Fomin?" Olympia said.

Maryusa turned away suddenly. She could not look at Olympia. Her back towards Olympia, she spoke.

"Fomin is gone."

"I knew he would go."

"Fomin is young," Maryusa said. "He is young and he is a patriot."

"Then you do not know what he did?"

"I forgive him for what he did."

Maryusa was silent for a few moments. Then she turned about and faced Olympia. Both women sat down. Maryusa began to speak as though she welcomed the hurt which speaking of Fomin gave her.

"There was first the big portrait," she said. "He wanted to hang the portrait in the room where the children gather. It was premature. He is a patriot. He is young. It was premature."

"I did not know about the portrait," Olympia said.

"The next thing was writing on the blackboard. He wrote slogans. But I was afraid. They were the usual slogans. There were also some new ones I had not seen before."

"The son-of-a-bitch," Olympia said.

"I rubbed them out. Some children repeated the slogans. I was afraid."

"I would be afraid," Olympia said, "with those children."

"They are just children."

"They are political children. I am a political child."

"I tried to prevent the slogans," Maryusa said. "But I knew that some children would remember them."

"All this time he was making love to you?" Olympia said.

"How can you say it?"

"Huh!"

"I am not sorry for that," Maryusa said.

"You are a woman. It is nothing. With a man it is nothing. They all lie. What else did he do?"

"There was nothing else. He went away."

"There was something else. Because the SS came to the school."

"How do you know the SS came?"

"I know all that," Olympia said. "I heard it from my Soedermann."

"He is brave," Maryusa said. "He went through the window even as the SS came through the door."

"So, you were denounced, and an SS man came and found all the schoolbooks changed back to Soviet books, all the pieces of paper covering the Communist words torn off, and he took some books away."

"Nothing has happened since," Maryusa said.

"Of course, nothing has happened since. The Red Army is outside the city and the SS has other things to think about. But we have not time to talk. Listen to that whistle!"

"It is terrible the propaganda they make," Maryusa said. "It is possible to see the reason for it. But it is terrible."

"Soon the Germans will go," Olympia said, "and everything will be propaganda again. But now let us go. Let us hurry!"

"There was even Lydia Artemova here to warn me," Maryusa said.

"Lydia Artemova! That old one came to warn you? What did she say?"

"She said I had contaminated the children."

"You see," Olympia said, "she was telling you to go."

"She did not say it."

"She was telling you that *you* are to blame. It is not the fault of the children. It is *your* fault."

"I have done nothing."

"Oh, it is not real," Olympia said. "Do you not understand? Someone must be to blame. If you go it is your fault. If you stay they will condemn you all. They *have* condemned you all, you and the children together. But if you go alone, you alone will be to blame."

Maryusa did not reply for a moment.

"Yes," she said, at last. "I see."

"That is what Lydia Artemova was saying. Do you think for a moment the Party sent her to say that? She came on her own account because she is a woman. But she does not know how to say it. She is an old fool who knows only the Party language."

"She has always been like that."

"But she knows what the Party intends. Yes, she knows that. And she came to you because she saw a way out. She was saying for you to go now, because then only you would be responsible."

"Do you think they would harm the children if I stayed?"

Olympia did not answer. She sat looking at Maryusa. How far can you go with innocence? Yet she must persuade Maryusa quickly to go with her to the train. Only then could she pass herself off as Maryusa's comrade, another teacher.

"I cannot tell you," Olympia said. "I cannot tell you more than this: you *must* go."

Maryusa went to the door of the large room.

"Goodbye." It was the voice of a child.

"It is Kotkin," Maryusa said. "He is sick."

"Come," Olympia said.

"I cannot leave them," Maryusa said.

Maryusa entered the big schoolroom. The fire in the stove had died down. The room was in gloom. The morning sun filtering through cracks in the window shutters cast little rods of light that touched a face here and there, pale, wedge-shaped faces with large luminous eyes too big for such heads. It was quiet in the big schoolroom. The sound of the locomotive whistle, soft, incessant, seemed to have its source in the room, or to be sourceless, like the faint funnelling of the wind in a chimney.

As Maryusa stood there a voice began talking.

"They come with the sun behind them, golden men in great numbers, and the forests do not stop them, nor do the rivers. . . ."

"It is the *Deda,*" a boy's voice cried.

"Quiet! Let the *Deda* talk."

"Not even the great Volga. Though there at Tsaritsin, at Stalingrad, where begins the long delta through which the river issues into the Caspian Sea, the west bank is a high bluff and the east blank a flood-riven marshland. It is not new. Across the islands of this marshland, from times unrecorded, have come the enemies and plunderers of the western plains, the forgotten men of the forgotten dynasties of the dried-up seas, nomads from the black sands of the Kara Kun and the tamarisk forests of the Kopet-dagh, wanderers from the Hindu-Kush and the Koh-i-Babn, soldiers of the great Khanates of Khiva and Bokhara, swordbearers from the cities of Kokajand and Samarkand and Merv, men of Tartary, the golden men. So the high bank at Tsaritsin, at Stalingrad, has always been a place to stand. Here the Scythians had a stockade and Persians' caravans wintered behind mud walls. Here camped Alexander's men, bringing back with them the little star-marked lizard which Pliny called the stellion. Here the blue-eyed Kievan Rus, looking out over the flat Kirghiz steppe, saw cities in the sky, strange palaces with blue domes, minarets, stairways cut out of mountainsides, inland seas bearing ships with lateen sails . . . mirages. . . ."

"He has come back to us again," Maryusa whispered.

She felt a touch on her arm. Lydia Artemova was standing beside her. Olympia joined them. They listened quietly.

"I am so glad," Maryusa said.

"Why did Fomin send him away?" Olympia asked.

"Fomin did what the Party told him to do," Lydia Artemova said.

"You mean the Party had some use for him?" Olympia said.

"Every time they send him away he comes back," Maryusa said.

"This time he brought me back," Lydia Artemova said.

"And you will stay?" Olympia asked.

"I shall stay with the children," Lydia Artemova said, "so that you can go. It is necessary for you to go."

"I see that now," Maryusa said. "But they will hold you responsible."

"I *am* responsible."

"Lydushka," Maryusa said, "you no longer love the Party!"

"We who have lived through it," Lydia Artemova said, "only we know. They must not be allowed to take our experience from us."

Olympia puzzled over this remark, then the meaning became clear to her.

"*They,*" Olympia said. "She means the NKVD."

"Yes," Maryusa said.

"Then she is an Enemy of the People, too," Olympia said.

Maryusa turned to Lydia Artemova.

"Will the *Deda* stay here also?" she asked.

"I shall send him away to a place of safety,'" Lydia Artemova said.

The development outpaced Olympia's thinking. All she could guess now was that Lydia Artemova knew as much as she herself knew about the fate of the schoolhouse, only from a different source, from a Party source. This knowledge filled her with admiration for Lydia Artemova.

But the locomotive whistle was an unbearable urgency.

"Now we can go," Olympia said.

"Yes, now I can go," said Maryusa.

The two young women kissed Lydia Artemova. Olympia's kiss was the stronger, less affectionate but more understanding.

When they had gone Lydia Artemova sat quietly listening to Professor Shevchenko, fully absorbed, a gentle smile on her face.

"Strange," she said to herself, "that in the Party one never had this feeling of being forgiven."

The sound of the locomotive whistle penetrated the room occupied by Dr. Karandash like a faint spirit wail. For a feverish moment Dr. Karandash was prepared to believe that he was in the presence of the supernatural. Then, as the soft shriek continued at a regulated volume, he realised that this was the signal he had been told to expect.

A moment later the electric light failed. The power at the Kushney station had been cut off. Dr. Karandash rose from his bed where he had been lying fully dressed. He heard the guard outside his room rise from his chair.

Since his arrest at Stalingrad Dr. Karandash had been

confined to his hotel room under guard. There had been no explanation, no confrontation. He was being held at the Obergruppenführer's pleasure. The day before he had been told to prepare to leave Kharkiv.

Slowly Dr. Karandash gathered his few possessions. The grey faceless uniform he had worn for so many months lay in the bottom of the wardrobe. He picked it up, held it for a moment, and then tossed it into a corner of the room. The wardrobe was a mess of papers. They puzzled him; then he remembered them for the dossiers he had taken from the NKVD files sixteen months ago. He did not disturb the papers, but added to them those bulky notebooks he had compiled on the operations of the SS.

Dr. Karandash jammed on his battered Homburg and went out.

Walking ahead of the SS guard he crossed the Paulus Platz, not looking up, not noticing the empty streets, the quiet of the city under the snow. Outside the SS building, the former NKVD, stood Obergruppenführer Rauch's Mercédès. Beside it was a *Dushegubky* van, its airtight steel-lined body half-filled with office material, typewriters, box files, all the paraphernalia of an efficient bureaucracy. Inside the building the odour of *mahorka* was reasserting itself over the sweet smell of Turkish tobacco.

As he mounted the stairway Dr. Karandash paused at the landing outside the vast archives room. Somewhere in there, indexed under his birth name, was that dossier containing the only pertinent information existing anywhere in the world about himself. Was this the moment to look for it?

The SS guard nudged him in the back. Dr. Karandash went on up to the big room occupied by Obergruppenführer Rauch.

The big room was in darkness; but Dr. Karandash could hear the Obergruppenführer's voice.

"We are going back," he was saying, "reversing a little, temporarily moving our quarters to Poltava until we are able to take up the slack overextension of the enemy's forces. It is a war of manoeuvre. In a war of manoeuvre such movements are performed many times. It is a movement which will be repeated many times this century."

"Yes," said Dr. Karandash.

"At the present moment we are all but surrounded. The enemy's forces are of the lightest kind, however, an infantry screen. In general we see that the enemy would like to take the city intact, as it is, with only such demolitions of a military character as General von Mannstein is now preparing, the airport, the bridges, the railroad station, the military barracks, but still a city which could be a capital, a prize, to prove something to the people, the Ukrainians, to show them that, after Stalingrad, their resistance to Germany is not inevitably accompanied by total destruction. The SS is here, gentlemen, for that reason. To frustrate the enemy's political objectives."

Dr. Karandash saw that he was not, as he had first thought, alone in the room with Obergruppenführer Rauch. At the long committee table, indistinct in the gloom, a number of SS officers stood at frozen attention. He saw that he was present at a staff conference. He was about to retreat when a sign from the Obergruppenführer, a sideways, unglanced gesture of his heavy hand, commanded him to remain. At the same time Rauch rose from his desk and, with his hands clasped behind his back, his head slightly bowed, walked down the length of the room to where the seven officers stood around the table. One of the officers went to a cabinet and brought to the table two large brandy-sniffing glasses. In each of these he set a squat candle. When the candle flames began to burn, a soft yellow light was cast about the table. Dr. Karandash saw that a large survey map of the city of Kharkiv was spread over the table. The light, reflected upwards from the surface of the map, illuminated the faces of the officers and was reflected again from the shining black leather and the orders and insignia of their uniforms. Dr. Karandash saw that all were officers except a very tall wolf-like man whom Dr. Karandash remembered, out of his village experiences, as Scharführer Schewe.

"The granaries!" shouted Obergruppenführer Rauch. "Do not forget the granaries!"

The seven men at the table bent more closely over the map. They laid heavy forefingers on the map. Scharführer Schewe covered their fingerprints with heavy red crosses.

Obergruppenführer Rauch turned to Dr. Karandash.

"In the Ukraine food is a political weapon? Correct?"

"Yes."

Rauch turned back to the table, called out: "The former Commissariat of Agriculture, the Technological Institute, the Veterinary Institute, the Museum of Agronomy . . ."

Dr. Karandash heard them but vaguely. In each section of Kharkiv there were a number of buildings to be destroyed: theatres, meeting houses, newspapers, educational buildings.

". . . The Marxist-Leninist Institute, the Red Teachers Club, the Red Co-operator Club, the Central Scientific Library, the Artem Museum depicting the former bourgeois society of Kharkiv, the so-called Revolutionary Museum . . ."

Obergruppenführer Rauch turned aside from the table and spoke to Dr. Karandash.

"I am impatient for the future," he said. "For I see now the fine buildings that we shall build here, those structures superb in utility, perfect in harmony, in that good taste and simplicity of line, the very essence of modernity, for which the Germanic mind is renowned."

He drew a circle on the map around the area of the University Mount; then threw down the crayon.

"There is one building we have forgotten," he said. "I am surprised that none of you has mentioned it."

The officers drew up to attention.

"It is the building in which we now stand. You are covering the operation, Schewe. Your last act will be to fire this building."

Scharführer Schewe saluted.

"Seig Heil!"

"Seig Heil!"

"Come, my friend," said Rauch, "we shall go to the train."

The Obergruppenführer's Mercédès was drawn up in front of the building. As Dr. Karandash climbed in he saw Sturmführer Gruber already seated there.

"So," said Dr. Karandash, "we arrive and depart together."

"I wish he would hurry," said Sturmführer Gruber.

He was looking at Obergruppenführer Rauch standing on the pavement, issuing final orders to the *Sonderkommando* which would cover the withdrawal.

"It is that nerve-wracking locomotive whistle," said Dr. Karandash; "it seems to have been blowing for hours."

"By the way," said Sturmführer Gruber, "I have this for you."

He opened his briefcase and drew out a large envelope. Dr. Karandash took the envelope, staring at his birth-name spelled out in Cyrillic script on the flap. The envelope was identical with those of Professor Shevchenko and Zeta Yarmoslansky which, more than a year ago, Dr. Karandash had filched from the NKVD archives.

"So all the time you have had this," said Dr. Karandash.

"An innocent document. What were you worried about?"

"Not only did he know my real name, but all the time he has known my position," said Dr. Karandash.

"It was in one of the old files reserved for those condemned to death in absentia, if that's what you mean. The Obergruppenführer was reassured."

The twenty-year-old envelope weighed heavily in Dr. Karandash's hands. He put it in his own briefcase.

"Why doesn't he hurry," said Sturmführer Gruber, "there is so little time."

As though he had heard the Sturmführer's plaint Rauch stepped into the Mercédès and ordered the chauffeur to drive to the Yusnei station.

Taut, vibrant, he addressed Dr. Karandash:

"You have brought your notes on Stalingrad?"

"No."

"You were present at the conference on capitulation, yes? You have a good head for such matters, you will remember everything. We must get to the very roots of the treachery."

"You mean Von Paulus?"

"Already Von Paulus is plotting a revolt against *Der Führer*. But it goes deeper than Von Paulus. I suspect Von Seydlitz and the old General Staff gang." He paused, added: "Soon we will begin killing the generals."

"And the war? What of the war?"

"It strengthens us," said Rauch.

Dr. Karandash said nothing.

"My optimism surprises you, yes? I must tell you that we were last week visited by the SS Reichsführer himself. I cannot tell you all he said. But you may know this: that our eastern frontier will be a boundary of permanent fluidity. The exclusive task of maintaining that frontier has been given to the SS. Here, each age group of the SS will fight on alternate years, so that we shall never become soft, will avoid falling into the pitfalls of stylism and the vanity of past glories. For, as you have no doubt realised, the black coat will be very attractive to wear in peacetime, but those who decide to wear it will know that every second year they will not dance in Berlin or attend the carnival at Munich, but will be posted to the eastern frontier in arctic winter. Thus we shall have a healthy elite for all time."

Dr. Karandash noted that the Obergruppenführer was wearing a shining new order: the Iron Cross, First Class.

"From time to time, whenever the pressure is powerful we may give way a little, as at present, and then we shall push it further back, each time gaining a little more space for ourselves, for the West. Thus Europe, controlled, ordered, and led by us, the Germanic people, will be able in future generations to stand the test in the battles of destiny with Asia. For you know and I know that this which we now have seen in Russia is only the beginning of the total organisation of all the peoples of Asia, of the Mongols and the Indian peoples, as well as the Slavs. Then when this mass of Asiatic humanity of one-and-a-half milliard lines up against us, the Germanic peoples, the West, numbering, I hope, two hundred fifty to three hundred millions, and the other European peoples, the Latins, the Anglo-Americans, making a total of six hundred to seven hundred millions, and with this outpost area stretching as far as the Urals, or, in a hundred years, beyond the Urals, then we must stand the test of survival. With time our weapons may be more mechanical, impersonal, vaster in scope, in proportion to the problem, but the burden of the struggle will rest with the SS man, his successors, his kind."

They had driven down the Paulus Platz, crossing the Lopansk River at the former Rosa Luxemburg Square. In a few minutes they were at the Yusnei station.

A crowd of people stood waiting outside the station gate.

"The whole city would like to come with us," said Rauch, "but we have space only for a limited number of our collaborators."

A Feldwebel shouted: "All schoolteachers in the last car."

"You are saving the teachers," said Dr. Karandash. "I am glad."

He looked at the group of poorly-dressed women who were climbing into a box car at the end of the train.

"That reminds me," said Obergruppenführer Rauch. He turned towards Sturmführer Gruber. Dr. Karandash saw the face of the archives expert go suddenly pale.

"Gruber, go back to the big room," Rauch said. "On my desk there is an order. You will recognise the order because there is attached to it a Ukrainian schoolbook. You will say to Scharführer Schewe that I wish him to execute this order. When you have done that take the Poltava Road. Avoid capture."

Rauch turned to Dr. Karandash.

"A little thing," he said. "In the rush of these last days I overlooked it."

The floor of the box car was covered with straw. The men and women who climbed through the open door settled themselves. It had not been easy for them to pass through the crowd outside the station gate. They had tried to hold their faces away, as though from shame, or fear of recognition, but they were too well known to go unrecognised. When it became clear that the Germans would admit no more than schoolteachers to the train there were mutterings outside the station gate. "Traitor schoolteachers," a voice said.

But very soon the schoolteachers began to share a warm feeling of complicity in their good luck.

Olympia, feeling wonderfully safe, lit a cigarette. She drew on the cigarette. Everybody in the box car began talking at once.

"I heard," Olympia said to Maryusa, "that Sophia Samoilov was caught in Moscow."

Immediately she knew it was the wrong thing to have said.

"I am worried. I would like to go back," Maryusa said.

"It is too late," Olympia said.

"The Red Army is not yet here."

"The Red Army!" Olympia said, stung to anger by Maryusa's vacillation. "What has it got to do with the Red Army? Don't you understand that it was not propaganda that Fomin was making at your schoolhouse, but a provocation."

There was the sound of an explosion close at hand. Above the shear and crackle of flames they could hear the distant sound of a sub-machine-gun.

It was a short train. Next to the box car containing the schoolteachers there was an open gondola on which an anti-tank gun had been mounted. Ahead of the gondola there were two "hard" carriages crowded with soldiers, *Kommandatura* personnel. Forward of the "hard" carriages were two *wagon-lits* and then the locomotive. There were machine-guns mounted on the locomotive and ahead of the locomotive there was a flat car loaded with steel rails and wooden ties.

Dr. Karandash followed the Obergruppenführer into the second *wagon-lit*. Here an orderly in a smart, newly-pressed uniform took charge of him. The *wagon-lit* was heated and the warmth was balm to Dr. Karandash's bruised nerves. The orderly halted and slid back a door. Dr. Karandash was ushered into a pleasant compartment. The upholstered seats were draped with lace antimacassars. The metal of the luggage rack was polished. The compartment had the pleasant odour of ironed bed sheets and footwarmers faintly tinctured with coal smoke. The sensation was overwhelming; it was the sensation of setting foot once again in Europe. Dr. Karandash, without being aware of doing so, groped in his pocket for a coin.

"You do not have to tip the orderly," a voice said.

Dr. Karandash looked in the direction of the voice and saw a face he remembered. It was the face of Prince Dolov, that gentle, refined, aloof and weak face.

"How are you, my friend?" said Prince Dolov.

Sitting beside Prince Dolov was Hetman Horopadsky.

"Good afternoon," said Dr. Karandash.

"It has been a long time," said Hetman Horopadsky. "I am too old for such winters."

"You are returning to Berlin?" Dr. Karandash asked.

"Paris," said Hetman Horopadsky.

"Ah, yes. I had forgotten that Paris is available."

"Paris is the only possible place to live," said Hetman Horopadsky. "Prince Dolov will agree, I think."

"I prefer Italy," said Prince Dolov.

"I have never been to Italy," a third voice said, "but now I may go. Yes, it is more than likely I shall go. A beautiful country and deeply religious."

The third voice was that of Father Wròbel. He was sitting in a corner of the compartment.

"You too?" said Dr. Karandash.

"The food has been abominable," said Prince Dolov.

"They are blowing up the city," Hetman Horopadsky said.

"Yes," said Prince Dolov, "they will destroy the whole Soviet world."

"A good thing," said Hetman Horopadsky. "My visit here has convinced me that there is nothing else to be done about it."

"After twenty-five years," said Prince Dolov, "it is too late to undo what has been done."

"It is never too late," said Father Wròbel. "The material condition does not matter."

"What I want to know," said Hetman Horopadsky, "is how so many people who ordinarily belong to the Orthodox Church were able to accommodate themselves to *you*."

"I can only say this," said Father Wròbel, "that I was besieged. Yes, that is the word. From morning to night, in every way, openly and secretly, I was begged to minister my office. I will tell you frankly, gentlemen, that God is needed in this dreadful country."

The passengers in the compartment looked at Father Wròbel. The expression on his face was a kind of complacency. None of the other passengers could have spoken so surely out of an experience of any comparable order.

Dr. Karandash was moved to shatter the complacency.

"I think," he said, "that you underestimate the Communists. The Communist Party today is founded on faith. There is a mystery in the connection between the Leader-Teacher and the pupils. It is not rational. It comes of necessity, out of hardship perhaps. It is emotional. It cannot stand analysis or argument. It may be cynical, or self-indulgent, but at its simplest level it is more likely to be selfless. It may seem wholly bureaucratic, but it is really submissive, impersonal, humbled. We must not underestimate the powerful urge of the Russian character for moral righteousness. It is true that the Orthodox Church has been revived, but it is also true that Party members are immune. They, perhaps, have a deeper, more disciplined mystery. I think it is also an error to underestimate the employment to which this mystery, this faith, may be put in war. Let us not be so foolish as to think that this reversal at Stalingrad is a temporary one. It was brought about by the harnessing of immense forces. Having achieved that much do you think they are going to stop there?"

Prince Dolov looked startled. Hetman Horopadsky was nervously twisting his moustaches. Father Wròbel, however, was smiling.

"I shall tell you something," he said. "During my sojourn I had the privilege of converting a Communist. He was a German who had gone to Russia, an intellectual, one whose life had been wholly dedicated to communism. You would imagine him to have been a hard man, a firm man, a man of faith, in the sense you have described faith, yes? I have never met such a confused man in my life! This poor man was at the end of his tether. He had committed a crime. There was guilt in his soul. Inexpungnable guilt. I brought him to God. So you see that there is in every Communist a profound weakness which may not always show itself, but which is there because his creed is a false creed, a blasphemy."

Out of a great weariness Dr. Karandash asked:

"Can we possibly be acquainted with the same man? Is it possible that the name of the man of whom you speak was Müller?"

"Yes. His name was Müller."

"He was, at the time you converted him, in the SS?"

"Yes."

"I often wondered what happened to him," said Dr. Karandash. "May I ask whether he was still a member of the SS after you had converted him?"

"His position was difficult," said Father Wròbel. "He undoubtedly could not withdraw from the SS. But it was a matter of slight concern. I have no doubt he found a way."

Dr. Karandash was about to reply when there was the sound of a huge explosion. The vibration rattled the windows of the carriage. Prince Dolov lifted a corner of the curtain and peered out.

"It is the Palace of the Soviets," he said. "It is on fire."

"A hideous building," said Hetman Horopadsky.

"They are very thorough," said Prince Dolov.

"It will be an experience to remember," said Father Wròbel.

Dr. Karandash stood up. The sense of living in a dream had become unbearable. He took his briefcase from the luggage rack and without a word slid back the door of the compartment and stepped out into the corridor.

The locomotive gave out a final shriek.

Standing in the corridor Dr. Karandash realised that Obergruppenführer Rauch was at his elbow.

"I wish to ride with the schoolteachers," Dr. Karandash said.

"You show too much distress," Rauch said, "for one whose youth was dedicated to the destruction of all human institutions."

"It is true," said Dr. Karandash, "I was once an Anarchist. You have known it all the time. But anarchy . . . how shall I explain what anarchy meant to us?"

"You have heard me order the destruction of the old centres of culture in your native city. But culture is a legitimate political objective. Here, in Kharkiv, the Communists have shown us that he who captures a country's culture captures its people."

The train began to move. Swaying gently on the rails the train began to curve around the long platform over the last undestroyed track.

"When we stop I shall go to the box car," Dr. Karandash said.

"You will have to go a long way," Rauch said.

Through the window Rauch pointed back along the length of the train. The train was moving out of the curving platform. The box car was stationary. The train was drawing away from the box car. The box car had not been coupled to the train. With each second the distance between the box car and the train increased.

Obergruppenführer Rauch had his helmet under his arm. He had taken off his large round glasses and was polishing them with a clean handkerchief.

"Schoolteachers are also cultural monuments," he said.

The Obergruppenführer finished wiping his spectacles. He covered the deepset blue eyes. Today there was no flutter in the boldly bossed jaw; the cleft chin was firm. He set the squat black helmet on his head, turned, and strode down the corridor of the *wagon-lits*.

The stationary box car had disappeared from view. For a long time Dr. Karandash stood looking out of the window at the rolling white steppe.

The Yusnei station was blown up at 5 p.m. on February 15. The blasts shattered the station buildings and brought down the overpass. (An empty box car standing on the tracks was undamaged.) A few minutes later the bridges across the Kharkiv and Lopan rivers were blown and the demolition parties prepared to depart. It was the moment for the Kharkiv *militsia* to demonstrate its solidarity with the incoming army and there was some sniping. Scharführer Schewe remembered that he had still to check the destruction of the SS headquarters. He was in time to see the Mercédès speeding away down the Chernyshevskaya. The evacuated building was open; the black-white-and-red sentry box was empty.

Scharführer Schewe was alone. A movement of infinite surreptitiousness, stealthy, like a flurry of rats, was behind him. He swung about, saw them. Five, six of them. Grey figures in cloth caps and old patched jackets, lean, dark, running crouching towards him, now like wolves, not looking at him, running sideways, loping easily towards him, towards the building in front of which he stood. They came from doorways and they deployed across the street, unhurried, deliberate, only conscious of his being in the way of their objective, not yet aiming at him, five, six, now eight guerillas. Their leader was within a few paces of Schewe and Schewe saw him to be a gaunt youth with agate-coloured eyes, like the eyes of a wolf pacing a sleigh, in one hand a huge Parabellum pistol.

In this gaunt Slav face Schewe saw the quarry he had always hunted. He raised his Luger and fired.

There was no falter in the steady loping advance of the youth coming towards him, the eyes now direct upon him, unflinching.

Schewe aimed again, squeezed the trigger and there

was a click. (Thinking back: after the schoolhouse, I forgot to reload.) And now this figure, of whose hunting he was now the quarry, was almost upon him, now lifting, in an almost careless movement, the huge Parabellum pistol, had already fired, and in the red-blinding there was the staggering blow that knocked Schewe off his feet so that he fell forwards into the snow, the Luger snatched, and already the hard calloused hand reaching into him for the spare clip. (Schewe thinking: after the *Judenaktion* in the schoolhouse in the Sadovo-Kulikovskaya I should have inserted this clip into the magazine.) There was the smell of Russian above him and then they were gone, gone without seeming to halt, without pause in that loping movement which carried them, the eight Red guerillas, across the road and into the building which had been, until that day, headquarters of the SS *Einsatzgruppe* and was now, by this action, reclaimed, reinstated to its former function, the *Narodny Kommissariat Vnutrennikh Djel.*

The City of Kharkiv was liberated by the 215th Rifle Division commanded by Major General Georgi Mikhailovich Zeitsov. The division had been among those in Rokossovsky's army group which had passed through the local battles of the Don breakthrough and had marched across the Don steppe to the Donetz. Zeitsov's division had crossed the Donetz at Chuiguick and had advanced along the railroad through Marovkia and Rogan. Southeast of Kharkiv they had encountered elements of the SS divisions Gross Deutschland and Adolph Hitler. The SS divisions were covering a general *Wehrmacht* withdrawal to the southeast. After a delay of two days in the area southeast of the tractor factory the SS disengaged.

On February 17, Zeitsov, a modest grey-haired soldier of forty-two years, entered Kharkiv at the head of his division. The Red Army soldiers passed quickly through the deserted streets, taking up positions on the city's western perimeter, beyond contact with the city or its people. There now arrived in Kharkiv a number of officers and a company of special troops who took charge of the city.

Soon there appeared in a number of places in Kharkiv those little letter boxes, ubiquitous at that time in all Russia, for the convenience of vigilantes or informers, according to your view, bearing the initials NKVD. Even before the little boxes could be put to use, however, the yard at the rear of the NKVD building in the Chernyshevskaya had its complement of prisoners. Mostly they were women, but they were not working women. There was even one wearing a leopardskin coat. Hopefully they carried little bundles of food and toilet articles. They stood in attitudes of strange relaxation, not speaking to one another, indeed quite detached from one another, as though each were isolated, standing there in attitudes of tense listening.

Every now and then there was the sound, from within the basement of the brick building, the clamour of a walled-in rifle shot. At the sound of the shot the women changed their positions, shifted their weight from one leg to another, but they did not speak.

It was a time of great victories, and in a mood of vainglory, or merely of careless optimism, Moscow now dispatched to Kharkiv that party of foreign correspondents which had attended the capitulation of Stalingrad.

For one whole day the foreigners were at liberty in Kharkiv.

The city lies whitely in the morning sunshine with smoke rising in slow spirals as from a score of peaceful chimneys. In the big square stands the Palace of the Soviets and each flame-lashed window is like an astonished eye and through the windows the sun falls gently into floorless space. All over Kharkiv there are such buildings. It is a city of shells, a city of façades. The frost which has had its grip on the outer surfaces of these buildings has preserved the surfaces well, even the wooden surfaces, against the flames. The side of a building may stand complete while behind it there are only charred embers. The façades of these gutted buildings are like gigantic theatrical sets erected on waste ground. Some of the older wooden buildings, designed in styles popular during the eighteenth and nineteenth centuries, now bear a curious resemblance to those architectural backdrops, romantic and ruinous, favoured by some modern choreographers. Voided, charred, but still holding the beauty of classical line, unreal, disembodied, they are yet more effective, more emphatic now than in their former utility. Leaning in from the wings are the street signs. Boldly in black Gothic letters on a white ground they proclaim the Paulus Platz. And here, standing boldly next to a burned-out building, also in neat Gothic letters, is the sign of a German shop-keeper. None takes the signs down. None has authority to take them down.

And now the players come on, coming in from the wings, up from the cellars, coming out in the quiet morning air. Women carrying water from wells. An old man, alone, pulls an unpainted wooden coffin mounted on runners. Edging onto the stage, barely able to walk, are some strange creatures, gaunt scarecrows, the survivors of the massacres in the ravine beyond the tractor factory. The streets fill up and some of the foreigners, wandering at large without escort, are recognised for what they are, foreigners not from Moscow. Suddenly men and women are edging close to the foreigners, an excitement in their eyes, a hunger for the tobacco they smell on the foreigners' clothes, the intelligence of something hitherto not believed, pressing in with their black soiled caps, pressing close, stories to tell. (It is not a pleasant or an easy thing to write about and, this being a time of optimism, there is no use for it; thus it will be simpler for the foreign correspondents to make a story about this youth, this boy partizan, who, it is said, performed gallantly in the liberation of the city, and who is to receive the gold star of Hero of the Soviet Union. His name: Fomin something-or-other.) But now the people are thrust back, on the throaty order of a soldier with a rifle and fixed bayonet. Before him marches a woman. The people draw back, but do not disperse, for it has been seen often today. And this is a young woman wearing a kerchief tied over her head and a man's boots. Her face is white, the high ridges of her cheeks flushed red, her lips are parted and trembling, her eyes are tearlessly bright, almost starry. The people make way for her. She hears the suck-back of spittle behind yellow teeth and Maryusa feels on her cheek the wet pellet of a demonstrable patriotism. She does not flinch.

In these cold battlefields and devastated cities there are no grotesqueries. The dead lie as in sleep, quietly not-sleeping, may lie there for as long as there is frost, the snow sweeping over them like a soft lace shroud, the flesh waxed and pink as with health. Nor does high explosive make that much difference or, as with this old woman, the rifle butt. Lying there on the floor her face broken, she is yet human, real, still clutching the old string bag with which, evidently, she attempted to fight her aggressors. And the children about her skirts! The children in the corners of the room! In the other rooms! Difficult even to see where they had been shot, lying there in sleeping attitudes, little bundles of ice-starched clothes, bullet-tinctured somewhere, frozen, perfect small angular faces, thin drumstick legs. There in the old schoolhouse, in the ruin of broken-in windows, torn-up floor, overturned stove, in the confusion of rags and refuse, they are not in themselves horrifying; when the life-ending is less pathetic than the life-in-living, death may seem even pretty and peaceful. This is what Maryusa is thinking as she walks through the streets, a pace ahead of her captor: there are no lives any longer, therefore no responsibility; all that for which she has fought so stubbornly is now disposed of. She is not thinking of punishment; there being none to punish the doer, that is, none above the human authority by which this action was condoned. In her mind there is only peacefulness. It is not bad that the children are dead. The struggle was carried on, but now it is ended. Already in the basement room of the NKVD she awaits her own prompt demise with the same expectancy.

The Interrogator asks many questions and she answers him without thinking about him.

From her position, standing before the Interrogator, she can hear, clearly, the words of the interview in the adjoining room. The questions are not personal and then, suddenly, they are personal. And even while the Interrogator is questioning her she can hear this Party Worker voice declaiming: "You will make us another University! The Ukrainian culture will rise again! There will be a new Republic! It has been decided that Ukrainian will be the second language! You will have facilities for the production of all the needed textbooks! The principle of cultural autonomy has never been yielded. Long live Comrade Stalin!"

Stepping back, glancing through the rooms, through the doorways, Maryusa sees Professor Shevchenko standing there, the pince-nez wobbling on his nose, the old bicycle suit crushed and soiled, the sealskin *shapka* in his hand, standing there, nodding his head. And Maryusa cannot forebear to smile, an innocent smile which so utterly confuses, enrages, the Interrogator that, barely glancing at her dossier, he orders the appropriate action.

Later (we remember) there were some in Moscow who thought the liquidation of the Kharkiv schoolteachers precipitate. But the matter was soon forgotten, for not much over a week later (it seems so long ago now as to be hardly worth mentioning), the Germans were back in Kharkiv.